P9-CCD-451

Praise for the Spice Shop mystery series

Kill 'Em with Cayenne

"Oust excels [at] serving up another seasoning-themed cozy complete with a guide to peppers and a rub recipe."
—*Kirkus Reviews*

"Plenty of spice lore adds flavor to this amiable mystery."
—*Publishers Weekly*

"Ms. Oust knows just how to simmer her story to bring out its full flavor."
—*Back Porchervations*

Rosemary and Crime

"[A] quality first in a Southern cozy series . . . The practical, vulnerable Piper turns to her colorful BBF, Reba Mae Johnson, for help in proving her innocence. Two possible love interests add spice—and that's not counting Piper's former husband. This is a must-read for fans of Carolyn Hart's Death on Demand series, as well as those who like culinary mysteries."
—*Publishers Weekly*

"Gail Oust has crafted an excellent mystery, chock full of savory treats including a charming small town atmosphere and a lively, engaging heroine, accented with a sprinkling of delicious spices. Truly a cut above—and highly recommended!"
—Donna Andrews, *New York Times* bestselling author of *The Hen of the Baskervilles*

"Piper's real-life problems as she negotiates her peril, along with some sassy small talk from Reba, will have fans of Oust looking for the sequel."
—*Kirkus Reviews*

"Struggles with her teen daughter and problems trying to keep business going add dimension to the story of Piper's sleuthing efforts. A strong cast of secondary characters add to the appeal. Fans of Jenn McKinlay and Ellery Adams will want to add this series to their reading lists." —*Booklist*

"Gail Oust has whipped up a killer read featuring the snappy new amateur sleuth Piper Prescott. Added into the mystery mix are a sweet puppy, a troublesome ex, a charming new beau and a smokin' hot chief of police. *Rosemary and Crime* is a character-driven zip zap of a tale with a robust mystery that readers will relish."

—Jenn McKinlay, *New York Times*
bestselling author of *Book, Line, and Sinker*

"A down-but-not-out divorcee deals with a new life, an appealing but challenging teenage daughter, and murder, teaming up with a spunky dog in a delightful Southern romp. Fast, freewheeling, and fun."

—Carolyn Hart, national bestselling
author of *What the Cat Saw*

"A delicious new mystery series guaranteed to make you hungry for more. Gail Oust's warm, witty characters bring Southern charm to life."

—Krista Davis, national bestselling
author of *The Diva Digs Up the Dirt*

"*Rosemary and Crime* is a custom blend of humor and suspense with an added dash of flavorful characters. Piper Prescott is a tasteful addition to the world of amateur sleuths. Gail Oust has created a delicious new addition to the world of cozy mysteries. I'm definitely adding her to my must-read list." —Jacklyn Brady, national bestselling
author of *Arsenic and Old Cake*

CINNAMON
Toasted

GAIL OUST

St. Martin's Paperbacks

This is a work of fiction. All of the characters, organizations, and events portrayed in this novel are either products of the author's imagination or are used fictitiously.

CINNAMON TOASTED

Copyright © 2015 by Gail Oust.
Excerpt from *Curried Away* copyright © 2016 by Gail Oust.

All rights reserved.

For information address St. Martin's Press, 175 Fifth Avenue, New York, NY 10010.

ISBN: 978-1-250-09670-8

Our books may be purchased in bulk for promotional, educational, or business use. Please contact your local bookseller or the Macmillan Corporate and Premium Sales Department at 1-800-221-7945, ext. 5442, or by e-mail at MacmillanSpecialMarkets@macmillan.com.

Printed in the United States of America

Minotaur hardcover edition / December 2015
St. Martin's Paperbacks edition / October 2016

St. Martin's Paperbacks are published by St. Martin's Press, 175 Fifth Avenue, New York, NY 10010.

10 9 8 7 6 5 4 3 2 1

To Caden Alexander and Emma Grace.

Love you to the moon and back.

ACKNOWLEDGMENTS

Everyone should have a friend like Fran McClain. Not only does she lend me prized cookbooks and handwritten recipes, but she also hosted a German Oktoberfest for me in July so I could sample sauerbraten and spaetzle. And to Greg, my son, who truly gets what it's like to be a writer— and lets me know he's proud of me. Have I told my friends in the Purple Gang and Sweet T's how much I appreciate you welcoming me back into the fold after lengthy absences while I've been in the "basement" writing? If not, forgive me. I treasure your friendships. No less appreciated is my husband, Bob, who never complains about egg sandwiches for dinner. My acknowledgments wouldn't be complete without a shout-out to the wonderful readers who love nothing more than to curl up with a cozy. May that addiction never end.

CHAPTER 1

Cinnamon from Ceylon. Nutmeg from Grenada. Cloves from Madagascar. A regular United Nations lined the shelves of Spice It Up! Pleased, I stepped back to admire the window display I'd just finished. The collection of baking spices paired with the large wicker basket of red Cortland apples as nicely as cheese did with crackers.

In spite of naysayers, Spice It Up!, my little spice shop on the town square in Brandywine Creek, Georgia, was flourishing. Certain folks—they shall remain nameless— were reluctant to admit that a former country club wife who'd been dumped by her ambulance-chasing, skirt-chasing husband of twenty-some years could morph into a successful shopkeeper. But I'd done it. I'd showed them.

With a contented sigh, I returned to my place behind the counter, intending to check inventory. I'd no sooner clicked on the computer than Melly Prescott, my former mother-in-law, burst through the door.

"Piper," she gasped. "I practically ran all the way over."

I stared at her, aghast. *Melly, run?* Never in a million years. Not even if her house were on fire. It simply wasn't her nature to hurry. "Melly, are you all right?"

Melly pressed a blue-veined hand against her twinset-clad chest. "I'm fine, dear, really," she panted. "Give me a minute to catch my breath, is all."

I went over to her and, taking her elbow, guided her toward one of the stools I kept behind the counter. I studied her more closely. She looked . . . different. Her usual not-a-hair-out-of-place silver pageboy was mussed. If that weren't alarming enough, she'd ventured out in public without first applying lipstick.

Melly managed a laugh, albeit a breathless one. "The way my heart's pounding, you'd think I'd just won a dance contest."

"Sit down. I'll get you some water." Racing for the small fridge at the rear of the shop, I patted the pocket of my sunny yellow apron with its chili pepper logo for the reassuring outline of my cell phone. I might need to dial 911. Melly not only looked different, but she was behaving strangely as well. Was this a warning sign of a stroke?

Casey, my mutt of many breeds, woke from his snooze at the foot of the back stairs leading up to my apartment. My scruffy pet raised his head, one ear cocked, as if to ask what all the commotion was about. When I ignored him, he resumed his afternoon nap.

I snatched a bottle of water from the fridge, twisted off the cap, and hurried to Melly's side. "Here you go."

"Thanks, dear." Melly took an unladylike gulp.

Although her breathing was less ragged, Melly's color was still high, her cheeks flushed, and her eyes mirror bright. I berated myself for not taking the CPR course offered at the fire station. One never knew when that information might come in handy. *What is the rule of thumb these days?* I wondered. Were people still doing mouth-to-mouth? Was it chest compressions only? Or both? I made a mental note to Google this later.

"You haven't stopped taking your blood pressure medication, have you?" I inquired, eyeing her nervously.

"Mercy sakes, no," she said. "I'm fit as a fiddle."

I regarded her thoughtfully. Melly had to be in her seventies, but other than that, I didn't have a clue which end of the spectrum her birthday fell upon. I doubted even CJ—her son, my ex—knew his mother's exact age. According to the *Melly Prescott Book of Etiquette,* never ask a woman her age. *Never.* And if—I shuddered at the prospect—a person unwittingly breached the etiquette protocols, a bald-faced lie was perfectly acceptable.

"Melly"—I channeled my inner yoga instructor—"why don't you take a deep, calming breath, then tell me what's going on."

She withdrew an envelope from the pocket of her A-line skirt. "I wanted you to be the first to see the letter that arrived in the afternoon mail."

Before she could explain further, a woman who looked startlingly familiar, yet drastically different, charged through the door. "Honeybun, wait till I tell you . . ."

Melly and I gaped at the new arrival dressed in red with blond hair styled in a beehive. Hoops the size of tangerines dangled from her earlobes. Strappy sandals with three-inch wedge heels were also a clue. Big earrings, high heels, and bright colors pointed in only one direction. I was the first to recover from surprise. "Reba Mae Johnson, that you?"

Opposite as opposite could be on the outside, Reba Mae, my BFF, and I were two peas in a pod when it came to things that mattered. Where I was barely five foot two, with unruly red curls and eyes as green as a tomcat's, Reba Mae was tall and statuesque, with fair skin and eyes a pretty soft brown. Her hair color varied with her mood—or maybe the moon. Yesterday it had been jet black; today it was sunflower yellow. The two of us had bonded years ago over diapers, teething, and soap operas.

Melly pursed her lips, her urgent news temporarily forgotten. "Girl, what have you gone and done to yourself this time? You look like a floozy."

Unabashed, Reba Mae patted her sky-high do. "You know what they say, Melly. The higher the hair, the closer to God."

"Hmph." Melly sniffed. "If that's true, you oughta be close enough to whisper in his ear."

"Stop!" I held up my hand like a traffic cop. "Will one of you kindly tell me what's going on?"

Both of them began talking at once.

"I just received the most wonderful—," Melly gushed.

"Y'all won't believe—," Reba Mae said—so excited, she couldn't stand still.

They stopped midsentence and glared at each other.

"I was here first," Melly pointed out. After sliding off the stool she occupied, she insinuated her smaller self between me and Reba Mae, who towered over us. "Piper, dear, I wanted you to be the first to hear my news."

Reba Mae, not about to be outdone, gently but firmly elbowed Melly aside. "Piper, you're gonna freak once I tell you—"

"Not so fast, missy." Melly glowered at Reba Mae.

"Ladies, ladies," I said, shaking my head in disbelief. "You're behaving like a pair of six-year-olds. Don't make me give you a time-out."

Again, Melly sniffed, affronted. Reba Mae, on the other hand, pouted—she actually pouted. I hated to see a forty-something woman pout. It wasn't a pretty sight.

"Fine," Reba Mae conceded grudgingly. "Age before beauty."

"Reba Mae Johnson," I scolded. "Shame on you. That's no way for you to speak to my mother-in-law."

"Ex-mother-in-law," Reba Mae and Melly chorused in perfect two-part harmony.

"Right," I muttered. "Nice to see that you finally see eye to eye on something. Now, someone, please tell me what the heck's going on."

Melly took the high ground. "Go on, Reba Mae, you first."

Reba Mae, not to be outdone, folded her arms across her impressive bosom. "No, you go first. I insist."

Unbelievable! We had apparently reached a stalemate. I tucked an errant red curl behind one ear. "Why don't we just flip a coin and settle this thing once and for all?"

I fished a shiny copper penny from the need-a-penny dish next to my antique cash register.

"Very well," Melly agreed in a put-upon tone. "I'll take heads."

"Fine," Reba Mae said, sounding equally prim. "Tails."

I rolled my eyes, a gesture I'd acquired from my daughter, Lindsey, who turned seventeen in late July. Teens, I'd discovered, were hands-down experts when it came to eye rolls. "All righty, then." I placed the coin on my closed fist and tossed it into the air. It landed on the heart pine floor and spun around a few times before coming to rest.

"Tails," Reba Mae crowed. "I got the part."

"And I'm going to be rich," Melly announced, not missing a beat.

"Part? What part?" My head swiveled from one woman to the other. "Rich . . . how rich?"

"I'm gonna be Truvy Jones." Reba Mae enveloped me in a hug that nearly cracked my ribs. "The opera house is puttin' on *Steel Magnolias*. Since I own and operate the Klassy Kut—the best little ol' beauty shop in Brandywine Creek—the director said I'd be perfect for the role."

I hugged her back. "That's wonderful, Reba Mae. You'll make the best Truvy ever."

Melly cleared her throat to regain my attention. "My turn for a hug." She put her arms around me in a stiff embrace, gave me an anemic squeeze, and just as quickly released me.

I tried not to show my surprise at this unprecedented display of affection. Now, I know hugging is second nature to most Southerners, but Melly Prescott didn't number among them. I swear the woman must have been at the hairdresser's the day the good Lord dispensed the hugging gene.

Melly's face was wreathed in a smile the size of Texas. "I'm going to be rich, Piper. Not just rich, but filthy rich. And I owe it all to you."

"Me? What did I do?"

"You feelin' okay, Melly?" Reba Mae asked, genuine concern on her face. "You look a mite feverish. Maybe you should sit a spell."

"Never felt better." Melly waved a sheet of paper, which by this time was a bit crumpled. "I'm too excited to sit still, although I do feel a little flushed."

Melly, excited? Flushed? Reba Mae and I exchanged nervous glances. Melly was scaring me. I regarded her worriedly. Eyes—the same blue gray as my ex-husband's and my daughter's—sparkled, her cheeks rosy. "How long has it been since your last physical?"

"Here, read this." She shoved the letter into my hands. "This will explain everything."

"What's it say?" Reba Mae huddled closer so she could read over my shoulder.

I scanned the contents. It seemed a company called Trustychipdesign.com was prepared to make Melly a generous—make that very generous—offer for software she'd developed. After attending a trade show in Atlanta, the owners of the company planned to stop by Brandywine Creek and seal the deal in person. If all went according to plan, Melly would soon be a wealthy woman.

"Melly, this is wonderful news," I said, "but I can't take credit for your accomplishment."

"Of course you can, dear," she corrected. "If I hadn't been so bored one afternoon while you were out running errands, I never would have been tempted to experiment with the software on your computer. I never would have discovered where my true talents lay."

I recalled how upset I'd been several months ago when I returned to Spice It Up! and, much to my chagrin, discovered Melly had tinkered with my pricey point-of-sale software program. Guess all that tinkering had paid off.

"Next to yours, my grand announcement seems like small potatoes," Reba Mae complained.

"Now, now, don't say that." Melly, no doubt feeling magnanimous, patted her arm. "*Steel Magnolias* is a wonderful play. Why, I saw it years ago and cried my eyes out. It was funny yet poignant. I loved seeing how all the women supported one another."

"I never saw the play," I confessed, "but I saw the movie version. Sorry, but I can't remember who played Truvy."

Reba Mae patted the blond confection atop her head. "Dolly Parton."

"Well, then, that explains the do."

"It's a wig," she explained needlessly. "The director, Sandy Granger, let me borrow it. Said she used it last year as part of a Halloween costume. Sandy claimed wearing it would help me get into character."

"All this good news calls for a celebration. And I have just the thing." Not waiting for an answer, I turned and ran up the stairs to my apartment. I returned minutes later with a bottle of champagne. "I've been saving this for a special occasion, and as occasions go, they don't get any more special than this."

"I'll get cups." Reba Mae dashed toward the rear of my shop and brought back three dainty teacups.

"Mmm, I don't normally imbibe in spirits." Melly eyed

the bottle of bubbly, then broke into another smile. "But I suppose it won't hurt to indulge just this once."

I filled the teacups, then handed one to Melly and one to Reba Mae. I raised mine in a salute. "To Melly, soon to become the toast of the town. And to you, Reba Mae, a star is born. You, ladies, rock!"

"Hear! Hear!" they said as our cups clinked together.

The three of us proceeded to get comfy as we sipped and chatted. Melly and I claimed the pair of stools. Reba Mae perched on the edge of the counter, crossed her long legs, and let them dangle. I felt my chest swell with pride at seeing the pair looking so happy, so pleased with themselves.

Melly chuckled. "I can't wait to see the expressions on everyone's faces when I make my grand announcement at computer club."

"Wish I could be a fly on the wall," Reba Mae said.

"Yeah, me too," I replied.

Melly smiled again, smugly. "Just because Thompson Gray's the president, folks think he is the be-all, end-all when it comes to computers. They tend to overlook comments from a woman of a certain age. Will they be surprised at hearing my news!"

Thompson owned and operated Gray's Hardware, down the block from Spice It Up! He'd returned to Brandywine Creek several years ago after his father passed away suddenly. He lived with his mother, and as far as I knew, he'd never married, never even had a serious relationship. And, if rumors were true, it wasn't for lack of trying on Thompson's part. "When's the next meeting?" I asked idly.

"Tonight at seven o'clock," Melly replied. "I volunteered to bring refreshments. How well do you think gingersnaps go with champagne?"

"Honey, everythin' goes well with champagne," Reba Mae drawled as she motioned to refill our cups.

"I really shouldn't," Melly demurred, then changed her mind. "Oh, why not? What harm can it do?"

We were giggling like schoolgirls at a pajama party when my ex-husband strolled in, looking dapper in his designer duds. CJ took in the scene at a glance, then fixed his gaze on the nearly empty champagne bottle. His sandy brows drew together in a frown. "Y'all ought to be ashamed. Drinkin' like fish, and it's not even five o'clock yet."

Melly raised her cup. "It's five o'clock somewhere, son. Care to join us?"

CHAPTER 2

"What's the occasion? Did Scooter here"—CJ gave me a patronizing wink—"manage to break even for a change?"

I cringed at hearing the nickname I'd once found endearing but now loathed. As for his snide remark, I refused to take the bait. "Sorry to disappoint you, CJ, but I'm happy to report business is brisk at Spice It Up!"

"That so?" CJ surveyed the exposed brick and wood beams of my shop. He was an attractive man with golden blond hair, styled not cut, and slate blue eyes. His thickening waistline—blame it on a fondness for fine Kentucky bourbon and prime rib—was camouflaged by an expertly tailored suit. "You might want to consider usin' some of those big bucks to spruce up this place," he continued. "Might want to ask Amber for advice. That girl's got style."

Mention of Miss Homewrecker set my teeth on edge. Reba Mae sucked in a breath; Melly pressed her lips together in disapproval. I may not have been number one on my ex-mother-in-law's personal hit parade, but she wasn't happy her only son had sullied the family name by discarding his wife and hooking up with a former beauty queen. The lovebirds were planning a destination wedding over the Christmas holidays. The honor of my presence hadn't been requested at the nuptials.

"What brings you here, CJ? Can't find an ambulance to chase?" Reba Mae asked.

CJ snapped to attention. "Reba Mae, that you? What have you gone and done to yourself ? You look like a floozy."

Floozy? Hadn't I heard that same word from Melly's mouth? It was "déjà vu all over again," to quote Yogi Berra, my father's favorite philosopher.

Reba Mae patted her blond wig and batted her lashes. "You should be so lucky, darlin'."

As usual, CJ's attention skidded from Reba Mae's hair to her 38DDs framed to full advantage in a cherry red scoop-neck top.

"What *did* bring you here, CJ?" I repeated.

After digging into his pants pockets, CJ fished out a set of car keys and placed it on the counter in front of me. "Thought I'd stop by and drop off Lindsey's car keys. Tell her I had Reba Mae's boy rotate the tires and change the oil."

"Sure thing," I said, taking the keys and tossing them into a drawer. Lindsey's red Mustang convertible had been a bone of contention when CJ presented it to her on her sixteenth birthday. A consolation prize of sorts for having divorced parents.

CJ returned his attention to Reba Mae and flashed his chemically whitened choppers. "I hear your boy is doin' a fine job of keepin' Cloune Motors in business."

"Caleb has a God-given talent tinkerin' with motors." When it came to her twins, Reba Mae couldn't keep her pride from showing.

"Heard Diane Cloune is huntin' for a buyer for the place. She's lookin' at real estate in Atlanta. Got her eye on a place in Buckhead and needs the cash."

"That so?" Reba Mae replied, her tone noncommittal. "And accordin' to the grapevine, I heard talk you're thinkin' of hirin' yourself a personal trainer. Any truth to the rumor?"

At Reba Mae's question, CJ's expression turned stormy.

"Reba Mae just found out she landed a role in *Steel Magnolias*," I interjected before the thundercloud burst.

"*Steel Magnolias?*" CJ scratched his head. "Piper, isn't that the chick flick you dragged me to years ago? For the life of me, I don't know why women like to cry in movies till their mascara runs. Gimme a good shoot-'em-up and car chase any ol' day."

"Son, are you certain I can't interest you in a bit of the bubbly?" Melly asked, as gracious as a hostess at a soiree.

I took the offer of champagne as my cue to hop down from the stool. "I'll get another cup."

CJ flicked his wrist to glance at the gold Rolex I'd once given him for an anniversary gift. In exchange, I received a dozen roses. I swear they were the same sorry-looking bunch I'd seen in the produce aisle at the Piggly Wiggly. "Don't bother," he said. "I'm meetin' a client in fifteen minutes. Seems this guy slipped on a bar of soap and wants to sue the manufacturer for pain and sufferin'. I told 'im he's got a good case. Things that slippery oughta carry a warnin' label."

Ain't that the truth? I wished CJ had come with a warning label. Something along the lines: BEWARE OF SLIPPERY SMOOTH-TALKERS OOZING SOUTHERN CHARM. I brought myself up short, thinking of the lovely daughter and smart, good-looking son our marriage had produced. CJ and I'd had plenty of good times, lots of good memories until he decided he needed his "space." Needed to "find" himself. Fortunately for me, I'd moved on.

CJ rocked back on his polished loafers. "So, just to be

clear, all this celebratin's just 'cause Reba Mae's gonna try her hand at actin'?"

Melly, Reba Mae, and I exchanged conspiratorial looks. I traced the rim of my teacup with a fingertip. Melly sighed. "You might as well hear it, son, straight from the horse's mouth, so to speak."

CJ's forehead creased in another frown. "Out with it, Momma," he demanded. "Don't tell me you've gone and invested in some fool get-rich-quick scheme and now you need me to bail you out. I don't want to hear that you used your last twenty bucks for a bottle of cheap champagne to drown your sorrows."

Melly climbed down from her stool and went around the counter to confront him. "I did no such thing."

CJ aimed a finger in her direction. "If you're tryin' to get up the nerve to ask if you can come live with Amber and me, you might want to consider one of those senior citizen homes. The kind that cater to folks your age. We got plenty of room, but between my work schedule and what with Amber busy with weddin' plans, neither of us are home much. You'd be lonesome and spend all your time mopin'."

Fisting her hands on her hips, Melly looked her son dead in the eye. "Chandler Jameson Prescott, mind your tone. Stop treating me like some doddering old fool. For your information, I haven't lost my last red cent to some harebrained scheme. Quite the contrary. I'm about to become quite wealthy—and I owe it all to Piper."

"Momma, you're startin' to scare me. You comin' down with old-timers' disease?"

"It's not old-timers', you idiot," Reba Mae informed him. "It's Alzheimer's."

"Really, Melly, I can't take any credit for—," I protested.

"Nonsense," Melly cut me off. "For the record, CJ, I'm

in full possession of my faculties. Matter of fact, I might even decide to put the house on the market and buy myself a condo in some place like Hilton Head."

"Momma, you're not makin' a lick of sense. I think you should go home and rest a spell."

Melly whipped out the letter she'd received from the software firm. "Here, read this."

CJ's brow furrowed once more as he read the letter. "Sounds like a scam, if you ask me," he said, handing it back. "No way a woman your age could come up with an idea to make a company hand over that much money."

"Well, she did, and they can," I said, summing it up.

CJ shot me a look before turning back to his mother. "Momma, don't sign a thing without the advice of a good lawyer."

"And who might that be?" Reba Mae inquired oh-so sweetly.

CJ ignored her. "I'm tellin' you, Momma, it's a trick of some sort. Folks your age should be content to take life easy. To sit in a recliner with the TV tuned to the Weather Channel, and not fool around tryin' to design software."

"I didn't design. I merely *modified* preexisting software."

"Melly made some changes on my point-of-sale while I was out one afternoon. And I have to admit, I was amazed at how much more efficiently it operated. I can understand your doubts, CJ, but—"

"It's a scam," he repeated obstinately.

"CJ Prescott, that's quite enough!" Melly's patience was wearing thin. "I researched Trustychipdesign.com long before ever submitting my idea. I assure you Chip Balboa and Rusty Tulley are highly respected in their field and very successful businessmen. If they think my . . . modifications . . . are valuable, then who am I to quibble?"

"Hmph!" CJ snorted. "Well, I'm going to check them out

myself. In the meantime, Momma, don't sign any contracts until I look them over. Take advantage of your son's free legal expertise."

"When are this Chip and Rusty expected?" I asked.

"Gracious." Melly looked flustered. "I'm afraid I was in so much of a hurry to share my good news that I didn't pay attention to minor details. I confess I might've been temporarily blinded by the dollar signs."

"There's no time like the present. Give it up, hon. Let me take a gander." Reba Mae stuck out her hand, and Melly gave her the letter.

Spice It Up! grew so still that the only sound to be heard was Casey snoring softly in the storeroom at the rear of the store. Although we'd quickly skimmed Melly's letter earlier, none of us paid much attention to the closing paragraph.

"Well?" I asked impatiently. "When are they coming?"

CJ edged closer. For all his skepticism, I knew he was every bit as interested as we were. Reba Mae looked at me, her expression dazed.

"Well . . . ," I prompted again.

"Tomorrow," she said. "Their letter states they're arriving tomorrow afternoon. They plan to spend several days in Brandywine Creek before headin' to Savannah."

Melly clapped her hand to her chest. "Goodness! Tomorrow? I've got a thousand and one things to do before they get here. Reba Mae, can you squeeze me in for an early morning appointment? I want to look my best when I meet Chip and Rusty."

"I'll check my appointment book the minute I get back to the Klassy Kut."

"I'll go with you." Melly hooked her arm through Reba Mae's and steered her toward the door. "Soon as I get home, I'm going to bake a fresh batch of gingersnaps. Nothing says welcome like homemade cookies."

The instant the door swung shut behind them, CJ turned

to me. "Thanks to you," he growled, "Momma's talkin' about tradin' in the family home for a condo on the beach."

I tuned him out and proceeded to stack the teacups.

"What next?" he ranted. "A villa in Tuscany? Momma's led a sheltered life. When Daddy was alive, he treated her like a queen. She never had to lift a finger. Never had to balance a checkbook or pump her own gas."

I stopped what I was doing and tried to reason with him. "Your mother is an intelligent, self-sufficient woman, CJ. I'm sure her talent with computers came as a shock, but chill. Relax and let her enjoy her time in the limelight."

"Easy for you to say." He glared at me. "The way I see it, this whole thing is gonna be nothin' but trouble. I'm warnin' you, Piper, quit interferin' in Momma's life."

CHAPTER 3

Me, interfere? I fumed as I watched CJ stalk out of my shop. How dare he accuse me of interfering in his mother's life? I'd never dream of doing such a thing. And if the thought ever did occur to me, Melly would squash it like a June bug.

Melly Prescott had a mind of her own. And an opinion on most every subject. Times too numerous to mention, she'd made her opinion of me quite clear. Seems I never measured up to her image of the wife she'd envisioned for her precious son. Not only did he marry a Yankee, but also one who hailed from—of all places—Detroit. Then, to add insult to injury, it snowed on our wedding day. Anyone familiar with Michigan knows an early snowfall in late October isn't impossible. Snow, however, was a foreign concept to a Southern belle born and bred in the Peach State. As God is my witness, she declared to everyone within earshot, I'll never again step foot north of the Mason–Dixon Line. Her theatrics would have made *Gone with the Wind* star Vivien Leigh green with envy.

I carried the teacups to a sink at the rear of the shop, near the storeroom where I'd installed a small kitchen with

the intention of hosting occasional cooking demos. My
first attempt, however, had been a disaster of tsunami pro-
portions. Maybe the time had come for me to get back on
the horse that threw me. I made a mental note to ask
Dr. Doug Winters, one of the best cooks in a town full of
good cooks, in to show off his culinary skills. Doug wasn't
only a great cook and a terrific veterinarian but he was also
a wonderful human being, too. He and I had been seen together so often, people were starting to think of us as a
couple. Truth be told, even I'd begun to think of us that
way. Doug was sweet, affectionate, easy to be with, and I
was seriously "in like" with him. For the time being, however, we had an unspoken agreement to take things slow.

I turned on the tap and added a generous squirt of detergent. I was up to my elbows in soapy water when the
front door opened. I could've kicked myself for not locking up behind CJ when I'd had the chance. Thinking to
see a last-minute shopper, I forced a welcoming smile.

Wyatt McBride—make that Chief of Police Wyatt
McBride—sauntered toward me as if he had all the time
in the world and nothing better to do. He looked his usual
tall, dark, and dangerous self in a starched navy blue uniform and a big, bad gun strapped to his waist. Actually,
he'd look tall, dark, and dangerous regardless of what he
was wearing—or wasn't. Not that I have firsthand knowledge of the latter, because I didn't. Blame it on women's
intuition.

"I'm surprised to find your shop still open after your
usual closing time," he said. A hint of Georgia lingered in
his smooth baritone.

I rinsed suds from the cups and set them in a rack to
drain. "Are you here in an official capacity, McBride? Or
are you in the market for spice other than salt and pepper,
your old standbys?"

"Nothing wrong with good old salt and pepper."

"Boring." I reached for a dish towel to dry my hands. "Food tastes better if you spice it up a bit."

He hooked his thumbs in his belt and grinned. The dimple in his right cheek made a brief appearance. "Would you believe my visit is part of a community outreach program? Sort of a 'make nice with the local business owners' project of mine?"

"Nice try, but no." I hung the towel on a hook to dry.

Something in my tone caused my faithful mutt to wake from his nap. I swear Casey slept as much as a newborn. The pup yawned broadly, then padded over to the lawman to sit at his feet. Casey's tail swished back and forth like a metronome in a pathetic bid for attention.

McBride squatted on his haunches and scratched the sweet spot behind Casey's ears. The small dog practically writhed in ecstasy. "How you doing, boy?"

Judging from Casey's unabashed behavior, I concluded my pet was doing quite well indeed. I'd lecture him later on the pitfalls of being too "easy." A more discerning animal would have held out for a doggy treat before surrendering in a undignified display of adoration.

"So how's business?" McBride asked as he got to his feet.

"Why the sudden interest?" I swept past him, headed for the front of the shop.

McBride joined me as I started tidying up. Grabbing the champagne bottle, I debated whether to save what was left or dump the contents. McBride raised a brow. "Since when have you started drinking in the middle of the day? Experts say drinking alone is a bad habit."

"I wasn't drinking alone." I dropped the bottle in the waste basket with a resounding thud. "I had company."

He waited for me to continue.

"*Plenty* of company." I huffed out a breath. "Reba Mae and Melly were here. We were celebrating."

"Celebrating?" A corner of his mouth twitched in another smile. "I'm having a hard time picturing prim and proper Melly Prescott sipping champagne in the middle of the afternoon—and out of a teacup, no less."

"Well, I'm fresh out of champagne flutes." I hoisted the trash bag from the basket, tied it shut, and set it by the back door as a reminder to put it in the Dumpster later. Then I returned to the front of the shop where McBride waited. "Reba Mae won a role in a play the opera house is putting on this season."

"Don't tell me—Melly Prescott is also a budding thespian, and there was a part for an older woman who is never without her pearls."

The thought of Melly onstage in her signature pearls and twinsets made me laugh. "No," I said. "Melly isn't destined to be an actress, but she's about to come into a nice sum of money."

"How's that? She win the Georgia lottery?"

"No lottery ticket needed in Melly's case. Seems she has a God-given knack with computers. She redesigned a software program. Some company's convinced it'll be their next big moneymaker."

McBride shook his head, bemused. "Never would have guessed she'd be the type to even own a computer."

"Goes to show, you can't judge a book by its cover." I opened the cash register to tally the day's sales. "Not only is Melly a computer whiz, she can also program a DVR, converse on Facebook, has more apps on her smartphone than Lindsey, and—" I paused for dramatic effect. "—she can text with her thumbs."

"Both thumbs, eh?" McBride said, sounding suitably impressed. "Gotta admire someone with that kind of skill set."

I glanced up from my neat piles of fives, tens, and twenties. "You're not the type for idle chatter, McBride. Now that we've exhausted the subject of drinking in the middle of the day, why not tell me what's on your mind?"

An uncertain expression crossed his too-handsome-for-his-own-good face. "I . . . ah . . . need a favor."

Apparently, asking favors didn't come easily for the man, so I stopped counting cash and waited for him to continue. "Go ahead, ask away."

He dug into his back pocket and brought out a wrinkled page torn from a glossy magazine. "Here," he said, handing it to me. "I wanted you to look at this and give me your honest opinion."

"Sure." Curious, I placed it on the counter and smoothed out the wrinkles. It was a photo of a kitchen, complete with stainless steel appliances, gleaming hardwood floors, granite countertops, and ceramic backsplash.

"So, what do you think?" He shifted from one foot to the other. "Like it?"

"What's not to like? It's every cook's dream kitchen." I returned the page. "I take it you're planning on doing some renovating."

He carefully tucked it into his pocket. "You mentioned awhile back that kitchens are a good place to start. My Realtor agreed. Thing is—when it comes to renovating, I don't know the first thing about it."

I tried to hide a smirk, though don't think I succeeded. "If memory serves, McBride, you've admitted to owning a hammer. You even confessed you are that rare breed of man who occasionally reads directions."

"Are you suggesting I buy more tools? Do the job myself?"

"Heavens no!" I exclaimed, horrified by the notion. "From the little I've seen, you don't have a domestic bone in your body. Since you seem to want my opinion, I suggest you hire a good contractor."

Relief washed across his features. "Any recommendations?"

I went back to sorting bills. "Well, Reba Mae's son Clay works for various contractors in the area. He might be a good one to talk to. Might even be able to do some of the work himself. Pick up a little extra cash on the side."

"Sounds perfect." He smiled again, showing off that danged dimple. "I'll swing by and have a chat with him."

I followed him as he turned to leave. This time I intended to turn the OPEN sign to CLOSED. I could use a power nap before Lindsey returned from cheerleading practice. The champagne I'd consumed was making me drowsy.

McBride stopped in the doorway. "I'm considering your advice to knock out the back wall and have a deck built. I might even do something wild and crazy such as invest in a gas grill and retire my George Foreman."

"Now you're talking." I stifled a yawn as he walked away.

The midafternoon drinking must have slowed my reflexes because before I could twist the lock, Thompson Gray's face appeared on the opposite side of the glass door.

"Thompson," I said, stepping back and allowing him entry. "I was just about to close up shop."

Tall, lanky, and with a prominent Adam's apple, Thompson never failed to remind me of Anthony Perkins, the actor who played Norman Bates in *Psycho,* my all-time-favorite scary movie. Like the character in the movie, Thompson lived with his widowed mother and ran the family business. Thankfully, hardware—not motels. Also unlike the movie, Thompson's mother was alive and well.

"Glad I caught you." He ran a hand over thinning mouse-brown hair. "Mother's making apple cobbler for dessert. She told me not to come home unless I brought some of your special cinnamon with me. Ever since trying it, she refuses to use anything else. Claims even everyday recipes taste better with spices from your store."

"Well, that's music to my ears."

Casey glanced up, but seeing it wasn't one of his favorite patrons, put his head on his paws and regarded us through heavy-lidded eyes.

Mrs. Gray, I knew, favored the Vietnamese variety for its rich, sweet flavor. Her cinnamon rolls were a surefire hit at every bake sale. "This one's on me," I told him when he started to go for his wallet. "I wish everyone would follow your mother's example instead of using spices that have stood on a pantry shelf for years."

"Thanks, Piper. That's mighty nice of you." Taking the sack I handed him, he sniffed the air. "It sure smells good in here. A little bit like being inside a bakery."

I glanced at my watch, hoping he'd take the hint. No such luck.

"Your mother-in-law dropped by earlier. She was with Reba Mae."

"Melly's my ex-mother-in-law, seeing as how CJ and I are divorced," I reminded him.

"Right, right," he said. "Melly said she's making a grand announcement at computer club tonight. Refused to give me any details. I don't suppose you'd like to give me a heads-up what's so all-fired important?"

"Sorry, Thompson, I promised Melly. Mum's the word."

"Guess I'll just have to wait along with the rest of the members." He gave me a halfhearted wave as he left.

"Guess so," I muttered, locking the door behind him. I wouldn't spoil Melly's time in the limelight for all the spice in Grenada.

CHAPTER 4

The following morning, customers drifted in and out. Everyone was talking about the Oktoberfest bash Sandy Granger and her husband, Craig, were throwing. A pair of Brandywine Creek movers and shakers, the Grangers loved big splashy affairs—Mardi Gras parties, Fourth of July celebrations, and pig roasts on the final day of the Masters Golf Tournament. This year, in a nod to their busy travel schedule, they planned to host an Oktoberfest that promised to be an all-out, no-holds-barred event. Sandy, an attractive woman in her mid-fifties with a stylish chin-length bob, had told Reba Mae that after the party, she intended to give her undivided attention to her directorial debut in *Steel Magnolias*.

It seemed most of the town had been invited, but thus far, I hadn't received an invitation. I suspected Sandy was still miffed by a comment I'd once made. No sooner had the couple returned from their condo in Grand Cayman than Sandy told me about a trip around the world they were about to embark upon. "Don't you two ever stay home?" I'd blurted, part admiration, part envy. I hadn't meant that as an insult. Maybe my lack of an invite was payback time.

Oktoberfest guests were asked to bring a German dish of some sort. Foods like sauerkraut, goulash, schnitzel, and strudel were hot topics among my clientele. Dottie Hemmings, the mayor's wife, quizzed me about German desserts. Gerilee Barker asked my advice on German potato salad. "Add a teaspoon of celery seed," I'd told her, "but not too much. It has a strong flavor."

Finally, a lull. I'd just been about to unwrap a tuna sandwich I'd made for lunch when Melly waltzed in. From her freshly washed and styled hair, I could tell that Reba Mae had squeezed her in for an appointment. She was accompanied by two men I'd never seen before, but I had no doubt as to their identities. They were the pair destined to make Melly wealthy.

"Piper, dear," she cooed, her voice dripping honey. Apparently, with little or no effort on my part, she'd forgiven my past transgressions as a daughter-in-law. Seems it no longer mattered I'd once held the dubious honor of having the highest handicap on the women's golf league. Or that my finesse at bridge had been nonexistent.

I shoved my sandwich back into the wrapper and stashed it under the counter, out of sight. "Melly, how nice of you to stop by."

"These are the gentlemen I was telling you about yesterday—the brains behind Trustychipdesign.com. Allow me introduce Mr. Russell Tulley and Mr. Charles Balboa."

The taller of the two stuck out his hand. "No need for formalities. Call me Rusty."

The second man popped the remainder of a Snickers bar into his mouth, wiped sticky fingers on a pant leg, then offered his hand. "Not even my mother, God rest her soul, called me Charles. I'm Chip," he said around a mouthful of chocolate, nougat, and caramel.

"Nice to meet you both," I said, intrigued by the disparity between the partners.

They couldn't have been more different if they'd tried. Rusty Tulley was the neat-as-a-pin pretty-boy type. The top layer of his dark hair was skillfully lightened to a burnished chestnut and swept back from a handsome face with deep brown eyes and strong features. Fashionable stubble shadowed his jaw. Chip, on the other hand, was frumpy and overweight. His pale blond hair was falling victim to male-pattern baldness. His rumpled slacks bore food stains; his shirt was partially untucked at the waist. I estimated them to be in their early to mid-thirties.

Rusty looked around. "Nice place you have."

"Thanks," I told him. The term "metrosexual" popped into my head. I'd heard the word used a time or two on TV. If my assumption was correct, it referred to an urban male with discretionary income to spend on grooming products and shopping. They had facials, manicures, and knew the best clubs, gyms, shops, and hairdressers. Until Rusty, I'd never met one in the flesh. Not many metrosexuals in a town the likes of Brandywine Creek.

"I'm giving the boys a guided tour," Melly announced.

From the corner of my eye, I saw Rusty flinch at hearing himself referred to as a "boy."

"Do you plan on staying in Brandywine Creek awhile?" I asked. "Or are you just passing through?"

"We're on a road trip," Chip said. "We started in Stanford, then worked our way across the country."

"We rented an SUV," Rusty volunteered. "We'll fly home out of Miami."

"Sounds like fun."

"It has been," Rusty agreed. "We're managing to mix business with pleasure."

Chip shoved his hands into his pants pockets. "We've made it a point to stop at various trade shows and leading distributors along the way."

"They've already been to L.A., Phoenix, and Birmingham," Melly informed me. "They just attended an international computer conference in Atlanta."

Rusty picked a jar of anise from a shelf and read the label. "Anise," he said. "Great for baking. My grandmother used to put this in cookies."

Chip, evidently uninterested in Grandma's cookies, cleared his throat. "Since Brandywine Creek and Atlanta are close, we thought we'd pay Mrs. Prescott a visit. So much nicer when one can conduct business in person, don't you think?"

"Um . . . I suppose." I didn't feel qualified to answer, since except for my customers, my business was conducted either over the phone or online. I'd met very few of my wholesalers face-to-face.

Melly chattered on. "Rusty and Chip are staying at Felicity's bed-and-breakfast while they're in town."

"I'm sure Felicity will treat you to some good old-fashioned Southern hospitality." The town's historic Turner-Driscoll House had been restored to its antebellum state through the dint and determination of Felicity Driscoll. She'd invested a great deal of her savings restoring a ramshackle building to its former glory.

"Felicity's done a great job," Rusty agreed. "Not only does she have impeccable taste, but a keen eye for antiques as well."

"The upkeep on a house that old must cost a small fortune." Chip looked as though he mentally calculated the price of heating and cooling a home dating back to the 1800s and found the sum astronomical.

"Don't mind Chip. My partner's always looking for ways to cut corners. He's the chief financial officer. The money man behind Trustychipdesign." Bored with the anise, Rusty picked up a container of vanilla beans imported from Madagascar. He raised a brow when he saw the price.

"Felicity offered us use of her parlor to discuss business," Melly said.

Before I could respond, Lindsey bounded through the door, swinging her backpack. "Hey, y'all."

I had to give Lindsey credit—the girl knew how to make an entrance. Her blond hair fell in loose curls around a pretty face with eyes the same blue-gray as her grandmother's. Her Southern accent notwithstanding, she could have passed for the quintessential California girl.

"Hey, sweetie," I said. "What are you doing home this early?"

She dropped her backpack next to the counter. "Teachers' workshop this afternoon."

"Right, right. I forgot." Now that she'd reminded me, I vaguely recalled finding a crumpled reminder to that effect protruding from an algebra textbook. "Meet your meemaw's . . . um, business associates. Mr. Tulley and Mr. Balboa."

"Call me Rusty," said Rusty.

"Call me Chip," said Chip.

I swore both men stood a little taller at the sight of an attractive girl. I smiled proudly as Lindsey politely introduced herself, using manners I'd drilled into both my children since they were knee-high. The formalities over, she gave her grandmother a peck on the cheek. "Hey, Meemaw. Is it true you're going to be famous?"

Melly's eyes sparkled with pleasure. "Mercy! Where did you hear that nonsense?"

"All the kids in school are talking about how smart you are. My friends can't believe anyone your age even owns a computer."

"Then they'll really be impressed to learn I have a Facebook page *and* a Twitter account."

Chip smiled indulgently. "Your—meemaw—could give

your classmates a lesson or two about navigating their way around a computer."

Lindsey's eyes widened as she regarded her grandmother in a new light. "Joey Tucker told me that Mayor Hemmings told his dad that he might even award you a key to the city—whatever that means."

"Joey Tucker is a know-it-all." Melly waved her hand in a dismissive gesture. "Who needs a key to a city where no one even locks their door at night?"

"So, Melly," I said, "what have you shown Chip and Rusty so far?"

"We just came from the Brandywine Creek Opera House. Sandy Granger happened to be there. You know, don't you, she's directing *Steel Magnolias*. Anyway, Sandy very graciously gave us a tour of backstage as well as its history. For instance, did you know it once hosted vaudeville acts and dance revues? According to local legend, Fanny Brice made an appearance back in the day."

"Speaking of tours, weren't you going to introduce us to your friend from the computer club?" Rusty smoothed his already smooth hair.

"Mr. Black or was it Mr. White?" Chip frowned. "Never can remember names."

"Thompson Gray," I said, amused at hearing a computer whiz confess to memory problems. Goes to show geniuses are human after all. "Thompson runs the hardware a couple stores down."

"We'd best be off," Melly said. "See you later, dear."

Melly marched out like a commanding general leading her troops. Rusty and Chip trailed obediently. Melly was queen for a day. The toast of the town. And enjoying every second of her fifteen minutes of fame.

"You're going to the game Friday night, aren't you?" Lindsey asked as she walked into the storeroom and emerged with Casey's leash. Casey immediately jumped to his feet, his furry brown body wriggling in anticipation.

"Who do the Bearcats play this week?"

"The Johnsonville Giants." She clipped Casey's leash to his collar. "Wait till you see the awesome routine we've been practicing at cheerleading. Brittany used to take gymnastics. You'll freak when you see her backflips."

I confess, backflips made me a trifle nervous. I was happy Lindsey's arm had been in a cast the fall her friends had registered for gymnastic lessons. By the time the cast came off, Lindsey's interest had shifted. Tap, jazz, and ballet had become her passion. Now, although she was a cheerleader, she left the backflips to others.

"I'll be at the game—provided the Band Boosters are selling their deep-fried Oreos."

Lindsey grimaced. "Do you know how fattening those things are? Good thing you're into jogging to burn off extra calories."

"Fattening, yes—but oh-so scrumptious." All things in moderation was my motto, including Oreo cookies dipped in pancake batter, deep fried, then dusted with powdered sugar.

"And if you're at the game, you'll get to see Sean in action. He's hoping for a football scholarship at University of Georgia."

"Mmm," I said, trying to keep my tone noncommittal.

"He is sooo cute—and sooo nice! He's been voted team captain."

"Really?" I was bursting with curiosity to find out more about Sean Rogers, the boy who'd captured my daughter's fancy. The mother of a teenage girl has to walk a tightrope. Too interested, your daughter clams up. Yet at the same time, you want to find out all you can. I wanted to ask what kind of student he was. Learn about his family. What his plans were for after graduation.

"Taylor thinks Sean might ask me to homecoming." With this parting salvo, Lindsey and Casey departed.

Hmm. I went back to the counter. I noticed my tuna sandwich waiting where I'd left it, but realized I was no longer hungry. I idly thumbed through a catalog from a supplier, my thoughts on Sean Rogers. Due to his prowess on the football field, Sean was everyone's favorite son. I'd heard he transferred here from a much larger school in Atlanta to live with his father following his parents' divorce. I hadn't met him yet, but I had the feeling that would soon change.

I was tying the laces on my poison-apple green running shoes the next morning in preparation for jogging. The autumn morning had a chill in the air. Temperatures dipped overnight, and it took the day awhile to recuperate. After debating what to wear, I'd chosen a pair of leggings that I'd used for yoga in my former life. A nondescript gray hoodie over a faded UGA T-shirt with a grinning bulldog prominently displayed across my modest bosom completed my ensemble. My cell phone rang just as I was about to tuck it into the pocket of my hoodie.

No good news ever arrives before nine o'clock. My first instinct was to let it go to voice mail, but guilt kicked in. Lindsey might be calling to tell me she'd forgotten her Language Arts assignment. Or it could be one of the rare, sporadic calls from my son, Chad, begging me to send chocolate chip cookies—and a check. Reluctantly, I pulled out the phone and checked the display.

Melly's name appeared on the screen. Odd, she never called this early.

"Hello," I answered warily.

"Piper, I need you. Drop what you're doing and get over here this instant."

"Melly, what's wrong?"

"Hurry . . . ," she whispered, her voice strained.

I stared at the phone as if looking for answers, but the line had gone dead.

After snatching my keys, I raced down the back stairs and outside. I jumped into my VW Beetle and drove the short distance to Melly's house on Jefferson Street. I chased away images of her falling, then crawling, helpless and in pain, to summon help. I pulled up in front of Melly's old Victorian on a street lined with old Victorians. She was waiting for me on the front porch, already dressed for the day in one of her signature twinsets and pearls. Her face was bone white, and as I climbed from the car, I noticed she clutched her cardigan tightly around her shoulders against the early-morning chill.

"Melly, are you ill? Let me drive you to the emergency room."

"Come with me," she said.

Taking the porch steps two at a time, I hurried to catch up with her. She passed through the living and dining rooms into the kitchen. Wordlessly, she opened a door that led to the basement, and pointed.

I peered over her shoulder. The light in the basement could best be described as murky. Melly's entire lower level was filled with splotches of dim light interspersed with shadow. I made a mental note to have CJ replace his mother's low-wattage bulbs with higher-powered energy-efficient ones.

My eyes slowly traveled downward and came to rest on a crumpled form at the base of the steps.

CHAPTER 5

From my vantage point at the top of the stairs and judging from the clothing, the body appeared to be that of a male. I scooted around Melly for a closer look. My heart knocked furiously against my rib cage. Fear and dread turned my mouth as dry as dust.

"Who is it?" I croaked.

"I don't know," Melly replied, her voice quavering. "I asked, but he didn't answer."

Being careful to hold on to the handrail, I slowly descended the steep stairs. I could see that whoever it was had been dressed casually in a plaid shirt and khakis. A shirt and pants that looked vaguely familiar. I'd seen that same combination recently, but where? My gaze happened to settle on a smudge of brown along one side of the man's khakis.

And a memory flooded back.

In that instant, I remembered the remains of a Snickers bar being popped into a hungry mouth, and sticky fingers wiped on a pant leg before a hand was offered in greeting. The crumpled heap at the bottom of the steps now had a name—Charles "Chip" Balboa.

"It's Chip," I called over my shoulder.

"Well, I don't care who he is, I want him out of my house. Please tell him to leave, right now. Right this instant!"

I edged closer. "I don't think he's going to leave any time soon." *Or under his own power,* I added silently.

"Gracious! What's wrong with him?"

"Um . . . he's not moving."

"That's not a good sign, is it?"

Gingerly, I bent and placed two fingers on the side of his neck as I'd seen dozens of times on TV crime shows. Chip's skin felt cold enough to send shivers down my spine. I quickly withdrew my hand. His myopic eyes had a cloudy cast as they stared up at me.

"Did he pass out? Is he all right?" Melly inquired from the top of the stairs.

I stared at blood the color of beet juice that formed an obscene halo around dishwater blond hair. Chip's neck was bent at an unnatural angle. The poor guy looked so uncomfortable, I felt an irrational urge to tuck a pillow under his head.

"Should I call an ambulance?"

"Mmm, Melly," I hedged, reluctant to send her into a tailspin. "I think you'd better call nine-one-one."

"Oh, dear." She wrung her hands. "Do you know the number?"

The number? Melly's reaction—or lack thereof—was beginning to scare me. "Don't worry, Melly, I'll call. I have it on speed dial."

That was meant as an ill-timed joke. A lame attempt at levity. Inappropriate, perhaps, but I'd atone for my sin later. I dragged my cell phone from the pocket of my hoodie and keyed in the three digits.

Dorinda, the police dispatcher on the day shift, answered on the first ring. "Hey, Dorinda," I said, trying to sound more cheerful than I felt. "Could you send Chief McBride over to Melly Prescott's ASAP?"

"You are aware, aren't you, Piper"—the woman either recognized my voice or had ESP—"that this line is reserved for emergencies only? I know you and the chief are on friendly terms, but if you want to chitchat, call his cell. Need the number?"

"I have his number," I replied. I probably shouldn't, but I did.

"All right, then," she said, her voice curt.

"Dorinda, wait!" I shouted when I sensed she was about to hang up. "This *is* a police emergency."

I rattled off Melly's address, then disconnected before Dorinda could question me further. Not that McBride needed to rush. I knew death when I stared it in the eyes—in this case, cloudy, wide-open eyes. The only place Chip Balboa was going anywhere soon was the morgue.

I trudged up the steps. Melly hadn't budged from where I'd left her. "Melly . . . what's Chip Balboa doing in your basement?"

"I haven't a clue." She shook her head, bewildered. "Do you think I should put on a pot of coffee before the police arrive? Or do you suppose the men prefer tea?"

Coffee? Tea? What was she thinking? This wasn't a meeting of the garden club. Now, I'm no shrink, but it seemed to me like a textbook case of shock or denial. Putting my arm around her shoulders, I steered her away from the coffeemaker. "Why don't we wait for Chief McBride in the living room?"

"Whatever you think best, dear," she said as I led her away. "I baked gingersnaps yesterday. They always go nice with coffee, don't you agree?"

"You can never go wrong with gingersnaps," I said as I guided her out of the kitchen. What was taking McBride so long? I wondered. The Brandywine Police Department was on Lincoln Street, only a few blocks away. Had he stopped for breakfast first? Shame on me. McBride was a professional through and through when it came to his job. Duty first, coffee and doughnuts second.

I urged Melly down onto the sofa, where she perched on the edge, her hands folded primly in her lap, a lost expression on her face. "Chip said he'd never tasted better gingersnaps than mine. I told him my secret ingredient—cardamom. Not all recipes call for cardamom, you know, but I like the extra flavor boost it gives."

"Cardamom's popular in Scandinavian countries," I said, hoping talk of a spice would distract her—and me as well. A little taste of normal before harsh reality sank its fangs. "Scandinavians use it in breads and pastries. Cardamom comes from a shrub in the ginger family. It's also used quite extensively in India."

"Hmm, India. I'm not much on foreign food."

I crossed the room, pulled aside the sheers, and peeked out the picture window. Still no sign of reinforcements. "The cost of cardamom is right up there with saffron and vanilla," I continued in the same vein, "because harvesting is labor intensive."

Melly hugged the lightweight cardigan of her twinset tighter around her shoulders and shivered. "When Chip stopped by last night, I offered him tea and cinnamon toast. Tea and cinnamon toast seem to go together like . . . ham and eggs . . . peanut butter and jelly . . . shrimp and grits . . ." Her voice trailed off.

In spite of a corpse in the cellar, my stomach made an unladylike noise. What did that say about my character? I asked myself. Not much, probably. It wasn't as if Chip Balboa and I were bosom buddies. We'd met only once. I'd mourn his loss later, but on a full stomach.

I started to pace. Food temporarily forgotten, my thoughts returned to Chip Balboa, dead in Melly's basement. So far, I'd blocked out a rather nasty, unsettling thought, but now it returned with a vengeance. Chip's skin had felt cold. It should have been warm if the accident had just occurred. That meant the fall had happened hours—and not minutes—before Melly called me. What had taken her so long to phone for help?

"Melly?"

My question went unanswered because McBride picked that moment to make his arrival. I released a pent-up breath when two squad cars screeched to a halt in front of the house. McBride sprang out of the lead car. Sergeant Beau Tucker, CJ's whiskey-drinking, cigar-smoking, poker-playing buddy, followed at a more leisurely pace.

I hurried to open the door. McBride groaned when he saw me. He actually groaned out loud before his cop mask slipped into place. How unprofessional was that? I wanted to ask. Beau stared at a point somewhere over my left shoulder and hitched his trousers higher over his paunch.

"Dorinda failed to tell me you made the nine-one-one call. Please, don't tell me you stumbled over another dead body."

"No," I said with all the dignity I could muster. "I didn't stumble. I merely opened the basement door and . . . there he was."

"He . . . who?"

"Chip Balboa," I said. "Come, I'll show you."

Melly gave McBride and Beau Tucker a parody of a smile. "Can I offer you gentlemen coffee? Sorry, but I don't have any doughnuts. Have to watch my cholesterol these days, so I never buy them. I read that they're high in trans fat."

Beau frowned at Melly, then spoke to me in a stage whisper, "What's goin' on with the ol' gal? She okay?"

"Shock," I whispered back. "It's not every day someone tumbles down her basement stairs." As I led the way to the kitchen, I couldn't help wondering what had happened after the tea and cinnamon toast last night.

"Don't touch anything." McBride tugged on a pair of latex gloves. Beau Tucker followed his example and did likewise.

I fidgeted at the head of the stairs, the same spot Melly had occupied not long ago. McBride, aping my earlier actions, felt for a pulse. I might have saved him the trouble, but checking a dead body for a pulse was probably protocol.

Grim-faced, McBride reached for the two-way radio clipped to his shoulder. "Dorinda, call the coroner. Tell him we have a body. Tucker," he ordered, "get the crime scene kit out of the trunk. Soon as you get back, start taking photos."

Beau brushed past me without a word.

McBride peered up at me. "Are you certain the victim is this Chip Balboa person?"

I swallowed. "Yes, I'm sure."

"I don't suppose you were here when Balboa took a header down a flight of stairs?"

"No." I shook my head so vigorously, my curls bounced. "I came after Melly called and told me to come right over."

He mentally cataloged the information. "How well do you know the victim?"

"Melly introduced us yesterday when she brought him by Spice It Up!" I darted a glance at the body sprawled at the foot of the steps. "Chip and his partner, Rusty Tulley, are from California. They're in town to see Melly on a business matter."

McBride's eyes narrowed. "Business? What kind of business?"

"Something to do with computers. You'll have to ask her for the details."

"I'll do that." McBride removed a pad and pen from his

uniform pocket and jotted notes, my presence seemingly forgotten.

I cleared my throat to regain his attention. "Mm, Mc-Bride, is there anything I can do?"

"Keep Mrs. Prescott occupied while we do our job," he said without looking up. "She seemed pretty shaken. I'll need to talk with both of you later and take your statements."

I started to leave but turned back. "McBride?"

He shot me an impatient glance over his shoulder. "Yes?"

I fumbled around, trying to find the right words. "This was just an accident. That's all, a tragic accident. People trip and fall down the stairs every day. Surely, you don't think—?"

"At this point, I'm still gathering information. For the time being, however, this is being treated like any other crime scene."

A crime scene? I swallowed a lump in my throat. Impossible. Ridiculous.

Or was it?

CHAPTER 6

I felt dazed as I walked through the dining room and back into the living room. Surely McBride was simply flexing his hotshot homicide detective muscles. Chip's fall had been just that—a fall. An accident. Why did McBride have to turn it into a federal case?

Poor Melly. I couldn't help feeling sorry for her. Nothing in her sheltered existence had prepared her for finding a dead man in her basement. I also worried about her. Her color wasn't good, much too pale. Though we hadn't always been on the best of terms, we'd reached a detente of sorts. Our current relationship could best be described as borderline friendly. Guess you could say we'd come a long way since the early days of my marriage to her only child.

The screen door opened and slammed shut. Beau Tucker stalked past me clutching a stainless steel box with FORENSICS stenciled on the side. The thing looked big enough to satisfy an avid bass fisherman. I knew that for fact, since Reba Mae's late husband, Butch, had regularly competed in fishing tournaments. It was his love of bass fishing that did him in. He'd been so excited at the hefty striper dangling from his line, he lost his balance and toppled overboard, striking his head on the bow of his boat, and drowned. It had been a sad, sad day in the Johnson household.

I heard the wail of sirens. Anyone with an official title of some sort was about to descend on Melly's place like a swarm of boll weevils in a cotton field. The entire Brandywine Creek police force—off duty and auxiliary—along with EMTs in their brand-new ambulance, and firefighters who didn't want to be left out of the action, all felt obligated to hear the details firsthand, spurred by the "need to know." They were the town's first line of defense. And just as often, its first line of gossip.

Before I had time to take a seat next to Melly on the sofa, John Strickland, county coroner and owner of the Eternal Rest Funeral Home, rushed in. "Which way to the basement?" he asked, not bothering with pleasantries.

"Straight through the dining room," I told him.

"All these folks in and out," Melly murmured. "Where are my manners? I'm not being a very good hostess."

I patted her shoulder. "Don't worry about a thing, Melly, you're doing just fine."

As soon as McBride released us, I was going to insist Melly see a doctor, get checked over. She'd had quite a shock. At her age, most anything could happen healthwise.

The front door opened again, and CJ charged into his mother's home like the proverbial bull in a china shop. If this kept up, Melly might want to consider installing a revolving door.

"Police cars at the curb. Coroner's van out front. A crowd congregatin' on the lawn," he ranted. "Momma, what in tarnation's goin' on?"

I sprang to my feet. "CJ, don't speak to your mother like that. Can't you see she's upset?"

He glared at me. "What in blue blazes you doin' here,

Piper? Trouble seems to follow you around like that damn fool mutt of yours."

I bridled at hearing this. It was one thing to attack me, but leave my dog out of it. "I'm here because your mother asked me," I informed him.

Melly fiddled with her pearls. "Seems a gentleman caller took a rather nasty fall."

CJ scowled at her. "Momma, shame on you. You been seein' some man behind my back?"

"CJ!" I gasped, caught between outrage and outright laughter. I had a hard time wrapping my mind around the thought of Melly dating.

"Really, son," Melly said with a hint of asperity in her tone. "Mind you, even if I did have a gentleman friend, it's none of your concern."

I was relieved to see a trace of color return to her cheeks. "Mr. Balboa—Chip—was a partner in Trustychipdesign .com," I explained. "If you recall, that's the firm interested in your mother's software expertise."

"Whatever," he said dismissively. "Thanks to Beau's heads-up, I got over here before all hell broke loose."

"Sorry to disappoint you, CJ," McBride drawled. His tall frame filled the arched doorway separating the two rooms. "If you're worried about hell breaking loose, you're a day late and a dollar short." He turned to Melly. "Mrs. Prescott, I'm aware these are trying circumstances, but I need to ask a few questions."

Melly let out a fluttery sigh. "Very well, if you must."

I sank down next to her, hoping my nearness would lend moral support.

"Please explain why you didn't call nine-one-one immediately upon finding Mr. Balboa? Why you called your former daughter-in-law instead?" McBride asked, pen and notebook at the ready.

"Now, just a cotton-pickin' minute." CJ raised a hand, which made him look like a cross between a traffic cop and a first-grader in need of the little boys' room. "Don't you go upsettin' an old lady."

"Don't you call me an 'old lady,'" Melly snapped. "Must I remind you, son, age is a number, not a state of mind."

I silently cheered her on. Evidently, CJ had forgotten that with many women—and his mother in particular—age was a sensitive subject.

"I believe you wanted to know, Chief, why I called Piper and not the police." Melly took a moment to collect her thoughts before answering. "I admit I panicked. I had no idea why a man would be lying on my basement floor. Or even who he was. Piper's levelheaded in an emergency. Who better to call?"

McBride continued his questioning. "Mrs. Prescott, when did you last see Chip Balboa?"

"Let me think." Melly's brow knit in concentration. "It must have been around nine or so last night."

"You certain about the time?"

"Listen here, McBride," CJ interrupted. "I don't like the direction these questions are headin'."

"It's all right, son. The man's just doing his job." Melly stopped fiddling with her pearls and smoothed her skirt. "Yes, Chief McBride, I remember the time quite well."

"And why is that?" McBride asked.

The room grew so still, you could've heard a pin drop. All eyes were fixed on Melly.

"Chip complained of a headache, so I went upstairs to fetch him Tylenol. When I happened to glance at the clock on the nightstand, I realized it was time for *Vanished,* my favorite TV show, to start. Even though I set my DVR to record, I thought, what's the harm in watching for a minute or two while I freshen my lipstick? By the time I returned to the kitchen, Chip was gone. I assumed he grew tired of waiting and left. I cleaned up, then went upstairs to finish watching my program."

"There, McBride." CJ smirked. "Satisfied?"

McBride ignored him. "Describe how you happened to find Mr. Balboa this morning."

"It was breakfast time." Melly clenched her hands together to keep them from trembling. "I like strawberry preserves on my toast, but I remembered I'd used the last of it yesterday. I knew I had another jar or two in the fruit cellar. I opened the basement door, switched on the light, and that's when I noticed something—or someone—at the bottom of the steps. I had no idea what to do, so that's when I decided to call Piper. If I hadn't needed preserves, it could have been days before poor Chip's body was discovered."

"That all?"

"Maybelle Humphries gave me the preserves. Shame she's still off gallivanting with that Texan she met up with at the barbecue festival. Maybelle's preserves were the best, don't you agree, Piper?" Melly looked to me for confirmation.

"Absolutely," I concurred. "Maybelle's preserves won first place at the county fair more times than I can count." Melly's mind seemed to be veering off topic again. She was obviously more comfortable talking about cinnamon toast and strawberry preserves than about a corpse in the cellar. Can't say I blamed her.

McBride flipped through his notes. "According to the coroner, body temperature and lividity indicate the victim's been dead for nearly twelve hours."

"Twelve hours!" I gasped.

"Twelve hours?" CJ echoed. "John Strickland may be one hell of an undertaker, but that doesn't make the ol' boy a whiz-bang coroner."

I quickly did the math. That meant Chip had suffered

his fatal fall at tea-and-toast time, not at the strawberry-preserve hour when Melly had reported the incident. That confirmed my earlier suspicion that Chip's death had occurred long before Melly's frantic phone call.

Melly appeared genuinely perplexed. "B-but that's impossible! He was fine last I saw him."

"Body's in full rigor," McBride stated matter-of-factly.

Who were we mere mortals to dispute forensic science? I tugged my lower lip between my teeth. This didn't bode well for Melly. Surely she was telling the truth about the events, but convincing McBride of that fact was a whole other matter.

"What are you inferrin', McBride?" CJ asked, sounding belligerent.

McBride zapped CJ with a look from his laser blue eyes. "Seems strange your mother's visitor suffered a fatal fall down the basement stairs without her knowing anything about it until the next day."

Melly opened her mouth to protest, but CJ cut her off. "Momma, I'm warnin' you, don't say a word. Not a single word, and that's on the advice of legal counsel"—he thumped his chest for emphasis—"and that would be me."

My stomach clenched at hearing this. If CJ intended to act as Melly's lawyer, she was in even greater trouble than I'd first imagined. She'd have a better chance of him winning her case if she'd tripped over her bedroom slippers and stubbed her toe.

McBride was relentless in his quest for information. "Mrs. Prescott, tell me everything you can remember about the last time you saw Mr. Balboa. You mentioned he complained of a headache?"

"How many times do I have to go over this?"

"Let's run through it one more time, step by step."

"But I've already told you everything that happened."

"Really, McBride, is it necessary to badger my mother-in-law?" I protested.

"Ex-mother-in-law," CJ and Melly both corrected automatically.

McBride, after some consideration, relented. I was pleased to see that he wasn't completely hard-hearted. "All right," he agreed, albeit reluctantly. "Let's continue this line of questioning later. I'll need a full statement from both of you ladies."

Happy at the temporary reprieve, I heaved a sigh of relief. "Fine by me, but it'll have to wait till after business hours. I have a shop to run."

He nodded. "CJ, you might want to take your mother someplace quiet where she can get a little rest while we process the scene."

"Sure, good idea." CJ rubbed his jaw and, frowning, turned to his mother. "Wish I could take you home with me, Momma, but I'm afraid the painter's there. Amber complained the rooms were too vanilla for her taste. Said she wanted colors that 'popped.' Whatever the hell that means."

"Melly's welcome at my place. She can use Lindsey's room for a few days."

"Where's Lindsey gonna sleep?"

"She'll have to make do with the sofa bed, like Chad does on semester breaks." Our son, Chad, was in premed at the University of North Carolina at Chapel Hill. On his infrequent visits home, he preferred to stay at my small but cozy apartment rather than his father's spacious new golf course home. Although Chad hadn't come right out and said so, I didn't think he was enthralled with CJ's future bride, Miss Amber Leigh Ames, any more than I was. I privately referred to the home wrecker and former beauty queen as Miss Peach Pit.

McBride replaced his notebook in his uniform pocket.

"Sorry to interrupt housekeeping details, but I don't suppose either of you could tell me where I might find Mr. Balboa's business partner. I'll need to notify the next of kin."

I pointed behind him toward the front door. "Turn around," I said. "He's right behind you."

keeping details. No, I don't
you couldn't the screen, he need
turned to say to reach the next

little uncertain, morning said. Then
"He's" put himself

CHAPTER 7

Rusty Tulley, his hand poised to knock, stood on the front porch. Spotting me through the screen, he gave me an uncertain smile. "Sorry, looks like this is bad timing, but I just need a minute."

I opened the door for him and stepped aside but avoided eye contact. CJ and Melly, I noticed, took the same cowardly route. CJ stared at the polished toe of his shoe. Melly twisted the gold wedding band she wore on her right hand around and around. None of us, it seemed, wanted to be the bearer of bad news. None of us wanted to tell Rusty his friend and business partner was dead.

"Why are police cars out front?" When no answer was forthcoming, Rusty turned to the man with a badge. "What's up?"

McBride wordlessly took Rusty Tulley's measure from the top of his two-toned head to the turned-up collar of his polo shirt down to the bare feet stuffed into pricey loafers.

Rusty shifted under McBride's scrutiny. "Um . . . look, I can come back later if this is inconvenient."

His appraisal completed, McBride introduced himself and asked, "And you are?"

"Rusty Tulley." Rusty stuck out his hand for a handshake, then apparently had second thoughts and slipped it into his pocket instead. "I thought I'd find my partner, Chip Balboa, here, but I see I was mistaken."

I fixed my gaze on an African violet plant on an end table by the window. The plant seemed to be thriving under Melly's care. Too bad the same couldn't be said for Chip.

"Is there a problem of some sort? Care to clue me in?" Rusty's expression seemed more puzzled than worried. "Curious" might have been an even better word choice.

"I'm sorry to inform you," McBride said. "Mr. Balboa took an unfortunate fall down a flight of stairs."

"Chip's always been something of a klutz. I assume he's already been transported to the local hospital?"

CJ cleared his throat. Melly smothered a sob. I wished I were in the Caribbean, shopping for nutmeg or cloves.

"You're starting to worry me." The look on Rusty's face changed from puzzled to concerned. He shoveled his fingers through his hair. Every strand fell perfectly back into place. "How seriously was he hurt? Which way to the hospital? I want to see him."

Impatient, he half turned toward the door when McBride detained him with a shake of his head. "I'm afraid that's impossible. Mr. Balboa is dead. He suffered a broken neck in the fall. I'm sorry for your loss."

Rusty's knees buckled, and he sank into a nearby armchair. Beneath the California tan, his complexion turned pasty. "No, I don't believe it. This must be some mistake. A joke of some sort."

"Let me get you some water," I offered. Not waiting for a reply, I raced to the kitchen, took a glass from the cupboard, and twisted the tap. I wished I had something fancier to give him. Evian or Perrier. Rusty was sophisticated, a possible metrosexual, probably accustomed to costly

bottled brands, not the kitchen-sink variety. Funny, the in-
consequential thoughts that can run through your mind
during periods of stress.

I hurried back. Everyone was still locked in the same
pose as when I'd left them. The only amendment to the
tableau was that McBride had retrieved his pen and
notebook from his shirt pocket.

"Here you go," I said, handing the water to a stunned-
looking Rusty.

"Thanks," he mumbled before downing half the contents.

I wasn't exactly sure why people worked up a thirst at
hearing bad news. I made a mental note to ask Doug Winters. Even though Doug was a vet and not a people doctor,
his medical knowledge wasn't limited to animals alone.

"When did you last see Mr. Balboa?" McBride asked.

"Last night."

"Do you recall the time?"

Rusty stared into his half-empty glass as if he might
find answers floating in the water. "Must've been eight
thirty or so, give or take. We had dinner together at the
Mexican place, then I needed to catch up on some work
on the computer. We agreed we'd meet for breakfast to talk
over strategy. When he didn't show, I went to his room and
was surprised to find his room was unlocked and his bed
hadn't been slept in."

"What made you come to Mrs. Prescott's in search of
your friend?" McBride asked.

"Chip wanted to visit Melly one more time before we
headed out. If he had plans for the remainder of the evening, I thought he might've mentioned them to her." Rusty
raised his eyes to search Melly's. "What happened?"

She lifted her hands, then let them drop. "I don't know."

"Just for the record," CJ snarled, "my mother had nothin'
to do with your friend's death."

"Just for the record," McBride replied, his tone even, "no one implied that she did."

"This morning I went to get a jar of strawberry preserves from the basement and found Chip. He was lying at the bottom of the steps."

Rusty's grip tightened on the glass he held. "Oh my God, you don't suppose he—?"

McBride cut him off. "Can you tell me who I might contact for next of kin?"

Rusty nodded and swallowed. "Chip really didn't have any family to speak of. Cheryl, his ex-wife, would know whom to call. I think I still have her number somewhere."

While Rusty fumbled in his pocket for his cell phone, the coroner, John Strickland, made a loud *hrmph* noise from the doorway. McBride glanced his way, and John beckoned him over. The four of us watched the men confer, but they kept their voices low, and we weren't able to overhear their conversation.

After a minute or two, McBride returned. "You're all free to leave for the moment, but, Mr. Tulley, I'd like you to stick around town another day or two until this is all sorted out." He turned to address Melly and me. "I'm going to need an official statement from both of you ladies later today."

"If you think you're going to browbeat Momma without an attorney present, McBride," CJ growled with lawyerly fervor, "then think again."

I fought the urge to roll my eyes at his theatrics. "C'mon, Melly," I said, pulling her to her feet. "After the doctor checks you over, I'll make you a nice cup of chamomile tea and tuck you in for a nap."

Although it was only midafternoon, it felt like I'd already put in full day's work. I'd just finished the last of my yogurt—a late lunch—when I heard the front door open. I looked up and saw Reba Mae enter the shop.

"I ran all the way over," Reba Mae explained, sounding out of breath after her mad dash from the Klassy Kut. "Tried to come sooner, but I was booked solid all morning with back-to-back perms. Then, wouldn't you know, Mary Lou Lambert messed up another do-it-yourself dye job. This time, her hair turned pea soup green. I swear a woman who never reads directions is a freak of nature."

I dumped my yogurt carton into the trash. "One in every crowd."

Reba Mae headed for the fridge at the back of the shop and helped herself to a Diet Coke. "Mary Lou came in cryin', wantin' me to turn her hair back to its original color. Said she's done experimentin'. Problem was, it'd been so long, she didn't remember what her natural color used to be."

I eyed Reba Mae's jet black locks. "Sounds like someone else I know who shall remain anonymous," I commented dryly. She was letting it grow out from the short, sleek Vampira style she'd worn the last couple months. Knowing my friend, she was itching to dip into her Crayola box for a color change.

Reba Mae perched on the edge of the counter, crossed her legs, and popped the tab on her Coke. "Whole town's buzzin' about you findin' a body in the old girl's cellar."

"Technically, I didn't find the body." I straightened a pile of spice catalogs and food magazines I'd yet to browse through. "Melly phoned in a panic, then hung up on me. I drove over to see why the fuss, saw Chip at the bottom of the basement stairs, and made the nine-one-one call."

"Better have that number on speed dial, honeybun. You're gettin' quite the reputation. No need for a cadaver dog long as you're around."

Casey, who had been snoozing under the counter, raised

his head at hearing the words "cadaver dog." He listened with one ear cocked, but when no further mention was forthcoming, he resumed his nap.

Reba Mae sipped her soda. "Melly all right? Must've been quite a shock."

"CJ had the doctor check her over before bringing her here."

"What did the doc say?"

"She's fine other than her blood pressure being a little high. The doctor blamed it on her being upset, told CJ not to worry. He wrote a prescription for something to relieve the stress."

"Where's she now?"

"Upstairs in Lindsey's room, sound asleep."

Reba Mae was gearing up to grill me like a burger on the Fourth of July. When you'd been friends as long as we'd been, you could recognize the warning signs. Thankfully, Doug Winters picked that moment to make an appearance. I wanted to rush over and hug him—and not just out of gratitude. Doug had that kind of effect on me.

He greeted us with a smile. "Hey, ladies."

"Hey, yourself," I said. "Was the seminar a success?"

Doug had spent the week in Charlotte, learning new surgical techniques at a regional veterinary conference. My pulse did a happy dance at the sight of him. In spite of the prematurely gray hair and wire-rimmed glasses, Doug's face was boyishly handsome. While he reminded me of *American Idol* winner Taylor Hicks, Reba Mae insisted he looked more like a scholarly version of George Clooney. Way I saw it, didn't matter which one, Taylor or George, both were easy on the eyes.

"Not only was the conference successful, but I managed to get in a round or two of golf with my buddy, Josh, too."

"Golf, eh," Reba Mae drawled, "that explains the casual attire."

Doug subconsciously smoothed the collar of his buttery-yellow golf shirt. "What's all this I've been hearing, Piper, about you and your mother-in-law finding a dead body?"

"Ex-mother-in-law," Reba Mae and I corrected, sounding like a duet.

"Are you both all right?" Brown eyes the color of melted chocolate brimmed with genuine concern.

"Melly's shaken. She'll be staying with me for a few days."

"What happened?"

"Yes, Piper, what happened? Do tell." Dottie Hemmings, the wife of Brandywine Creek's mayor, had apparently overheard the last of our conversation as she burst through the door. Her blond beehive hairdo was sprayed stiff enough to qualify as a motorcycle helmet. Resplendent in hot pink polyester, she advanced with the assurance of an ocean liner sailing into home port. "I've been in Augusta, shopping all day. I stopped at the Piggly Wiggly on my way home to buy one of those roasted chickens they sell in the deli and ran into Jolene Tucker. Jolene said you'd found *another* dead body. Really, Piper, that has to stop. Keep that up, folks are going to start avoiding you."

"Excellent advice, Dottie," I said, but I think she failed to detect my sarcasm. Jolene was the wife of Beau Tucker, otherwise known as Sergeant Blabbermouth of the Brandywine Creek Police Department. Who needed fiber optics to speed communications along when they had Beau and Jolene?

"When I came in, you were about to tell Doc Winters all the juicy details. Pretend I'm not here," Dottie instructed.

I sighed. How many times would I have to go over this? "Let me set the record straight," I said. "Melly discovered a man at the foot of her basement stairs, called me to come over, and I called the police. That's it in a nutshell."

"A man?" Dottie gasped. "Don't tell me Melly was seeing someone on the sly?"

I didn't know if Melly would be outraged or flattered to learn some viewed her as a femme fatale—senior citizen style.

"Did you recognize him?" Doug asked.

Reba Mae had probably already heard this part of the story from one of her clients, but she listened attentively nonetheless.

"I identified him as Chip Balboa, one of the partners in Trustychipdesign.com." I realigned the stack of magazines even though it didn't need realigning.

"Isn't that the company that was going to make Melly rich?" Dottie didn't wait for an answer. "Shirley Randolph over at Creekside Realty told Jolene that Melly planned to put her house on the market. Said Melly wanted to buy herself a condo in Hilton Head."

Reba Mae swung her foot back and forth. "I overheard Ruby Phillips say Melly wanted to move to Key West."

"Key West?" This was the first I'd heard about a move to Florida. "What did she plan to do in Key West? Look for Jimmy Buffet's lost shaker of salt?"

Undeterred by talk of real estate, Dottie cut to the chase. "According to Jolene, poor Mr. Balboa had been dead for hours before it was reported."

Reba Mae choked on a swallow of her diet soda. "That true?"

Doug looked at me quizzically while I silently counted to ten. Beau Tucker needed a come-to-Jesus talking-to. And I knew just the man to do it. I'm no Miss Manners when it comes to police protocol, but it doesn't seem very professional for an officer of the law to embellish details of a simple trip and fall.

"C'mon, out with it, Piper. The whole town's buzzin'."

I was tempted to borrow a line from McBride's rule book, stick my nose in the air, and say smugly: I can't comment on an active case.

"Don't be coy." Dottie waggled a plump finger at me. "You can always tell your friends. When do you suppose he fell? Last night?"

Doug scratched his head. "How could Chip have fallen and Melly not have known about it?"

Reba Mae set down her Diet Coke. "Why would Melly wait so long to report it?"

Doug, Reba Mae, and Dottie all looked to me for answers, but I shook my head. I had none to give. "How," "when," and "why" were the same questions swimming inside my own head. I shuddered inwardly. Melly was in trouble all the way up to her pearl-draped neck.

CHAPTER 8

An hour later, I filled Lindsey in on all the details regarding her grandmother's situation while Casey waited patiently at our feet for his daily run in the park.

"Joey said Meemaw called you even before she called the police. Is that true?"

I stifled a groan at hearing the Tucker name again. The boy had apparently inherited the blabbermouth gene from his father. Whatever information went into Sergeant Beau Tucker's ears came out his mouth in the form of gossip. McBride needed to stuff a cork in it. "Yes," I said, "it's true."

"Why do you think she called you first?"

"This is just a wild guess on my part, but maybe your grandmother was scared, nervous, and in a state of shock."

"And because she knows you're experienced when it comes to finding dead bodies." Lindsey reached into a jar under the counter and pulled out a doggy treat for Casey, which he accepted with alacrity. "I bet Chief McBride gave both of you the third degree."

"Not yet, but our reprieve is about to come to an end.

Your grandmother and I are due down at the station"—I glanced at my wristwatch—"in ten minutes."

"Want me to come along for moral support?"

"Don't you have a report due for World History?"

"Yes, but—"

"No 'buts,' young lady. You need to dig in, get it finished." Lindsey's lower lip jutted out, the same way it used to when she didn't get her way as a toddler, but I stuck to my guns. "If you don't keep up your grades, you're off the cheerleading squad. Period."

"Fine," she said, infusing the word with life-and-death drama the way only a teen can.

My daughter was a pro when it came to procrastination of the written-report variety. I needed to be on her like white on rice. I shuddered to think what would happen to her grades without my nagging once she entered college.

"You know how busy I am. There's always new routines to learn. Our coach is constantly after us to practice, practice, practice. I haven't even been able to get my nails done lately."

"What's all this about not having time for a manicure?" Melly asked as she came downstairs. I was happy to see that she appeared well rested after her nap. Hair, makeup, twinset, and pearls, she looked good to go.

"Hey, Meemaw." Lindsey greeted her grandmother with a peck on the cheek. "Mom's being a slave driver. I offered to go to the police station with you guys, but she's making me stay home and work on that stupid history report."

"It's sweet of you to offer, dear, but with this place all to yourself, you ought to get that old report done in record time."

"I suppose," Lindsey grumbled, then brightened. "Meemaw, are you coming to the football game tomorrow night?"

"I hadn't planned on it, honey. Heavens, it's been years

since I've been to a game. I never could tell the difference between a tight end and a split end."

I picked up my purse, took out my compact, and inspected my reflection in the mirror. "Lindsey wanted you to keep your eye on number seven."

Melly smiled indulgently. "And who might number seven be?"

"Sean Rogers." Lindsey fairly beamed. "He's the quarterback. He's sooo hot!"

"'Hot'? Is that the word you young people use nowadays for 'attractive'?"

I snapped the compact shut, dropped it back into my purse. "Sean happens to be Lindsey's crush of the month."

"I think Sean is going to ask me to homecoming." Lindsey took Casey's leash from a hook on the wall and snapped it on his collar.

Melly gave a Lindsey another fond smile. "Then a new dress is in order. I foresee a trip to the mall in your future."

I was struck in that moment by how much my daughter resembled her grandmother. They shared the same eye color, had the same oval-shaped face, and fair skin. Melly, I'd heard, had been quite a heartbreaker in her prime. I might have been a trifle prejudiced, but my girl was as pretty as a picture.

Casey pranced about, his toenails making little clicking sounds on the heart pine floor. Lindsey reached down and petted him. "I want my dress for homecoming to be amazing," she said.

I remembered the prom dress fiasco last spring. I'd bought her a lovely pale pink confection at a bridal salon. One suitable for a Disney princess. Instead Lindsey, confident I wouldn't make a scene, showed up at the last minute in a short strapless number Amber had selected. Pageant material, she'd informed me. Pageant, my foot, the skimpy little thing was more suitable for clubbing.

Lindsey must've seen my scowl, because she hastened to assure me. "I won't get anything you don't approve of, Mom, but you have to promise you'll try to be more with-it. I'm not a little girl anymore."

I checked my purse to make sure I had my car keys. "Just because I prefer more fabric and less skin doesn't make me old-fashioned. It makes me a mother."

Melly smoothed her already smooth pageboy. "We'd best be on our way, dear. It would be impolite to keep Chief McBride waiting."

"Good luck, Meemaw." Lindsey gave Melly a hug.

"Thank you, sweetheart. This is just a formality. It's not as if I'm going to an execution."

Lindsey headed off in one direction with Casey trotting alongside. Melly and I started in the other. Although it was only a short distance to the Brandywine Creek Police Department, in view of Melly's rather harrowing day, I'd elected to drive.

"CJ phoned to say he's running late, but he'll meet us there," Melly said as she slid into the passenger seat of my kiwi green VW Beetle. "He said we're to stall McBride until he gets there."

"Peachy," I muttered under my breath. Stalling McBride was like trying to halt the progress of a logging truck barreling down the highway.

A few minutes later, I pulled into a parking slot reserved for visitors. I was happy to find Precious Blessing and not Dorinda behind the reception desk when we pushed through the double glass doors of the police department. Not that I have anything against Dorinda, she's nice enough and all, but Precious is the sort who almost always wears a smile. I'd often thought her disposition would be better suited for a Walmart greeter than as a welcoming committee for miscreants and felons.

"Hey, y'all." Precious's round, dark face beamed with

good humor. Her black polo with its BCPD logo strained to contain her plus-size figure.

"Hey, yourself." I smiled in return. "Will you let Chief McBride know we're here?"

"He's been waitin' on you. Right now, he's on the phone with the GBI. Have a seat. He shouldn't be long."

Melly gingerly lowered herself onto one of the wooden benches that ringed the outer office. I settled next to her and picked up a dog-eared copy of *Car and Driver*.

"Either of you care for a nice cup of coffee?" Precious asked. "Or I might could find a couple tea bags some-where."

Melly declined the offer. "Thank you, but no. My stom-ach's been in knots ever since finding that poor man in my basement."

"Yes, ma'am. Must've been a shock." Precious nodded so vigorously that the colorful beads woven into a dozen or more thin braids clacked together. "Times like this call for a change of subject. You plannin' on goin' to the fancy Oktoberfest party the Grangers are throwin'?"

Melly sniffed. "I am, but Piper hasn't been invited."

"I'm sure it's an oversight," I added hastily. "My invi-tation probably got lost in the mail."

"I hear tell it's gonna be somethin' else. Bigger even than Becca Dapkin's funeral. My brother Zeke and his blues band are providin' the entertainment. Sort of a jazzed-up oompah band."

Just then, the buzzer on Precious's desk sounded. She pressed the intercom button, and we heard McBride order me into his office. As I got to my feet, Precious lowered her voice. "Between you, me, and the fence post, the man's grumpier than a bear with a sore paw."

"Thanks for the warning," I said. Tossing aside the magazine, I started down the hallway leading to his office. I knew the way by heart. It wasn't this gal's first rodeo.

"Remember," Melly called after me, "stall him till CJ gets here."

Sure thing. Piece of cake. How does one stall a bear with a sore paw? The door to McBride's den—oops, I meant office—was ajar. "Come in," he growled before I had a chance to knock.

I found McBride seated behind a scratched and scarred oak desk piled high with file folders. A desktop computer that looked old enough to collect Social Security was turned on, the monitor facing away from me. The walls had been painted pale butterscotch yellow, which was a marked improvement since my last visit. Diplomas and certificates in walnut frames hung next to a large map of Brandywine County.

"Have a seat." He indicated the chair across from him. "I had Dorinda type up everything you told me this morning." He reached into a manila folder, and withdrew a sheet of paper, then slid it across the desk. "Read it over carefully and make any additions or corrections. Precious can retype it and have you sign."

"All right." I did as he directed. The statement was brief and to the point but accurate. Unable to find fault with any of the details, I signed my name at the bottom.

"That's it?" he said. "You didn't find anything to quibble over? That's not like you."

"I've mended my evil ways." I slid the form back to him. "Besides, there wasn't anything to quibble about: Melly called me. I went to her house. Found Chip Balboa, felt for a pulse, then called nine-one-one."

He drummed his fingers on the statement I'd just signed. "Tell me, Piper, off the record, did you notice anything unusual about the scene?"

I shifted uncomfortably in my seat. I'd like to blame my sudden uneasiness on the cheap chrome and faux leather chair I was sitting in, but I knew better. It wasn't the chair;

it was McBride's cold blue stare that made me squirm. "Unusual how?"

He leaned forward, his cop mask securely in place. "You've discovered more dead bodies than archeologists in Pompeii. Did anything strike you as odd?"

What was McBride getting at? I inspected my nails to buy some time. I wasn't quite sure what to say—or what not to say. I didn't want to make things more difficult for Melly than they were already.

"Well?"

"Chip's skin felt cold and stiff," I admitted cautiously. "I suspected the accident happened hours prior to Melly's call. But that's hardly front-page news. The coroner confirmed that himself this morning."

"Sure you're not holding back?"

"Of course I'm sure."

"I'd hate to think you're withholding information from the authorities—the authorities in this case being me. If so, you'd be guilty of obstruction of justice."

I surged to my feet, angrier than I'd been in ages. I felt a hot rush of blood heat my cheeks. "Now, just a frickin' minute, Mr. Law and Order. I told you exactly what happened. You can take it or leave it."

McBride was studying me like I was a crawfish in Biology 101. "I realize Melly Prescott is . . . was . . . your mother-in-law, and you might harbor a certain loyalty, but we're talking a man's death. I'm just trying to get my facts straight."

"Chip Balboa's death was an accident, a tragic accident." I started for the door, then stopped and turned. "Stop trying to make it into something it's not."

His expression stony, McBride slipped my signed statement back into a folder. "For the time being, we're calling Chip Balboa's death 'suspicious.'"

"We? Who's 'we'?"

"The medical examiner and Georgia Bureau of Investigation, that's who."

Stunned, I digested this in silence. What could possibly make them think Chip's accident wasn't a simple fall down a flight of stairs but a possible homicide instead?

"Sorry to lay this on you, Piper, but things aren't always what they seem."

I left McBride's office with his words ringing in my ears.

CHAPTER 9

"How was Melly when she got back to your place last night?" Reba Mae bit into her Italian sub with gusto.

"Hard to tell." I unwrapped my sandwich and popped the tab on my Diet Coke. Reba Mae and I were enjoying lunch on a park bench in the town square. Actually, the impromptu picnic had been Melly's idea. Watching the shop for an hour or so, she said, would help take her mind off her troubles. And if she needed anything, I'd be close by.

"What did CJ have to say?"

"He dropped her off, but didn't come in. When I asked Melly how her meeting went with McBride, she refused to talk about it and went straight to bed. She didn't even want dinner."

"I'm worried about her."

"Me, too." It was comforting to know that worry had company. That's the beauty of having a BFF.

"Mmm, Pizza Palace subs are the best." Reba Mae broke off a piece of her roll and tossed it to a gray squirrel rummaging through fallen leaves for acorns.

"Agree," I said. "I love the combination of capicola,

mortadella, Genoa, and provolone, but Tony's special dressing is what sets them apart."

"I'd ask him for the recipe, but I know better."

"I've been experimenting with a mix of my own—basil, thyme, oregano, garlic, a dash of salt and pepper, olive oil, balsamic vinegar. Next time, I'm going to add a tiny bit of rosemary."

"Sounds like a winner." Reba Mae wiped her fingers on a napkin. "You never said how your session with McBride went. You holdin' out on me?"

I took a bite of my sandwich, washed it down with a swig of Coke. "Pretty straightforward. Not much to tell."

"Did he ever get hold of Chip's ex-wife—whatsher-name? How'd she take the news?"

"Name's Cheryl. If he did, he didn't mention it."

"Sounds like McBride. The man can be as close-mouthed as a clam."

"Unlike his right-hand man, Sergeant Blabbermouth," I said. "McBride did say something that gave me pause."

By her raised brow, I knew I had Reba Mae's undivided attention. "Out with it, honeybun," she ordered. "It's not nice to leave a friend danglin' by a thread."

I brushed crumbs from my capris. "Just as I was about to leave his office, he said, 'Things aren't always what they seem.' What do you suppose he meant?"

"McBride's a sneaky buzzard. I don't think he'd leak a secret if you threatened him with Chinese water torture."

"When I arrived at his office, he was talking to someone at the Georgia Bureau of Investigation. I can't help but think McBride was trying to tell me something, you know, without coming right out and saying it. Does that make any sense?"

Reba Mae shrugged. "The whole thing's a mystery, if you ask me. It's all folks talk about. Jolene Tucker let it be known around town that Chip had been dead for twelve hours before Melly phoned the police. No one can figure out why she waited so dang long."

"According to Melly, she dialed me the instant she saw a man on her basement floor."

"You think she's tellin' the truth or fibbin'?"

I stared at my friend, surprised at her question. "Of course she's telling the truth," I said. "She's Melly."

Reba Mae balled up her sandwich wrapper and stuffed it into the bag it had come in. "No need to get your panties in a twist, girlfriend. I'm just askin' is all."

I idly watched a redbird land in a nearby holly bush and peck at the berries. "Melly told me Chip complained of a headache. She went upstairs to get him Tylenol but realized it was time for her favorite show. She turned on the TV to watch for a couple minutes and probably lost track of the time. When she went downstairs, Chip was gone. She assumed he got tired of waiting and left. She tidied the kitchen, then went upstairs to finish watching her program."

"I guess it makes sense. Still . . ."

"Still?"

"If a man fell down your stairs, don't you think you would have heard something and gone to see what it was?"

It was a question I'd asked myself a dozen times. "I admit it's been awhile since I've been in Melly's bedroom, but to the best of my knowledge, her room is in the front of the house. The kitchen's at the back. Who knows, maybe Melly is a little hard of hearing. That happens as people age."

"Melly would sooner bite off her tongue than admit she's gettin' old." Climbing to her feet, Reba Mae smoothed wrinkles from her swingy patterned skirt. "Well, I'll be glad when this whole thing blows over. Then I can focus on rehearsals for *Steel Magnolias* and decide what I'm bringin' to Oktoberfest."

There it was again, Oktoberfest. I was beginning to feel

paranoid. Was I the only one in the entire town who hadn't been invited to the Grangers' party? With each passing day, I was becoming more and more convinced that the snub was intentional. By withholding an invitation, Sandy was letting me know in no uncertain terms that she didn't like little ol' me criticizing her lifestyle. Never again would I question the couple's propensity for travel.

Reba Mae glanced at her watch. "Uh-oh. Gotta run. My cut and color is due any minute. You comin'?"

I let out a sigh. "No, I think I'll enjoy the sunshine a bit longer."

"Okay, see you later." She gathered our trash and hurried off. I noticed she took the empty soda cans with her. Reba Mae never missed a chance to recycle.

The October sun was high in a cloudless sky, the humidity low. There was little traffic to disturb the quiet. Birds chirped; squirrels scampered. It should have been peaceful sitting here . . . but it wasn't. Surely McBride didn't think Chip's death was anything other than a tragic fall? If so, did he seriously suspect Melly of . . . ? My mind shied away from "murder." It scared me to think people already doubted her version of what had happened.

Rather than sit and ponder what was going on in that mind of his, I decided to go straight to the source. No time like the present. Before I could talk myself out of it, I hightailed it over to the police station.

Dorinda scowled at seeing me. "Can I help you?"

"I need a few minutes of the chief's time." I tried to disarm her with a smile, but it didn't work.

"He's busy." Dorinda went back to pecking at the keyboard.

"No problem. I'll wait." Not about to be dismissed so easily, I took a seat on the same wood bench I'd occupied yesterday, a bench worn smooth by the backsides of anx-

ious relatives and friends of those accused of crimes, big
or small.

"Suit yourself." Dorinda didn't look up.

Picking up the same dog-eared copy of *Car and Driver*
I'd flipped through yesterday, I studied Dorinda, who was
doing an excellent job of ignoring me. She was a tall,
broad-shouldered woman in her fifties with a no-nonsense
demeanor. Silver strands crept through medium-brown
hair. Her eyes, small, dark, and as bright as a sparrow's,
didn't miss a trick.

She must have sensed me watching her, because she
glanced my way. "Chief's with someone. Shouldn't be long."

I nodded and went back to my magazine browsing. I
couldn't help wondering if McBride's visitor happened to
be the driver of the snazzy black BMW angled across not
one but two parking spaces marked RESERVED.

I'd no sooner scanned an ad for a pricey Range Rover
when I heard a loud wail come from the direction of Mc-
Bride's office. This was followed by a series of harsh gut-
tural sobs.

"The Widow Balboa," Dorinda said.

"Widow? I thought Chip was divorced."

"So did the chief."

More wailing and sobbing followed. Nothing—not rain,
sleet, or hail, nothing—was going to make me budge from
my ringside seat. I had to see for myself a woman capable
of such gut-wrenching sounds.

Fortunately, I didn't have a long wait before a door
opened and I heard McBride say, "I'm sorry for your loss,
Mrs. Balboa. If you don't mind, I'd like you to stick around
for a few days until matters are resolved."

I eavesdropped so blatantly, my ears twitched like antennas. Even Dorinda stopped typing and cocked her head
to listen.

"Very well, since you insist," Cheryl Balboa sniffled. "When will my husband's body be released?"

"Soon, I expect. The ME should release it by tomorrow at the latest."

"Not until then? Tomorrow's Saturday," the widow whined. "That means I probably won't be able to have my husband cremated until Monday."

"Cremation isn't my department," McBride said. "You might want to stop at the Eternal Rest Funeral Home and talk with John Strickland, the undertaker. John also happens to be county coroner."

"Fine, I'll do that," Cheryl replied. "I'm eager to have things settled and return to California. I plan to call my attorney this afternoon and apprise him of the situation. I'll want to set up an appointment as soon as I get back. Seeing how Chip and I were still married, I'm the sole beneficiary of his estate. There's a great deal of business to attend to."

I heard the click of high heels on tile. Pretending interest in a Porsche ad—it could have been an ad for Cheerios, for all I cared—I peeked over the top of the magazine for my first glimpse of the widow. Cheryl Balboa paused not more than three feet in front of me. I watched her toss a wadded-up tissue in the general direction of a corner trash can, then extract an iPhone from a Kate Spade handbag.

She was pretty in a mannequin sort of way. Thin almost to the point of emaciation, she wore a short skirt showing a mile of slender, tanned leg. I estimated her salon cut with its highlights and lowlights cost more than Reba Mae earned in an entire day.

"Hey, babe," Cheryl said into the phone as she walked toward the exit. "You hungry?"

I stared after her, thinking I was missing something. Then it hit me: There wasn't a single drop of moisture on her cheeks, no reddened eyes, no runny mascara. In spite of all the wailing and carrying on, her makeup remained flawless. So much for her grieving widow act.

McBride peered down the short hallway and noticed me sitting on the bench. He didn't seem particularly pleased to see me, but him being a public servant and me being a taxpayer, he crooked a finger and beckoned. I didn't wait for an engraved invitation.

Dorinda narrowed her beady eyes and shot me a warning look as if to say, State your business but make it brief. Ignoring her, I hurried toward McBride before he changed his mind.

"Something you wanted to add to your initial statement? Or is this a social call?"

"Neither." After skirting past him, I plopped down in the chair reserved for visitors.

He closed the office door, then sat on the edge of his desk, his gaze never leaving my face. "Then what brings you here?"

I tucked an errant curl behind one ear. "I keep thinking of what you said last night when I left your office. A cryptic remark about how things aren't always what they appear. What exactly was that supposed to mean?"

His expression impassive, he picked a pen off his blotter. "What do you think I meant?"

If I wanted to play word games, I'd get an app for my phone. "I took your parting comment to mean that just because something looked like an accident, sounded like an accident, or smelled like an accident, didn't necessarily mean it was an accident. Am I hot or cold?"

He studied the logo on the pen for a protracted moment before zapping me with his laser blues. "As I told you last night, we're treating Chip Balboa's fall as suspicious."

"Suspicious," I repeated. "Is that because the coroner ruled Chip died hours before Melly reported it?"

"That and because of the ME's preliminary report.

Seems he found an unusual pattern of bruising. A pattern
more consistent with a shove than a fall."

"A shove?"

Call it denial if you will, but I had a hard time wrapping my mind around the notion that Chip's death was a
homicide. I rubbed my arms against a sudden chill. If that
were true, McBride would come gunning for the killer . . .
and he had Melly lined up in his sights.

CHAPTER *10*

Melly gave me a wan smile. "Enjoy your lunch, dear?"

My idyllic lunch with Reba Mae on a park bench seemed eons ago. In reality, it was less than an hour. I'd returned to Spice It Up! more confused—and more worried—than ever. "It's a beautiful day to be outdoors," I said as I slipped on my apron. "You should take a walk, get some fresh air."

"Maybe later." Melly neatly restacked a pile of cooking magazines that I subscribed to in the hope inspiration would strike for new and novel uses for spices. "I looked across the way, but you weren't there." Melly made no effort to disguise the mild rebuke: Shame on me for not being in plain sight.

"Since I haven't jogged the last couple days, I decided I'd go for a little stroll, get some exercise."

I had no intention of informing Melly of my conversation with McBride. She'd learn soon enough that Chip's death was deemed suspicious. That the ME's findings were more consistent with a shove and not a fall.

A shove not a fall?

The words rattled around my brain like tiles in a bingo

cage. What really happened the night Chip died? Was McBride the only person who was being closemouthed? Or did Melly know more than she was telling? What secrets hid beneath the sweaters and pearls? No time like the present to polish my Nancy Drew, girl detective, skills.

I ran a hand over my unruly curls and opted for casual: "You never told me what brought Chip over to your house the other night."

"He wanted to talk."

"Talk?" I tipped my head to one side, imitating an attentive pose I'd seen actors do on soap operas. "About what?"

"Business," Melly snapped. "Software things that don't concern you."

All righty, then. I guess she'd put me in my place. Time for another tactic. "You're absolutely right, Melly. When it comes to computers and such, all I need is for them to work. You, on the other hand, are a natural."

"Hmph!"

Flattery wasn't helping me gain much ground, either. What would Nancy do? Or, for that matter, Jessica Fletcher or Miss Jane Marple? I opted for a direct approach. "You never said any more about Rusty and Chip's proposal. Was the amount they offered satisfactory?"

"No! Not even close to what they initially led me to believe. And before I forget"—she abruptly changed the subject and pointed to a cardboard box partially hidden at the base of the counter—"the FedEx driver dropped this off while you were off gallivanting."

Picking up the box, I cleared a space on the counter, then set it down and read the label. "This is a shipment of spice from my supplier on the West Coast. Before you know it, people will start thinking of holiday goodies. I wanted to make sure I had an ample supply of cinnamon, nutmeg, and cloves."

"The delivery man insisted on a signature, but since you

weren't here, I signed for you." She whipped the yellow apron over her head. "I hope that was all right."

I slit open the box. "Thanks."

"Doug phoned." Melly painstakingly folded the apron as if her life depended upon perfect creases. "He said he'd be here at six o'clock to pick you up."

I struggled to corral my thoughts, which flitted between a tumble down the stairs to baking Christmas stollen. Finally it dawned on me what she meant. Football. Friday Night Lights. Football was a big deal in small towns across America. I'd promised Lindsey that Doug and I would be in the bleachers to cheer the new routines she'd been practicing all week.

Melly stowed her apron under the counter. "Doug mentioned you were having a bite to eat at High Cotton before the game. I've never been there personally. I've heard the place is rowdy."

"Maybe late at night, but not early on." I unpacked a bundle of cinnamon sticks and couldn't resist sniffing their sweet, spicy fragrance before setting them aside. "High Cotton is known for its great burgers and chili cheese fries."

Melly shuddered. "All those calories and cholesterol can't be good for a person."

"Probably not," I agreed. Melly, it seemed, was more willing to talk about the hazards of chili cheese fries than about what had transpired between her and Chip Balboa. However, I wasn't about to abandon my inquisition so easily. "So," I said, "did you and Chip argue when he came to visit?"

Melly's lips flattened. "Both those young men mistook me for a dotty old woman without a lick of sense. I wasn't about to sign over my software modifications and lose all my equity. I told them straight-out I wasn't interested. Chip thought he could soften me up, convince me to change my mind."

Mental alarm bells sounded. Some people might construe that as motive to give the cheap dot-com guy a shove or two. "Have you mentioned this to McBride?"

"He didn't ask, and I didn't volunteer." Her back ramrod stiff, Melly turned on her heel and marched off.

Perplexed, I stared after her. Melly had a delicate build. It was hard to imagine her strong enough to push a seemingly healthy, mildly overweight thirty-something down a flight of stairs. And heartless enough to let him lie there until the following morning. No, I told myself: That wasn't the Melly Prescott I knew.

I've found nothing soothes me like performing some mundane task. After taking out a feather duster, I methodically ran it over shelves lined with spices from the four corners of the earth. Those spices had become my extended family, my friends. I knew their countries of origin, how they were harvested, and how they were used. Studying about them had been a virtual tour of places I'd never heard of, could barely pronounce, and definitely couldn't spell.

Casey trailed after me as I systematically worked my way around the shop. He eventually tired of my slow progress and settled down in a patch of sunlight streaming through the front window.

I'd progressed to a display of various salts and peppercorns when the shop door opened. I recognized the newcomer instantly as none other than Sandy Granger, Brandywine Creek's hostess with the mostess. I wedged the duster between jars of sea salt from the Mediterranean and peppercorns from Borneo. "Hey, Sandy," I greeted. "What can I do for you?"

"I've been meaning to stop by ever since Craig and I returned from our trip around the world."

"I heard you were home." *And planning a huge party to which I haven't been invited,* I added silently. "How was your trip?"

"Fabulous, just fabulous." Sandy's green eyes sparkled at the memory. "Eight countries on five continents. We were so exhausted, we stayed in London a couple extra weeks to catch our breath."

"Sounds wonderful."

"I'd love to tell you all about it, but I don't have time. You've probably heard from Reba Mae that I'm directing *Steel Magnolias* at the opera house. It's scheduled to kick off the winter theater season. I'm on my way to a meeting with the set designer, but I wanted to stop by for a few items first." She dug through a designer tote and produced a shopping list. "I need saffron, a gram ought to do it—I prefer coupe," she added. "Vanilla—beans, not extract—and cardamom. Seeds, no shells."

"No problem." Humming to myself, I plucked the requested spices from the shelves. Any sale of saffron always lightened my mood.

Sandy handed me her American Express card. "I know saffron is horrendously expensive, but a little goes a long way."

Still humming, I rang up the items and bagged them. "Here you go."

"Thanks," she said. "But before I run off, I wanted to extend a personal invitation to a party Craig and I are throwing next Saturday—an Oktoberfest. I'm asking all my guests to bring a German dessert or side dish to share."

At last, the long-awaited invite. "Can't wait. I'll be there," I said, but she was already out the door. Apparently, all was forgiven. My thoughtless remark about her extensive travel was now water under the bridge.

I resumed dusting the shelves, my mind now on food. What should I take? Potato dumplings with a sprinkle of grated nutmeg? Or apple strudel with a generous teaspoon of Vietnamese cinnamon? Maybe lebkuchen, a German spice cookie. Oh, how I wished all my problems were this simple.

Doug was prompt as usual, dressed casually in jeans, a long-sleeved rugby shirt, and a sweater draped across his shoulders in readiness for later, when the temperature dipped. I'd dressed even more casually than Doug, in jeans and a sweatshirt in red and gold, the team colors.

"Hey"—he grinned—"no one can say you don't have school spirit."

"Is this too much? Does the sweatshirt clash with my hair?"

He tugged a curl and pulled me in for a kiss so warm and sweet, it made my toes curl. A noise from the floor above startled us apart. "Your houseguest, I presume."

"'Fraid so," I said. "I offered to fix Melly dinner, but she said she'd make something later."

Doug placed a hand at my waist and steered me toward the door. "Any idea how long she'll be staying?"

"I'm not sure." I had a sinking feeling that Melly's house would remain off-limits for some time. I turned my key in the lock. "It could be awhile."

"Why's that?"

"You know what a stickler McBride is for detail." For some odd reason, I felt reluctant to discuss the ME's preliminary findings with Doug. After all, "preliminary" meant just that—preliminary. It might amount to nothing. Nothing at all. Melly was entitled to the benefit of the doubt. *When did I turn into such a Pollyanna?*

"No telling when the painters will finish at CJ's," I said. "Amber insists on having the entire house redone. She consulted an interior designer at some fancy furniture store in Augusta, who told her the current color scheme is all wrong. And," I added, "I think Melly's leery of broaching the subject of her return home with McBride."

Doug held open the door of his SUV. "If she has nothing to hide, she has no reason to worry."

I slid inside the car. It sounded simple enough—provided Melly had nothing to hide. But what if she did?

Doug climbed into the driver's side, and we headed in the direction of High Cotton. As Doug talked about everyday things, my thoughts wandered. Melly had admitted Chip's visit was for more than milk and gingersnaps. She'd been disappointed with Trustychipdesign's offer. Had their last conversation been friendly? Or contentious? She'd mentioned Chip complained of a headache, but what had preceded it?

Even stranger, I thought as the SUV turned into the gravel lot of High Cotton, was the ME's impression that the bruising on Chip's body was more consistent with a shove than with a fall. I'd bet my last jar of saffron that McBride knew more than he was letting on.

The situation called for a quarterback sneak. I knew just the person to ask in order to gain some yardage.

CHAPTER *11*

By the time Doug and I arrived at Brandywine Creek High School, the football field was lit up as bright as day. Doug parked the SUV in the adjoining lot. Friends and acquaintances called out greetings as we strolled hand in hand toward the ticket gate. Judging from the *rat-a-tat-tat* of drums punctuated by blares of trumpets, trombones, and French horns, the band was in top form for the school's big game against their archrivals.

After Doug paid for our tickets, we wormed our way through the crowd. We stood at the foot of the bleachers, scanning the sea of red and gold for a place to sit. Gerilee Barker, a large-boned woman with permed hair a determined shade of brown, sat next to her husband, Pete, the town's butcher, halfway up. She caught my eye and motioned for us to join them. Amidst a chorus of apologies to those already seated, Doug and I edged along the row toward Gerilee and Pete.

Gerilee scooted over to make room for us on the hard metal bleacher. "Hey, y'all. Seems half the town turned out for the game."

"Everyone's sayin' the team has a good chance to go all

the way to the state championships this year." Pete dipped his hand into a striped tub of popcorn nearly as big as his head.

Just then, the two opposing teams ran out onto the field and were met with a cacophony of cheers, catcalls, and stomping feet. I craned my neck to watch Lindsey, who along with her fellow cheerleaders, shook giant red and gold pompons and exhorted the crowd to give them a *B*. The crowd roared back.

A voice over the loudspeaker introduced each player and his position on the team. In turn, each boy stepped forward to a smattering of applause. "Which one is Lindsey's current heartthrob?" Doug asked.

I nodded toward the player who had garnered the noisiest response from the crowd. "Number seven. Sean Rogers."

"The quarterback?"

"The one and only." I strained forward, trying to get a better glimpse of the young man everyone was talking about. Other than being tall, the boy was hard to make out beneath the helmet and protective padding. "Lindsey's keeping her fingers crossed he'll ask her to the homecoming dance."

"I've heard there's a good chance he'll be recruited by one of the college scouts. Georgia Tech, maybe Georgia Southern or even University of Georgia. Have you met the kid?"

"Not yet." The kickoff return interfered with any more conversation.

Several plays later, Doug grimaced at a pileup of young bodies, then turned to me. "Clients of mine know Rogers's father. Apparently, he and his son moved here from Atlanta following a messy divorce. The mother remarried recently, and the stepdad didn't want a teenager underfoot. My clients say Sean's a good kid."

"I hope so. Lindsey hasn't always been wise in her choice of boyfriends."

My gaze fastened on the cheerleaders, who were performing choreographed gymnastics. Lindsey's blond ponytail danced and swayed as she bobbed up and down. The sight of her tugged on my heartstrings. My girl seemed impossibly young yet impossibly grown-up. In the blink of an eye, she'd be graduating high school and off to college, just as my Chad had done.

And my nest would be empty. I'd be alone.

Gerilee nudged me in the ribs. "How's Melly holding up? Pete tells me she's staying with you these days."

"She set up camp in Lindsey's room until McBride gives her the go-ahead to return home."

Pete offered popcorn from the half-empty tub. "I noticed Sandy Granger coming out of your shop this afternoon. She put in a big order for all kinds of German sausages. Bratwurst, knockwurst, mettwurst, you name it."

"Sandy and Craig want the real deal," Gerilee continued while the teams gathered in a huddle. "Luckily, Pete knows a butcher in Helen who can help supply what he needs."

Doug winked at me. We'd talked about visiting Helen, Georgia, located on the Chattahoochee River in northeast Georgia. The town resembled an alpine village, complete with cobblestones and old-world towers. Doug had read about a charming bed-and-breakfast, perfect for a romantic weekend getaway. So far, that's all it had been—talk. Work was the excuse we used most often to postpone our trip, but deep down, I think both of us were being cautious when it came to dipping our toes into the relationship pool.

"Have you decided what you're taking to the Oktoberfest?" Gerilee asked Doug.

"I'm thinking of trying my hand at sauerbraten," he said. It hadn't taken long for Doug to earn the reputation of being a "foodie." I had to hand it to him; the man certainly knew his way around a kitchen. Fortunately for me, he liked to experiment with various cuisines—many that called for unusual spices. As a matter of fact, we'd first met when he wandered into Spice It Up!—even before its grand opening—to purchase saffron.

A grin spread across Pete's face at the mention of sauerbraten. "I'll set aside a couple real nice bottom rounds."

"Great." Doug chuckled before turning to me. "The recipe I found calls for lots of spices, including juniper berries, so I hope you're well stocked."

"Doesn't sauerbraten also include gingersnaps?" Gerilee, not waiting for an answer, continued, "Why don't you ask Melly to supply the cookies? No one makes better gingersnaps than Melly."

Poor Melly, I thought. I wondered if she'd forever associate her favorite cookies with Chip Balboa's visit to Brandywine Creek and his subsequent tumble down her basement stairs. There was no time to ponder the question further, because just then, the crowd erupted in a frenzy of excitement. Sean Rogers sent the football sailing down the field, where it was caught by a receiver for a touchdown. By halftime, the Brandywine Bearcats led by a score of 21–3.

"Kid's got an arm," Pete commented, climbing to his feet. "Gonna get me some of those deep-fried Oreos the Booster Club always sells."

Gerilee stood and stretched. "I'll go with you. There's always a long line for the ladies' room."

Doug shrugged on his sweater. "Temperatures really drop at night, now that fall's here. How about some hot chocolate to warm up?"

"Sounds great."

We scrambled down from the bleachers to join the throng headed toward the concession stands. As luck would have it, CJ and Amber materialized alongside us. Amber was dressed in football chic: dark slimming jeans that accentuated her mile-long legs, a cashmere turtleneck the shade of ripe apricots, and a waist-length coffee-brown leather jacket. I felt frumpy—and short—walking next to her in my jeans and sweatshirt.

"Hey, y'all." Amber flashed a smile, revealing a mouthful of teeth whiter than God ever intended. "Fancy runnin' into you."

"Hello, Amber." I forced a smile as well. The two of us would never be friends. I couldn't even pretend. My acting ability just wasn't that great. I'm sure even Bette Davis had limitations.

CJ stuck out his hand, and the men shook. "That Rogers kid got an arm on him," he said, parroting Pete Barker's assessment.

"You come to check out Lindsey's new beau?" Amber asked, falling into step beside me.

"No, not really," I said. "I wanted to show my support for all the hours she poured into learning the new routines."

"Our girl looked good out there, didn't she?" CJ multitasked by nodding and grinning at the same time. "Prettiest one on the squad."

Amber tossed glossy mahogany locks. "When it comes to boyfriends, I told Lindsey if she wants to be homecoming queen, to set her sights on the quarterback. It's a sure-fire way to win votes."

I fumed at the implication Lindsey was interested in Sean Rogers only because of his prowess on the football field. My girl wasn't that shallow. I bit my tongue to hold back an angry retort.

CJ placed a possessive hand on Amber's waist. "Quarterbacks, in my estimation, are overrated. Give me a good running back any ol' day."

"Wasn't Wyatt McBride quarterback the year your team went to state?"

I knew my barb hit its target when a dull red flush crept up CJ's neck. The animosity between McBride and my ex dated back to their high school days. I had never learned all the details, but knew enough to know there was no love lost between the two men.

As we neared the concession stand, Amber's gaze swept over a balding, overweight man carrying a plate heaped with deep-fried Oreos. A vertical line formed between her penciled brows at the sight. "Those things kill one's figure. They go directly to the hips. I wouldn't touch them with a ten-foot pole."

"Well, you're in luck," Doug said with a smile I knew wasn't genuine. "There's not a ten-foot pole in sight."

Failing to recognize the thinly veiled sarcasm, Amber patted CJ's tummy. "I keep tellin' Pooh Bear he needs to start workin' out if he wants to be in shape for our weddin'."

"Have you lovebirds set a date yet?" I asked, bolstered by Doug's hand in mine.

Amber gave another head toss. I wondered if she ever worried about dislocating a vertebra. "Sometime between Christmas and New Year's," she said. "Mother's havin' a procedure done and wants us to wait until she's fully recovered."

It was a poorly kept secret that Amber's mother was a frequent passenger on the cosmetic surgery express. Amelia Ames's obsession with her appearance might explain her daughter's self-absorption.

CJ waved at a well-dressed couple standing off to one side. I recognized Dennis and Bunny Bowtin from our country club days. He was a successful banker; she, the reigning queen of the tennis courts. "Glad we had a chance to chat," he said. "Gotta run."

"Dennis just hired CJ's firm. Quite a coup on Pooh Bear's part," Amber explained as they ambled off. "Their son's on the team. He's the runnin' back."

So that explained why CJ was at the game. It wasn't his love of high school football. It wasn't interest in his daughter's cheerleading. It wasn't a promising young quarterback. No, CJ's sole purpose tonight was to cozy up to a new client. One with deep pockets. He'd never once asked how his mother was getting along. Whatever happened to the idealistic young attorney I'd married?

Doug squeezed my hand. "You all right?"

I squeezed back. "People change over time, drift apart. Seeing CJ and Amber together used to upset me, but not anymore. It's been downgraded to minor annoyance. Goes to show I'm making progress. Quite frankly, I'm happy with the life I've created without him."

Doug scowled. "Looks like the line at the concession stand is a mile long. Why don't you find a spot to watch the band's halftime show while I get the refreshments."

"Fine," I said.

"Seeing we've already clogged our arteries with burgers and chili fries, let's have some deep-fried Oreos with our hot chocolate?"

"You sure know how to treat a gal," I teased, waving him off. I've even seen Double Stuf deep-fried Oreos on a menu at a popular restaurant in Augusta. To add insult to injury, the restaurant topped these off with Hershey's chocolate syrup and served them with vanilla ice cream. A heart attack on a fancy plate.

I found a vantage spot not far from the main gate to observe the goings-on. The band struck up the school fight song and strutted up and down the field, drums rattling and trumpets blaring. I glanced over my shoulder to check on Doug's progress in time to see Beau Tucker, out of uniform and casually dressed, separate from the crowd at the concession stand. Beau balanced a cardboard tray loaded with snacks and sodas as he threaded his way back to the bleachers.

"Hey, Beau." A kernel of an idea burst into bloom as I hailed him. Now, I don't usually prey on a man's weakness, but I was about to make an exception in Beau's case. I knew he loved to boast about his experiences in the police department. McBride might be closemouthed, but no one could accuse Beau of that.

"Hey, Piper." A broad grin wreathed his round face. "Some game, ain't it?"

"Sure is. That Rogers kid has quite an arm." That seemed to be the comment du jour.

Beau made to move off and take my opportunity with him.

"Wait up, Beau. Mind if I ask a question before you go?"

He readjusted the tray he carried. "Shoot."

"Chief McBride said something that's still bothering me. I hope you can shed some light on the subject. Put my mind at ease."

Beau eyed the nachos dripping gooey yellow cheese and loaded with jalapeños with obvious longing. "Yeah, I guess. What exactly did the chief say?"

"McBride told me Chip's death was being viewed as 'suspicious.' He said the preliminary findings were more consistent with a shove rather than a fall. I keep wondering what he meant by that."

Beau stared down at his cache of goodies. The yellow cheese dripping over nacho chips was beginning to congeal. He seemed eager to get back into the stands and chow down before it cooled completely. "Since McBride told you about the prelim, guess there's no harm telling you why the ME said what he did."

I affected a casual shrug. "Guess not."

"The ME reported there was less bruising than expected." Beau shifted his weight from one foot to the other. "If Balboa had hit most of the stairs on the way to the bottom, there would've been considerably more bruising, more fractures, as a result of coming into contact with the risers. Only fracture the vic suffered was a broken neck."

"A broken neck's bad enough," I said.

Beau nodded. "The theory is that Chip Balboa was propelled down the stairs with a force great enough to send him directly to the floor below. Sort of like in the Monopoly game. You know: Do not pass go. Do not collect two hundred dollars."

"Interesting," I murmured. From the corner of my eye, I saw Doug approaching.

"Yeah, interesting. Same thing the chief said." Beau half turned to leave, then stopped. "One other thing—there was a bruise shaped like a handprint between the vic's shoulder blades. Suspicious, don't you think?" Not waiting for my response, he hurried off, muttering how Jolene was going to give him whatfor if the nachos were ruined.

Handprint?

I stared after Beau, watching him get swallowed up by the crowd. I'd lost my appetite for deep-fried Oreos. The chili cheese fries I'd eaten earlier weren't sitting too well, either. The roar from the stands nearly drowned out the buzzing in my head. Like it or not, Melly had become the prime suspect in a murder investigation. I vowed then and there to do everything in my power to find out who was really responsible for killing Chip Balboa. Melly's freedom—her life—hung in the balance.

CHAPTER *12*

"Point me toward the ginger," Dottie Hemmings requested the next morning as she reached for one of the small wicker baskets.

My jaw dropped. Dottie tended to be a looky lou. Although she frequently visited Spice It Up!, it was to gossip. She never purchased a thing. Dottie was convinced spices retained their freshness into the next millennium. I'd been trying to convince her otherwise but thus far had failed.

"Ginger?" I asked, coming around the counter to offer assistance. "Do you want ground, crystallized, or root?"

"Better give me some of each," Dottie instructed.

Before she reconsidered, I snatched a jar of ground, grabbed a bag of crystallized, and added handful of knobby rhizomes to her basket. "Planning to do some baking?"

"Good gracious, no." She chuckled. "Piper, shame on you. You know me better than that. Whenever my husband the mayor gets a hankering for baked goods, I head straight for the Piggly Wiggly."

"Sorry," I mumbled. "What was I thinking?"

Dottie plucked two jars of cloves from a shelf, dropped them into the basket. "Did you hear Fred Higgins has shingles? Irma's been nagging him to get the vaccine—but did he listen? No, he's stubborn as a mule."

"Ginger happens to be one of the most widely used spices," I said, in hope of diverting her from tales of misery and suffering. "I have a collection of recipes you might be tempted to try if you ever decide to experiment."

"Nice of you to offer, Piper, but if I want homemade goodies, I'll wait for the next funeral. In my opinion, the Methodist women are the best bakers in town. Harvey and I always take a sample or two home with us."

Dottie and her hubby were notorious for asking the kitchen crew for to-go boxes, then filling them with choice tidbits from the dessert table. Since Harvey was "Hizzoner the mayor," folks tended to look the other way.

"Can't tell you how disappointed I was when I found out Chip Balboa was gonna be cremated. Here I was hoping the Thursday Night Bingo Ladies would step up to give the man a decent send-off. Show him some old-fashioned Southern hospitality."

I moved toward the cash register with Dottie trailing. "It's my understanding Chip lived in California. Whatever made you think his service would be held in Brandywine Creek?"

"Ned Feeney was at the Eternal Rest when the deceased's widow came to call on John Strickland. She demanded her husband be cremated the instant his body's released. When John questioned her, she said since her husband had no family to speak of, she saw no reason to dawdle."

"I suppose that makes sense," I said, unloading the bags, jars, and rhizomes onto the counter.

"Mr. Balboa's widow complained about the high cost of transporting a corpse. Said the price was astronomical, and the money would be better spent elsewhere." Dottie fished a credit card out of her purse. "Don't understand why all the rush."

Frankly, I didn't, either. My first impression might've been wrong, but Cheryl didn't strike me as a grieving widow. She seemed more interested in meeting someone for lunch than in mourning her dearly departed. Added to that, Rusty Tulley, trusted friend and business partner, had been under the impression that the couple was divorced. However, as I'd learned at the police station, the couple was still married. Had they reconciled? Or had one or the other delayed signing the final papers?

"Now, take me, for instance"—Dottie patted her lacquered blond beehive—"when I pass, I've given my husband the mayor strict orders that I expect standing room only at First Baptist. Have you given any thought to arrangements?"

My mind went blank. "Arrangements?"

"Don't leave the important decisions to others," Dottie counseled. "There are dozens of things to consider—casket, favorite hymns, type of flowers. Don't forget to put in writing what clothes you want to be wearin'. You'll be wantin' to look your best when folks come to pay their final respects."

This conversation was creeping me out, so I abruptly changed the topic. "You never mentioned what you were going to do with the ginger."

"Spiders," Dottie replied succinctly.

"Spiders?"

"Noreen McCarthy, a friend in Florida, uses ginger to rid her house of the pesky little buggers. Noreen said she hasn't needed an exterminator in years. Saves her a bundle."

"Interesting," I replied for lack of a better word.

"I'm going to make little sachets, fill them with ginger, and place them in strategic spots all around the house.

Thought I'd add some cloves and nutmeg for good measure. Noreen swears by this method. It's so much better than those noxious sprays most folks use. Heavens, it can't be good to breathe those fumes. My niece's second cousin twice removed met a very untimely end, and all because of a spray can."

I handed her a receipt along with her purchase. "I'll keep that in mind."

"Toodle-oo," she sang out as she departed with a merry wave.

"I thought I heard Dottie Hemmings's voice."

I turned to find Melly coming down the stairs. Casey's tail thumped in greeting, but when no doggie treat was forthcoming, he resumed his snoozing.

"Thanks to Dottie, I have to order more ginger. The woman's on spider patrol." As Melly neared, I noticed she looked wan. Her blue-gray eyes were shadowed with worry and fatigue. "You don't look as though you slept well."

She gave me a weary smile. "I tossed and turned half the night. I'll be glad when I can sleep in my own bed again."

"McBride should finish his investigation soon, and things can return to normal."

"Normal?" Melly shuddered. "I keep thinking of that poor man lying in my basement the whole time I was sound asleep. I hope he didn't suffer in the fall."

"It's a beautiful day outside. Why not take a little walk? Some fresh air will do you a world of good."

"Maybe I'll do that," she said, brightening. "I think I'll stop by Gray's Hardware and surprise Thompson with a visit. We always seem to find some computer-related topic to discuss. One nerd to another, as Thompson is fond of saying."

Melly had no sooner left than the phone rang. It was Doug calling to break our date for that evening. Seems he had a sick dog with anxious owners who needed his attention. Apologizing profusely, he promised to make it up to me, then disconnected.

Restless, I rapped my fingertips on the counter. Saturday night stretched ahead of me like a long and winding country road. But I had more on my mind than a broken date. A nasty thought worked its way into my mind. I knew Melly hadn't killed Chip—but that meant someone else had. Did Cheryl Balboa have reason to want her husband dead? I needed a sounding board. So I did what came naturally. I dialed my BFF.

Reba Mae slipped into the booth across from me at North of the Border. Nacho, one of the owners, dropped by our table with a basket of warm tortilla chips and spicy salsa, and then left and returned minutes later with our drinks. After an eventful week, Reba Mae and I were both ready for a little R & R, which translated into margaritas and girl talk. For a short while, I allowed myself to set my worries aside and relax.

"I thought you might bring Melly along," Reba Mae said after taking a sip from a frosted glass rimmed with salt.

"I invited her, but she had a better offer. Thompson Gray's mother's bridge group had a last-minute cancellation, and she asked Melly to fill in. Melly was hesitant at first, but I convinced her it would help take her mind off things."

Reba Mae dipped a chip into the salsa. "Never could get the hang of bridge."

I picked up a menu. "Me neither. I'm still hunting for a game I'm good at."

"Well, besides bridge, you can rule out golf and tennis."

I grimaced at the reminder. When I was a country club

wife back in the day, I tried tennis. My backhand was non-existent. My forehand wasn't much to brag about, either. Golf wasn't much better. Seems I had no muscle memory whatsoever when it came to sports. Nacho returned to our table, order pad in hand. I ordered my favorite chicken chimichanga while Reba Mae was more in the mood for quesadillas. "How's my favorite premed student doing in Chapel Hill?" Reba Mae asked as the owner scurried off.

I warmed to the mention of my son. "Chad's more determined than ever to keep up his grade point average so he can get into one of his top picks for medical school."

"Wish my Clay was as motivated as your Chad." Reba Mae twirled the stem of her margarita glass, her expression wistful. "Caleb is happy as a clam when he's tinkerin' under the hood of a car, but Clay seems to be driftin'. He's taken a class here or there at the community college and works construction pretty steady, but has no clear plans for the future."

"It takes some kids longer than others to figure out what they want to do with their lives. Take Lindsey, for example. In the last couple months, she's wanted to be a veterinarian, a videographer, and lately she's talking about going to New York to study fashion. Who knows what next week will bring?"

Reba Mae grinned. "Maybe she'll decide to be a brain surgeon."

I took a swallow of my margarita, enjoying its sweet-tart taste, and let my gaze roam the colorful surroundings. Since it was Saturday night, most of the tables and booths were occupied. Red, green, and yellow sombreros, along with posters of Mayan ruins, sunny beaches, and quaint adobe churches, hung on the bright orange walls. The photos reminded me of vacations in Mexico with CJ. Reminded me of the good times. During the last year or so, I'd let the bitterness of our divorce overshadow happier memories. I was proud to say I was overcoming that tendency.

"Earth to Piper." Reba Mae snapped her fingers in front of my face. "I almost forgot to tell you, McBride asked Clay's help with some renovations he's doin'."

"Hmm." As I dipped a chip into salsa generously seasoned with cilantro, I noticed a woman seated at the rear of the restaurant. After straightening in my seat, I leaned forward for a better look.

"What's up, honeybun?" Reba Mae turned, curious to find out what had captured my attention.

"See the blonde in the back booth? That's Cheryl Balboa. Chip's widow."

"Who's the guy she's with?"

Now, I have to admit, it's difficult to recognize someone by the back of their head, but Brandywine Creek is a small town, and I knew many of its residents by sight if not by name. The sun-bleached mop of hair and bronzed nape didn't ring a bell. "Don't have a clue."

"Maybe he's related to Chip?" Reba Mae suggested.

I frowned. "Somehow, I doubt it. According to the grapevine, Chip doesn't have much family."

Reba Mae helped herself to another tortilla chip. "His wife probably needed a shoulder to cry on. Might've brought a friend along from California for moral support."

Before I had a chance to speculate further on Cheryl's dinner companion, our meals arrived. I cut into my chimi, but without my usual gusto. All the while, my attention kept straying to the couple in the far corner.

Reba Mae added a dollop of sour cream to her quesadilla. "Have you decided what you're taking to Oktoberfest?"

"I'm not sure," I answered absently. I saw the mystery man reach across the table and take Cheryl's hand. Was that a simple act of comfort? I wondered. Or was there more to the gesture? Cheryl's openly flirtatious manner confirmed the notion. Even from a distance, it was clear to me she'd already found a replacement for her pudgy, disheveled husband. I tried to tell myself I was being overly suspicious, even cynical. Yet I couldn't help wondering—since they were still legally wed—if Chip had been less eager than she to dissolve their marriage. Had he stalled signing the divorce decree? Could that have prompted a frustrated, impatient woman to give the poor guy an angry shove down a steep flight of stairs? Or perhaps Chip had a large life insurance policy with her the recipient? Money topped the motive list when it came to murder, so I'd heard on *48 Hours*. Or was it on *Dateline*?

"I'm thinkin' of makin' apple strudel," Reba Mae said, unmindful of my mental meanderings.

I took a bite of my chimi. "Why do you think Cheryl is in such a hurry to have Chip cremated?"

Reba Mae shrugged. "She's probably just anxious to get on home."

"Maybe . . ." I told myself I was making a mountain out of a molehill.

"I ran into Doug at the Piggly Wiggly. He said he's going to try his hand with sauerbraten." Reba Mae pushed her plate aside.

From the corner of my eye, I saw Cheryl Balboa laugh at something her companion said. In my humble opinion, she seemed too animated, too carefree for a woman who'd recently lost her husband. She acted as though she was on a date rather than in mourning.

We'd barely finished our dinners when Cheryl and her "friend" got up to leave. Sun-streaked hair, Hollywood handsome, tall and tan, all the dude lacked was a surfboard. Although I tried not to stare, I noticed him casually drape an arm around Cheryl's shoulders. To my mind, the gesture seemed more affectionate than consoling.

The instant the couple disappeared from sight, I jumped to my feet and tossed some bills on the table. "C'mon," I said to a startled-looking Reba Mae. "Let's go on a little road trip."

CHAPTER *13*

We hopped into Reba Mae's five-year-old Buick, parked at the curb in front of North of the Border. I pointed at a set of taillights moving down the street. "Follow that car."

Reba Mae gave me a puzzled look, but didn't question me. Shifting into gear, we headed down Washington Avenue, then turned onto Main Street in hot pursuit of a car that bore a striking resemblance to one I'd seen outside the Brandywine Creek Police Department earlier that day.

"Keep a couple car lengths behind. I don't want the occupants to get suspicious." '

"Jeez Louise," Reba Mae grumbled. "What do you think this is—an episode of *Hawaii Five-0*?"

"Good analogy. Pretend I'm Detective Steve McGarrett."

Reba Mae pouted. "Guess that makes me Danno. Why can't I be McGarrett?"

"Next time." I peered through the windshield, trying to make out the logo on the car's trunk.

"Mind tellin' me what's goin' on?"

"I'm pretty sure that's the rental car Cheryl Balboa's driving. I want to see where she and her friend are going."

Keeping the sedan in sight wasn't a problem, since traffic was a rare commodity in a town no bigger than a flyspeck on a map. The difficult part was remaining inconspicuous. I was grateful for Reba Mae's Buick. My gecko-green VW Beetle would've stood out like . . . a gecko-green VW Beetle.

The car ahead of us sped up as it left the business district behind. A mile farther down, the driver slowed and turned onto a county road that eventually led to the interstate. When the flash of brake lights revealed the distinctive BMW logo on the vehicle's trunk, I knew my instincts were spot-on. "It's Cheryl Balboa, all right," I said with satisfaction.

Reba Mae darted a look my way. "What next? A stakeout?"

"Humor me, okay? I just want to see what Cheryl and her guy friend are up to. Consider this my early birthday present, if you will."

"Your birthday is in February," she reminded me. She flicked on her turn signal and kept the BMW in sight. "This is only October."

"Don't tell me you've never heard of paying it forward?"

"By the time February rolls round, you'll have forgotten I did you a favor back in October. That's the drawback of payin' it forward. Folks tend to forget. They still expect cards, presents, and cake when their big day comes."

Up ahead, the yellow and green neon sign of a small motel lit up the night sky. The Beaver Dam Motel. Part of the sign, however, was currently malfunctioning. It now read THE   DAM MOTEL.

The BMW pulled into the paved lot. "What are you doing?" I shouted when Reba Mae kept driving.

"You'll see." She smirked. She braked to a stop in front of a defunct gas station, executed a perfect three-point turn, and headed back in the direction we'd just come.

Smiling, she shut off her headlights and dimmed the dash while she eased to a stop at the far end of the motel parking lot.

Fortunately for us, the couple under surveillance was too engrossed in each other to notice our arrival. In the flash of neon, I saw the silhouette in the front seat separate into two separate figures. A man climbed out, then hurried around to the passenger side. Cheryl was let out of the car, embraced her companion briefly, then laughing, disappeared with him into one of the rooms. A light flicked on, visible through a narrow slit in the drapes.

"Why's Cheryl stayin' at the no-tell motel?" Reba Mae switched off the ignition. "Judgin' from the way she's dressed and car she's drivin', it doesn't look like she's hurtin' for money. Her purse alone cost more than a week's stay at this fleabag."

"Good question." I stared at the motel through the windshield. It was a low one-story redbrick building built in the '70s and had seen better days. It consisted of two wings separated by a shabby office. "My guess is Cheryl brought a friend along but wants to keep it quiet."

"Well, if they're 'friends,' they're mighty good ones," Reba Mae observed. "Considerin' she's a recent widow, Cheryl's not lettin' any grass grow under her feet."

"Rusty, Chip's partner, is under the impression that the Balboas' divorce was final." I lounged back on the cloth seat. "I found out only by accident that they were still married."

Reba Mae leaned back, too, and drummed her nails on the steering wheel. "I bet she was cheatin' on Chip with this dude. Bet five bucks he's the reason for the divorce. Think he's her pool boy?"

"What I think is, you've been watching too many reruns of *Desperate Housewives* on Lifetime."

"Cheryl's guy friend is hot." Reba Mae made a fanning

motion with her hand. "Never met an honest-to-gosh pool boy, but he's got that look. All sun-streaked hair and fabulous tan."

I shifted, trying to find a more comfortable position. "I'd be willing to wager half the people in California don't even own a pool—and most of those who do clean it themselves."

"*If* I lived in California—and *if* I had a pool—I'd hire someone who looked like Cheryl's guy friend to clean it whether it needed cleanin' or not. I'm just sayin' . . . ," she added. "Why all the interest in the Widow Balboa?"

"I'm worried Melly might be charged with killing Chip," I admitted.

"Ridiculous!" Reba Mae shook her head so emphatically, her dangly earrings swayed. "Surely, no one who knows Melly believes she's that coldhearted."

"There's more." I fiddled with the radio to buy time to organize my thoughts, settling for an oldies station. "Beau Tucker told me—off the record—that the ME's preliminary report stated there was less bruising, fewer fractures than expected. All Chip suffered during the course of the fall was a broken neck.

"And if that isn't bad enough, Beau said the ME found a bruise between Chip's shoulder blades the size of a hand."

"Whoo-ee!" Reba Mae whistled. "That's pretty heavy stuff."

"If McBride pursues the case as a homicide and not an accident, Melly is going to top his persons of interest list. I intend to find out if others might've had a motive to want Chip dead. Try to draw attention away from Melly and force McBride to consider other possibilities."

Reba Mae considered this thoughtfully. "And you're thinkin' Cheryl Balboa might've had somethin' to do with her husband breakin' his neck?"

"With Chip dead, Cheryl is set to inherit all his assets,"

I said, voicing thoughts that until now had remained un-spoken. "I've read enough about celebrity divorces in *People* and watched enough *Entertainment Tonight* to know California is a community property state. If the divorce were final, she'd only have been entitled to half."

Reba Mae's jaw dropped. "You're not sayin' what I think you're sayin'?"

"It's something to consider is all, I replied."

The implication hung in the ensuing silence. Finally Reba Mae spoke. "Aren't you overlookin' one important fact, hon? I know women have been known to kill for money, but Cheryl was in California the night Chip bought the farm."

I hated whenever logic interfered with a perfectly thought-out motive, but instantly perked up when a new thought occurred to me. "What if . . . what if . . . she of-fered to pay someone to do the dirty deed for her?"

"Murder for hire?" Once more, Reba Mae nodded slowly. "Saw a movie on Lifetime just last Saturday—"

Just then, the light in Cheryl's room blinked out.

We sat and stared at the darkened motel room for an-other twenty minutes before Reba Mae said, "Let's blow this pop stand before one of my boys drives by and won-ders what his momma's car's doin' at the Dam Motel." With that, she switched on the headlights and pulled out of the lot. "I like to set a good example for 'em."

Once home again and in bed, I couldn't sleep. Who would want to hurt Chip? Who wanted him dead? My mind kept sorting through the puzzle pieces. I turned on my side and punched my pillow. Cheryl Balboa had the most to gain from her husband's death, but she'd been clear across the country at the time of his death. Try as I might, she didn't fit my image of a grieving widow. Her weeping and wailing in McBride's office could've been heard clear out on the street, yet I didn't notice a single tear when she'd waltzed out. Seeing her behavior tonight, first at North of the Border, then at the Beaver Dam Motel, led me to believe she'd been having an affair.

I flounced onto my back and stared at the ceiling as though the answers to my questions would magically appear on the plaster. Who was the man Cheryl was with? They acted like lovers. Had the two conspired to kill Chip? While Reba Mae binged on the Lifetime channel, had I spent too much time watching shows like *48 Hours* and *Dateline?* Only thing I knew for sure was that Melly was innocent. True, she was annoyed Chip and Rusty had reneged on the amount of money they'd initially offered, but that irritation didn't constitute motive. Or did it? Of course not! Melly was a paragon of virtue. She didn't drink hard liquor, smoke, or cuss. And she certainly never lost her temper.

Even before I heard the *snick* of a key in a lock, Casey woke and growled deep in his throat. I tensed, waiting, then let out a sigh of relief when I recognized Melly's light footsteps. "Melly?"

"Sorry if I woke you, dear," she called. "I tried to be quiet as a mouse."

Casey relaxed his guard, put his head down on his paws, and resumed his interrupted night's rest in his doggy bed near the bedroom door.

"No problem." I yawned. "Have a good time tonight?"

"Absolutely. I'd forgotten how much I enjoy playing bridge. Mavis is going to put me down as a regular substitute."

"Good for you, Melly. G'night." Another yawn. Rolling over, I punched my pillow a final time and promptly dropped off to sleep.

When I opened my eyes again, Sunday morning sunshine streamed through the blinds. The clock radio told me I'd slept much later than usual. The apartment was still. Lindsey had spent the night at her friend Taylor's, and Melly was most likely at church.

I lay there for a moment, enjoying the peace and quiet, knowing I had the day to do as I pleased.

I hauled myself out of bed, but judging from Casey's prancing and dancing, I knew my pooch needed out more than I needed coffee. I threw a hooded sweatshirt over my pajamas, clipped on his leash, and let him roam the vacant lot behind my shop until he took care of business.

Once I got back inside, I discovered Melly had left a note on the kitchen table. She informed me that she was going to brunch after church and not to expect her until midafternoon. Since McBride insisted on treating her home like a crime scene, she asked if I'd do her a favor and retrieve more of her clothing.

Casey yipped impatiently while I scanned her list. "Sorry, pal," I told him. "Breakfast is on the way."

I poured pet food into his doggy dish, then brewed a pot of Jamaican Blue Mountain coffee. My taste buds clamored for something sweet. A quick search of my cupboards and refrigerator revealed I had the necessary ingredients for morning glory muffins. Raisins, coconut, crushed pineapple, carrots, and apple. Healthy with a capital *H*. To add even more zing, I'd add a teaspoon of the special baking spice I'd concocted from cloves, nutmeg, and several types of cinnamon.

While the muffins baked, I showered then blow-dried my unruly mop of red curls, pinning them back with tortoiseshell clips. I dressed for the day in rust-colored denims, oversize cream and rust sweater, and slipped my feet into soft-soled ballet flats. A swipe of mascara, blush, and lip gloss, and I was all set.

Over a second cup of coffee—and a second muffin spread with the delicious cinnamon honey butter I'd whipped up—I reviewed Melly's wish list. It should be a quick in and out. Easy peasy.

CHAPTER 14

It was Sunday, my only day off.

A distant church bell tolled the hour of noon. I finished loading the dishwasher and reached for my purse. Casey, his eyes like shiny black buttons, watched hopefully. "Want to come along, boy?"

Casey didn't need coaxing. He answered my question with enthusiastic tail wagging.

Usually I walk the short distance to Melly's, but since I'd be carrying an armload of clothes when I returned, I elected to drive instead. Within minutes, I turned down Jefferson Street. Two blocks later, Melly's Victorian came into view. I groaned out loud as I spotted McBride's black Ford F-150 pickup in the driveway. I pulled in behind it and cracked the window for Casey. "Sorry, buddy, but I don't think the chief would appreciate a canine—even a cute one—traipsing through his crime scene."

The door was ajar, so I let myself in. I stood for a moment, expecting McBride to appear any second, but instead heard someone moving about in the basement. Assuming he wouldn't appreciate an interruption, I went directly upstairs to Melly's bedroom. With luck, I'd complete my mission and be on my way before McBride even knew I was here.

Thanks to Melly's detailed list, it didn't take long to gather the specified items. I filled a tote with undergarments, being careful not to look too closely. It made me uncomfortable knowing what Melly wore under her twinsets. An invasion of privacy. Next, I moved on to the closet. She'd underlined the words "don't wrinkle" several times, so I took the outfits, hangers and all, and draped them over my arm.

Pleased with myself for being so efficient, I started downstairs, my arms piled high. My ballet flats made little sound on the carpeted steps. Just as I predicted: In and out. Easy peasy.

"Police!" a male voice thundered. "Hands in the air."

Startled, I dropped the tote bag. It thudded down the stairs, strewing the steps with Melly's unmentionables. The slacks, skirts, and blouses in my arms flew through the air like snowflakes in a blizzard.

Wyatt McBride materialized from around the corner of the hall closet, his gun in a two-handed grip aimed at my midsection, his expression as serious as sunstroke. My eyes widened at the sight.

Seeing me, he slowly lowered the weapon. "Should've known it was you."

My heart rate gradually returned to normal. "McBride," I gasped, "you scared the living daylights out of me."

He tucked the pistol into a holster at the small of his back. "What do you think you're doing?"

"When was the last time you had an eye exam?" I made a sweeping motion with my hand to indicate the clothing all helter-skelter. "What does it look like?"

"This place is off-limits."

I descended several stairs, pausing along the way to pick up a blouse here, a skirt there. I found a small button—

probably from one of Melly's many cardigans—that must've come loose and slipped it into the pocket of my jeans. "If it's 'off-limits,' then you should've had enough sense to lock the door."

"I did," he growled.

"It's an old house." I picked up a dove gray pleated skirt. "The door needs an extra nudge to engage the lock."

McBride stooped to help. "I'll try to keep that in mind— provided there is a next time."

"Since you're out of uniform, what are *you* doing here on your day off?"

"I wanted to check the handrail on the basement stairs one more time."

"Why?" I added a pair of camel slacks to the steadily mounting heap.

McBride shrugged his broad shoulders. "Wanted to see if a piece was missing."

I paused to stare at him. "Do you think the handrail was defective?"

"No, nothing like that. Don't suppose there's any harm in telling you. The ME found a long wooden splinter embedded in the vic's palm. I wanted to confirm that it happened during the fall."

"And did it?"

"Looks like a strong possibility." McBride handed me Melly's favorite silk blouse, the one she claimed enhanced the blue in her eyes. "Can't say for sure, but my guess is it'll be a match."

I nodded. "Melly's been asking when she can return home."

"Not until I get the toxicology back."

"You think Balboa had drugs in his system that contributed to his fall?"

"We're exploring all avenues." McBride picked up a pair of lavender panties and hurriedly shoved them in my direction. I felt my cheeks warm. I snatched the panties, and I stuffed them into the tote bag. Who would have guessed my former mother-in-law favored lacy and frilly when it came to lingerie? Next time her birthday came around, I'd surprise her with a gift card from Victoria's Secret.

I surveyed the staircase. Satisfied I'd retrieved the last of Melly's scattered belongings, I straightened. Standing as I was on a step above McBride, I was able to almost look him in the eye. "How would drugs explain the hand-sized bruise between Chip's shoulder blades?"

McBride's jaw clenched. His blue eyes narrowed, icy cold. "Who told you that?"

I smoothed imaginary wrinkles from a pair of navy permanent press slacks. I was a terrible liar, and I hated to rat out Beau Tucker. My face grew warmer, the curse of being a redhead. "I . . . ah . . ."

McBride shook his head in disgust. "As if I didn't know—Sergeant Blabbermouth."

I'd overstayed my welcome. Shifting the bundle of clothing I held, I decided a dignified retreat was in order. McBride watched me go. At the front door, I turned for a final parting shot. "Surely you can't believe Melly had anything to do with Chip's fall?"

For a fraction of a second, I thought I detected a flicker of regret. "Sorry, Piper. I know you're fond of your mother-in-law, but the evidence will speak for itself."

I hurried out the door and toward my car, feeling as though I'd been kicked in the solar plexus. McBride seemed fixated on Melly's culpability in Chip's death. I needed to prove him wrong . . .

. . . before it was too late.

I drove around aimlessly for a while. Lindsey had called earlier to ask permission to have dinner at a friend's house, promising to be home no later than eight o'clock to finish a report for Language Arts. And even though Melly had probably returned from brunch by this time, I wasn't in the mood to deal with her just yet. Reaching over, I scratched Casey behind his ear.

"I need to find out what really happened, Casey." The little dog thumped his tail to show he listened attentively.

Before I realized where I was going, I cruised past the Beaver Dam Motel—minus the BEAVER. I noticed a maid's cleaning trolley parked outside the door to Cheryl and her guy's love nest. There was no sign of Cheryl's rental car. I wondered where she and her "friend" were off to this sunny October afternoon.

Before I could talk myself out of it, I executed a U-turn, pulled into the lot, and got out of the car to investigate. An ancient Hoover propped open the door to Cheryl's room. "Excuse me," I called out, poking my head inside.

The maid, an overweight girl in her late teens with a bad case of acne and bleached blond hair scraped back in a pony-tail, peered out from the bathroom she'd been scrubbing. Thankfully, she was someone I didn't know and who didn't know me. "Guests s'posed to check in at the front office."

"Ah, I'm not a guest." I tried to portray a friendly stranger while my mind scrambled to come up with a plausible excuse for my visit. "I . . . ah . . . I'm expecting company from out of town, and since I don't have an extra bedroom, I was wondering—"

"Feel free to look," the maid said. "But if I had company, I wouldn't put them up in this dump."

"Thanks," I told her. I'd hoped the girl would resume her cleaning, but instead she stood sentinel in the bathroom doorway, arms folded across her chest. I don't claim to have ESP, but I knew from her watchful expression she didn't trust me not to filch the occupants' possessions.

My gaze swept over the room. King-size bed with rum-pled sheets. Tan slacks draped over the back of a chair. A smattering of coins on a faux walnut dresser. Designer-brand perfume bottles. Jars of expensive skin-care products. Supplies belonging to a contact lens wearer, which included a travel-size container of wetting solution, a bottle of Visine, and a blue plastic lens case. Nothing that flashed "clue" in bright neon letters.

Disappointed, I murmured my thanks to the maid and turned to leave.

"No skin off my nose," the girl called after me, "but if I was you, I'd put my company up in one of them newer motels off the interstate."

As I headed toward home, I couldn't escape a ballooning sense of urgency to uncover the truth. I'm no expert, but it seemed to me that *if* Chip's death had been deliberate, not accidental, it had possibly been a crime of passion. A crime of opportunity. Rage, resentment, or greed could've precipitated the act.

But if Melly wasn't responsible, then who? Who would be brazen enough to kill a person in another person's home—especially when the homeowner could reappear at any given moment? It angered me to think whoever that person might be, he—or she—was content to sit back and let Melly shoulder the blame.

A sudden thought occurred to me. Sitting up straighter, I slapped the steering wheel. Casey cocked one ear as if to ask why the excitement. I rubbed his head. "It's okay, boy. I just had a brilliant idea and got a little carried away."

No one knew Chip better than his partner, Rusty Tulley. The two had been friends since college. Maybe Rusty could shed some light on the sort of man his partner was. And whom Chip might've angered. I was also curious to learn if Rusty knew Cheryl's male companion.

With that in mind, I headed for the historic district.

I parked at the curb in front of the Turner-Driscoll House and walked up the curving drive. Casey trotted alongside as if he owned the place. The Turner-Driscoll

House, the bed-and-breakfast where Rusty was staying, never failed to remind me of Scarlett O'Hara's beloved Tara in *Gone with the Wind*. I spotted Rusty slumped in one of the white rocking chairs, his smartphone and an untouched drink sitting on a wicker table beside him. I wondered why he was still in town, but assumed McBride had ordered everyone to stay put until the case was resolved. Rusty raised his head when he heard me call his name. I sat next to him; Casey curled at my feet. "I thought I'd drop by. See how you were doing."

"Not good," he admitted glumly. "Still can't believe Chip's dead."

I felt sympathy for Rusty. Unlike Cheryl's theatrical performance, his grief seemed genuine. The guy looked in need of a hug. "Losing a close friend must be difficult."

Rusty plowed his fingers through his longish hair. "Yeah, we've been buddies since sophomore year at Southern Cal."

Nudging the porch floor with the toe of my shoe, I set the rocker in motion. "College? Is that where Chip met Cheryl?"

"They might've been in a couple classes together early on but didn't really start dating until they hooked up at an alumni party. Cheryl was more interested in performing arts."

I stole a page from McBride's book and kept quiet. When it came to the school of pregnant pauses, the lawman was a graduate student.

Rusty hunched forward, hands between his knees, eyes downcast. "I told Chip right from the start, Cheryl was nothing but trouble. But Chip refused to listen. He couldn't believe his luck—that a woman with her looks would be interested in a nerd like him."

"He sounds like a man in love."

"Ha, he was a fool!" Rusty snorted. "Cheryl wouldn't

have given him the time of day if Trustychipdesign hadn't already made its first million."

"I only met him once, but Chip seemed like an easygoing sort of guy."

"He was, and except for Cheryl, he was no pushover. Besides owning half interest in Trustychipdesign, Chip was also our company's CFO. Losing him is a blow in more ways than one."

I recalled Melly complaining that the two men were reneging on their original offer to purchase her software. "Being chief financial officer of a successful company must mean having to make some hard decisions. Did Chip have any enemies that you're aware of?"

Rusty slanted me a look. "What are you getting at?"

"Nothing," I said hastily. I wasn't ready to stick my foot into the homicide versus accident quagmire. I'd leave that for McBride. "I suppose with Chip dead, you'll have to share control of the business with his wife."

Rusty's expression darkened. "You mean ex-wife, don't you?"

I hesitated a moment, then took the plunge. "Cheryl and Chip were still married at the time of his death."

"What?" He stood so abruptly, his chair violently rocked to and fro.

I stood, too. Casey immediately jumped to his feet, not sure why everyone was standing but ready to leap into the fray nevertheless. "I don't know what happened," I said, "only that, apparently, their divorce papers were never signed."

Rusty's face reddened with anger, his hands bunched into fists. "Why, that . . . greedy . . . money-hungry . . ."

Rusty never got a chance to finish his sentence because Cheryl Balboa picked that moment to cruise up the winding drive in her rented BMW and announce she was checking into Felicity Driscoll's bed-and-breakfast.

CHAPTER 15

"Then what happened?" Reba Mae prompted the following afternoon. I'd been regaling her at my store counter.

"Rusty was furious, that's what happened! And who could blame him?" Melly asked as she walked into Spice It Up! carrying a tray with a pitcher of sweet tea and a plate of gingersnaps. "The two were supposed to be best friends, yet Chip failed to disclose that he and his wife were still married."

I cleared a space, and Melly set the tray on the counter. Melly took a seat on one of the stools. I took the other while Reba Mae rested one hip against the counter. We were enjoying a midafternoon lull. Reba Mae had had a last-minute cancellation and dropped by for a visit. Melly had volunteered to go upstairs to my apartment for refreshments. In this case, refreshments translated into the cookies she'd spent most of the morning baking.

"What did you do?" Reba Mae helped herself to a cookie. "Try to calm 'im down or enjoy the ringside seat?"

I poured the tea into glasses. "Rusty looked ready to pitch a fit. Fortunately, Felicity's timing was impeccable. Her arrival helped avoid a showdown. The display of

Southern charm she turned on would have made Paula
Deen envious."

Reba Mae took a sip of tea, a bite of cookie. A strange
expression came over her face as she chewed.

"Wish you could've seen Rusty glare at Cheryl. If looks
could kill, she would have keeled over right then and
there." I sampled a gingersnap, curious to learn what had
caused Reba Mae's pained look. It immediately became
apparent that Melly's cookies weren't up to her usual high
standards. They were bland rather than spicy. Something
was obviously missing. Ginger? Coriander? Ginger *and*
coriander?

Reba Mae pointed to the plate of gingersnaps. "Melly,
I hate to be the one to—"

I cut her off. "Reba Mae hates to be the one to tell you,
it's supposed to rain tomorrow."

"Ohh," Melly said, confused at the abrupt change of
topic. "Well, I suppose we could always use a good
rain."

Judging from the look Reba Mae shot me, Melly wasn't
the only one confused. When Melly wasn't looking, I held
my finger to my lips and signaled Reba Mae not to mention the flavorless gingersnaps. Melly had enough troubles
as it was.

"Did Cheryl mention why she bailed out of the no-tell
motel?" Reba Mae slipped her half-eaten cookie into the
wastebasket.

I discreetly did the same. "I heard tell they have a cock-
roach problem."

Melly sipped her sweet tea. "I heard bedbugs."

"Cockroaches, bedbugs, whatever. Cheryl refused to
spend another night in a rinky-dink hotel if she didn't have
to. I heard her complain that seeing an exterminator's truck
there made her itch."

Reba Mae scratched her arm. "Can't say I blame her.

Hate creepy crawlies. That's why I signed a contract with Bugs-B-Gone."

"Here, I thought it was the twenty-five-dollar discount coupon."

"That too."

I pushed my sweet tea aside untasted. "Once she stormed inside, Rusty intimated Cheryl wasn't the type to stay in a fleabag. She'd become accustomed to luxury. According to him, she expected Chip to become the next Bill Gates."

"What happened to the hot guy Cheryl was with at North of the Border?" Reba Mae idly toyed with her chandelier-style earring. "Did he check into the Turner-Driscoll House with her?"

"Nope," I said. "She was alone."

"Goodness gracious!" Melly pressed a delicate hand to her chest. "Chip's wife has a new man in her life? Already?"

Reba Mae smiled thinly. "From the way they were carryin' on when we saw 'em at North of the Border, I suspect they've been friends with benefits for some time."

"Tsk, tsk." Melly clucked her tongue. "I wonder if Chip suspected his wife of being unfaithful?"

The front door of the shop burst open. "Yoo-hoo!" a familiar voice sang.

The three of us quit gossiping as Dottie Hemmings, clad in a royal blue pantsuit and frilly blouse, sailed into the shop. Her blond bouffant beehive was lacquered to withstand gale force winds.

"Hey, Dottie," I said. "What can I help you with?"

Dottie ignored my question and reached for a cookie. "Oh, lucky me. Just in time for a tea party."

I nudged my tea in her direction. "Here, have mine. I haven't touched it yet." Truth was, I really didn't care for sweet tea. My Yankee taste buds rebelled at the syrupy

sweet drink so many loved here in the Deep South. Melly
always kept a pitcher on hand when she was at home, and
I wanted her to feel at ease while at my place.

"Don't mind if I do." Dottie took a big bite from her
cookie and grimaced. "Melly Prescott, what have you gone
and done to these? They taste terrible."

Melly looked stricken. "Why, Dottie, I don't know what
you're talking about. It's the same recipe I've been using
for years. I've made these gingersnaps so often, I know the
recipe by heart."

Dottie wasn't about to back down. "Don't take my word
for it. Taste one for yourself. You'll see what I mean."

Reba Mae and I swapped nervous glances as Melly did
what Dottie suggested. She immediately reached for her
tea and washed down the cookie. "I must have forgotten
some of the spices—the ginger and coriander. And the cardamom," she added in a small voice.

"They're not so terrible as Dottie said," I consoled, pat-
ting her back.

Reba Mae's head bobbed in agreement. "Just not quite
up to snuff, is all."

Melly's eyes filled with tears, but she sniffed them back.
"I'm so absentminded lately. I don't know what's come
over me." With that, she slipped off the stool, picked up
the plate of gingersnaps, and marched off, leaving us staring after her openmouthed.

Dottie was the first to recover. "Well, don't that beat all.
I didn't mean to insult her. The cookies weren't all that
bad, just not as good as usual."

"You still haven't said what brings you here, Dottie," I
said, trying to steer the discussion away from Melly's
cookie disaster.

She polished off the last of her gingersnap and brushed
the crumbs from her fingers. "I got to wondering if you
had more cloves or ginger?"

"I'm afraid you cleaned out my stock the other day," I said. "I've reordered, however, and expect to get a shipment later this week."

Dottie beamed happily. "Call me when it comes in. I'll hurry on over."

Reba Mae crossed one ankle over the other. "Long as I've known you, Dottie Hemmings, you've never been of a mind to spend time slavin' over a hot stove."

"Can't teach this old dog new tricks." Dottie laughed. "It's my turn to host bunco this month. Thought we'd do something a little different than roll dice. I want to show the ladies how to make those little spice sachets to keep the spiders away. No sense payin' top dollar for an exterminator."

"I'll call my supplier, double my order, and ask him to put a rush on it."

"You've turned into a regular businesswoman, Piper. Who knew?"

At the sound of the front door opening, the three of us glanced up. Rusty Tulley, as dapper as ever, entered wearing a pale pink mesh polo shirt with its collar turned up, stone-colored chinos, and loafers sans socks. A pair of aviator-style sunglasses was shoved on top of his head. He smelled faintly of expensive men's cologne. "Ladies," he said.

Dottie rushed over to him. "You must be Mr. Tulley, the dear departed's best friend," she gushed. She took his hand in hers and squeezed. "I'm so sorry for your loss. Tragic thing, him falling down a flight of stairs like that and breaking his neck."

Rusty disengaged his hand, then flexed his fingers to make sure they were still in working order. "I beg your pardon. Have we met? Who are you?"

Dottie smiled. "I'm Dottie Hemmings. My husband, Harvey, is the mayor."

I stole a peek at Reba Mae. She hadn't met either of the dot-com partners during their brief visit to Brandywine Creek. From the expression on her face, I could tell she was waffling between a hug and a handshake. In the end, she extended her hand, opting for the traditional. "I'm Reba Mae Johnson," she said. "My condolences."

Rusty shifted his weight from one foot to the other. "Thanks."

"Is there something I can help you with, Rusty?" I asked.

"Ah, yes . . ." He smiled a bit sheepishly. "This might seem odd, seeing as how Chip and I are strangers to your town, but I'm having a reception of sorts—I'm calling it a remembrance—in Chip's honor. I'd be pleased if you'd attend."

"A memorial service?"

"Memorial services I've attended always seemed so . . . depressing. I'd like something more relaxed, less formal. More a celebration of life. I need a chance to talk with others about the Chip Balboa I knew—a remembrance. I suppose I could postpone this until I return to California, but what's the point? As long as Chief McBride wants me to stick around, I thought, why wait? Selfish of me, but I'm hoping this will bring closure."

Touched by his thoughtfulness, I reached over and lightly placed my hand on his arm. "Of course I'll be there."

"Chip was a loner. His job was his life, so that didn't leave much time for socializing. Except for a few distant cousins, he didn't have family. If I don't do something to mark his passing, no one will."

"Aww . . ." Reba Mae's constraint broke, and she hugged Rusty.

"I'll come, too." Dottie's eyes gleamed with anticipation. "Just tell me when and where."

I refrained from rolling my eyes at hearing this. To the best of my knowledge, Dottie had never even seen Chip Balboa, but couldn't ignore the chance for free food and juicy gossip.

"You're welcome also, Ms. Johnson," Rusty said, including Reba Mae in the invitation.

"Folks call me Reba Mae," she told him. "And I think it's real sweet what you're doin' for your friend."

"It didn't seem . . . right . . . not to have a gathering of some sort." Raising his hand, Rusty massaged the back of his neck as if to erase tension that had settled there. "His wife refuses to make any effort."

"Guess that's understandable, considering they were on the verge of divorce. Still . . ." My voice trailed off.

An awkward silence fell.

"Well, at least Chip had a loyal friend in you," Reba Mae said to fill the void.

"A friend in need is a friend indeed," Dottie intoned solemnly.

"What time do you want us?" I asked.

"It's set for four o'clock tomorrow afternoon. Felicity said we could use the front parlor at the Turner-Driscoll House. She even volunteered to provide refreshments." He started for the door, but turned back. "Be sure to include Melly in the invitation. Tell her that I don't hold her responsible for what happened to Chip."

"What a nice young man," Dottie cooed as the door closed behind him. "No sense in dyin' if no one's around to mark the occasion."

Buzz Oliver showed up just before closing time. Buzz—short and stocky, dressed in a blue uniform and ball cap with a smiley-face insect logo—was the senior exterminator at Bugs-B-Gone, a job he'd held since graduating from high school. "Hope I'm not too late," he said, refer-ring to the three o'clock appointment the office manager had scheduled.

"No problem," I told him, glancing up from a pile of mail order catalogs I'd been studying.

"My truck blew a tire, or I woulda been here sooner," Buzz explained as he hauled in paraphernalia. Casey took one look at all the equipment and hightailed it upstairs to join Melly.

I went back to making notes about items I wanted to stock, now that the holidays were fast approaching. Things that would make good gifts, like chef's aprons, saltshak-ers and pepper mills, and an assortment of recipe cards. I also hoped to sell the soup cookbooks the ladies at the Lutheran church had compiled to benefit a women's shelter. Since my business was now on more solid finan-cial footing than in the past, I planned to diversify. I'd start small, but would include a variety of cooking ac-cessories if my ideas proved profitable. The production of *Steel Magnolias* was bound to bring in groups such as Red Hatters and senior citizens by the busloads. And those folks loved to shop.

"Reba Mae's boy Caleb was busier than a one-arm pa-perhanger at the garage." Buzz took off his cap and ran a hand over his bristly crew cut, which had earned him his nickname.

"There isn't a car made that he can't fix," I said. Ca-leb managed Cloune Motors while its owner, Diane Cloune, searched for a buyer. Her husband, Dwayne, was currently a guest of the Georgia Department of Correc-tions as a result of killing his third cousin once removed. So far, no one had shown much interest in the garage. Diane bragged about wanting to move soon to Buckhead, a ritzy suburb of Atlanta, and leaving Brandywine Creek in the dust.

Buzz replaced his cap. "Heard Miss Melly was staying here."

"Only until Chief McBride gives her the okay to return home. Shouldn't be much longer." I continued leafing through the glossy catalogs, pausing here and there to earmark a page.

Buzz energetically pumped a large metal canister containing chemicals. "Darn shame about what happened, ain't it?"

"It certainly is," I replied, my tone neutral, my gaze fastened on the page in front of me.

"Ran into Ned Feeney down at the Cloune Motors while waitin' to get my tire fixed." Buzz walked around the shop's perimeter, the nozzle of his sprayer aimed at the baseboards. "Ned overheard the widow talkin' to Mr. Strickland at the Eternal Rest. She told 'em not to expect her to shed no crocodile tears. Said she's been tryin' to get that husband of hers outa her life for nearly a year. She was sorry he was dead, but life goes on. Ask me, she sounds more coldhearted than brokenhearted."

"Mmm. Interesting."

Ned stopped spraying long enough to mop his brow with a red bandanna. "The wife's a real looker. Not my type, but a looker all the same. Her and her male friend seemed pretty chummy when I saw them check into the Beaver Dam Motel."

Cheryl and her companion seemed "pretty chummy" the night Reba Mae and I had spotted them, too, I mused. I made a check mark next to a couple of cute chef's aprons. I thought briefly about ordering one for Doug that read REAL MEN BBQ AND GRILL. He'd love it. Another apron had OCD stitched in bright letters. Underneath was written OBSESSIVE CUPCAKE DISORDER. That might work for Melly if I could get it customized as OBSESSIVE COOKIE DISORDER.

Buzz seemed oblivious of my preoccupation with aprons. "The whole time, the wife kept askin' me what I was doin' at the motel. Wanted to know if I'd inspected all the rooms. Asked if I was usin' organic pesticides."

With a sigh, I closed the catalog. "When was this?"

Buzz stopped spraying and squinted, his round face screwed up with concentration. "Wednesday, late afternoon. I was just finishing up my last job of the day."

Wednesday?

Chip's body wasn't discovered until early Thursday—but the coroner had ruled that Chip died the night before. Everyone had assumed Cheryl was in California, thousands of miles away, at the time. Unless Buzz Oliver was mistaken, Cheryl had been as snug as a bug in a rug—pardon the play on words—at the Beaver Dam Motel.

"Buzz," I said, choosing my next words carefully, "are you certain you saw Cheryl and her friend on Wednesday, not Thursday?"

"Yep, positive. I remember 'cause Wednesday's my bowlin' league. I knew I had to hurry if I wanted to grab a shower and a bite to eat before meetin' the guys. The woman insisted that I spray her room a second time to make sure I didn't miss anything. Because of her, I showed up late, and my team had to forfeit points."

I practically shoved Buzz out the door the instant he quit spraying. I could barely contain my excitement. Cheryl would benefit if Chip died while they were still married. She might even have an accidental-death benefit written into his life insurance claim. Did double indemnity still exist? I remembered seeing an old movie with Barbara Stanwyck and Fred MacMurray with the pair plotting to kill her husband for the insurance money, an almost perfect crime that involved a train track. Train track. Flight of stairs. Either way, dead was dead.

"Melly!" I called up to her. "Dinner's in the Crock-Pot. If I'm not home in an hour, you and Lindsey eat without me."

Not waiting for a response, I grabbed my purse and flew out the door. I couldn't wait to tell a certain somebody what I'd just learned.

CHAPTER 16

McBride's truck wasn't in its usual space, but I didn't let that deter me. He could just as easily have commandeered one of the marked cars for his use. I jumped out of my Beetle and shoved through the door of the Brandywine Creek Police Department.

Precious Blessing sat ensconced behind the front desk, munching on a submarine sandwich. Her face broke into a wide grin at seeing me. Other than Precious, the office appeared deserted. "Is the chief in?" I asked, not bothering with our usual pleasantries.

Precious set her sub next to an opened bag of potato chips and a can of Dr Pepper. Her smile faded when she saw my expression. "Don't go tellin' me you found another dead body?"

I blew out a breath. Folks were starting to think that finding dead people had become an occupation of mine. Technically, I'd found only one. Melly and Casey had discovered the others. "No, no dead body," I said.

"Praise the Lord!" Precious pushed the bag of chips in my direction.

I pushed them back. "I need to speak to McBride."

"The chief left 'bout a half hour ago. Let me page him for you."

"No thanks," I said when her hand reached for the phone. "I need to talk to him face-to-face. Did he say where he was going?"

"He mentioned somethin' about pickin' up a pizza before headin' on home. Offered to get me one, too, but I was in more of a mind for a meatball sub."

"Thanks, Precious." I was out the door in a flash and in my car.

I wanted to witness McBride's reaction from up close and personal when I relayed the information that Cheryl Balboa had been in town the night her husband died—not thousands of miles away, as she'd led everyone to believe. Motive, means, and opportunity, McBride liked to preach. Well, I'd been taking notes. Cheryl possessed two of the unholy trinity, motive and opportunity. All she'd needed to complete them was a steep flight of stairs, which Melly had unwittingly provided.

Shadows lengthened as I drove the two-lane county highway out of town. Days were growing noticeably shorter, now that October was here. Leaves on the oaks and sweet gum trees lining both sides of the road had started to change color. Not the blazing oranges and reds I'd known growing up in Michigan, but more mellow tones of gold and yellow.

Five miles farther, I turned into a driveway marked by a shiny black mailbox with MCBRIDE stenciled on the side. Gravel crunched beneath my tires. McBride's house, partially hidden by a giant magnolia tree in the front yard, came into view. I caught sight of a deer poised at the edge of the woods that bordered his property—so still it might have been a statue. Then, its head lifted as though sensing danger, the deer vanished among the towering loblolly pines.

McBride's Ford pickup was parked next to the house. I pulled up behind it, got out, and went up the walk. McBride—or someone—had done extensive yard work since my last visit. The hydrangeas and viburnum had been trimmed, the holly tamed. I also noticed another difference: A refrigerator stood on the porch in a spot previously occupied by an aluminum lawn chair. I felt like I'd wandered into an episode of *The Beverly Hillbillies*— minus the Beverly Hills. My knock was answered almost immediately.

"Come in." McBride stepped aside and motioned for me to enter. He'd taken time to exchange his uniform for jeans and a sweatshirt. "You're just in time for supper."

I found myself in the midst of a work in progress. A kitchen that had formerly been on my right now lay gutted and bare. A wooden plank resting across two sawhorses held a toaster, salt- and pepper shakers, and McBride's George Foreman grill. The outdated red and black linoleum in the kitchen, along with threadbare carpeting in the rest of the house, had been ripped out and replaced with a plywood subfloor.

"Cozy," I commented.

"The lady's being facetious," McBride said with a smile. "Eventually, I'll have hardwood floors throughout."

I gestured to a large sheet of plastic taped over a gaping hole. "Don't tell me," I drawled. "You lost your temper and put your fist through the wall."

"Funny," he said. "I'm having a French door put in, which will lead onto a deck." He led the way to a drop-leaf table covered with chipped and yellowed paint with an unopened pizza box as its centerpiece. "Like anchovies?"

"Anchovies?" I blinked at the sudden change of topic. "No, not really."

"Good, neither do I." He flashed a grin that showed off

the dimple in his cheek that I found so appealing. "Have a seat."

I sat. "I came here to talk, not interrupt your dinner."

"Heard women are good at multitasking. Now's your chance to prove it." He sorted through a cardboard box that held an assortment of kitchen items and produced two paper plates. "I even have china."

"That isn't china," I said, laughing in spite of myself. "It's Chinet."

"China or Chinet, they both hold food. What would you like to drink? I don't have Diet Coke, so it's either beer or water."

"Water works for me." I served up the pizza while he went out to the porch and returned with beverages—bottled water for me, a can of Bud Light for him.

I bit into my slice, savoring tomato sauce richly flavored with basil, oregano, thyme, marjoram, and garlic. The recipe was local chef Tony Deltorro's carefully guarded secret. "No one makes better pizza than the Pizza Palace."

"I've heard folks rave about Chicago-style deep dish." McBride tore off several sheets from a roll of paper towels and handed me one to use as a napkin.

"Never been to Chicago, but I don't know how it could top this." I scooped up a mushroom that had managed to escape from the gooey mozzarella. "What's your trick for getting pizza home while it's still hot?"

"I keep one of those hot-and-cold insulated bags in my truck. It also keeps ice cream from melting between the Piggly Wiggly and here."

I looked at him skeptically as I helped myself to a second slice. McBride was fit and trim. He didn't carry an extra pound. I wished I knew his magic formula. "I'd never have taken you for an ice cream–loving kind of guy."

McBride took a swig of beer. "Strawberry's my favorite. What's yours?"

"Blue Bell's butter pecan," I answered, naming not only the flavor but also the brand. "In my humble opinion, they make the best. I think it's all the pecans they add." I took a sip of my water. "Gee, McBride, this conversation's turning personal. What next, favorite TV shows?"

He took another slice of pizza—it might have been his third, but who was counting? "Okay, I'll play along. You go first."

"I'm a big *CSI* fan, and, of course, I love the Food Network."

"Figures."

I ignored his sarcasm. "Now your turn."

He studied the label on the beer can before confessing, "I like *Dancing with the Stars*."

I couldn't have been more surprised. Leaning back in my chair, I decided to test him. "Humor me, McBride. If you like *Dancing with the Stars* so much, which winners were your favorites?"

"Hines Ward, for one."

"Hmm." I nodded. "Wasn't he a professional football player?"

"Fourteen years with the Pittsburgh Steelers, voted MVP of the Super Bowl. Also played for the University of Georgia. And"—he grinned as he snatched the last slice of pizza—"Hines won perfect scores for both the Argentine tango and the quickstep."

"You probably read all that in *Sports Illustrated*. If you're such a huge fan, who else?"

"Emmitt Smith."

"Another football player?"

"Dallas Cowboys most of his career. A great running back." He took a long swallow of his beer. "I've got two left feet when it comes to dancing. Never did learn the shag. I turned green with envy, watching Doug and Reba Mae take home the trophy at the barbecue festival for their fancy footwork."

I felt a stab of guilt at the mention of Doug's name. I was enjoying Wyatt McBride's company far too much. Doug Winters was the one I should have been with sharing likes and dislikes with, not McBride. My loyalty rightfully belonged to Doug, a mild-mannered veterinarian. Not a hunky policeman who looked better than he ought to in faded jeans and scruffy sweatshirt.

"Dessert?" Unmindful of my inner turmoil, McBride rummaged through the cardboard box and unearthed a half-eaten bag of Oreos.

"Sure." Pizza *and* cookies? My metabolism couldn't compete with his. I made a mental note to resume jogging, a habit I'd fallen out of since Melly's grisly discovery.

McBride wolfed down a couple of Oreos, then leaned back, arms folded across his chest. "Now, what brought you out here in the first place?"

I felt a frisson of anticipation, now that the "reveal" was at hand. "You can cross Melly off your persons of interest list."

"That so?"

I nodded so vigorously, my curls bounced. "You need to check out Cheryl Balboa. She should be your number one suspect."

"Exactly why do I 'need' to do this?"

"Motive, means, and opportunity," I replied succinctly. "Cheryl has all three. With Chip dead, Cheryl is entitled to inherit everything—house, cars, cash, and half of Trustychipdesign."

"Aren't you overlooking one important fact? Cheryl Balboa was in California the night her husband was killed."

"That's where you're wrong." I paused for dramatic effect, then played my trump card. "Cheryl was right here in Brandywine Creek the entire time."

McBride lifted one dark brow, the one bisected with a small scar, ever so slightly. "And you came by this information how?"

"Because Bugs-B-Gone offered a twenty-five-dollar coupon to customers who signed a year-long contract. Termites, spiders, ants. They promised to spray every other month, whether you need it or not."

"You lost me." He tapped the empty beer can on the tabletop. "What do bugs have to do with any of this?"

"Nothing, but Buzz Oliver does," I said. "If you recall, Buzz is the senior tech at Bugs-B-Gone. Buzz came by Spice It Up! this afternoon to perform routine pest control. While he was there, he let it slip that Cheryl and her boyfriend checked into the Beaver Dam Motel late Wednesday afternoon."

"Is he sure about the date?"

"Not just sure, he's positive. Cheryl was the reason he was late for bowling. His team had to forfeit points."

I could almost see the cogs in McBride's brain start to grind.

"Chip's body wasn't found until Thursday morning," I reminded him needlessly. "Both the coroner and ME concluded he died Wednesday evening. You've been under the impression Cheryl was two thousand miles away when you called to inform her that Chip was dead, but she was right here in Brandywine Creek the whole time."

He leaned forward, hands loosely cupped around the empty beer can, his expression thoughtful. "When I phoned Cheryl Balboa, she told me she'd be here as soon as she could make travel arrangements."

"Some travel arrangements," I scoffed. "All the way from the Beaver Dam Motel to the police department, where she auditioned for the role of grieving widow."

"You referred to Cheryl Balboa's 'boyfriend.' Tell me what you know about him."

"The guy looks like he was born with a surfboard tucked under his arm. He's the Ken doll to her Barbie. You know the type—tall, bronzed, and built. Lots of sun-streaked blond hair. Reba Mae wants to hire him for a pool boy."

He seemed puzzled. "Reba Mae doesn't have a pool."

"Point made."

"How long have you been aware of Cheryl's friend?"

I shifted my weight. Had the chair suddenly gotten harder? "We—Reba Mae and I—saw them canoodling in a back booth at North of the Border on Saturday night. So we tailed them to the Beaver Dam."

"Tailed them?" McBride pinched the bridge of his nose between thumb and forefinger. "Please don't tell me you women are playing detective again. How many times do I have to warn you to stay away from trouble?"

I raised my chin defiantly, but the action was wasted on him. "We saw them embrace, then go into a motel room together."

"Interesting." Climbing to his feet, he discarded the pizza box and paper plates in the nearby trash can.

"Interesting? Is that all you're going to say?" I huffed out an impatient breath. "Aren't you going to bring Cheryl in for questioning? Subpoena her? Grill her? Find out why she lied about being in Brandywine Creek? See if she has an alibi? Ask her the last time she talked to Chip? The last time she saw him?"

One side of McBride's mouth quirked in obvious amusement. "I'm looking for someone to replace Sergeant Blabbermouth. Care to fill out an application?"

My mouth dropped open. "You've fired Beau?"

"I put him on probation. The man needs to learn the meaning of privileged information in an ongoing investigation. And to keep his mouth shut."

"Don't blame Beau." I tugged my lower lip between my teeth. "It's my fault. I cornered him at the football game and forced him to tell me everything he knew."

McBride's beer can clanged as he dropped it into a plastic bin labeled RECYCLE. "Did you use thumbscrews? Or did you resort to water boarding?"

"Beau was caught between a rock and a hard place. It was either answer my question or the cheese on his nachos would congeal."

"Tough choice."

I rose from my chair and neatly pushed it against the table. "You still haven't told me what you're going to do about Cheryl. Why not get a copy of her cell phone records like they do on TV? They should be undisputed proof to show where she was when you called to tell her about Chip."

"Since you seem to know so much, you ought to know I can't do that without a court order."

"So," I challenged, "what are you waiting for?"

A loud meow sounded before he could reply. My head jerked around at the cry. I watched a cat slink out a door that I assumed belonged to a bedroom. The feline looked dressed for the opera, its fur like a black tux with a snowy-white shirt front. Its eyes glowed like twin emeralds. Half of one ear was conspicuously absent, ruining the cat's haughty pose.

"A cat? You have a cat?" I asked in amazement.

"She's a feral cat. At least part feral. She sort of adopted me. Kept coming up to the porch, looked half-starved, so I started feeding her. When the temperature dropped a couple weeks ago, I finally let her inside. Now she doesn't want to leave the house."

I stooped down. "Here, kitty, kitty," I crooned.

The cat responded with another plaintive meow, turned tail, and retreated back into the bedroom.

"Well, I guess she told me in no uncertain terms," I said, both irritated and amused at the animal's behavior. "Does your pet have a name?"

"Fraidy."

I rolled my eyes. "As in 'fraidy cat'?"

"The name suits her. Fraidy doesn't trust people," he admitted. "I keep her in the bedroom when workmen are around."

Would wonders never cease? Not only did the man love watching *Dancing with the Stars,* but he'd befriended a homeless feline, too. What else was hidden beneath the tough-guy exterior?

"G'night, Wyatt," I said.

"G'night, Piper."

I left him standing in the center of his self-proclaimed work in progress. It wasn't until I was almost home that I realized I'd called him by his given name.

CHAPTER 17

Lindsey practically floated through the front door of my shop. "Sean asked me to homecoming."

I stopped sorting credit card receipts at the counter. "That's wonderful, sweetie."

"I worried he was going to ask Brittany Hughes, but he was waiting by my locker after French class." She plunked her backpack on the floor, grabbed me around the waist, and twirled me in a circle. "Can you believe it? Sean Rogers asked *me* to homecoming."

Casey, who had been indulging in his favorite pastime—napping—woke up and wanted to be part of the celebration. Barking excitedly, he wagged his tail back and forth and pranced about.

"You'll really like him, Mom," Lindsey said, releasing me and scooping up Casey.

I gazed into my daughter's flushed face, her sparkling eyes, and felt my breath catch. Before I knew it, she'd be off to college. The years had flown. One minute it's diapers and teething; the next, they're finishing high school and choosing a career. I cleared my throat. "I think Sean Rogers is one smart guy for picking you."

She stroked Casey's shaggy brown fur until the pup almost purred like a kitten. "Sean's cool. He listens, he really listens when I talk."

I smiled once more. I knew exactly what she meant. Doug Winters did that very same thing whenever we talked. My smile dimmed when it dawned on me I hadn't heard from him recently. That wasn't like Doug. Was something wrong? I made a mental note to find out.

"I want to meet this young man you talk so much about. Why not invite him for dinner soon?" I said, taking the receipts up again and tucking them into an envelope.

"I will, promise." Casey licked Lindsey's chin with his wet, raspy tongue, making her giggle. "And we need to shop for a dress. Something amazing. There's a good chance Sean will be voted homecoming king."

I put the envelope in a drawer of the cash register. "Does that mean you might be elected queen?"

Lindsey set Casey on the floor. "Oh, Mom, there are a lot of girls prettier than me who'll get votes."

Still, I could read my daughter's mind. I knew she knew that she was in the running for that coveted honor. "Let's set time aside soon to go to the mall. I heard there's a new Italian restaurant nearby we might like to try."

"Sure, sounds like fun." Lindsey found Casey a doggy treat from a jar under the counter and handed it to him. "Okay if Amber comes along? She knows the managers of all the boutiques from her pageant days."

Two's company; three's a crowd. That might be a cliché, but in this case, no truer words were ever spoken. I forced a smile again even though I feared my face would crack. "No problem."

"Great. I'll text her."

A glance at my watch told me I'd better hurry if I didn't want to be late for Chip Balboa's remembrance. I intended to keep a close eye on the Widow Balboa. Could she—

would she—shed a tear for her dearly departed? Or merely display the cool detachment of an about-to-be ex-wife who's already moved on? Better yet, maybe I'd detect a flicker of guilt for having hastened her husband's untimely demise. "Are you sure, Lindsey, that you can manage the shop by yourself?"

"It's never very busy this time of day." She went over to her backpack and leaned down to pull out a three-ring notebook covered in hearts and flowers. "This will give me time to study for the history quiz tomorrow."

"Great." I fished my compact out of my purse and inspected my makeup a final time. I hoped the heavier-than-usual coat of mascara would draw attention to my eyes and away from the blasted freckles peeking through the light foundation I'd applied earlier. I wasn't sure what the appropriate attire was for this afternoon's final tribute, so I'd chosen every woman's go-to—the little black dress. Equally suitable for cocktail parties or funerals. "See you later," I said as I went out the door.

Cars filled the drive of the Turner-Driscoll House, so I parked at the curb and walked up the circular drive as quickly as my slim skirt and three-inch heels allowed. I spotted Cheryl's rental parked in front of Reba Mae's Buick. Reba Mae, bless her heart, had squeezed Melly in for a wash and set, then volunteered to give her a ride over. The dark Cadillac belonged to Dottie Hemmings. I wasn't sure who owned the Toyota Corolla.

Felicity greeted me at the door, her somber expression befitting the occasion. "Everyone is congregating in the entrance hall. The remembrance will begin in just a few minutes in the front parlor."

Felicity effortlessly oozed charm and chic. Her silver hair was worn in a short, no-nonsense style. Smile lines bracketed lively brown eyes. She'd been married to a prominent Birmingham physician. After his death, she'd moved to Brandywine Creek determined to restore a house that had been in her husband's family for decades. She was a people person, loved to entertain, so operating a bed-and-breakfast proved a perfect fit.

The entrance hall, which ran the length of the house, was large enough to accommodate a marching band. I stood for a moment to get my bearings. Guests formed small clusters on the black and white marble checkerboard floor. A staircase with a mahogany banister gracefully curved to bedrooms on the second level. An ornate gilded mirror hung above an antique console decorated with a gorgeous centerpiece of white hothouse roses and rosemary. Unable to resist, I leaned forward for a whiff of the peppery-pine fragrance.

"Rosemary is for remembrance," Felicity said from over my shoulder. "I thought it would add a nice touch."

"I'm sure Rusty appreciates the gesture."

"He's been struggling to deal with the loss of his friend. The two had a terrible row the night of Chip's unfortunate accident. I think this is Rusty's way of making amends for the harsh words." Felicity nodded toward the doorway of the parlor. "Now, if you'll excuse me, I need to check on the refreshments."

Before I had a chance to fully process what Felicity had just told me, Reba Mae separated herself from a group that included Melly, Dottie, and Thompson Gray. "Hey, honeybun," she said. "I been waitin' on you. You're not usually late. Thought you might've had a change of heart and decided not to come."

The front door opened to admit a latecomer. McBride stood for a moment, his cool blue eyes surveying the assembled guests.

"Whoo-ee!" Reba Mae fanned herself. "That man sure cleans up well."

"Mmm." I tried to keep my tone neutral, although I secretly agreed he looked handsome in dark blazer, pale blue shirt, and gray pants.

"By the way," I said, hoping to sound offhand, "I drove out to his place last night. We shared a pizza."

Reba Mae waggled her eyebrows suggestively. "Anythin' else you care to share?"

I leaned closer and spoke softly, "Cheryl Balboa wasn't in California the night her husband died. She was here the entire time."

Reba Mae's eyes widened. "You're kiddin', right?"

"I think she might've had something to do with Chip's death."

The babble of voices in the entrance hall faded into silence. I glanced around to find the cause. Everyone's eyes were trained on the staircase. Cheryl Balboa, stunningly dressed from head to toe in black, befitting a recent widow, her blond hair swept into a fashionable chignon, slowly descended the stairs. I had to give the woman points. She knew how to make an entrance.

"I saw an actress with that hairdo on *The Young and the Restless*. Been wantin' to try it ever since," Reba Mae said, referring to the off-center knot at Cheryl's nape.

"Nice," I murmured. Out of the corner of my eye, I studied Rusty's expression. His face looked pinched as he observed Cheryl's slow descent. I wondered where Cheryl had stashed her boyfriend. Had she sent him packing? Or was he still holed up at the Beaver Dam Motel while she called on her limited acting skills to portray a grieving widow?

Felicity rang a little silver bell to get people's attention. "Ladies and gentlemen, shall we adjourn to the parlor, where Rusty will share memories of his dear friend, Chip Balboa."

With Felicity leading the way, we filed after her. The parlor still retained its formality from when the house was first built. Brocade draperies, velvet settees, Aubusson carpet, and precious antiques all contributed to the ambience. Late afternoon sunlight filtered into the room through double-hung floor-to-ceiling windows along two walls. A mahogany sideboard held a series of photographs chronicling Rusty and Chip's friendship through the years.

Rusty stood next to the fireplace. Cheryl, I noted, preferred to stand apart from the others. "First of all," Rusty began, "I want to thank you all for coming this afternoon to honor a man you didn't know. I hope when you leave today, you'll feel acquainted with a man I regarded as a brother."

A strangled sound that might have been a sob—or a laugh—came from the widow.

Rusty pretended he hadn't heard anything and continued. Hands stuffed in his pants pockets, he spoke about meeting Chip in college, sharing a dorm room, and about their decision to form Trustychipdesign.com.

"Tell us about the road trip you and Chip were on," Melly encouraged when he seemed to falter.

Rusty's smile was tinged with sadness, but he readily complied. He held up a photo showing the two of them with the Golden Gate Bridge in the background. "We started our odyssey in San Francisco, then moved on to the Grand Canyon, Las Vegas, New Orleans, and Birmingham before traveling to Atlanta and eventually Brandywine Creek."

Cheryl cleared her throat loudly. "I didn't come prepared for this little show-and-tell, but I do happen to have our wedding picture with me." She drew out a framed photograph that had been hidden behind Rusty's display.

Her face screwed up until she looked like she was going to burst into tears.

"There, there, dear." Dottie reached out and patted her arm. "You're among friends."

At the sight of Dottie's plump hand on her forearm, Cheryl sniffed her unshed tears into submission. "I want everyone to know our wedding day was the happiest day of our lives. True, our marriage had hit bumps in the road, like many marriages often do, but Chip and I loved each other in spite of our . . . differences."

I swore she was about to say "divorce" but changed it into "differences" at the last second.

Cheryl dabbed at her eyes with a tissue. "Chip phoned, and after a long talk, we agreed to work on our problems. We planned to reconcile."

Rusty snorted at hearing this, and Cheryl returned a look as lethal as a poisoned dagger. "My husband and I loved each other—deeply," she concluded, her lower lip quivering.

"You poor thing." Dottie enfolded her in a bear hug. Cheryl's arms flailed as she tried to wriggle free, but Dottie only clung tighter.

I placed a hand over my mouth to stifle a giggle. Shame on me. I didn't dare glance at Reba Mae for fear we'd both break down and laugh. Once the giggling started, stopping wasn't easy.

Felicity clapped her hands, much like Mother Superior back at St. Agnes Grade School. "If y'all will follow me, refreshments are waiting in the dining room."

Everyone trailed out except for Reba Mae and me, who lingered to examine the photographs. I picked up a candid shot of the partners high-fiving with a Trustychipdesign logo in the background. "They look so happy in this one. I wonder what they argued about the night Chip died. I'm going to have to ask Felicity if she knew."

Reba Mae didn't answer. Instead she was staring intently at Chip and Cheryl's wedding picture. "Take a gander," she said. "I swear it's been Photoshopped. Looks like the groom was cut out of the photo, then put back in. What do you think?"

I examined the photo, too. "You might be right. Chip's face is identical to the one in the Trustychipdesign snapshot. Right down to the smudge on one lens of his eyeglasses."

"Well, don't that beat all?" Reba Mae murmured. "Why do you suppose she'd go to all the trouble?"

I thought of Cheryl Balboa's theatrics and histrionics and knew the answer. "Because she wants people to think they were a loving couple. And to point suspicion away from her."

"It's most always the wife or the husband, isn't it?" Reba Mae linked her arm in mine. "Let's go eat."

Halfway across the entrance hall, we paused. Red and blue lights strobed through the sidelights of the front door. Seconds later, someone jabbed the doorbell three times in quick succession. Felicity hurried to answer. I noticed the others guests, including McBride, had migrated into the entrance hall to find out why the commotion.

Sergeant Beau Tucker stood on the doorstep, puffed with self-importance. He adjusted his utility belt with one hand while his other hand clutched a document of some sort. "I have something for the chief that can't wait."

McBride shouldered his way between Dottie and Thompson Gray, who gawked unashamedly. "What is it, Sergeant?"

Beau Tucker shoved the sheet of paper at him. "Thought you'd want to see this ASAP."

Seeing McBride's expression upon scanning the document, I felt a sinking sensation in the pit of my stomach. "What is it?" I asked.

"Toxicology report," he replied.

CHAPTER 18

"It was nice of Thompson to go to Chip's remembrance, wasn't it?" Melly asked.

Melly and I had just returned to Spice It Up! from the Turner-Driscoll House. The clock on the wall told me it was almost time to lock up for the day. Upon seeing us, Lindsey had been more than happy to take a break from her schoolwork and take Casey for a romp in the park.

"Thompson has always struck me as the thoughtful type," I said as I opened the drawer of my antique cash register and began to count the day's receipts.

Melly watched, her fingers toying with her strand of pearls. "Thompson met Chip only the one time when I'd introduced him as president of our local computer club. He's such a lovely man. You can see that in the way he treats his mother. Shame he never married. He would have been a good catch for some lucky woman."

I half listened as Melly droned on. Instead of concentrating on the cash I was counting, my mind roamed. I kept wondering about the significance of the toxicology report. McBride indicated it was important for reasons he didn't care to divulge. Beau Tucker's attitude when he'd arrived at the bed-and-breakfast reinforced the notion of its importance.

Seeing how the amount never tallied, I finally gave up counting bills and switched tasks. As I slipped quarters into coin rollers, I made a mental note to ask McBride if he'd made any progress in obtaining Cheryl Balboa's phone records. The woman certainly would reap enormous financial rewards as Chip's widow rather than as a divorcée. If McBride could prove she'd trailed her husband across the country and was in Brandywine Creek the night of Chip's fatal fall, well, that would certainly move her up a notch on his persons of interest list.

"I don't understand why Chief McBride was at the remembrance." Melly shot me a disapproving look when she saw me slip a nickel in with the quarters. "Doesn't that man ever smile?"

I started separating dimes from pennies. "I suppose McBride was there to observe. That's part of his job description, his training."

Melly pursed her lips. "Well, if you want my opinion, it seems disrespectful. Let the dead rest in peace, I always say."

I snatched a penny in time to keep it from rolling off the counter, then looked up as the door opened, expecting to see Lindsey and Casey. Instead McBride strode into Spice It Up!, trailed by Officer Gary Moyer. My stomach lurched at the sight of McBride—and this time it had nothing to do with him being tall, dark, and hunky. McBride, I noted, had changed out of civvies and back into uniform. The expression on his face spelled trouble. "Well, speak of the devil . . . ," I muttered.

Ignoring me, McBride went directly to Melly and handed her a folded document. "This is a warrant signed by Judge Herman to search the premises at 239 Jefferson Street."

Melly's mouth opened and closed in astonishment.

I snatched the paper from her and scanned the contents. Anger and frustration sizzled in my blood as I returned the document to her. "Unbelievable!" I fumed. "Why the search warrant? What do you expect to find in Melly's home besides an AARP card?"

"New evidence has come to light," he said, still not looking at me. "We initially treated Balboa's death as accidental and didn't do an extensive search. Now, because of the report from the GBI, we have probable cause."

Before I could question him further, Lindsey burst into the shop. And she wasn't alone. The young man with her was tall with short, wavy brown hair and hazel green eyes. If there were a shred of doubt in my mind as to his identity, it would have been dispelled by the name embroidered on his varsity jacket—SEAN ROGERS. I groaned silently. What a time she'd picked to introduce her family to her homecoming date.

Lindsey skidded to halt when she spotted McBride. Her gaze traveled back and forth between me and her grandmother. Sean hung back, uncertain. "What's wrong?" Lindsey asked.

"Chief McBride dropped by to present your meemaw with a search warrant," I told her. No point in sugar-coating the facts, I thought glumly. News like this spreads faster than kudzu.

"What for?" Lindsey cried. "What did she do?"

"I didn't do a thing," Melly replied, indignant. "The man is trying to justify his salary by harassing a law-abiding senior citizen."

Under ordinary circumstances, I would have smiled at hearing Melly play the senior citizen card. She did that only on rare occasions and only when it worked to her advantage. These, however, weren't "ordinary" circumstances.

Lindsey unfastened Casey's leash, and the little mutt trotted over to sit at McBride's feet, expecting his usual scratch behind the ears. Not even the hopeful gleam in the pup's dark eyes softened McBride's demeanor.

I cleared my throat. "The warrant specifies chemical substances. Precisely what type of substances are you looking for, McBride? Illegal drugs?"

Melly gasped at the implication. "That's preposterous! The only drug I take is for high blood pressure."

Which was probably about to shoot through the roof, I thought. "When is this warrant going to be executed?"

"My men are standing by, awaiting the word." With that, McBride turned and left the shop with the silent Officer Moyer close behind.

I dived into my pocket for my cell phone. "I'll call CJ," I told Melly. "I'll ask him to meet us at your place."

Melly reached for her purse. "Tell him to get a move on."

We formed a caravan of sorts. McBride and Moyer in their squad car led the parade. Melly accompanied me in my Beetle, and Lindsey and Sean brought up the rear in his beat-up Impala. Much to Sean Rogers's credit, the kid didn't bolt and run at the first sign of trouble. Or maybe he just wanted a front-row seat at what would turn out to be a circus.

Soon, drawn like fleas to a hound, a crowd began to gather on porches and sidewalks near Melly's house. Gerilee Barker chanced to be taking Bruno, her black Lab, for a stroll. Thompson Gray's mother, Mavis, muttered something about returning a book she'd borrowed. Jolene Tucker, no doubt alerted about the festivities by her husband, Beau, didn't bother with pretense. In her haste, she hadn't paused long enough to take the rollers from her hair. Everyone, it seemed, wanted to be an eyewitness to the most exciting event since the Brandywine Creek Barbecue Festival.

CJ's sleek Lexus screeched to a halt behind one of the police cars at the curb. He leaped out and jogged to where I stood with Melly. Lindsey and Sean remained at a short distance apart from the others. "What in Sam Hill's goin' on?" he thundered.

"Apparently, McBride and his troops are looking for a chemical substance of some sort," I explained.

"Does the fool think Momma's runnin' a meth lab in her cellar?"

"CJ, really!" Melly darted a look around. "What will the neighbors think at hearing that kind of talk?"

CJ draped an arm across his mother's slim shoulders. "Momma, you should be back at Piper's restin'. Watchin' all this can't be good for a body."

"Nonsense." Melly drew her sweater tighter. "I'm not going to sit by while a bunch of men ransack my home."

"Daddy," Lindsey wailed. "Can't you do something?"

"Wish I could, baby."

"Isn't Judge Herman an old friend of the family?" I asked. "He and your mother were bridge partners not long ago."

CJ frowned. "I gave Cot a call on the way over. He claimed his hands were tied. Told me to assure Momma this is nothin' personal."

I could make out men's figures moving back and forth inside the house. "What do you suppose they're looking for?"

"Damned if I know." CJ tunneled his fingers through his salon-styled hair. "Chemical substances could be any-thin' from cough syrup to furniture polish."

"I'm scared, CJ," I confessed in a low voice. "I don't like the direction this is all heading."

"I'm scared, too, darlin'." CJ slipped his free arm around my waist and pulled me closer.

Leaning against him, I rubbed my cheek against his

starched shirt and inhaled the familiar scent of his cologne. He felt strong, solid. Comforting. For a moment, it seemed almost like old times.

The search of Melly's house turned out to be mercifully brief. I straightened and drew away from CJ as McBride bounded down the steps, an evidence bag clutched in one hand. Lindsey and Sean moved closer until the five of us resembled refugees huddled against a storm.

McBride went directly to Melly and held up an official-looking bag containing a small plastic bottle. "This yours?"

"Yes, of course it's mine," she snapped. "Whom else would it belong to?"

"What did you find, McBride?" CJ, his shoulders braced, stood as tall as his five-foot-ten-inch frame allowed. "As her attorney, I have a right to know what you consider evidence."

"Check your law books, CJ," McBride said. "You're jumping the gun. Far as I know, evidence isn't shared until the discovery phase of a trial, and we're not there . . . yet."

Clearly upset, Melly wrung her hands. "I don't understand why I'm being treated like a common criminal. All this fuss because of a little disagreement about the low offer Trustychipdesign wanted to pay me. Why, any red-blooded person would've been insulted. Naturally, I was angry and upset. Who wouldn't be?"

"Momma"—CJ held up his hand—"on the advice of your son—and your attorney—*don't* say another word."

Hearing CJ volunteer to represent his mother made me shudder. While he fancied himself Perry Mason, he lacked Perry's finesse in front of a jury. His specialty was trip-and-falls that were settled out of court. Heaven forbid if Melly needed a criminal defense lawyer and chose him.

CJ motioned toward the evidence bag. "What's this all about, McBride?"

A tick would have merited more attention. "Mrs. Prescott," McBride addressed Melly, "you need to come down to the department for fingerprinting."

Melly's eyes widened with shock. "Whatever for? I'm no felon."

"Just routine," McBride informed her, his tone neutral. "We need to exclude your prints in case more than one set are present on the container."

"Don't you worry none, Momma," CJ said, then turned to McBride. "I'm comin' along."

McBride headed for his patrol car. "Suit yourself."

"We'll all go," I said with finality. "Times like this, families need to stick together."

"We're coming, too, Meemaw," Lindsey called out. I noticed she and Sean were holding hands.

"Remember, Chief McBride said this is only routine."

Melly shook her head. "All this bother over a little bottle of eyedrops. I swear, I don't know what this world's coming to."

"Eyedrops?" CJ's voice rose. "Is that what McBride took as evidence? You sure 'bout that?"

"Son, I saw the container plain as day." She took my arm as we turned to leave. "I often suffer from eyestrain after staring at a computer monitor hours on end. I keep eyedrops on my kitchen table along with a few pens and pencils in a sweetgrass basket I bought years ago at the City Market in Charleston. You know . . . the kind of basket the Gullah ladies make."

CJ stood planted on the walk and scratched his head. "Don't see how eyedrops could get you into a heap of trouble. McBride's had it in for me ever since our scuffle in high school. Might be this is his way of gettin' back at me."

I steered Melly through the looky lous, toward my car. "This isn't about you, CJ," I reminded him over my shoulder. "It's about your mother."

And a bottle of eyedrops—not to mention Chip Balboa's dead body.

CHAPTER 19

Why are good habits so difficult to acquire and so easy to lose? The morning after Melly's fingerprinting, it was time to get back in the saddle, so to speak. That is if sneakers, hoodie, and ball cap could be equated with a saddle. I needed to resume my jogging routine, which had been disrupted ever since Melly had found a body in her basement.

Casey watched me tie the laces of my sneakers, his tail thumping rhythmically on the floor. His button-bright eyes gleamed with anticipation. He was telling me in doggy terms he'd also missed our morning runs.

"All righty, boy," I whispered, reaching for his leash. I quietly closed the kitchen door behind us, not wanting to wake Melly. Lindsey had already left for school. Together Casey and I ran down the stairs as noiselessly as possible and slipped out the rear door into the vacant lot behind my shop.

"Hey, Scooter. Care for company?"

I nearly jumped out of my skin at the sound of CJ's voice. My hand flew to my chest, where I could feel my heart thudding against my rib cage. Casey, bless his furry little soul, growled low in his throat, read to serve and protect.

"Chandler Jameson Prescott!" I nearly shouted. "Don't you dare sneak up on me that way ever again!"

Now that my heart rate had returned to near normal, I noticed he'd dressed for the occasion in a navy blue track-suit that looked more suitable for sipping wine in front of a roaring fire at a ski resort than for zipping down side streets of small-town USA.

Casey sniffed CJ's thick-soled, name-brand, and obviously expensive running shoes and began to lift a hind leg.

"Don't even think about it, you mangy mutt," CJ snarled.

"Don't you insult my dog!" I shot back. Casey, unused to being reprimanded so harshly, backed off and relieved himself in a clump of weeds.

Resting my palms against the rough brick of the building, I performed a few simple, gentle stretches to limber up muscles in my calves and thighs. "Okay, CJ, why are you masquerading as an athlete?"

"What's wrong with what I've got on?" CJ asked, instantly on the defensive. "Accordin' to Amber, this is Nordstrom's finest in men's sportswear."

I pointed at his red, white, and blue striped headband. It looked like something the front man in a rock group might wear. "The headband Amber's idea, too?"

CJ mimicked my warm-up routine. "Amber thinks I need to work out. Wants me in tip-top shape for the nuptials. Lindsey mentioned you'd started joggin'. Thought you might give me a few pointers."

"It's best to start at a brisk walk," I said, my warm-ups over. "Try to keep up." I headed for the street, Casey at my side.

CJ matched his stride to mine. "No problem. You're forgettin' I used to play sports. Football, baseball, tennis."

"From the paunch you're developing, I'd say the only

exercise you get these days is punching the buttons of the remote control."

"Amber's turnin' into a regular slave driver. She's after me to skip the prime rib and order salad. I didn't spend years eatin' tuna casserole and meat loaf so I can deny myself a good piece of meat now I can afford it."

"Poor baby," I said, picking up the pace.

CJ, not about to be outdone, followed my example. "Amber's talkin' about me signin' up for a Pilates class at the club. She's thinkin' about hirin' a personal trainer."

Why, oh why, had I fallen for CJ's sob story during our divorce? He'd convinced me that we were strapped for cash with Chad's plans for medical school and Lindsey's upcoming college expenses. Like an idiot, I'd believed him. I took him at his word and agreed to a cash settlement. All of which I'd invested in Spice It Up! Owning a business of my own had been a long-held dream. Now, while I struggled to make ends meet, CJ lived in relative luxury. But to quote a cliché, money can't buy happiness. True happiness, I'd learned, came from within. I felt good about the woman I'd become, confident and proud of my accomplishments.

I broke into a jog. "A personal trainer, eh? Must be nice."

CJ gamely kept up with me. "Amber met this guy by the name of Troy at the drivin' range the other day. He claimed to be a personal trainer visitin' here from California with a friend. Amber invited him over for dinner and drinks tomorrow night—and a free consultation."

Alarm bells sounded in my head. A visitor from California? Were Troy-at-the-driving-range and Cheryl Balboa's surfer dude one and the same? McBride wasn't the only one who didn't believe in coincidence. I hadn't figured out the particulars, but I planned to be an uninvited guest for CJ's "free consultation."

"Can you slow down a bit?" CJ whined. "I'm not trainin' for a marathon."

"Fine." I obliged. "Now, are you ready to tell me the real reason you showed up at my back door this morning?"

"I'm worried about Momma," he confessed. "How was she after you got 'er home last night?"

"Frankly, I've never seen her more upset," I admitted. "She kept complaining about the fingerprinting ink. Must've washed her hands a dozen times. Made me think of Lady Macbeth: 'Out, damned spot.'"

"Didn't know you knew any, ah, ah," he panted, "Shakespeare."

"There's probably a lot about me you don't know." I turned down a side street and once again lengthened my stride. Casting a sidelong glance at CJ, I frowned. "Sure you're okay?"

"Just dandy," he puffed. "Give me a second."

I was in the zone and felt I could run forever. I even had breath in my lungs enough to speak. "If all you wanted to do was break a sweat, you could've stayed home and used your treadmill."

"You're a hard woman, Piper Prescott. A hard woman." He chugged to a halt.

I jogged in place next to him. "Want me to call nine-one-one?" I inquired sweetly.

He shot me an angry look, then bent forward, hands on his knees, while he caught his breath. Casey stared at him curiously, with his head canted.

Eventually, CJ straightened and swiped the perspiration from his upper lip. "I'm damn near killin' myself, all because I need a favor from you."

"Ask away."

"Momma's got herself in a fine pickle. McBride's a regular pit bull. He's not gonna let go until he finds out why

Chip Whatshisname showed up deader 'n' a skunk in her cellar."

As much as I would've liked to, I couldn't fault his logic. "So what's the big favor?"

"Momma needs your help. Hell's bells, I need your help. You've got a good head on your shoulders, Piper, when it comes to figurin' things out. I want you to do everythin' in your power to find out what really happened."

Does he think he has to ask me to help Melly? If so, ours was a sorry state of affairs. Rather than jogging in place, I kept raising my feet—first right, then left—to keep the muscles from seizing. "I'm already trying to get to the bottom of this, CJ, but I'm not a detective. McBride's the one with all the experience. Maybe he's the one you should be having this conversation with."

"McBride doesn't know Momma the way we do. We both know she didn't push that man down the stairs—but, sure as shootin', someone did. Think how easy it would be for the police to take things as they appear on the surface. To never dig any deeper. Promise you'll help sort things out. If not for me, do it for our children. Surely you don't want Chad and Lindsey to have to visit their meemaw in prison."

It occurred to me that this was the longest—and the most civil—conversation CJ and I'd had in a coon's age. "I give you my word, CJ," I said. "I'll do everything I can to find out what really happened that night."

Satisfied with my response, he nodded. I watched as he turned and hobbled back the way we'd come.

After returning home, I fed Casey, showered, and made egg-white omelets with tomatoes, mushrooms, and Swiss cheese for Melly and myself. I kept the seasoning simple, with kosher salt and a pinch of ground white pepper. Slices of whole wheat toast completed the menu.

When breakfast was over, I went downstairs to my shop and spent the morning fielding questions from those neighbors who'd heard Melly's home had been searched. Talk gradually drifted to the Grangers' Oktoberfest party, which was to take place in just a few days. Pinky Alexander mentioned her husband, Del, served in Germany while in the army. He'd once sent her a pretty velvet vest embroidered with wildflowers that she thought would be appropriate to wear if paired with one of her square dance skirts. Lottie Smith, on the other hand, said she wouldn't be caught dead in some ridiculous outfit. Happily for me, most people left with spice of one sort or another. Cloves and cardamom seemed to be leading the pack, with cinnamon not far behind. Someone—it might have been Ruby Phillips—confided she used cardamom to give her meatballs their unique flavor.

The morning's discussion of German recipes and the various spices used prompted me to give more serious consideration to what I was going to take to the party. Lebkuchen, I decided with finality, a spice cookie and one of Chad's favorites. Since business had slowed, I went to the small kitchen at the rear of my shop and started assembling and measuring ingredients. The dough needed to be thoroughly chilled before rolling out and baking. I'd make the dough today, then refrigerate it overnight.

I was stirring dark molasses into a mixture of egg, brown sugar, and honey when a woman with curly blond hair and hoop earrings the size of bangle bracelets shoved open the door. "Why do you suppose McBride took Melly's Visine?" she asked.

"Reba Mae, you meet up with Lady Clairol again?" By now I should have been used to my BFF's constantly changing hair color, but the transformations always came as a mild surprise.

Preening, she patted her curls. "This time the blond hair's the real deal. Thought the change of color would help me get into character for Truvy Jones. Play practice for *Steel Magnolias* begins next week. Like it?"

I tipped my head from side to side, studying the difference. Black hair one day, blond the next. Both were a vast improvement, however, over the magenta she'd favored for a while. "It'll take a little getting used to, but since it's for the sake of art . . ."

"You didn't answer my question: Why did McBride take Melly's Visine? He lookin' to find DNA?"

I sighed. "How would DNA get inside a bottle of eye-drops?"

Reba Mae shrugged. "Just askin', is all. I'm no CSI. No need to get testy."

"Sorry." I added flour and spices to the batter. "I've got the feeling we're sitting on a time bomb about to explode."

Reba Mae rested her hip against the edge of my worktable. "I'm puttin' my money on the wife. I bet Cheryl and the boyfriend did it. Speakin' of boyfriends, have you seen him around lately?"

Slivered almonds and candied fruit peel went into the mix. "Funny you should mention him. He sounds like Troy, the guy Amber met at the driving range. He's supposedly a personal trainer, so Amber invited him over for dinner and drinks tomorrow—to advise CJ how to get into shape."

"He'd have to be a hypnotist in order to get CJ away from Kentucky bourbon and red meat." Reba Mae picked up a food zine I subscribed to and flipped through the pages. "Wonder if Cheryl and the dude are still hookin' up at the Beaver Dam Motel?"

"Maybe we should do another drive-by. Check things

out and see if we can spot her car in the motel lot," I said
as I wrapped the cookie dough in plastic wrap first, then
aluminum foil before sticking it in the fridge "I'm not busy
tonight—are you?"

Reba Mae brightened. "Nope. I'll bring the snacks.
Stakeouts and drive-bys always work up an appetite."

"Great. Pick you up soon as it gets dark."

We were debating whether cheese dip was considered
a serving of protein when Doug Winters walked into Spice
It Up!

"Hey, stranger." I smiled and wiped the flour from my
hands. The sight of him lifted my spirits. I realized I hadn't
heard from him in days, which was unusual. I rationalized
that Melly's predicament was the reason behind our lack
of communication.

"Hey, yourself." Doug's usual easygoing smile was absent, his tone frosty.

Reba Mae, sensing the chill in the air, decided to beat
a hasty retreat. "Guess I'd best be goin', honeybun. Nice
seein' you, Doug."

Traitor, I mouthed. It would have been nice to have
Reba Mae as insulation against Doug's unexpected cold-
ness. "Anything wrong?" I asked the instant we were alone.

He slid his hands into his pants pockets. "I could ask
the same of you."

Something was definitely off. Doug usually greeted me
with a hug, often a kiss. Smoothing my apron, I ran through
a mental checklist, but other than worries about Melly, I
couldn't find any transgressions.

Doug made a big production of looking over my shoulder. "Melly around? There's a favor I need to ask."

"Sure thing," I replied. This seemed to be ask-a-favor
day. I walked to the foot of the stairs and called Melly's
name.

"I'll be down as soon as my soup comes to a boil," Melly called back.

Awkwardness stretched between us like a wad of Double Bubble. Doug rocked back on his heels and looked at everything in the shop except me.

"What did you want to see Melly about?" I finally asked, braving the silence.

"I was going to ask her to bake a batch of gingersnaps for me to use in the sauerbraten I'm bringing to the Oktoberfest. Gingersnaps thicken the sauce that goes over the meat. They give sauerbraten its distinctive flavor."

"I'm sure Melly'd be happy to do that for you. Besides, it'll help keep her mind off her trouble. Doug," I said hesitantly, "if there's a problem, you know you can always talk to me about it."

He met my eyes for the first time since entering. "I thought the problem might be on your end."

My mind flashed back to the pizza I'd shared with McBride the other night. That was followed immediately by a pang of guilt. I reminded myself I had no reason to feel guilty. I had no interest in the lawman; he had none in me. "I haven't a clue what you're talking about," I said.

"I find it . . . strange . . . that you haven't returned any of my phone calls. I've left messages with Lindsey each time, but you never call back."

I felt a wave of relief wash over me that it wasn't anything more serious. "I didn't know you called! Lindsey must've forgotten to relay the messages. Between cheerleading practice, schoolwork, and now with her grandmother's predicament, well, she's got a lot on her plate."

"Guess, you're right," he relented, his smile both boyish and sheepish. "I've overreacted ever since Lindsey mentioned you and CJ have been spending more time together."

"Teenagers." I laughed, moving in for a long-overdue hug. "You know how they exaggerate."

"Can you forgive me for acting like an idiot?" Seeing my smile, he bent down and kissed me, making me feel all warm and melty inside.

Suddenly, a loud clanking, banging, and grinding noise emanated from upstairs. We broke apart and raced up the steps to find Melly staring at the kitchen sink, a stricken expression on her face.

Doug identified the problem immediately and pulled the switch for the garbage disposal. Blessed silence prevailed.

Tears swam in Melly's eyes. "I just ruined one of your good pieces of flatware—along with your garbage disposal. I'm so sorry, dear. I don't know what's the matter with me these days."

If this weren't disaster enough, the pot containing Melly's vegetable soup boiled over, sending carrots, peas, beans, and potatoes cascading over the rim, onto the stove top, then to the floor.

Turning off the stove with one hand, I yanked a length of paper towel with the other. My drive-by and impromptu picnic would have to stand in line behind driving to Lowe's for a new garbage disposal.

CHAPTER 20

The nearest Lowe's was twenty-odd miles down the highway, near the interstate. Stores, restaurants, a Cineplex, and motels had sprung up around the exit like dandelions after a spring rain. "Build me and they will come" seemed to be the motto. Walmart was open 24/7 and attracted kids even on prom night.

I'd tried to convince Reba Mae to accompany me, but she said no thanks. Unless Lowe's had a shoe department, she wasn't interested. Besides, she'd added, now that our stakeout had been canceled, she needed to start memorizing lines for her upcoming stage debut.

I stood in the center of an aisle and pondered my choices of garbage disposals. Horsepower seemed to be a major concern. Warranty another. One-, two-, or three-year? I finally settled for one in the middle of the pack that claimed to be perfect for a small household.

After loading my selection into a buggy—as shopping carts are called in the South—I decided to take a look around the rest of the store. While I wasn't in the market for new appliances, it was always fun to play "pretend." I rounded the corner and nearly plowed into Wyatt McBride.

Deep in concentration, he stood in front of a long row of refrigerators while other shoppers streamed around him.

"I suggest stainless steel."

His head jerked up and he noticed me for the first time. "What are you doing here?"

"For your information, this store happens to be open to the general public—not just befuddled law enforcement."

He winced. "Is my confusion that obvious?"

"I've seen less confusion on faces of toddlers trying to decide between orange and red lollipops."

"Why stainless?" He gestured to a nearby side-by-side.

I angled my buggy closer. "I watch a lot of HGTV— *Property Brothers, Love It or List It, House Hunters.* Stainless steel appliances seem to be a hot ticket item for home buyers these days. If you should ever decide to relocate, it'll increase your resale value."

"I'm never going to sell this blasted house once it's fixed up. They'll have to carry me out feetfirst."

I clucked my tongue. "Now, now, that's no way to talk."

"Here I am, spending all my money on things like refrigerators and ranges when I could be buying a bass boat," he groused.

"If you had a boat, you'd probably go fishing, right?" When he nodded, I continued, "If you caught fish, you'd need a place to keep them. That's where a refrigerator comes in handy."

"Be easier to buy a cooler and a bag of ice at the fillin' station. That oughta suffice till I could fry 'em up."

I ignored his twisted male logic. "A range is a must for frying up a whole mess of stripers, crappies, or catfish. No kitchen is complete without a range. Think about property values. Think marketability. While you're at it, you might want to consider purchasing a dishwasher and microwave."

His expression turned even glummer. "I could've bought a small yacht for all of my money you just spent."

"Don't be ridiculous," I chided. "There isn't a body of water anywhere near here large enough for a yacht. We're Brandywine *Creek*, remember. Nothing bigger than a canoe or a kayak."

He treated me to a genuine smile. The dimple in his cheek winked in and out. "Don't suppose I could persuade you to help me select an appliance or two?"

I smiled back. "Thought you'd never ask. I happen to have a God-given talent when it comes to spending other people's money. But my services are going to come at a price. I want something from you in return."

"Are you attempting to bribe an officer of the law?"

"Mmm," I said, pretending to ponder the matter. "I prefer to think of it as barter rather than bribery."

"I'll take the matter under advisement," he countered.

"Fair enough." I motioned toward the large selection of shiny kitchen appliances. "I'm talking a trade. My priceless expertise in exchange for answers to a few simple questions."

"Questions such as?"

"The toxicology report, for starters."

A dark brow rose sharply. "Some starter. You know I can't divulge privileged information in—"

"—an active investigation," I said, completing his sentence. "Pity to invest all that hard-earned money in appliances, only to realize later you made poor decisions." I put on a sad face and made to move my buggy around him.

"Wait up." He placed a hand on the buggy to waylay my progress.

I noticed Band-Aids on two of the knuckles. Poor guy. He was more adept with a handgun than with a hammer. I quashed the spurt of sympathy and pressed my advantage. "Ticktock."

He raked his fingers through his hair. "Tell you what I'll do," he said at last. "For every appliance you help me select, I'll answer one question—provided I'm not jeopardizing the case. I can't very well hold Beau Tucker to one standard and me to another. Agreed?"

"Agreed." I grinned. "Now, let's get down to business, shall we?"

A half hour later, I steered my buggy through the checkout line while McBride talked with a salesman and jotted down model numbers. After debating the merits of various refrigerators, he'd decided on side-by-side with an ice and water dispenser on the door. He said he wanted one that dispensed beer and acted disappointed when informed that wasn't an option. He also purchased a stainless steel range with a self-cleaning oven, since he didn't strike me as the type who'd don a pair of rubber gloves and wield a can of Easy-Off.

McBride suggested coffee, so we convened at a nearby restaurant, part of a popular chain. "Had dinner yet?" he asked as I slid into a booth.

I thought of Doug. For a nanosecond, I wondered if I was being disloyal. Then, just as quickly, I dismissed the notion. My meetings with McBride were strictly business. Nothing personal. Though I was tempted to tell him I wasn't hungry, my stomach rumbled and gave me away. A waitress brought us coffee—decaf for me, heavy duty for McBride. He ordered a rib eye steak, medium rare, and fries; I ordered a Cobb salad.

"So," he said after the waitress disappeared with our orders. "Two appliances—two questions."

The first was easy. "What was in the toxicology report that made you get a search warrant?"

Leaning back, he rested an arm along the top of the booth. "The lab found an ingredient in Chip Balboa's stomach contents that raised suspicion."

"An ingredient? What ingredient? Is that why you left

with Melly's eyedrops in an evidence bag? Are you saying Chip was poisoned?"

"Whoa!" He raised a hand. "You had one question left, not four."

"You'll also need a washing machine and a dryer. Did you know front-loading washing machines are energy efficient?"

"Good try, but I'm already energy efficient. Final question."

I was framing what to ask next when I happened to see the hostess lead a couple past our table. My eyes widened in surprise when I recognized the pair. "What do you suppose Cheryl Balboa and her boy toy are doing here?"

"Having dinner, same as us?" He smirked. "Consider your final question asked and answered."

"B-but, that's not fair. That wasn't the one I wanted to ask." Darn McBride, anyway! The man was as slippery as an eel. He had managed to answer my questions without giving away any information of importance.

His smirk widened into a grin. "Life isn't fair, sweetheart. Thought you'd learned that by now."

I felt blood rush to my cheeks. I stifled an urge to kick him in the shins, but fear of being charged with assaulting a police officer made me behave. "Just wait until you need advice on cabinets, countertops, and flooring." My salvo succeeded in erasing the smugness from his handsome face.

The waitress returned with our orders and refilled our coffee cups. Still fuming, I drizzled dressing over my salad, then speared a tomato wedge. McBride sliced into his rib eye. "So that's the guy Reba Mae wants to hire for a pool boy?"

I mixed the contents of my salad with a fork. "Have you ever heard of double indemnity?"

"Sure. Classic film noir," he said, dipping a french fry into a puddle of ketchup. "Barbara Stanwyck and Fred MacMurray. Filmed back in the '40s. One of my all-time favorites."

"It's one of my favorites, too," I admitted. "But I wasn't referring to the movie. I was referring to the real deal—an insurance clause. Those things still exist, you know."

"Where are you going with this?" McBride stabbed a piece of steak.

"In a double indemnity policy, the insurance company agrees to pay the face value several times over if the death is accidental. This includes murder, unless, of course, the beneficiary is the guilty party. Have you ever stopped to consider the possibility that Cheryl—or a hired hit man— might have killed Chip for the money? If Chip's death was ruled an accident, collecting the insurance money would be a snap."

McBride continued to eat his dinner, his movements precise and methodical. "Where did you learn all this stuff?"

I dug into my salad. "I might not be as savvy as Melly when it comes to computers, but I can navigate my way around the Internet."

"So according to this theory of yours, Cheryl followed Chip to Brandywine Creek, Georgia, where she slipped her husband—let's call it a mystery substance—then shoved him down a flight of stairs. Or"—he looked over his shoulder where Cheryl and Troy were seated—"had her friend do the job for her?"

"I'm just saying, is all," I said, borrowing a page from Reba Mae's phrase book. Maybe it did sound a little far-fetched when spoken out loud, but I wasn't ready to throw in the towel.

"You want dessert?"

"Ah, no thanks." I realized McBride had cleaned his

plate while my salad was still half-finished. "But go ahead if you want."

He signaled the waitress and asked for the check. "You're doing it again, Piper. How many times do I have to warn you not to stick your cute freckled nose where it doesn't belong?"

It was hard to appear offended when someone was giving you a backhanded compliment, but I tried. "Did you even attempt to get a court order for Cheryl's phone records?"

"Judge Herman signed the order yesterday. I expect to get the printout from the phone company tomorrow latest." He sipped his coffee. "Hate to be the bearer of bad news, Piper, but there's a glitch in your theory."

I sat straighter and leaned forward. "Glitch?"

"Seems your prime suspect has an alibi."

"Alibi?" Hearing that word certainly took the starch out of my petticoat. "Who? What?"

McBride seemed amused that my speech had been reduced to monosyllables. "When I questioned Cheryl Balboa more specifically on her whereabouts the night her husband was killed, she admitted she was in Brandywine Creek the entire time. She went on to elaborate that she'd placed an order at the Pizza Palace around the time the murder took place. Danny Boyd confirmed he made the delivery himself."

"How long does it take to eat pizza?" I flung up my hands, not ready to concede defeat "Maybe Cheryl left right afterwards."

"I checked with Danny. Seems he ran over some metal debris in the Beaver Dam's parking lot and blew a tire. He had to wait over an hour before a buddy showed up with a spare. He swears that if Cheryl had left her room, he would've seen her."

Disheartened, I slumped back against the booth. I'd

been so sure Cheryl was the culprit. Now I'd have to widen my net of suspects if I hoped to find the guilty party and clear Melly.

"If it makes you feel any better, I still intend to look at the widow's phone records."

McBride withdrew bills from his wallet and placed them on the table next to the check. When I attempted to pay my share, he shook his head and pushed the money back toward me.

"Mark my words, Wyatt McBride," I warned as I climbed to my feet. "Someday this situation will be reversed. You'll have questions, and I'll be the one with the answers."

CHAPTER *21*

When I returned from Lowe's, I found Lindsey doing her homework at the kitchen table. Casey lay at her feet, his head resting on his paws. At seeing me, he flopped his tail once or twice in a lazy welcome.

"Hey, Mom," Lindsey greeted me. When she saw that I was struggling with a large box, she jumped up to help carry it. "This thing must weigh a ton."

"Close to it," I said, out of breath after lugging my spiffy new garbage disposal up a steep flight of stairs.

"I wasn't sure what time you'd be home, so I took Casey out to do his thing."

"Thanks, sweetie," I puffed as we set the box on the floor, where it would be out of the way.

I heard the sound of a television in the living room. I glimpsed Melly in an armchair reading *The Statesman*, Brandywine Creek's weekly newspaper. Upon seeing me, she clicked the remote and came into the kitchen. "I hope you didn't buy the cheapest model Lowe's carries. You should know by now that you only get what you pay for."

"This particular one was middle of the line. It's supposed to be perfect for small households."

"If you say so . . ." Melly eyed the box skeptically. "Remember, I insist on paying for the disposal, along with the cost of installation. It's the least I can do, seeing as how this is entirely my fault."

"Melly, we've been over this a dozen times. Accidents happen. That's why they're called 'accidents.'"

"Even so, I should have had enough sense to switch off the disposal immediately instead of standing there like a ninny. I just froze."

"It's okay, Meemaw," Lindsey said. "The stupid garbage disposal probably needed to be replaced anyway."

"Sweet of you to say that, dear, but I feel bad nevertheless." Melly smiled fondly at her granddaughter, then turned to me. "I've already talked to Ned Feeney. He's coming over bright and early tomorrow morning to replace the damaged one."

I had doubts about Ned Feeney's plumbing expertise but kept silent. Dottie Hemmings had once confided she'd hired Ned to unstop a stopped-up sink. In the process, Ned had accidentally dropped his wristwatch down the drain, and a real plumber had to be called to retrieve it. Ned was the local jack-of-all-trades and master of gossip and innuendo, in addition to working for John Strickland at the Eternal Rest Funeral Home.

"Besides, I feel sorry for the man. The funeral business has been slow lately, so I'm certain Ned will appreciate a chance to earn a little extra money." Melly sat down across from Lindsey and began work on the newspaper's crossword puzzle.

"Daddy used to do all the home repairs." Lindsey snapped her history text shut. "Did you know only six percent of divorced couples remarry each other?"

Melly glanced up, pencil poised in midair, crossword forgotten. The two of us exchanged puzzled looks. After reaching into a cabinet above the sink, I took down a glass.

"Where did you hear that?" I asked, trying to sound casual.

"Sean."

I turned on the tap, filled my glass, took a sip. "What else did Sean have to say?"

Lindsey aligned pages of notes. "He read that of the divorced couples who reunite, seventy-two percent stay married."

I leaned my hip against the sink and watched Lindsey stuff textbook, notes, pens, and highlighters into her backpack. The whole time, I kept wondering what scene was playing out in her pretty little head. "Hmm . . . ," I murmured. "Interesting statistic."

"Does Sean wish his parents would remarry?" Melly asked.

Lindsey shrugged. "It's too late for them."

"I'm sorry to hear that, dear," Melly murmured.

"Sean told me his father was the one who wanted the divorce. Later, he realized it was a mistake, but by then, it was too late. His mom had already met someone else and wanted to move on. She remarried, and his stepdad made it clear he doesn't want a teenager around 24/7." Lindsey zipped her backpack closed and set it next to the door, where she could easily grab it the next morning on her way to school. "I'm going to shower and get ready for bed."

"Shower" and "bed" were buzzwords telling Melly and me it was time to clear out so Lindsey could have the living room/temporary bedroom to herself. Melly stood, the newspaper tucked under her arm. "By any chance, Piper, have you spoken to Chief McBride recently? I'd like to know when that horrid man will allow me to return home."

I placed my glass in the dishwasher. For some reason I didn't care to explore, I felt oddly reluctant to tell her we'd had dinner together. I wanted to kick myself for not asking McBride Melly's question when I'd had the chance. Shame on me. I'd been too preoccupied helping him choose kitchen appliances. And by the couple in a back booth. Seems it didn't take much to distract me these days.

"I don't expect it'll be much longer," I finally said.

"Hmph!" she snorted. "When you do see him, be sure to let him know that my granddaughter wants her bedroom back. Tell him she's threatening to move in with her father if she has to continue sleeping on the sofa."

Ouch! Melly's comment hit home. Lucky for me, CJ's house-painting seemed to be taking forever, or Lindsey might make good her threat. Truth was, my apartment *was* feeling a bit cramped these days, with three women sharing one bathroom. I thought this might be a good time for a change of subject. "Melly, I said, "are you certain it was Visine that McBride had in the evidence bag?"

"Of course I'm certain," she snapped. "There's nothing wrong with my eyesight."

I let that remark slide as she marched off toward Lindsey's room.

I made up the sofa bed for Lindsey and plumped the pillows so all would be in readiness for her after her shower. Then I picked up my laptop from an end table and went into my room. Casey trotted after me, jumped on the foot of the bed, and made himself at home.

But sleep wasn't an item on my agenda. I felt as though I could samba all night. I'd asked the waitress for decaf at the restaurant, but wondered if she'd given me high-test instead. I tried flipping through channels on the small television on the dresser, but nothing held my interest. Next, I picked up the crime novel on my bedside stand but couldn't seem to concentrate. My thoughts tumbled like socks in a clothes dryer. I'd been mistaken to focus all my attention on Cheryl Balboa. Since she had a solid alibi, I was obviously overlooking something. Or someone. Who other than

Cheryl might want Chip dead? Where was Troy while Cheryl ate pizza? And what about Rusty "Trusty" Tulley?

I knew as well as I knew my own name that Melly had nothing to do with Chip's death. I was equally certain that if the real killer wasn't found, Melly would be upgraded from "person of interest" to "suspect." It was only a matter of time—and time was running out. Cheryl and her boyfriend weren't going to stick around Brandywine Creek forever. Rusty would either fly back to California or complete the road trip he'd started with Chip.

I tapped my fingers on my closed laptop. Thinking. Thinking. Thinking. I thought back to the remembrance Rusty had hosted in Chip's honor. What was it Felicity had mentioned? Something about a quarrel between the partners? What had they argued about? How much had Felicity overheard? I decided to pay the woman a visit the following day. Nothing like a face-to-face discussion.

Even if I did learn why the men had disagreed, it still wouldn't explain why a small bottle of eyedrops was significant. Plenty of people used eyedrops. Thousands, maybe millions. I'd seen an identical bottle on the dresser in Cheryl and Troy's motel room. Time to do a little sleuthing. I might not have been a whiz like Melly when it came to computers, but Google and I were BFFs. Smiling to myself, I powered up the laptop.

I typed in the name of a popular brand of eyedrops, the kind Melly kept in a small basket on her kitchen table. From that point on, the rest was simply following a trail of bread crumbs. I clicked on the eyedrops' ingredients. A chemical by the name of tetrahydrolozine was listed as the "active" ingredient. Curious, I Googled "tetrahydrolozine." In seconds, the search engine showed more than one hundred thousand hits.

A frisson of excitement raced through me as I read the

symptoms of tetrahydrolozine poisoning. Rapid heartbeat, difficulty breathing, blurred vision, nausea, nervousness, headache, irritability, and changes in blood pressure. Coma and even death could result when swallowed.

I leaned against the headboard as I digested this information. I'd be willing to bet that tetrahydrolozine was what the medical examiner found in Chip Balboa's stomach contents. Did McBride think Melly put eyedrops into Chip's drink—and when he started to feel ill and his vision blurred—gave him a hard shove down a flight of stairs?

Just then, Lindsey poked her head in the door, a towel wrapped turban-style around her newly washed hair. "G'night, Mom."

My girl, fresh from her shower, smelled of soap and lemon-scented shampoo. She half turned to leave when I stopped her. "Not so fast, young lady. There's something I need to talk to you about."

She came into my room and perched on the edge of the bed, absently stroking Casey's shaggy head. "What's up?"

"Dr. Winters dropped by the shop this afternoon," I said, closing the lid of the laptop.

Lindsey avoided looking at me by pretending an interest in a group of framed family photos that hung on the wall. But I recognized guilt when I stared it in the face. Lindsey seemed to forget I'd once been a teenager, too, trying to hide certain . . . shortcomings and transgressions from my parents.

"Doug was acting very strangely, standoffish. At first, I thought he was angry with me." I waited a heartbeat for Lindsey to say something, but when she didn't speak, I continued. "Turns out, he wasn't angry at all, but hurt. Seems he'd phoned a number of times, but couldn't understand why I never returned his calls."

Lindsey remained quiet.

"He said that each time, he'd left a message with you and asked that I return his call."

"Guess I forgot," Lindsey said, sounding defensive. "You know how busy senior year can be. Between cheer practice and getting ready for homecoming and pep week, there's never time."

Granted, there was a grain of truth in Lindsey's words, but it was what she didn't say that bothered me. "That's what I told Doug."

"If that isn't enough, there's always a quiz to study for or an essay to write. I hardly have a minute to myself," Lindsey whined. She stood and picked up Casey, who lathered her chin with kisses. "Are you finished?"

"Not quite. Is there anything else you might've forgotten to tell me?" I asked, giving Lindsey an opportunity to explain why she'd told Doug that her father and I had been spending time together.

Lindsey studied the ceiling. "Um . . . now that you mention it, Doc called tonight while you were out. I told him you were at Lowe's."

"Did he leave a message?"

"He wanted you to call him back if it wasn't too late. Is that all?" she asked plaintively. "I have to get up early and still need to dry my hair."

Oh, to have so many pressing demands on my time. "G'night, Linds." I sighed. "In the future when someone calls, write it down on the notepad next to the phone."

"Whatever." In her haste to leave, she'd shed the damp towel that had been wrapped around her wet hair.

I climbed out of bed, picked it off the floor, and folded it. I'd been under the impression Lindsey liked Doug. She had been on his pit crew during the annual Brandywine Creek Barbecue Festival last July. She occasionally worked at his animal clinic. Now she habitually "forgot" to relay his messages. What was that about? And then there was all the talk about divorced couples remarrying each other. Even with CJ's impending marriage to Amber, did Lindsey still harbor hope for the two of us reuniting like in some made-for-television movie?

The clock on the nightstand told me it was too late to return Doug's call. I resolved to phone him first thing in the morning. Yawning, I returned the towel to the bathroom towel rack. Lindsey wasn't the only one with a busy day ahead. A visit to the Turner-Driscoll House was in order. I planned to pump Felicity for information on Rusty and Chip's argument.

And I planned to be an uninvited guest at CJ and Amber's little dinner party. I was curious to learn more about Troy, Reba Mae's fantasy pool boy. What sort of man was he? Did he possess a volatile temper? Or was he the type easily manipulated by others? And last but by no means least, did he stand to benefit from Chip Balboa's death? Tomorrow promised to prove interesting.

CHAPTER 22

"I can't tell you how sorry I am," Melly said for the zillionth time.

"It was an accident, Melly," I replied for the zillionth time. "Accidents happen."

I finished my morning coffee, rinsed my cup, and put it in the dishwasher. I was feeling virtuous after having gotten up early for my run. I'd half-expected to find CJ on my doorstep, but there'd been no sign of him. I couldn't wondering if he'd given up on being in tip-top shape or if he was delaying further exertion until his consultation with a personal trainer.

Melly brushed crumbs from her English muffin off her navy slacks. "Well, I insist on paying Ned for the installation."

No sooner had she spoken than a knock on the rear door signaled Ned's arrival. I hurried downstairs and let him in. He'd arrived promptly at nine o'clock, as promised.

"Hey, Miz Piper." He doffed his ever-present ball cap with its Georgia bulldog logo and gave me a loopy grin that never failed to put me in mind of the Gomer Pyle character ably played by Jim Nabors. "Heard you needed an expert."

"Come in," I said, stepping aside. I'd briefly considered doing the installation myself rather than trust Ned Feeney. I didn't share Melly's conviction that he was the right man for the job, but since she was holding the purse strings . . .

Ned followed me up the stairs. "I told Miz Melly that I'd be more 'n' happy to fix you up. Told 'er I wouldn't charge y'all an arm and a leg, either."

"We appreciate that, Ned," I said, entering the kitchen.

"Morning, Ned." Melly greeted him. "Care for a cup of coffee? Piper always likes those fancy kinds. Today she made us Blue Mountain coffee all the way from Jamaica."

She referred to an extravagance of mine. Kona from Hawaii. Blue Mountain from Jamaica. I usually hoarded them for special occasions—or when my sprits needed a boost. Once, feeling generous, I'd brought a thermos of freshly brewed Kona coffee and blueberry muffins to McBride. Of course, I'd hoped for something in exchange, in the form of information. Typical McBride, he was stingy as usual.

"No thanks, ma'am," Ned said. "Filled up on coffee at the Gas and Go. One more punch on my Coffee Club Lover's card, and I get a free twelve-ounce cup of their house blend."

Call me a snob, but anyone who prefers Gas and Go coffee—which tastes like varnish—over beans grown in Jamaica is unworthy of my precious cache.

Ned jiggled the tool belt sagging from his scrawny waist. Pliers, screwdriver, and wrench clanked together. "Brought my tools. Never know what you might need. Be prepared's my motto."

I was tempted to remind Ned that his motto "Be Prepared" also belonged to the Boy Scouts of America. If memory served, it was also the title of a song from *The Lion King*. Given more time, I'd hum a few bars.

"Show me to it," Ned said, rubbing his palms together.

I motioned at the box on the kitchen floor. Ned read the description printed on the label, then nodded knowingly. "You picked a good one, Miz Piper. Stainless steel flange and all. This baby oughta last a long time, unless you go droppin' spoons down the drain."

Melly winced. I rushed to sidetrack yet another apology that had started to form. "I'll leave you to get started on the disposal, Ned. If you need anything, Melly will be close by."

"Piece of cake. Nothin' to it." Ned hitched up his baggy jeans. "Could install this little number in my sleep."

"Great," I replied as I headed down to Spice It Up! "Nice to know I can leave the installation in your capable hands."

Since I still had time before opening for business, I grabbed the feather duster and started making the rounds. I'd barely had time to flick the duster over jars of cinnamon and cloves in the Hoosier cabinet when Melly hollered down for me. "Piper! Quick! Get up here!"

I dashed upstairs, taking the steps two at a time. Casey, instantly awake from one of his multitude of naps, bounded after me. I slid to a halt on the threshold of the kitchen. Casey, the victim of too much momentum, sailed across the floor on a sea of water and sewage that spilled from a pipe below the sink.

Ned—half in, half out of the cabinet—pressed his hand against the pipe gushing waste, futilely attempting to staunch the tide. Melly watched the goings-on, horrified. I grabbed a mop bucket and, sidestepping the mess, shoved it under the leak to catch what hadn't already drained out.

"Didn't see that one comin'." Ned eased out from beneath the counter and accepted the towel I handed him.

"Gracious!" Melly exclaimed.

"Not to fear, Miz Piper. I'll have this mess cleaned up in a jiffy," Ned assured me.

My cell phone buzzed just then. As luck would have it, Felicity Driscoll was calling to ask if I carried fenugreek. I assured her I not only stocked fenugreek seeds but would also be more than happy to deliver them personally. I overruled her objections and said I'd run them right over.

"Melly," I said, turning to my former mother-in-law. "I need to take Felicity something. I shouldn't be long."

She brightened. "Don't worry, dear. I'll mind your little shop if you're not back by ten."

Melly loved playing shopkeeper. If anything, she loved it a tad too much. Once, when I'd been running errands, she took it upon herself to rearrange all my spices alphabetically. Another time, she'd made changes on my pricey point-of-sale software without asking. I shuddered to think what creative "improvements" she might make in my absence.

"Thanks," I said. I snatched my purse and left.

Minutes later, Felicity, perfectly groomed, met me at her door. "So nice of you to do this, Piper. I'm making curry tonight. The recipe calls for fenugreek seeds. Naturally, I thought of you."

"The seeds need to be ground to release their flavor. They combine well with cardamom," I said, handing her the small jar. "I planned to call you later today. There are some questions I'd like to ask. Do you have a couple minutes?"

"Your timing's perfect. I was just about to sit down for a cup of coffee."

I followed her down the long marble entry hall to the kitchen. The kitchen, large enough to accommodate a small restaurant or café, was as modern as the rest of the house was antebellum. The appliances were high-end stainless steel; the countertops, pale quartz. White glass-fronted cabinets stretched to a high ceiling and were filled with neatly stacked china and crystal. The most stunning feature, however, was the view. A bank of windows over-looked a meticulously landscaped yard and gardens with flowering shrubs. Because the weather had been unseasonably mild, many plants, such as clematis and knock-out roses, were reblooming. A gazebo stood in the center, the perfect site for a wedding.

"Have a seat." Felicity gestured toward a table and six ladder-back chairs. She poured dark, rich coffee into thick white mugs and set them on the distressed wooden table along with a plate of iced cinnamon rolls speckled with dried currants. "I made these for my guests, but they decided to sleep in."

How could anyone in their right mind refuse homemade cinnamon rolls? It was downright uncivilized. I wouldn't dream of insulting my hostess by declining her gracious offer, so I took the only option open and helped myself.

"The coffee beans are from Ethiopia," Felicity said, taking a seat that gave her an unrestricted view of the garden.

I'd probably be hyper for the rest of the day, considering all the caffeine I'd consumed, but I'd take my chances. "Felicity," I said, breaking off a small piece of cinnamon roll, "you mentioned something at Chip's remembrance that started me thinking. You told me the two partners argued the night of the accident."

"Goodness, I'd nearly forgotten." Felicity spread a cloth napkin embroidered with violets across her lap. "I happened to be delivering fresh linens to one of my guest rooms when I overheard raised voices."

I sampled my coffee and wasn't surprised to find it as delicious as advertised. "Did you hear what the men were arguing about?"

Her mouth turned down in distaste. "I don't like to be a teller of tales."

"Normally, I wouldn't ask it of you." I crossed my fingers

under the table, where she couldn't see. "Problem is, I'm worried sick about Melly. I thought if I knew more about Chip and Rusty's relationship, it might shed some light on what happened later. Often even the smallest detail can turn out to be significant."

Felicity regarded me in silence for a long moment, then nodded slowly, her decision made. "Since you put it in that light," she said. "Their disagreement had to do with business. Rusty seemed angry that Trustychipdesign was losing market share. He blamed Chip for its recent poor performance. Rusty accused Chip of allowing his personal life to interfere with work."

I popped the last morsel of the roll into my mouth and chewed thoughtfully. "Do you recall anything else?"

"How shall I phrase this?" Felicity watched a Carolina wren flit through the boughs of a Japanese maple. "Rusty . . . suggested . . . Chip might consider stepping down, resigning."

I leaned back in my chair. That didn't seem like a simple disagreement.

"It's not as harsh as it sounds," Felicity said as though reading my mind. "I'm certain Rusty regretted the words he said in the heat of the moment. He was genuinely distraught after hearing his friend had passed. I'm convinced the lovely remembrance service he initiated was his way of making amends."

I finished the last of my coffee and neatly refolded my linen napkin. "One more thing, Felicity. Do you know where Rusty was the night Chip was killed?"

"Why, he was right here. He spent the entire evening in his room. I assumed he was working."

"Did you actually see him?"

Felicity pondered the question. "Well, I can't say that I did. He kept the door of his room closed, but his light was on, so I presumed he was there. I was arranging flowers in the entrance hall. I certainly would have seen him come down the stairs."

Rusty's alibi seemed a slam dunk. I'd reached a dead end. Nothing against Rusty personally, but after hearing about his argument with Chip, I'd hoped it would take the investigation in another direction.

"Thanks for the coffee and cinnamon roll," I said. As I rose to my feet, another thought struck me. "Felicity, is there another set of stairs, by any chance?"

"You're forgetting this house was built before the war." Felicity chuckled.

I'd lived south of the Mason–Dixon Line long enough to know she referred to *the* war—the War Between the States, as Southerners call it. They're quick to point out there was nothing "civil" about the conflict.

"Most of these homes," Felicity continued, "have a servants' stairs tucked away. The Turner-Driscoll House is no exception."

My mind churned with possibilities. In this day and age, a servants' staircase would nicely serve a teenager trying to sneak out after curfew. Or a guest trying to leave unnoticed. "Is it still in use?"

"My darlin' girl," she drawled, "everything here gets used. Waste not, want not."

I wanted to question her further, but my cell phone jingled. It was Melly. "Come home right this instant. It's an emergency."

"Melly!" I shouted into the phone. But too late, she'd already hung up. "Sorry, Felicity, gotta run."

I drove the short distance home in a panic. My panic ratcheted up a notch at the sight of an ambulance, lights flashing, outside Spice It Up! I parked haphazardly at the curb. A cluster of people was starting to gather on the sidewalk. I caught a fleeting glimpse of Thompson Gray from Gray's Hardware; Bitsy Johnson-Jones, the clerk at Proctor's

Cleaners; and Shirley Randolph, a real estate agent at Creekside Realty. Shirley put out a hand to waylay me, but I shook it off. Had something happened to Melly? A heart attack? A fall? Should I notify CJ? I flew up the stairs, the blood roaring in my ears.

I came to a screeching halt at the sight of two burly EMTs kneeling on the kitchen floor, tending to Ned Feeney. Melly hovered near the doorway, wringing her hands. From what I could see, she appeared upset but not injured. Ned, on the other hand, was another story. Casey was content to watch the proceedings from the relative shelter of the living room doorway.

Ned sat upright, legs splayed, a dazed expression on his face, eyes unfocused. One of the EMTs pressed a blood-soaked bandage against a gash on Ned's forehead. The other waved two fingers in front of Ned's face. "How many fingers do you see?" he ordered.

Ned blinked. "Four?"

"Mr. Feeney . . . Ned . . . ," the EMT said, "we're going to take you to the emergency room. Let the doctor check you out. You probably have a concussion."

"Okeydokey." Ned gave the men a slack-jawed grin. "Didn't see that one comin'. That durn garbage disposal has it in for me. Nowhere near as easy as it looks on You-Tube."

I turned to Melly. "What happened?"

"Ned was on his back under the sink. I don't think he realized how heavy, or how slippery, the old disposal would be once he removed the last bolt. It fell and struck him on the head. I heard the *thunk* clear from the living room." She wagged her head sorrowfully. "I found Ned knocked out colder than a cucumber."

First, sewage spilled all over the floor when Ned started to disconnect the plumbing. Next, the disposal had fallen on the poor guy's head instead of into his hands. Both

accidents, I knew, could have been avoided with a little
planning.

"Too bad that YouTube video didn't come with a warning to 'Be Prepared,'" I commented to Melly as the EMTs
hoisted Ned onto a gurney.

CHAPTER 23

From the way Melly fingered her pearls—which I was beginning to regard as worry beads—I could see she was still upset by Ned's unfortunate accident. "I'm afraid I'm not very good in an emergency," she fretted. "I just fall to pieces."

My kitchen resembled the aftermath of a tornado. Tools and bloody bandages, along with various and sundry parts of my new garbage disposal, littered the floor. Ignoring the mess, I took a box of tea bags and a pretty mug from the cupboard. "Nothing like a cup of chamomile tea to settle the nerves," I said, putting the kettle on to boil.

Melly sank onto the nearest chair. "I'll be more myself once I'm home again."

"You know you're welcome to stay with Lindsey and me as long as you like."

"No offense, dear"—Melly smiled wanly—"but nothing compares to being in your own home, surrounded by your own things."

While waiting for the water to boil, I straightened the kitchen. "I'll ask McBride how much longer he thinks that might be."

"I'd be forever grateful if you did. The less I have to speak to that odious man, the better."

I prepared Melly's tea, set it before her, and watched as she took a cautious sip. She seemed calmer now, more in control. I cleared my throat, then said, "Melly, there is a favor I'd like in return."

Melly wrapped her hands around the mug, savoring its warmth. "Certainly, dear. All you have to do is ask."

"I'd like you to put your computer skills to the test. Find out everything you can about Trustychipdesign's financial situation. Dig deep."

She raised a brow askance. "Their finances were in excellent condition when I researched them last spring."

I picked a bloody piece of gauze up by its corner and dropped it into the wastebasket, then scrubbed my hands. "Things may have changed in the interim. Nothing ever stays the same."

"I'll start on it as soon as I clean up this disaster area. Online research will keep my mind occupied. All I seem to do these days is worry that I'll be arrested for a crime I didn't commit." Tears pooled in her eyes, and she dabbed at them with a tissue from a box on the kitchen table. "I don't want my grandchildren to see their meemaw behind bars."

I went over to put an arm around her shoulders. "Don't worry, Melly. We'll get this figured out. It just takes time."

Ten minutes later, I went downstairs to open Spice It Up! I admitted privately that I wasn't feeling nearly so optimistic as I tried to make it sound. Time was proving to be Melly's enemy, not her friend.

People drifted in and out all morning to inquire about Ned's accident. Reba Mae's appearance following the noontime rush was a welcome diversion.

"Stopped by the Pizza Palace for calzones," she announced, brandishing a paper sack. "Hope you're hungry." Not waiting for my response, she handed me one.

"Not hungry, starved." I produced a couple cans of Diet Coke from the fridge in the back.

Reba Mae unwrapped a calzone, and instantly the shop was filled with the delicious aromas of tangy marinara sauce and spicy pepperoni. "The Klassy Kut's buzzin' about how Melly beaned Ned on the noggin."

I popped the tab on my soda. "Melly *didn't* hit Ned. When all the facts come to light, Ned will be the one to blame for the accident. I suspect the old disposal was heavier than he anticipated. It probably slipped from his hands and knocked him silly."

"I didn't really believe what the ladies were sayin'." She took a bite of calzone and washed it down with soda. "I heard the hospital's keepin' him overnight for observation. He keeps mumblin' about a stainless steel flange. Not makin' a lick of sense."

"Does he ever?" I was instantly ashamed of myself. Even though Ned was one sandwich shy of a picnic, he had a heart of gold. "Sorry, I shouldn't have said that."

"S'all right." Reba Mae plucked a piece of pepperoni from her sandwich and chewed. "I can't face tomorrow night starin' at the tube. Want to be my date for the football game? Unless you and Dr. Doug have plans."

"Sure. I'll go with you." I wiped my greasy fingers on a paper napkin. "Funny, but Doug hasn't mentioned the game."

"You two have a fight?"

"Not that I know of." It had become a habit of Doug's and mine to attend the Brandywine Creek Bearcats' home games together. Doug was convinced that it was a good policy for local business owners to be visible in the community. Talk of Doug only served to remind me I'd forgotten to return his call. I stifled a groan and promised myself I'd phone right after lunch.

"How's Melly holdin' up these days?" Reba Mae asked.

"Umm . . . she's doing okay, considering the circumstances. Right now, she's baking a batch of gingersnaps for Doug's sauerbraten."

Reba Mae swung her leg, causing her black suede clog with its three-inch cork sole to dangle from her foot. "Dottie Hemmings came in for a color and cut. She says her husband, Hizzoner the mayor, is pressurin' McBride to make an arrest. The mayor claims an unsolved murder is a black mark on the town in general—and McBride in particular."

"Hizzoner the mayor happens to be an old windbag."

"Maybe so"—Reba Mae shrugged—"but McBride still has to answer to him and the city council if he wants to keep his job."

For reasons I didn't wish to explore, I disliked the thought of McBride moving elsewhere. "I ran into McBride at Lowe's last night. Helped him choose a couple appliances."

"Clay wishes McBride would make up his mind on cabinets and countertops. The man might know his way around a Smith and Wesson, but he doesn't know diddly-squat about renovations."

"I don't suppose McBride has much time to be worrying about fixing up a kitchen with a homicide to solve." I balled up my sandwich wrapper and tossed it in the trash. "I'm going to crash CJ and Amber's dinner party later tonight. Care to join me? I want to get better acquainted with the lovebirds. Cheryl might have an alibi, but I'm not one hundred percent certain about the boyfriend. He could have a motive to want Chip dead." And after my conversation with Felicity, I was beginning to suspect Rusty might as well.

"Wish I could, honeybun, but I've got lines to memorize." She patted her recently dyed blond hair. "Truvy Jones is a central character in *Steel Magnolias*. She's in every scene. I need to be prepared."

I cringed. Seems "be prepared" was the slogan of the day.

Reba Mae wrinkled her nose. "What's that I smell?"

Now I smelled it, too. The scorched odor of burned baked goods. This was followed by the sound of metal clattering on floor tiles. Reba Mae and I looked at each other. "Melly's gingersnaps," we said in unison.

"I've got highlights waitin' on me," she said, moving toward the door. "If I were you, hon, I'd stay clear of upstairs and let Melly simmer down."

I took Reba Mae's advice. Discretion is the better part of valor, as a wise man once said. I was reaching for my cell phone to call Doug when a group of women garbed in red hats and purple outfits descended on Spice It Up!

"Fran," called a pretty woman with reddish-blond hair peeking out from a red hat trimmed with purple feathers. "Wait till you see this place. It's right up your alley. Fran's a gourmet cook," she explained.

A gray-haired woman with warm brown eyes laughed off the compliment. "Maureen's being kind. I just like to cook, is all. Try different things."

"It's true," Maureen insisted. "Fran even makes pasta from scratch."

I suffered an acute case of hair envy at the sight of Maureen's stylish and well-behaved reddish hair. My salesmanship, however, eventually overrode my spate of hair envy. "Feel free to browse," I told the Red Hat ladies. "I'll be happy to answer any questions you might have."

"What a cute place," commented a tall, athletic woman with short auburn hair graying at the temples. "Are you the owner?"

"Yes," I said. "I'm Piper Prescott. Where are you ladies from?"

"My name's Joan, by the way," she said, introducing herself. "We're from a small town you've probably never heard of in South Carolina."

"We're making a day of it," said a woman with a marked New York accent. "Our husbands are on their own for dinner tonight."

Curious, I said, "Brandywine Creek is off the beaten path. How did you ladies hear about our little town?"

"Maureen—she's our 'queen'—read an article about it in a magazine," Fran explained. "She arranged a fabulous lunch for us at Antonio's."

"And before lunch, we toured the opera house," offered a petite brunette, the most fashionably attired of the group. She turned to Joan. "What was the woman's name who showed us around?"

Joan shook her head in annoyance. "Oh, heavens, I don't remember. I hate that I can't recall names like I used to."

Fran laughed. "That's one of the advantages of living in a retirement community. None of us remember names."

The women all chuckled.

"I think it was Sandy," the petite brunette replied.

"Leave it to Janet to come up with the name," Joan grumbled good-naturedly.

"That must've been Sandy Granger," I said. "I'm sure she mentioned the opera house is over one hundred years old. Did she tell you about the resident ghost? There's even a chair reserved for it on the third-floor balcony."

Through an open doorway, the New Yorker spotted Casey lying in the storeroom at the foot of the stairs. Apparently he, too, had been avoiding Melly. "What a cute dog!" she exclaimed. "Is he a cairn terrier like Toto in *The Wizard of Oz*?"

"Rosemarie's secretary of our local humane society," Maureen explained.

"I'm afraid not," I said. "Casey's from a long distinguished line of mutts."

The women spread out in all directions. I was happy to see most of them took one of the small wicker baskets near the register.

"Hi, I'm Jan." A tall woman with short, light brown hair and a red visor approached me. Earrings with tiny red hats swung from her earlobes. "I'm chairing a golf outing at the club. I asked the food service to do a German theme. I showed the chef a recipe that calls for juniper berries, but he told me the Food Lion doesn't carry them, and he doesn't have time to drive to Augusta or Atlanta. I don't suppose . . . ?"

"Right this way," I said, leading her to a shelf where most of my ethnic spices were displayed.

"What about kala jeera?" asked Fran. "My husband, Mike, likes Indian cuisine."

Happy to oblige her as well, I plucked a jar from the shelf. I watched Fran lift the lid. An exotic, flowery scent wafted out. "Kala jeera is also called black cumin. Use these fairly soon because they lose their flavor rapidly."

Maureen glanced around, then asked in a raised voice, "Has anyone seen Carol? What about Ann and Claudell?"

"Carol spotted a garden shop around the corner." Rosemarie examined the label on a jar of pink peppercorns from the French island of Réunion. "I think Ann went with her. Ann and John are replacing some shrubs. Who better than a master gardener to tag along with?"

Maureen still looked worried. "Where's Claudell?"

"She ducked into the antiques store," Jan supplied.

Joan laughed. "Ever since we lost Fran at an outlet mall, Maureen started taking a head count."

Their shopping finished, the Red Hatters formed a

queue at the counter. I had to admit, Fran knew her way around a kitchen. In addition to kala jeera, she purchased mahlab used in Greek dishes and galangal, a frequent ingredient in Thai cooking. The attractive brunette, whom I heard referred to as Janet, turned out to be a baker.

"My husband's favorite pie is apple," Janet confessed, handing me her Visa.

"Then you'll love this combination I created from cinnamons of Indonesia and Ceylon, freshly grated nutmeg, and cloves from Madagascar," I told her while waiting for her receipt to print.

"Is it true allspice really isn't a blend of spices?" This question came from Jan, the golfer.

"Contrary to popular belief, allspice is a berry grown in the Caribbean and not a blend," I said, feeling as proud as if I'd answered the question on Final Jeopardy!

Joan lowered her voice and leaned forward. "Maybe you can tell us if the restaurant where we had lunch today, Antonio's, is the same one where a chef was found stabbed to death a few months ago."

I glanced up and realized I had a rapt audience. "Ah, yes," I murmured. "It is." Wouldn't these nice ladies be shocked to learn I not only discovered the body, but for a while was also the number one suspect in Chef Mario Barrone's murder.

"I remember reading about it in the newspaper," Janet said.

"There was another murder here, too, wasn't there?" Joan persisted.

Fran fished a couple of bills from a tote bag shaped like a large red hat. "I saw it on television. A show on the Cooking Network called *Some Like It Hot* ran the story. If I remember correctly, a woman was bludgeoned with a brisket."

"When my husband heard we were coming to Brandywine Creek, he wanted me to stay home. He said this town was dangerous," Rosemarie said. "I had to promise we'd stick together."

Maureen brought out an iPhone. "Piper, would you please take our picture?"

As the Red Hatters formed a tight cluster in front of a Hoosier cabinet filled with baking spices, my thoughts weren't on snapping a photo. I felt sick with dismay to hear Brandywine Creek was earning a reputation for murder and mayhem. Once word of Chip Balboa's death spread, the news would keep potential customers away in droves—or bring them here in tour buses.

CHAPTER 24

Spice It Up! seemed unusually quiet without the laughter and chatter of the Red Hatters. And I still hadn't called Doug. I hesitated phoning him in the middle of the day. I didn't want to interrupt him in the midst of a crucial nip-and-tuck procedure. Doug, I knew, planned to hire a full-time receptionist but so far hadn't found the right person.

I slowly walked up and down the aisles, stopping here and there to straighten or rearrange. With no customers to distract me, I felt restless, edgy. It was a relief hearing Melly's light footsteps on the stairs. I turned to find her standing tentatively on the threshold between the store-room and shop, a paper sack in her hand.

"I assume you'll be seeing Doug sometime between now and the Oktoberfest," she said. "When you do, would you kindly give these to him?"

"Be happy to," I said, taking the bag. "Matter of fact, if you don't mind watching the shop, I'll run this over right now. If he's busy, I'll just leave them at the desk."

"Don't mind a bit. I'm trying to stay busy, keep my mind off things."

The thought of vanishing from my shop for an hour or so filled me with guilty pleasure. I deliberately shelved any lingering qualms I had about leaving Melly in charge. Suddenly, I was a kid about to play hooky. After reaching for my purse under the counter, I retrieved my compact, snapped it open, and applied fresh lipstick. "I shouldn't be too long."

"No need to rush," Melly replied as she donned a Spice It Up! apron. "While you were busy waiting on customers, I took the liberty of starting a pot roast for dinner tonight."

"Pot roast?" I stared at her, my mind blank.

"You're forgetting that Lindsey invited Sean Rogers for dinner. A person can't go wrong with old-fashioned meat and potatoes."

"Right, right," I muttered. Though I had met Sean only once, I already liked him. A search warrant and subsequent trip to the police station had been a baptism of fire for the young quarterback. Certainly less than ideal conditions under which to meet your homecoming date's family. Instead of bolting, he'd stuck by Lindsey's side throughout the ordeal. He'd earned his pot roast. "Melly, do you suppose you'll have time to make biscuits? Mine are never as good as yours."

Melly smiled the first genuine smile I'd seen in days. "Piper, dear, Southern girls are born knowing how to make light and fluffy biscuits."

"So"—I returned the smile—"the secret's finally out. It's all in the DNA."

On impulse, I tucked a small jar of kala jeera into my handbag, a peace offering of sorts. Doug would be pleased to have the key ingredient for an exotic Indian dish he'd talked about making. If it turned out as tasty as predicted, I intended to corral him into doing a cooking demonstration sometime soon.

Ignoring the reproach in Casey's dark doggy eyes at

being left behind, I hurried to my car. I waved to Pete Barker, who was sweeping the walk in front of Meat on Main, then continued down Old County Road toward Pets 'R People. Not even the overcast sky could dampen my spirits. Cattle grazed in a farmer's field. The oaks and sweet gums were a blaze of gold. The scene was peaceful, bucolic. I could almost—almost—forget my troubles.

All too soon I reached my destination, a rambling ranch-style house with white vinyl siding and glossy black shutters. One end of the building served as Doug's living quarters; the other, an animal clinic. The first thing I noticed was the police cruiser in the drive. Worried, I snatched Melly's bag of cookies and my handbag, jumped out of my Beetle, and dashed inside.

The reception area was deserted with one notable exception: Wyatt McBride. He lounged in a visitor's chair, idly thumbing through an issue of *Modern Cat*.

"What are you doing here?" I demanded, hands on hips. "Shouldn't you be hiding behind a billboard, waiting to give speeding tickets to unsuspecting motorists?"

He flashed me a lazy smile that hinted of dimple. "Good afternoon to you, too."

I tucked a rebellious curl behind one ear. "Seriously, don't you have a murderer to catch? According to Klassy Kut gossip, Mayor Hemmings and the city council are breathing down your neck."

"That so?" He resumed his reading.

"And if that isn't enough, a group of nice Red Hat ladies informed me Brandywine Creek is on the road to wrack and ruin. It's time for you to put on your cape and save the town from destruction."

He flipped a page. "No can do. My cape's at the dry cleaners', and I have to pick up my cat."

I slumped into the seat next to him. "Guess we all have our priorities."

"Fraidy's here for her well-cat visit. I dropped her off on my way to work this morning."

The notion of McBride as a cat lover was taking some adjustment. I set the bag of cookies on an end table and picked up a magazine called—of all things—*Bark*. *Modern Cat* and now *Bark*? Who knew? I browsed through ads and advice columns before stealing a sidelong glance at McBride. "Don't suppose there are any new developments in the case that you'd care to share?"

"New developments? Can't say for sure, but I might could be bribed. For instance," he said, his expression sly, "how do you feel about countertops?"

"Well, let me think." I pretended to ponder the matter. "Countertops are a handy place to make sandwiches. They're useful when cooking—but, oops, I forgot—you prefer takeout. You're probably the only person I know who could get along *without* countertops."

He closed *Modern Cat*. "You're not going to make this easy, are you?"

"Nope." I hid my satisfaction behind a glossy ad for puppy chow. "Any advice comes with a price."

He appeared to mull this over, then nodded. "All right," he said, "but only on condition that you answer my question first. Laminate or tile?"

"Neither." My prompt retort was met with a frown. "While laminates are budget friendly," I explained, "they're prone to scratches, burns, and in some cases, stains. With tile, you need to make sure the grout is well sealed. Unsealed grout can result in staining, and any standing moisture can contribute to bacterial growth."

"So what would an expert such as yourself recommend?"

Hmm. This conversation had taken a serious turn. "Depending on your taste and price range, I'd go with quartz, which is an engineered stone. Granite or one of the solid-surface brands would also be good choices. They're durable and will be in it for the long haul. Or, as you so inelegantly phrased it, until they carry you out feetfirst. Okay, McBride, your turn to talk."

Just then, an angry feline yowled behind a closed door leading to the treatment rooms. McBride glanced over, looking as jittery as a dad-to-be in the maternity ward.

"Don't worry," I soothed. "Doug has a way with animals. Now give me an update before he appears with Fraidy."

McBride tossed his magazine aside and rose. "The only prints on the bottle of Visine belonged to Melly."

Duh! I surged to my feet, ready to do battle. The difference in our heights would have made this confrontation laughable to an outsider. David and Goliath. "That's it? Of course the prints were hers. They were her eyedrops."

"Since Miz Prescott's were the only prints found, we're ruling out the possibility that someone else put the drops in Balboa's drink."

"Did you check for prints elsewhere? If a person came into Melly's home while she was upstairs, they must've left prints behind."

McBride's jaw clenched, his blue eyes turned steely. "This isn't Mayberry, and I'm not Barney Fife. Of course we checked. The knobs on the back door of the house and the door leading to the basement had been wiped clean."

"B-but . . . ," I sputtered.

Approaching footsteps from the clinic side brought our conversation to a halt. I was determined, however, to continue it another time.

Doug appeared, the cat in one arm, a pet carrier in the other. He looked startled at seeing me but grinned, then switched his attention to McBride. "Except for being a little malnourished, Fraidy's an otherwise healthy two-year-old female," Doug announced.

Spying McBride, Fraidy sprang from Doug's arm to

McBride's in one graceful leap. McBride caught her easily and stroked his pet's sleek black fur. "Glad to hear that, Doc. How much do I owe you?"

"I'll have my receptionist bill you. Oops!" Doug smacked his forehead with the heel of his hand. "Forgot I don't have a receptionist."

"I'll spread the word you're looking to hire," McBride said. "The grapevine works better than an ad in *The Statesman*."

"Nice kitty," I said, reaching out to pet the cat now purring contentedly in the crook of McBride's arm. Fraidy hissed, and I quickly withdrew my hand.

McBride smiled smugly.

I frowned. "Animals usually like me."

"Felines can be selective about whom they like—and whom they don't," Doug said in an attempt to soften the rejection.

I watched McBride coax his cat into the pet carrier. He was zippering the carrier shut when I remembered Melly's request. She'd skin me alive if I forgot to ask him when I had the opportunity. "Melly wants to know when she can return home."

McBride straightened. "Tell her anytime she wants. I'll have one of my men take down the crime scene tape."

"That ought to please Melly," Doug commented as McBride left the clinic. He took off his glasses and polished the lenses on the sleeve of his lab coat. "I'll admit I was surprised to see you. For a minute, I thought Casey might be having a problem."

"It was too late to call when I got home last night, so I thought I'd pay you a visit instead." I was careful to leave out the part about Lindsey almost forgetting to give me the message—again. "You won't believe the day I've had."

He gathered me in for a much-needed hug. "Poor baby, tell me all about it."

I rested my head on his shoulder, inhaling a faint anti-septic smell along with the woodsy aroma of his after-shave. Doug felt solid, safe, dependable. I hugged him in return, grateful at having such a wonderful man in my life.

Leaning back slightly, I smiled up at him. "Where to begin . . ."

I fully expected Doug to cry "too much information" partway through my narrative. Typical Doug, he listened attentively while I recounted finding Ned Feeney bleed-ing on my kitchen floor. I ended by telling him about the Red Hatters who came to browse but stayed to shop.

Doug tunneled his fingers through his hair. "The rea-son I called was to explain why I haven't mentioned the football game tomorrow night. Josh, a colleague from vet school, wants to get together for dinner. Since we live a distance apart, it works best if we meet halfway. I hope you're not angry."

"Why would I be angry?" I asked. "Is this the colleague you left Casey with when your father had his heart attack?"

"One and the same."

"Well, by all means, give him our best."

Doug lowered his mouth to mine, his kiss slow and sweet. I felt my mind empty, my bones turn to jelly.

It wasn't till minutes later when brain cells started to fire again that I remembered the dual purpose of my visit. I retrieved the paper bag from the table where I'd left it and handed it to him. "This is for you."

"A present?" The brown eyes behind his rimless glasses gleamed with anticipation.

"Gingersnaps for your sauerbraten."

After peeking at the bag's contents, he scowled at me. "What in the blazes?"

Curious, I peeked, too—and couldn't believe my eyes. Melly had substituted a store-bought brand in place of her award-worthy gingersnaps. I managed a sickly smile.

"Well, that confirms what Reba Mae and I smelled burning."

"Don't worry." Doug shrugged it off. "Melly has a lot to deal with these days. I'm sure no one will be able to tell the difference."

Truth of the matter, I was more worried than ever. Not about store-bought versus home-baked cookies, but about Melly's state of mind. I kept thinking about that on the drive home. Melly's concern was justified. If the matter of Chip's death wasn't resolved soon, she could be charged with homicide. First, second, or third degree all resulted in jail time.

I tapped my fingertips against the steering wheel. Things hadn't been good to begin with—such as Chip dying long before it was reported—and they kept getting worse. McBride said the only fingerprints on the Visine belonged to Melly. What I didn't understand was why there were no prints on the door handles. That struck me as odd. Very odd. Since Melly lived alone, her fingerprints should have been everywhere.

Suddenly I felt a chill that had nothing to do with the damp, overcast weather. Some person—Chip's killer—had methodically erased evidence he left in Melly's kitchen. He, or she, had entered the house uninvited while Melly was upstairs. He then shoved a drugged, disoriented Chip Balboa down a flight of stairs to his death. What if Melly had returned downstairs in time to witness that shameful act? Would she have been the killer's next victim? If a stranger had entered undetected once before, could they, would they, try again?

Was Melly safe?

CHAPTER 25

Closing time had come and gone. I'd heaved a sigh of relief when I returned home from Pets 'R People to find everything in order. The mouthwatering aroma of roasting meat drifted from my upstairs apartment. Casey greeted me with an effusive display of affection, dancing about until his toenails clicked on the tile floor like castanets.

Melly stood at the stove, dressed in a flowered skirt and peach-colored twinset suitable for a high tea. Except for the fact she viciously jabbed a helpless roast with a two-pronged fork, she presented the picture of genteel womanhood.

"I hope Doug isn't upset with me," she said as she replaced the lid on the pot. "I know it was cowardly not to deliver the cookies personally, but I was just too . . . embarrassed."

I got out the makings for a salad. "Doug assured me that the sauce for his sauerbraten won't suffer any permanent damage as a result. The other spices—juniper berries, cloves, and bay leaves—will compensate."

"It's the cardamom that makes my cookies stand out." Melly wiped her hands on a dish towel. "Chip told me my gingersnaps were the best he'd ever tasted. Imagine, he even asked for the recipe."

"Aren't Lindsey and Sean here yet?" I said, veering the talk in a safer direction.

"Lindsey called to say the pep rally ran late. They should be on their way."

Melly took dinnerware from the cupboard and set the table using my best place mats and napkins. In another life, I'd entertained guests in a large formal dining room resplendent with wainscoting and a chandelier. Now, whether for guests or family, meals were served at the kitchen table. And I had to admit, I didn't mind a simpler lifestyle. Less is more I'd learned.

"I ran into McBride while at Pets 'R People." I sliced tomato and red onion and added them to the greens.

"Lord have mercy!" Melly opened the oven door a crack, then satisfied her biscuits were browning nicely, closed it again. "What business did that man have with a veterinarian?"

"Seems McBride adopted a cat." I added a sprinkling of blue cheese to the salad. "Or more accurately, the cat adopted him."

"A cat!" Melly shook her head in disbelief. "Strange choice for that man. I can picture him owning a dog—a Rottweiler, maybe a Doberman—but not a cat. It just doesn't fit his image."

"Apparently, the animal showed up on his doorstep half-starved, so he started feeding it. Next thing you know, it's taken up permanent residence. I must say the cat doesn't have a very friendly disposition."

"No wonder man and cat are soul mates." Melly took several bottles of salad dressing from the refrigerator and set them on the table. "I don't suppose you remembered to ask him when I'm allowed back in my own home?"

"As a matter of fact, he's having one of his men remove

the crime scene tape today. You have the green light to return whenever you wish, but . . ."

Melly pursed her lips. "But?"

The salad finished, I picked up the dish towel, twisted it in my hands. "I wish you'd reconsider and stay with us awhile longer. At least until Chip's murderer is found."

Melly let out an un-Melly-like snort. "At the pace this investigation is progressing, it could take forever."

"I worry about you all alone in that big house," I persisted.

"You've been reading too many mystery novels," she said, pooh-poohing my concern. "Why, I've lived in that house over forty years and never locked the back door. Half the folks in town do the same."

"Hasn't it occurred to you that whoever came into your house unannounced could do it again?"

"You worry too much, dear." She checked the biscuits and, deciding they met her high standards, removed the pan from the oven. "If it makes you feel better, I'll have Thompson check the locks on all the doors and windows."

"Promise me you'll keep them locked in the future—front *and* back."

At that moment, a door slammed and Lindsey and Sean charged up the stairs. I heard Lindsey laugh at something Sean had said, and then the teens burst into the kitchen.

"Hey, Mom," Lindsey greeted me. "Hey, Meemaw."

"Hey, you two." In the nick of time, I caught myself from telling them to wash up before dinner, as I used to do when my children were small. Lindsey would have died of embarrassment if I'd said that to her in front of her new boyfriend.

"Hey, Miz Prescott, Miz Prescott." Sean dug his hands into the pockets of his jeans. Unlike the confident athlete on the gridiron, he looking shy and self-conscious at finding himself surrounded by three generation of Prescott women. "Whatever you're cooking sure smells good."

"Meemaw makes the best biscuits ever," Lindsey bragged. "Bet you can't eat just one."

"Supper's ready to put on the table," Melly said. "You youngsters go wash up."

I bit my lip to keep from smiling. Lindsey's face, I'd noticed, had turned petal pink as the teens headed for the bathroom sink. I thought I heard her giggle, and then the sound of water running.

"What would you like to drink with your meal?" I asked when they returned with clean hands.

"Milk, if you please, ma'am," Sean said, his good manners showing.

"Now," I said as we filled our plates with potatoes, carrots, and pot roast so tender, it fell off the bone, "your grandmother and I would like to hear all about homecoming and spirit week."

"Homecoming's still two weeks away. We play at home tomorrow and have an away game next week." Sean dived into his food with the gusto of a teenage boy who hasn't eaten for a week.

Lindsey speared a carrot. "The committee is planning an awesome spirit week, a different theme each day. Camo day, pajama day, hippie day."

"There's a bonfire in the school parking lot Thursday before the game—public invited," Sean said, slathering butter on a biscuit. "Even my dad's going to be there."

"What about your mother, Sean?" Melly asked. "Does she ever come to watch you play?"

Sean concentrated on slicing a piece of meat. Lindsey shifted restlessly in her seat. "No, not since the divorce," he mumbled.

Melly clucked her tongue. "I'm sorry to hear that."

Sean shoved bits of roasted potato around his plate with his fork. "My parents' divorce was partly my fault."

My heart ached for him. No longer a boy, not quite a man, he looked so terribly young, so vulnerable. So sad. "Sean, what could you have possibly done that would've made a difference?"

"I could've tried harder to keep 'em together." Self-condemnation was present in every word.

Lindsey squeezed his hand. "You know you tried."

Sean's jaw set stubbornly. "I was too busy with sports. I should've seen what was happening and done something to stop it. Now my dad's miserable and my mom's married to some jerk."

"They're adults, Sean," I reminded him gently. "They're accountable for their own actions—their own mistakes."

"I suppose, still . . ."

Melly took this as a signal to start clearing the dishes. "Dessert, anyone?"

After changing into cream-colored slacks with an earth-tone sweater, and adding a chunky gold necklace, I left Melly to supervise the teens while I morphed from mom into party crasher. I intended to find out shortly if I should upgrade Troy's status from boyfriend to person of interest. With a game tomorrow, Sean wouldn't stay late, I knew. He'd thanked me profusely for the invitation to dinner. My first impression had been confirmed: Sean Rogers *was* a nice kid. This time Lindsey had picked a winner.

CJ's palatial home with its three-car garage overlooked a golf course. It was lit up like a Christmas tree when I arrived. I parked in the circular drive behind Cheryl Balboa's rented BMW, marched up the walk, and rang the bell.

Surprise registered on CJ's face as he opened the door.

He held a heavy cut-glass tumbler filled with what I assumed was fine Kentucky bourbon. "Hiya, Scooter."

Not giving him a chance to protest, I brushed past him into the living room. I found Amber curled in a chair large enough for a mother and her quadruplets. Cheryl and the surfer dude, wineglasses in hand, cuddled on the far end of an Italian leather sectional the size of the Vatican. "Hey, y'all," I said cheerily.

Amber looked stunned by my intrusion. Then irritated. "Piper, what are you doin' here? Can't you see we have guests?"

"Don't mind li'l ol' me." I plopped myself down on a curvy leather and chrome job that looked European in design. When the time came, I hoped I'd be able to extricate myself without the assistance of a crane. "Thought I'd pop in and see the redecorating you've done."

With the ease of a well-greased politician, CJ stepped forward to make the introductions. The sun-streaked, tan Adonis now officially had a name, Troy Farnsworth. A moniker like that would look good on a marquee. Cynical me wondered if it was given to him at birth or something he'd invented.

"Have we met?" Cheryl frowned—or would have, had her face not been Botoxed. "I can't place you, but you look familiar."

"I was at the remembrance Rusty Tulley hosted for your late husband. You were probably too grief stricken to notice who was there and who wasn't." I was being facetious about the "grief stricken," but Cheryl didn't seem to notice.

Amber made a last-ditch effort to get rid of me. "Piper, this really isn't a good time for a visit. Stop by tomorrow, and I'll gladly show you the changes I've made."

"Oh, come now, Amber, it's not as if we're strangers." I swiveled to face Cheryl and Troy. "CJ and I were married once upon a time—pre-Amber, of course. It's hard to compete with a twenty-four-year-old former beauty queen. Amber's too modest. Did she mention that she was first runner-up in the Miss Georgia beauty pageant?"

Cheryl smiled at this. "As a matter of fact, she did. I was in a few pageants myself during my college days. Amber and I share a lot in common."

"Hmm." That didn't take any stretch of the imagination to believe. In spite of the difference in hair color, the women, both polished and pampered, could have been sisters.

"Guessin' you still like Chardonnay." CJ handed me a wineglass and ignored Amber's glare that clearly read "don't feed strays."

"Your mother sends her regards, CJ," I said, accepting the glass.

CJ took a swig of Wild Turkey. "How's Momma these days?"

"Just peachy, considering she's a murder suspect." I took a sip of my Chardonnay, enjoying the cold, crisp taste. I preferred my wines sweeter, but as Chardonnays go, this wasn't half bad. "I'm trying to convince your mother to stay with me until Chief McBride arrests the person responsible for Chip's murder."

Cheryl didn't meet my eyes. Neither did Troy.

"We'd have invited CJ's mother to stay with us," Amber hastily explained for the benefit of her guests, "but with paint fumes an' all, we didn't think it would be good for her. Poor dear, she's gettin' on in years."

I gazed around the room in frank admiration. As much as it irked me to admit, the new paint colors were . . . transformative. Instead of plain vanilla, the walls and throw pillows were soft muted shades of blues and greens. New artwork also added a nice touch. "The color palette your decorator chose is truly amazing."

"Mona referred to it as 'Summer in Savannah.'" Amber smiled condescendingly.

I smiled back. "Funny, I think of summers in Savannah as hot and sweaty. At least that's the way I remember from the times CJ, the kids, and I vacationed on nearby Tybee Island. Isn't that right, CJ?"

CJ sank deep into the sectional, rested his arm along the back. "Ninety-five in the shade—if you could find any—and humidity just as high."

"Before you barged in, Piper," Amber said stiffly, "Troy was about to tell us about a business venture."

"I'm all ears." I sipped my wine.

Cheryl gave a practiced head toss that sent blond highlighted hair whipping over her shoulder. If I tried that move, everyone would hear my vertebrae creak. "When we return to California, Troy intends to open a chain of fitness clubs."

Troy leaned forward, his handsome face earnest. "Going to start off small—one, maybe two—in key locations in L.A. If all goes well, we'll expand."

"Our goal is to have one in every major city. New York, Chicago, Dallas, Phoenix, San Francisco."

"Not Brandywine Creek?" My veiled attempt at humor bombed. No one cracked a smile. "Sounds ambitious," I said after clearing my throat. "But aren't there already a lot of fitness clubs?"

"Not like ours," Cheryl corrected. "Ours will be cutting-edge. We'll offer things like plyometrics, pound, Zumba, and spinning."

Troy nodded as vigorously as a bobblehead doll. "Once we're established, I want to add stand-up paddleboard yoga. Maybe even circus arts, provided I can find the right instructors."

I pretended I knew what they were talking about. I knew jogging, had a passing acquaintance with yoga, but as for the others, I didn't have a clue. "You must need a great deal of capital to set things in motion."

Troy rested his hand lightly on Cheryl's thigh. "Thanks to my girl, we'll be able to start the ball rolling as soon as we get back."

Not thanks to Cheryl. What he really meant was thanks to Cheryl's money. Money Chip had accrued. I circled the rim of my wineglass with an index finger. "So this is a joint venture?"

"We're still hoping to find investors." Troy aimed the full wattage of his charm toward CJ.

CJ gulped Wild Turkey and headed to the bar for a refill.

CHAPTER 26

When I arrived home from jogging the next morning,
Melly was busily packing her bags. "The coffee's on. I
used the Blue Mountain beans you seem to favor lately.
Your granola and yogurt are on the table."

Casey made a beeline for his water dish. I chugged
down a glass from the tap. "Who's going to have breakfast ready and waiting for me after you leave?"

"I'll miss you, too, dear, but it's high time I get out of
your hair. I must admit, in spite of your many shortcomings,
you've been a very gracious hostess. Some of our famous
Southern hospitality must've rubbed off on you." Melly
placed her coffee cup in the dishwasher. "For the life of
me, I don't know why a body wants to live in a place where
it's cold enough to snow every winter."

I placed a scoop of dog food in Casey's dish and watched
him chow down. "Lots of people enjoy the cold and snow.
They stay active with sports like snowmobiling, cross-
country or downhill skiing, even ice fishing on the lakes."

"Brrr." Melly shuddered. "If I'd grown up in Michigan
like you did, my favorite winter pastime would be hiber-
nation."

"It's not all that bad, really." I poured myself coffee as I thought about what to say next—and how to say it. I didn't want to frighten her, but I wanted her safe. I'd broached the subject last night, but without success. It was worth another try. "I know you're innocent, Melly, but *someone* murdered Chip. I'm worried whoever killed him might return and harm you, too."

"You fret too much." Melly patted my arm. "Everything will be fine once I sleep in my own bed again, just you wait and see."

As I sat down to breakfast, I vowed I'd keep close tabs on her. And I'd have CJ do the same.

Melly refilled my coffee cup before I knew it needed refilling. "By the way, I nearly forgot to tell you I researched Trustychipdesign like you asked."

About to add a generous spoonful of granola to my yogurt, I paused. "What did you learn?"

Melly sat down opposite me, her expression troubled. "Strange as it sounds, given its position earlier this year, the company seems to be struggling to hold on to its share of the market. Unless Trustychipdesign comes up with a new or an improved product soon, several up-and-coming software businesses are poised to overtake it."

"Interesting." I began to eat, barely tasting my breakfast. What Melly had just told me dovetailed nicely with the argument Felicity had overheard between the partners. Rusty had been eager for change—and replacing Chip had been at the top of his list. Hmm . . . interesting. Too bad Rusty had an alibi. Or did he? Could he have left the Turner-Driscoll House undetected? The servants' stairs would have provided an easy exit. The idea was worth investigating.

"Rusty and Chip never should have reneged on their initial offer," Melly complained, sounding bitter. "My modifications would have given their company a much-needed boost. I just wasn't about to hand over my hard work for a pittance. If they weren't willing to pay me what it was worth, someone else would. I told Chip as much the night he tried to persuade me to change my mind."

I hoped Melly didn't air her grievance to just anyone. I knew she wouldn't hurt a fly, but people like to talk, and some, I feared, could misinterpret what she said. And conclude she'd acted out of anger, frustration, or greed.

Glancing at the wall clock, I realized I'd better hurry if I wanted to open on time. "Melly, if your things are ready, I'll help you carry them out to your car, but we'll have to get a move on."

"No need to bother. CJ already offered his assistance. He's even going to follow me home and take my bags up to my room." She rose from the table. "I was going to ask Ned, but the poor man is still in the hospital."

The day passed quickly. Before I knew, it was time to meet Reba Mae for Friday-night football.

"Let's get the hot dogs the Booster Club's sellin'," Reba Mae suggested as we wandered through the crowd, stopping here and there to chat with friends and acquaintances.

"Hot dogs are fine with me," I said, nodding to Bitsy Johnson-Jones. "I swear the woman's lost two dress sizes since spring. I barely recognize her these days."

Reba Mae leaned in and lowered her voice. "Don't spread it around, but she had her tummy stapled shut. Everyone in the Klassy Kut was talkin' about how she went to Augusta to get it done."

I sketched a cross over my heart. "Won't tell a soul."

"Hey, Jolene," Reba Mae greeted the wife of Sergeant Beau Tucker, a plump blond loaded down with food and drinks. "Nice to see you without crutches. How's the ankle?" she asked, referring to a tumble Jolene had taken some months back after a wild night of bunco.

"Hey, yourself, Reba Mae. My broke ankle healed just fine." Jolene gave me a look that would have withered tomatoes on the vine, then stomped off without another word.

"What was that all about?" Reba Mae asked as we got in a line at the concession stand.

"I think she's mad at me."

"Why? What did you go and do now?"

I sighed a sigh worthy of Joan of Arc. "Beau thinks I'm to blame for him being put on probation."

Reba Mae raised a brow. "Are you?"

"Guess it's possible." I studied the menu scrawled on a piece of plywood. "I might have *coaxed* a few details from Beau that should've been kept confidential. McBride wasn't happy when he found out."

Reba Mae wagged her head until her dangly earrings swayed. "Girl, keep that stuff up, and I'll be the only friend you have left in this town. Tony Deltorro still holds a grudge for you pointin' a finger in his direction."

"Tony's Sicilian. They're programmed to bear grudges."

"Danny Boyd and Marcy aren't exactly members of your fan club, either," Reba Mae reminded me.

I placed my order with the balding man behind the counter. "Danny and Marcy are young yet. They'll get over it—eventually."

"To this day, Danny skimps on the cheese whenever you order the pizza. And once he 'forgot' the mushrooms."

"He needs time, is all. It's not my fault Danny was a person of interest in a murder case. His alibi checked out okay. Cut me some slack. I'm an amateur when it comes to homicide investigations."

"Whatever." Reba Mae nudged me in the ribs. "Speaking of the mozzarella-skimpin', mushroom-forgettin' devil."

Danny Boyd, a thin young man in his early twenties with fly-away hair and a wispy goatee, stood no more than three feet away, studying the menu board. I edged closer, an idea taking shape. Danny had provided Cheryl with an alibi for the night her husband was killed, but there were still questions I wanted answered. "Hey, Danny," I said, aiming for casual and friendly.

At hearing his name, he looked over and gave me an uncertain smile. "Hey, Miz Prescott."

"I've been wondering about something, Danny. Maybe you can put my mind at ease."

His narrow shoulders rose and fell. "I'll try."

"Chief McBride mentioned you delivered pizza to Mrs. Balboa the night her husband died. Did you happen to notice her *male* friend in the motel room?"

"Nope," he said. "Don't know about any guy. All I saw was the chick."

I made as if to turn away, then turned back. "One last question. Did you happen to notice a late-model BMW in the parking lot that night?"

"Not a Bimmer in sight. I would've noticed if there had been. That's my dream car. Gonna buy me one when I win the lottery."

"Next!" the man behind the concession stand bellowed.

Danny shuffled forward, digging for his wallet.

Our conversation might have ended, but my mind had shifted into overdrive. Reba Mae had listened to our exchange with a puzzled expression on her face. "What was that all about?"

I caught her arm and tugged her toward a table loaded with condiments. I lowered my voice. "What if Cheryl had been clever enough to establish an alibi for the night Chip was killed? Then, knowing the pizza delivery person could vouch for her whereabouts, she sneaked off down the road to where her lover was waiting with a car? The pair could have done the dirty deed and returned to the motel with none the wiser."

Reba Mae heaped relish and ketchup on her hot dog. "Honeybun, try to sell that story to McBride, he'll think you're crazy as a betsy bug."

I grimaced. That wasn't exactly the response I'd hoped for, I thought as we slowly wandered back toward the bleachers. Maybe Troy had been the designated hit man all along and tracked Chip to Melly's house. Or perhaps the pair had worked as a tag team. Cheryl could have spiked Chip's drink with eyedrops, then sent Troy off to finish the job.

"Tomorrow's the Grangers' party," Reba Mae said, taking a bite of her dog. "I finally decided what to bring— apple strudel."

Only half-listening to Reba Mae ramble, I pondered ways to prove my newly hatched theory regarding Cheryl's so-called alibi. Did the no-tell motel rooms have rear exits? A means to escape detection? If so, Cheryl Balboa was back on my persons-of-interest list. I decided, then and there, to scout out the Beaver Dam Motel soon as the game ended. But before I did that, I needed to check on Melly.

"You haven't heard a single word I've said," Reba Mae said, her tone accusatory.

"Of course I have. You were saying something about . . ." I drew a blank.

"Gotcha." She smirked. She licked a dab of ketchup from her thumb. "I was sayin' as how I was gonna make apple strudel."

"Strudel sounds good."

A cheer rose from the stands as the teams returned to the field.

"Clay bought a bushel of apples at a roadside stand

while up in the North Georgia mountains. Winesap, Mutsu, Jonagold, and Rome beauty. The farmer told 'im all of 'em were good for cookin' and eatin'."

I made a concerted effort to corral my wayward thoughts—at least temporarily. "What was Clay doing in apple country?"

"The owner of the construction company he works for wanted Clay to do some repairs on a cabin of his." Reba Mae's mouth turned up in a cat-with-a-canary grin. "Clay's seriously thinkin' of quittin' construction and gettin' a degree in criminal justice."

I stopped walking and stared at her. "You're kidding?"

"Nope." Reba Mae's grin grew wider. "My boy's finally got his head on straight. And I have Wyatt McBride to thank."

"What does he have to do with any of this?" I asked as we resumed walking toward the stands. The crowd had thinned considerably, I noticed, since the game started.

"Clay's come down with a huge case of hero worship. In his eyes, McBride can do no wrong. He's hoping to get hired on the police force soon as he turns twenty-one. Course, he might end up like your Lindsey and change careers every other month."

I took a bite of my hot dog while I processed Reba Mae's news. True, Lindsey kept switching career choices, but lots of young people did. Now, at seventeen, she was filling out college applications with no particular goal in mind. Lindsey happened to be one of the youngest in her class. At times, I wished I'd held her back a year, but she'd pleaded and begged to start school with her friends. Hindsight is 20/20. Clichés are clichés for a reason.

We'd reached the bleachers. Reba Mae scanned the packed seats for a place for us to sit. "I think what put Clay over the top was seein' a photo of McBride in an old *People* magazine. Wyatt was escortin' a starlet to a movie premiere at South Beach."

"Jennifer Jade."

We whipped around at the sound of McBride's baritone directly behind us.

"The starlet's name was Jennifer Jade," McBride said. He was in starched and pressed navy blues, obviously working, and looked formidable. "Ms. Jade was being stalked by some nut case. My lieutenant assigned me as her bodyguard."

Reba Mae wanted details. "Jennifer Jade—that her real name?"

"As real as the rest of her." McBride smiled and sauntered off.

Reba Mae caught the eye of Joe Johnson, former police chief and her uncle by marriage.

He motioned for us to join him, then wiggled his girth to make room beside him on the bleacher. "That your baby girl out there, jumpin' around?" he asked, pointing a chubby finger at Lindsey.

"That's her, all right, prettiest girl on the squad."

He chuckled, then returned his attention to the game.

The teams were evenly matched. For a time, the score teetered back and forth. However, when halftime rolled around, the Brandywine Bearcats were down by a field goal.

Reba Mae rose and stretched. "Don't know about you, honeybun, but I'm exhausted from all the cheerin' and such. I need me some deep-fried Oreos."

"I'll go with you," I volunteered, "but slap my hand if I try to grab one."

"Deal."

Outside the football field, people milled about or chatted in small groups. I trailed after Reba Mae, who had her heart set on cholesterol and calories. Suddenly, I gave her a nudge. "Look," I said. "Do you see who I see?"

Coming toward us, larger than life, were CJ and Amber, along with Cheryl Balboa and Troy Farnsworth. "Hey, Scooter," CJ said, greeting me like we were best buddies. "Didn't know you were a big football fan."

"I'm just one big surprise after another." I tried to sound mysterious, but there wasn't much mystery left after living with the same man for more than two decades.

Amber flipped long brown locks over her shoulder. "Reba Mae, is it true what I'm hearin'? You really gonna make your stage debut?"

"Rehearsals start next week."

Amber treated us to a dazzling display of teeth too white—and in my humble opinion, too big. As the ex-wife, I felt obligated to find fault with the "other woman." "Reba Mae's going to have a starring role. She's in every scene."

"Pity my friend Cheryl"—she indicated Cheryl Balboa with a nod—"won't be here. She majored in Performin' Arts at Southern Cal. She could teach y'all a thing or two."

"That so?" I filed this away in my bank of useless information. I'd witnessed Cheryl's theatrics from a front-row seat in McBride's office not long ago. If that had been an indication of her acting ability, she must have finished at the bottom of her class.

Reba Mae batted her lashes at Troy Farnsworth, her fantasy pool boy. "A small-town football game must seem pretty dull compared with an excitin' life in L.A."

He lifted one shoulder and let it fall in a lazy shrug. "One has to make do. Not many choices here on a Friday night."

"I, for one, can't wait to leave this town and never look back," Cheryl said petulantly.

"What's stoppin' y'all?" Reba Mae asked, though her attention was still fixed on Troy.

Cheryl's mouth tightened. "For starters, your chief of police is a control freak. He's gotten the notion into his head that I had something to do with my husband's death."

CJ stuck out his chest. "I went with her when McBride called her in for questioning. Never a bad idea to have an attorney present."

"Isn't that conflict of interest?" I fumed. "What kind of son are you, CJ? You should be jumping up and down with joy that McBride's looking for suspects other than your mother."

He had the grace to look shamefaced. "Business is business," he muttered. "Nothin' personal."

"McBride subpoenaed Cheryl's phone records. The audacity," Amber said indignantly.

"He insinuated I was a liar," Cheryl said. "That I had something to hide."

"Don't give him no never mind, darlin'," CJ counseled. "McBride's a small-town boy playactin' a big-city cop."

Cheryl looped her arms through Troy's. "It's not my fault he assumed I was in California when he called to tell me Chip had died."

"Hmm." I struck a thoughtful pose. "Think that might be because you told him you had to book a flight?"

Amber prodded the foursome toward the bleachers. "Y'all, halftime's nearly over. Let's get back to our seats."

I scanned the crowd for sight of McBride's navy blue uniform, but if he still circulated among the crowd, he was impossible to detect. I wanted to tell him about Troy Farnsworth's grandiose plan for a chain of fitness clubs—financed by Chip Balboa's estate. I also wanted to let him know what Melly's research had turned up.

"C'mon, hon," Reba Mae said. "I've lost my cravin' for Oreos. Let's watch us some football."

I couldn't really get my head back into the game. Judging from the way Reba Mae kept hopping up and down and hollering, she didn't share my problem. According to the brightly illuminated scoreboard, it was near the end of the third quarter. The game was tied and the Brandywine Bearcats had the ball. Sean Rogers, as quarterback, called the next play. Before he could find an open receiver, he was taken down hard by a player twice his size.

And he didn't get up.

The refs blew their whistles, halting play. The coach ran over and conferred with the referees. The rowdy crowd of fans grew eerily silent as EMTs trotted onto the field. Sean was lifted onto a gurney. As he was carried off the field, he raised a hand toward the spectators. The gesture was met with deafening applause. Through a haze of tears, I watched Lindsey chase after the gurney.

CHAPTER 27

After Sean was injured, I completely lost interest in the game and decided to leave early. Fortunately, since Reba Mae and I had driven to the high school separately, this didn't present a problem. I might not have been in the mood for football and crowds, but I wasn't quite ready to pay a late-night visit to the Beaver Dam Motel just yet. Lindsey had phoned to let me know she was accompanying Sean to the hospital. She'd gone on to add that she'd probably be home late, since the doctors were talking X-rays and CT scans.

The streets were nearly deserted. People were either at the game or snug in front of their televisions. Temperatures dipped into the fifties. I was glad I'd worn my Brandywine Bearcats sweatshirt to ward off the chill.

Rather than drive around aimlessly, I decided to check on Melly. This would be her first night back in her own home. I didn't really expect I'd be able to convince her to return to my place, but . . .

After turning down Jefferson Street, I rolled to a stop in front of her house. Even though Melly was a night owl, not a single light burned. Strange, I thought. Her Ford Taurus was in its usual spot in the drive, so I assumed she was home. I drummed my fingers on the steering wheel while I examined my options. I could drive on, pretend I was never there. I could phone and risk her wrath at waking her. Or I could march up the front steps, pound on the door, and insist she tell me what was going on.

Frustrated, I stared at the house. Still dark; still no signs of life. Tired of waffling in indecision, I got out of my car and ran up the steps. I rang the bell, and then when no one answered, knocked on the door. Feeling like a nosy Nellie, I cupped my hands around my eyes and peered through a narrow gap in the living room drapes.

I didn't see any cause for alarm. But I felt it. Danger. Every instinct screamed a warning. The feeling was as real and as creepy as finding a long-legged spider crawling up my leg. I hadn't lost sight of the fact that there was a killer on the loose. One who might be hidden in plain sight—or lurking in the shadows. I cast a nervous glance over my shoulder, half-braced to have an assailant burst from the shrubbery, and felt absurdly relieved when that didn't happen. I returned to the door, twisted the knob, and found it locked. Just then, I remembered a key Melly had given me years ago to use in case of an emergency. Did this qualify? Guess that depended on how one defined emergency. I dug my keys out of the pocket of my jeans. A sliver of moon shed only a feeble light as it ducked behind clouds. I fumbled, trying to find the right key—then fumbled again, trying to fit it into the lock. After a couple of unsuccessful attempts, I heard the tumblers click and felt the door give way.

"Melly," I called as I stepped inside. "It's me, Piper."

I'd feel like an intruder if she suddenly appeared and demanded to know why I was prowling around her house in the dark. Shadows cloaked the house in gloom, making the familiar seem unfamiliar. I gnawed my lower lip, wishing I were elsewhere—anywhere but here—knowing I couldn't leave until I knew Melly was safe.

"Melly," I called again, louder this time. A quick look around, top to bottom, I decided, then vanish. My look-see would be much easier if I could shed a little light on the subject. I groped for a wall switch, found one, and flicked it.

Nothing happened.

I tried again. Still the same results. Melly's house was old. Fuses probably blew all the time. No big deal. I wished I carried a flashlight. A small, powerful one like the techs did on *CSI*. I vowed to heed Ned Feeney's motto in the future and "be prepared."

Feeling distinctly uneasy, I rested my hand on the newel post of the staircase. "Melly!" I shouted. "Come out, come out, wherever you are." She had been so eager to return home, to sleep in her own bed. Could she be upstairs, sound asleep in spite of the racket I was making?

The grandfather clock on the landing bonged the hour of ten. The deep resonant tones aggravated a dull throbbing in my head. I rubbed my temples and tried to formulate a game plan. A bead of perspiration trickled down my spine. The house was warm, much too warm. Stifling. Melly must have the thermostat set at eighty-five degrees. It didn't help any that I wore a heavy sweatshirt.

I yawned, starting to feel drowsy. I needed to conduct my search and get out of Dodge. With both arms extended, I navigated around the living room furniture. I narrowly avoided tripping over an ottoman. My shin connected with a corner of the coffee table.

"Damn!" I cursed out loud.

I heard a soft thud when I knocked a knickknack off an end table and onto the carpet. I'd pick it up later, provided I didn't step on it first. Feeling a bit like Christopher Columbus upon reaching dry land, I arrived at the window at the far end of the room and flung open the drapes and sheers. Voilà! Meager light filtered in.

I stood still for a moment to get my bearings. My head felt as though tom toms beat against the skull. I had Tylenol in my purse, but I'd left my purse under the seat of my car. As I started to traverse the room, a wave of dizziness washed over me, causing me to lose my balance and fall across the sofa.

And find Melly.

"Oh my God, Melly," I stammered, scrambling to my feet. "I'm so sorry. I hope I didn't hurt you. I didn't see you lying there."

Melly didn't move. Didn't say a word.

I was relieved to discover her body felt warm to the touch. I sent up a prayer of thanks when I detected the shallow rise and fall of her chest. A heart attack? Stroke? Had the stress of finding a corpse in the cellar finally been too much?

I needed to call for help, but my cell phone was in the car, along with the Tylenol. I knew Melly had a phone mounted on the wall in her kitchen, near the pantry. "Hang on, Melly," I pleaded.

Hugging the wall to steady myself, I worked my way down the hallway toward the kitchen. I snatched the receiver from the cradle and held it to my ear. No dial tone. I tapped the plunger impatiently. "C'mon, c'mon."

Still no sound. The line was dead. Thermostat set to tropical. House darker than Hades. Now no phone. Overkill, I thought. The "kill" part of the word clanged repeatedly through my throbbing brain. Someone was trying to kill Melly.

I turned and half ran, half staggered back the way I'd come. The combination of heat and headache was making me nauseated. "Don't worry, Melly. I'm going to call for help."

I shoved open the front door and practically tumbled onto the porch. Bending forward, hands on my knees, I took in great gulps of cool night air to clear my head. That revived me enough to clumsily sprint to my car. I fever- ishly retrieved my purse and dug through its contents. Im- patient when I couldn't find my cell, I dumped everything on the seat. Finally, phone in hand, I punched in 911.

My knees sagged with relief when Precious Blessing answered. "Honey, please don't tell me you found another body."

"Precious," I gasped, "something bad's happened to Melly. Send an ambulance. I can't remember her address."

I hurried back inside the house as fast as my wobbly legs would carry me. And that was the last thing I remem- bered.

"Mom?" I opened my eyes, and Lindsey's worried face filled my vision. "You're going to be okay, Mom. The doctor said you'll be fine."

"Of course I'm going to be fine, sweetie. Why wouldn't I be?"

"You don't remember?"

"What happened?" I drew in a deep breath of pure ox- ygen piped through a plastic tube in my nose. Gazing around, I found myself in a small curtained-off cubicle. A series of green squiggles and red blips tangoed across a monitor affixed to a wall. A blood pressure cuff was se- cured to one arm. A sensor stuck to my index finger like a clothespin. Fragments of memory began to coalesce. I shoved myself into an upright position. "Melly?"

McBride pushed aside the curtain surrounding the gur- ney I lay on. "Your former mother-in-law is going to be all right, but the doctor wants to keep her overnight for observation."

Comforted at hearing this, I eased back down on the pillow.

McBride turned to Lindsey, who held my hand. "I need to talk to your mom for a couple minutes. I think your boyfriend would like some company, seeing as how most of his friends have gone home."

"Sure." She squeezed my hand, then left.

"Sean's here?" I asked, my thoughts still foggy.

McBride lowered himself on the chair Lindsey had just vacated. He looked a little rough around the edges. His dark hair was disheveled, as though he'd run his fingers through it a time or two. A hint of five o'clock shadow darkened his jaw, but rather than detracting from his rugged appeal, added to it. "The kid suffered a knee injury in the third quarter."

Details of the football game drifted back. The memory of Sean being carted off the field clicked into place. "Is he going to be all right?"

"They'll know more when they get the results of a CT scan." McBride withdrew his ever-present notebook from a shirt pocket. "Tell me everything you remember about your visit to Melly Prescott's."

"Okay." Easier said than done in this case. Why was thinking so difficult? "Since this was her first night home after discovering Chip's body, I drove over to check on her. I saw her car in the drive, but no lights were on inside the house. She didn't answer when I rang the bell or pounded on the door, so I used a key she'd given me years ago."

"And then what?

I frowned, trying to knit the pieces together. "The light switch didn't work—it must've blown a fuse—so I didn't see Melly at first. The heat was turned so high that it gave me a headache, made me dizzy. I lost my balance, fell, and landed on top of Melly. She was unconscious. I tried to call nine-one-one from her landline. When I couldn't get a dial tone, I ran to the car for my cell phone."

"That it?"

"Mm-hmm." I vaguely remembered being carried in a strong pair of arms, but I didn't think he needed to jot that in his little black book. "What's going on? Come on, Mc-Bride, I have a right to know."

"Now, that sounds more like the Piper Prescott I've come to know." He almost smiled before turning serious again. "The doctors are treating you and Melly for carbon monoxide poisoning. They'll know for sure when the lab results come back. Doc put a rush on them."

"Carbon monoxide?" I repeated in disbelief. "That can be deadly. I need to see for myself that Melly's really all right." I tore off the oxygen tube and swung my legs over the edge of the stretcher. Before my feet had a chance to reach the floor, my vision grayed, my ears buzzed.

"Easy now." McBride scooped me up as effortlessly as though I weighed no more than a child and laid me back down. He refitted the cannula in my nose. "Here, take a couple whiffs of oxygen before you try any more heroics."

I wanted to glare at him angrily, but simply didn't have the energy.

McBride stepped away from the gurney. "You done good tonight, Piper. You saved Melly's life. Doc said if you hadn't shown up when you did, she would've died."

"I still don't understand how this happened. What causes carbon monoxide poisoning?"

McBride shrugged. "Faulty central heating systems, hot-water heaters, gas fireplaces, or a blocked chimney flue are common culprits."

"Melly's house is old. She probably hasn't had the heating system checked in years."

"That's a possibility."

Something in his voice signaled a Code Red. "Out with it, McBride. What *aren't* you telling me?"

His expression turned impassive. "We found a note."

"A note?" I felt anxiety bubble inside me. "What kind of note?"

"Until we can rule it out, we're treating the incident as an attempted suicide."

CHAPTER 28

The following morning, I drove around the hospital to a side door marked DISCHARGE AND ADMISSIONS. I waited behind a sedan while an elderly man was wheeled out by a nurse's aide. The woman assisted him out of the chair and gently eased him into the vehicle's passenger seat. After handing over a large bag of personal possessions, she waved him off.

The glass doors slid open, and Melly appeared in a wheelchair. Judging from her sour expression, she wasn't happy. I got out of my car and ran around the hood to open the door.

"I wish everyone would stop treating me like an old lady," Melly fussed. "I'm perfectly capable of walking out of this place on my two feet."

"Sorry, ma'am, hospital policy," answered a beleaguered aide. The instant Melly was safely in my VW, the aide spun the wheelchair around and disappeared back inside.

"What took you so long?" Melly demanded querulously as she readjusted the air vents.

I snapped the buckle of my seat belt. "I got here fast as I could. As it was, I was afraid I'd get a speeding ticket."

"Hmph!" Melly snorted. "I hope I never see the inside of that place again. All this commotion over a faulty furnace. Unbelievable!"

"Carbon monoxide poisoning can be deadly," I commented as I put the car into gear.

"If someone says that to me one more time, I'm going to scream. I've heard that said at least a dozen times since last night. I don't need to hear it from you."

"Yes, ma'am. I got the memo."

Melly shot me a look. "No need to be a smart mouth. I've never been subjected to such a trial in my entire life." She stared out the windshield. "From the way everyone kept watching me, you'd think I was a criminal. Why, I couldn't even go to the bathroom without being followed."

Did she realize her situation was considered an attempted suicide? Had McBride told her about a note he or one of his minions found? Perhaps last night Melly hadn't been in any condition for questioning. I cast a sidelong glance her way. Except for the fact that without makeup she looked pale, and her orderly pageboy suffered a severe case of bed-head, she didn't seem any different after her ordeal.

"Don't bite my head off, Melly, but I need to ask: Are you feeling any aftereffects from last night? Headache, dizziness, confusion?"

"Confusion?" she snapped. "Do I seem confused?"

"No," I admitted. "Irritable, but not confused."

Instead of being insulted, she took that as a compliment of sorts and settled back in her seat. "CJ dropped by the hospital early this morning. He gave me an ultimatum. Until my heating system is thoroughly inspected, I either stay with you or with him—and Amber. I chose your place rather that mausoleum he calls a home."

"Good, it's settled then."

"I refuse to be treated as a child."

I hid a smile. "I'm brave, but not that brave."

Lindsey had manned the register at Spice It Up! while I was away. Upon seeing her grandmother, she rushed over to hug her. "Meemaw, I'm so glad you're okay. You had us so scared."

Casey danced around their feet, apparently echoing Lindsey's sentiments. Or not wanting to be excluded from the lovefest.

Melly stroked Lindsey's long blond hair. "No need to worry about me, dear. I'm a tough old bird."

Lindsey pulled back, satisfied her world had righted itself again, and asked, "Mom, mind if I go visit Sean? He texted. Said he's bored and wants company."

"Go right ahead. Tell him we're sending positive thoughts his way that his injury won't require surgery."

"Will do," she said as she bounded out the door.

I turned to Melly. "Why don't you go upstairs and rest."

"I will right after I call Reba Mae and ask her to squeeze me in. I can't go to the Grangers' party tonight looking a mess. What will people think?"

"They'll think you just survived a terrible experience." I donned the yellow apron that Lindsey had hastily discarded. "You can't be serious about going to the Oktoberfest after everything that's happened?"

"I not only can, but I *will* be at that party. I'm not about to give the gossipmongers in this town any more ammunition. Now," she said, heading toward the stairs, "I think I'll make a phone call and take that nap."

I longed for a nap, too. It had been after one o'clock in the morning before the doctor had signed my discharge papers. Lindsey had stayed the entire time and driven me home. But my siesta would have to wait.

A steady parade of customers passed through the shop. Most dropped by to tell me how happy they were that I suffered no ill effects after my harrowing escape. Others hailed me as a hero for saving Melly's life. Some lowered their voices and confided they were praying Melly would find a way out of the "depths of despair." One, who shall remain anonymous, had the gall to sympathize with Melly's "desire to end her life." The person expounded that no life at all was preferable to one behind bars. Fortunately, Melly was at the beauty shop and wasn't around to overhear the remarks.

My phone rang, and I excused myself from a particularly odious do-gooder. At hearing Doug's voice, my mood lifted considerably.

"I must be living in a vacuum," he said. "I just heard a few minutes ago about what happened. I can't believe Lindsey didn't call me last night. Are you all right?"

"Other than needing a cat nap, I'm fine," I assured him. "How's Melly?"

"She's at the Klassy Kut right now, having her hair done. She's determined to go to the party tonight, come hell or high water."

"Wish I could run over and see for myself that you're all right and not just putting on a brave front. Unfortunately, I can't leave the clinic untended. A Yorkie devoured a slice of chocolate birthday cake. He's recovering, but I need to keep an eye on him."

"Any luck finding a receptionist?"

"Not yet, but I think the situation is about to change. I'll keep you posted, but right now I've got a couple worried dog owners coming up the walk."

"See you tonight."

I'd no sooner disconnected than Dottie Hemmings charged in. "I couldn't believe my eyes!" she said, waving her hands wildly. "Here I was at the Klassy Kut, waitin' on Reba Mae to pick up a can of hair spray, and who waltzes in? Melly Prescott, bless her heart, that's who. Been me after what she's been through, I'da been curled up in bed, the covers pulled over my head."

"Melly's determined to go to Oktoberfest tonight."

"You sure she's up to all the excitement?" Dottie wagged her head. "She's not gettin' any younger."

"Well, far be it from me to break the news." Knowing Dottie wasn't here to shop, I used the temporary lull to re-stock a shelf with small bags of whole nutmegs. Ten seconds of rubbing one against a small-holed grater yielded a half teaspoon of aromatic fresh ground nutmeg, I liked to advise customers.

"Your mother-in-law's a strong-willed woman." Dottie sighed, then brightened. "Wait till you see the costume I made for my husband the mayor to wear at the party."

I didn't bother correcting Dottie about my relationship to Melly—or lack thereof. "Can't wait."

"Wish I could stay and chat, but I have to finish hot-gluing plastic flowers to the suspenders he's wearing with the lederhosen I made out of an old pair of overalls. Let me tell you, Herr Burgomeister will be the talk of the town."

Hizzoner the mayor in lederhosen? Oh my!

I didn't have time, however, to ponder the mental image Dottie had painted. McBride, his expression grim, strode into the shop. If the look on his face wasn't cause for alarm, the object he carried was. I pointed to the evidence bag. "My birthday isn't until February."

His expression lightened fractionally before dimming again. "I'm here to talk to your mother-in-law. She available?"

"I don't know why I have to keep reminding everyone that she's my *ex*-mother-in-law." I tucked a wayward curl behind one ear. "And no, she's not available at the moment, but she should be back any minute if you care to stick around."

"Guess I don't have much choice. I'm afraid I've delayed this interview too long as it is. She wasn't in any shape to be questioned last night. By the time I got to the hospital today, they told me she'd been discharged. I have some questions for you as well."

I gestured toward the rear of the shop. "Step into my office. Have a seat," I said, indicating a stool. While McBride looked on, I took the cookie dough I'd made days ago out of the fridge, unwrapped it, and placed it on the lightly floured surface of my worktable. To be honest, in all the commotion, I'd nearly forgotten about the lebkuchen.

"So that's how it's done," McBride muttered, watching me wield a rolling pin, then cut the dough into small rectangles.

Not looking up, I carefully placed the cookies on a baking sheet. "What did you want to ask?"

He cleared his throat. "Carbon monoxide can cause a hazy memory. I was wondering if you recalled any more details from last night."

"Just what I already told you." I tried not to stare at the evidence bag he'd casually placed nearby, but subtle wasn't part of my repertoire. "Is that the *alleged* suicide note?"

He nodded.

Before I had a chance to question him further, Melly, her hair freshly washed and styled, sailed into the shop. "Mercy!" she said, spotting McBride. "I can't seem to rid myself of Brandywine Creek's finest these days."

"Can't be helped." McBride rose. "I brought something along for you to examine."

"Very well," she said in a martyred tone. "For your information, my son is having the heating system inspected. I'll have the workman send you a copy of the report. I take full responsibility for what happened. I should have better maintained my furnace."

"Yes, ma'am." McBride slid the evidence bag toward her. "Do you recognize this?"

I slid the cookie sheet into the oven and scooted closer.

Melly studied it from several different angles, then handed it back. "It appears to be my notepaper and my handwriting. How do you happen to have it?"

"It was found on the floor of your kitchen last night."

Squinting, I tried to read Melly's spidery cursive through the thick plastic. "What does it say?"

"Two words," McBride said. " 'I'm sorry.' "

"Sorry for what?" I asked.

Melly gave her head an impatient shake. "That could mean any number of things."

"Such as?" McBride hooked his thumbs in his belt.

Melly threw up her hands. "I'm sorry I missed your birthday. I'm sorry I can't attend your garden party. I'm sorry I forgot to water your African violets while you were on vacation. Pick any one of the above."

"In view of what happened last night, there are those who think it might've been a suicide note."

"Rubbish!" Melly flung her purse on the counter. "Why would folks even think such a thing, much less say it out loud? Don't they have better things to do?"

"You know how people love gossip, Melly," I soothed. "Some thrive on drama."

Hands on her hips, Melly addressed McBride. "You can't actually believe I tried to take my own life."

He gave a small shrug. "That was the initial assumption after finding the note you'd written. The theory tossed about was that you were responsible for Chip Balboa's death and couldn't face the guilt—or the penalty."

Melly looked McBride square in the eye. "Seems to me, young man, I've already been tried and found guilty in the court of public opinion. Are you here to arrest me? If so, I'd like to call my attorney."

"I'll be honest with you, Mrs. Prescott. Granted the case against you is circumstantial, but it doesn't look good. However, I still have a few unanswered questions so I'm holding off on making an arrest for the time being."

I heard Melly gasp. Cocking my head, I studied the man with the shiny gold badge pinned to crisp navy blues. McBride was a "damn the torpedoes, full steam ahead" kind of guy. He'd do his sworn duty and worry about the consequences later. "You're leaving something out, McBride—and it isn't because you've developed a sudden fondness for grandmotherly types."

McBride brought out his notebook and flipped it open. "Let's review what happened last night."

When he finished reciting the details I'd recalled in the emergency room, he zapped me with his laser blues. "Did I miss anything?"

Where was this conversation heading? I wondered.

McBride turned to Melly. "I returned to your home, Mrs. Prescott, after leaving the hospital last evening. Just as Piper mentioned, the light switches on the main level weren't functioning. The thermostat on the furnace was jammed. And last but not least, the phone line had been severed."

Melly frowned. "Coincidence?"

"I'm not a big believer in coincidence," McBride admitted. "When I took a good look around, I discovered the fuse box in the basement, as well as the thermostat, appeared to have been tampered with. The phone line leading into the house had been cut."

"Surely, you can't think Melly did all that?" I asked in disbelief.

"No one doubts that your . . . ex- . . . mother-in-law is a very shrewd woman. She's perfectly capable of doing all three of those things. It's also possible the phone line could've been cut accidentally when someone mowed her lawn. It's possible, too, that someone wanted her death to appear a suicide."

Melly's brow furrowed. "But why?"

McBride slipped the notebook into his pocket. "With you out of the picture, Chip Balboa's case would likely come to a dead end and be closed. The real killer would be home free. Until I conclude my investigation, I want you ladies to stay extra vigilant."

His gaze lingered on me a couple of extra beats; then he was gone. Attempted suicide versus attempted murder?

I didn't like the choices.

CHAPTER 29

The Grangers must have invited the entire town to their Oktoberfest celebration. Even at a distance, I could hear the sounds of Zeke Blessing and his blues band performing a down South rendition of oompah music. My mind, though, wasn't on music, parties, or parking spots. It was on persons of interest. Instead of eliminating suspects, I'd gone and added one—Cheryl Balboa—back on my list. What did that say about my sleuthing skills? The answer was simple: not very much. Rather than add, I needed to eliminate. Cheryl, Troy, or Rusty? Where should I start? Cheryl Balboa, that's where. My plan to revisit the no-tell motel last night had been interrupted by a detour to the emergency room, but tonight would work just as well. A quick look-see was all it would take. A visit would either rule her out or keep her on my short list. Child's play, right? And I'd do it before the night was over.

Frustrated at seeing cars line both sides of the road, I heaved a sigh. Finding a parking space, even one small enough to accommodate my Beetle, would be a challenge. I disliked the thought of having to hike half a mile to reach the Grangers not so much for myself, but because I didn't cotton to the notion of Melly venturing over unfamiliar terrain in the dark.

"I'm going to feel as though I'm under a microscope," Melly fretted. "Maybe I should've stayed at your place."

I slowly cruised past a cavalcade of parked SUVs and sedans. "If the evening gets to be too much for you, Melly, we can leave early."

"Folks will either flock around me like carrion or avoid me like a pariah." Melly stared straight ahead. "I can't believe people I've known all my life would even think for a minute I'd try to take my own life."

"Umm . . . that's human nature." I debated the wisdom of trying to squeeze between the front bumper of a Cadillac and the rear bumper of Mercedes but thought better of it. My "squeezing" left a lot to be desired. "Give everyone time, and they'll find something new to gossip about."

"Mmm, I suppose," Melly said, but she sounded doubtful.

"Why don't I drop you at the foot of the drive so you can join the party while I look for a place to park?"

"Fine."

As soon as I slowed to a stop, Joey Tucker, Beau and Jolene's middle boy, ran to greet us. "Hey, Miz Prescott."

"Hey, Joey."

"Mr. Granger hired a bunch of us seniors to be parking valets. Guys got to drive some really cool cars. Carter parked Mr. Wainwright's Porsche. Neatest of all, Randall drove Mr. Bowtin's '67 Corvette Stingray, since he's the only one who knows how to drive a stick shift. How cool is that?"

"Pretty cool." I couldn't help smiling at Joey's unbridled enthusiasm for a classic car. It was good to know that at least one member of the Tucker family didn't bear a grudge for the patriarch's being on probation.

Joey opened the VW's passenger door for Melly, then

hurried around to open mine. "We drew straws to see who got to park the hottest cars. I lost."

"Sorry about that." I reached into the back for the leb-kuchen I'd brought. Joey hopped inside the Beetle and adjusted the seat. "Doc Winters said if I saw you that I should tell you he'd be waiting near the food tent."

Hundreds, maybe thousands, of multicolored lights sparkled among the tree branches. A blue and white banner strung across the drive bade guests *WILLKOMMEN*. Lanterns lit the walkway leading to the outdoor festivities. The throaty blast from a tuba and playful notes of an accordion signaled the party was in full swing.

"Showtime," Melly announced.

Upon seeing us, the crowd parted as if by magic. I stole a glance at Melly. Head held high, she sailed through undaunted, nodding and smiling at friends and acquaintances as though nothing out of the ordinary had transpired. I felt proud of her. Under her sweater sets beat the heart of a steel magnolia.

A large tent had been designated for food. Judging from the tall stacks of dinnerware, the meal would be served buffet style. Long tables covered in white cloths held an assortment of chafing dishes. Several smaller tables were set aside for desserts. A gas grill large enough to roast a cow occupied the far end of an outdoor kitchen Bobby Flay would covet. Pete Barker in a tall chef's hat and wielding tongs guarded a mound of sausages.

"Hey, pretty lady." Doug materialized at my side and snatched the plate of cookies from my hand. Not caring who watched, he kissed me soundly. Self-conscious at the public display of affection, I gently disengaged myself. Melly cleared her throat, but not the least bit repentant, Doug winked at her. I'd overheard people refer to Doug as my "boyfriend." Part of me wrestled with the term. It's probably just me, but "boyfriend" seemed more suited for kids Lindsey's age, not adults over forty. On the other hand, Doug and I saw each other frequently, didn't date others, and enjoyed each other's company. Maybe that did qualify to make us boyfriend and girlfriend. As soon as the situation with Melly was resolved, I promised myself to give more consideration to how our relationship was perceived by others.

Melly rearranged some platters on the dessert table to make room for my cookies. "You young people mingle. I'll be fine once I have a glass of wine."

"Liquid refreshments are over there." Doug pointed toward a tent with a red and white striped awning where people were lined three deep. "They're serving beer along with several German wines, including Riesling."

Melly was quickly swallowed up by the throng. Turning, Doug produced two glasses of wine he'd hidden behind a tiered plate of cookies. His boyishly youthful face wore a worried expression. Brown eyes usually brimming with humor looked anxious. "I'm not about to let you out of my sight for an instant. I don't want to lose you. It scares me to death to think what almost happened last night."

I summoned a smile. "Then let's not think about it."

"All right," he said, taking my hand. "Did I tell you that you look particularly fetching in that getup?"

"Women never tire of compliments." I dropped a curtsy. I'd resurrected a costume I worn ages ago to a Halloween party—a peasant blouse and red dirndl skirt cinched at the waist with a corset that laced. From what I'd seen so far, the dress code varied from pseudo-Bavarian to country club casual.

Hand in hand, we followed Melly's suggestion and began to mingle. We hadn't progressed far when we met CJ and Amber. CJ and I stared at each other for a protracted moment, then burst out laughing.

"You must be Gretel." CJ grinned.

I grinned back. "And you must be Hansel." CJ must have remembered that long-ago party as well, for he was in lederhosen—worn a little lower than the last time to allow for an expanding waistline—and a natty alpine hat set at a jaunty angle.

"Hansel and Gretel," Amber drawled. "My, my, don't y'all make a cute couple."

I eyed Amber's short, short skirt and low, low neckline. A wide girdle was laced so tightly that two grapefruit-sized medical enhancements threatened to spill over the bodice of her peasant blouse. Thigh-high white stockings were tied with black grosgrain ribbons. "And you must be Gretchen," I said, "the sexy beer girl."

Amber twirled a pigtail around an index finger. "Aren't you supposed to be babysittin' Melly?"

"Melly doesn't need a sitter," I said stiffly.

"Amber's fixin' to come over one day soon. Take Momma out to lunch. Maybe visit the mall for some retail therapy."

Amber rested her head on CJ's shoulder and smirked. "Like I told Pooh Bear, I think it best to wait a bit. Make sure his mother's . . . more stable."

"Melly Prescott happens to be one of the most 'stable' people I know," I snapped. "Present company included."

Sensing fireworks, Doug tugged my hand. "I just spotted our host and hostess. Why don't we say hello."

Murmuring insincere excuses, we made our escape. Sandy and Craig Granger held center court on the patio near the pool. Both wore traditional German attire. In addition to a dirndl skirt and peasant blouse, Sandy wore a wreath of fresh flowers in her hair with ribbon streamers. Craig's lederhosen were genuine suede and not the Halloween costume shop variety. He'd tucked a red feather into the band of a forest green alpine hat. He held a hefty-looking beer stein adorned with an elaborate hunting motif.

Sandy greeted me with a hug. "I'm so glad you're here. After hearing what happened last night, I was afraid you wouldn't come."

Craig pumped Doug's hand. "Carbon monoxide can be deadly, you know. We had detectors installed when we built our house."

"Even so, we have a company inspect our heating and cooling system every year. Craig insists one can't be too careful." Sandy beamed at her husband and patted his arm.

Craig beamed back. "Thompson told me his hardware store sold every carbon monoxide detector in stock. He has to reorder."

Beyond weary of carbon monoxide talk, I changed the subject. "Reba Mae said rehearsals are going to start soon for *Steel Magnolias*."

"I have a terrific cast," Sandy gushed. "I plan to do a ton of advertising. I'll settle for nothing less than a sellout crowd at every performance."

"All it takes is some expert marketing," Craig said in his smooth-as-a-radio-announcer voice.

Doug smiled. "Ever since moving to Brandywine Creek, I've been fascinated by the local history. There's even a Civil War battle site not far from here."

I sipped my Riesling. "Don't forget the mystery of the lost Confederate gold."

"What lost Confederate gold?" Doug asked, his interest piqued.

"Oh, that." Craig laughed. "The last recorded location of gold belonging to the Confederate army is supposedly buried somewhere in the vicinity. Legend has it that it was hidden to await the day the South will rise again."

"Others believe soldiers hid it to keep the Union forces from gaining possession," Sandy explained. "People have been searching for it for years, but without success."

"Ha!" Craig laughed again. "Personally, I think it's a hoax, but you can't convince people."

"How much money are we talking about?" Doug asked.

"In today's dollars, it would be worth a small fortune. We're talking at least a million bucks."

Doug let out a low whistle. "No wonder people keep looking."

Sandy waved at someone behind us. "Speaking of gold."

Curious, I cast a look over my shoulder as Cheryl and Troy, wineglasses in hand, wandered in our direction. Bronzed tans, sun-streaked hair, the two Californians did indeed appear golden.

"An amazing couple," Craig commented, sipping his beer. "Sophisticated, poised, well traveled."

Sandy motioned them over. "Amber introduced us. She thought we might want to get in on the ground floor in a chain of cutting-edge fitness clubs her friend Troy is opening."

"Cheryl!" Sandy greeted the woman effusively. The women exchanged air kisses while Craig slapped Troy's back. "Have you met Piper and her friend Dr. Doug Winters?"

Cheryl's eyes shot angry sparks at me. "You!"

Wary of getting singed, I took an involuntary step backwards.

"Don't pull that wide-eyed innocent act on me." She aimed a fingernail shellacked bloodred at my chest. "You're the reason I was dragged down to the police station and questioned like a common criminal. You're the reason why my phone records were subpoenaed."

Sandy turned on me. "Piper!" she scolded. "What were you thinking? Isn't it bad enough Cheryl just lost her husband without you causing her more heartache?"

Unfortunately, Zeke Blessing and his blues/oompah band picked that precise moment to take a break. I cast a furtive glance around to find everyone avidly eavesdropping. Matt Wainwright, CJ's law partner, and his wife, Mary Beth, had ceased conversing with Dennis and Bunny Bowtin. If Dottie Hemmings gawked any harder, she'd be in a neck brace. My cheeks burned with embarrassment.

"C'mon," Doug urged quietly.

"I detest Riesling," I heard Cheryl say as Doug led me away. "Is this the only white wine you're serving?"

"I have a chilled bottle of Chardonnay in my wine cellar that you might find more to your liking," Craig said smoothly.

Sandy looped her arm through Cheryl's. "Did you know Chardonnay originated in the Burgundy region of France?"

"Well, that was fun—not," I said once we were out of earshot.

Sweeping my gaze over the knots of people conversing, I observed Thompson Gray having an earnest discussion with Rusty Tulley. Thompson seemed intense while Rusty, on the other hand, appeared angry. As I watched, Rusty stalked off, leaving Thompson standing alone, nursing a beer.

"Wonder what that was all about?" Doug muttered.

"One way to find out." I nudged Doug in Thompson's direction. "Hey, Thompson, everything okay?"

A myriad of emotions flickered across his bland features. Irritation. Anger. Impatience. "Tulley refused some friendly advice from a lowly hardware store owner."

"Don't let him ruin your evening," Doug counseled.

"Yeah, you're probably right. I just hate to see stupid decisions ruin an otherwise fine company." Thompson ran a hand over thinning mouse-brown hair. "Think I'll get another beer and not let it get to me."

Sipping my wine, I scanned the crowd. Rusty Tulley, Cheryl Balboa. Troy Farnsworth. They were all gathered here tonight. Any one of the three could be responsible for

Chip's death. But which one? Too many suspects. Too little time.

Doug held up his empty wineglass. "Thompson isn't the only one who could use a refill. How about you?"

Out of the corner of my eye, I saw Rusty disappear into the house through a side door and decided to follow him. Time for us to get better acquainted. "I need to use the little girls' room," I improvised. "I'll meet you at the beer tent."

Doug nodded. "Fine, but if you're not back soon, I'm coming to look for you."

As luck would have it, there was no sign of Rusty when I stepped inside the house. There were plenty of women, however, all of them lined up outside the powder room. "There's another bathroom off a guest room down the hall," Gerilee Barker whispered as she passed me.

I reversed direction, hoping I'd find Rusty. Opening a closed door at the end of a long hallway, I found myself in a pink and purple room suitable for a Disney princess. Probably in readiness for a visit from the Grangers' young granddaughters. I heard the sound of voices approaching and ducked into the adjoining bathroom, but kept the door open a crack.

"You have some nerve parading around on the arm of Surfer Boy," I heard Rusty complain.

"Jealous?"

I recognized the woman's voice—Cheryl Balboa.

"Jealous?" Rusty retorted. "I've moved on."

"So I've heard," Cheryl sneered. "Tell me, Rusty, as one ex-lover to another, you must be overjoyed Chip's dead. You've wanted him to step down from Trustychipdesign for months."

Rusty and Cheryl? Ex-lovers?

"Don't act so righteous, darling," Rusty continued. "I'm not the only one who stood to benefit from Chip's death."

Suddenly, the bedroom door crashed open. I caught a

glimpse of a glamorous young woman with inky-black hair and milk-white skin. "So there you are!" the new-comer screeched.

"Tulip!" Rusty gasped. "What are you doing here? How did you find me?"

"I might've known I'd find you two scheming." Tulip Whatshername gave Rusty an unladylike shove, causing him to step backwards. "I thought with that idiot partner of yours out of the picture, you'd forget about his wife and focus on me."

Uh-oh. It seemed like the list of people who wanted Chip dead was growing, not shrinking. I'd thought it before; I thought it again. Too many suspects, too little time.

CHAPTER 30

"Red, white, or beer?" Ned Feeney asked from behind the bar. Except for a neat gauze bandage visible below the visor of his ball cap, he looked as fit as ever after his confrontation with a garbage disposal.

"White," I answered.

Doug, who had been waiting patiently, gave me a quizzical look. "What took so long? I was beginning to worry."

"A long line for the ladies' room." I took a gulp of wine from the glass Ned had handed me. I'd made my escape from the Grangers' guest bedroom the instant the trio left. Cheryl had stalked off after accusing Rusty of being a player. Tulip had twined herself around the guy like kudzu around a tree limb and reminded him of how good they were together. Fortunately, Vicki Lamont wandered into the guest room just then in search of a restroom and broke up the fond reunion. I mumbled some inane comment to Vicki as I scurried behind the pair to rejoin the party.

"Sure you're all right?" Doug asked.

"Just peachy." I summoned a smile for his benefit while my mind struggled to process the information I'd stumbled upon. Rusty and Cheryl had been lovers. That had come as a shocker. Did that give Rusty even more reason to want Chip out of the picture? And who was this Tulip person? According to the snippet of conversation I'd overheard, she assumed that with Chip dead, Rusty would lavish more attention on her.

Taking advantage of a momentary lull, Ned shoved up the bill of his cap. "Whole town's talkin' about how you and Miz Melly nearly bought the farm. I think that house of hers must be jinxed. First that computer fellow falls down the stairs and breaks his fool neck. Now this. Maybe she needs to call one of those extortionist guys."

Doug swallowed a chuckle. "I think you mean exorcist, not extortionist."

Ned shrugged. "Whatever. Her place has some bad juju. While you're at it, Miz Piper, you might want to ask the exhibitionist to do one of those powwows in your kitchen. That garbage disposal of yours durn near killed me."

"I'll take that under advisement," I told him.

"Say," Doug said, motioning toward where Melly stood conversing with a distinguished-looking gentleman. "Who's the old codger in the seersucker suit?"

"Judge Cottrell Herman—Cot to his cronies. He's been on the bench for as long as I can remember." Though we'd never been formally introduced, the man in question was a familiar figure in and around Brandywine Creek. He was far from handsome, craggy features forming an arresting combination with deep-set dark eyes and a hawklike nose above a bristly mustache. "Recently he's been Melly's bridge partner."

"From the way he's hanging on Melly's every word, my guess is he's interested in more than bridge."

Craig Granger reappeared on the terrace and announced dinner would be served. Guests formed a queue that snaked along the patio, ending at the food tent. Tables groaned beneath the weight of every German specialty imaginable.

Sauerkraut, German potato salad, potato dumplings, spat-
zle, red cabbage, schnitzel, along with pork in Madeira
sauce and a vast assortment of sausages and breads.

Doug balanced a bratwurst on a mound of red cabbage.
"I only wish I had a plate big enough to match my appetite."

We found an unoccupied table on the lawn somewhat
apart from the main flow and sat down. "Want company?"
Reba Mae asked as she approached.

I looked up and smiled. "Hey, there. Where've you been
hiding?" My friend had dressed for the occasion in a dark
green skirt gathered at the waist and an embroidered peasant blouse, a costume equally suitable for an Oktoberfest
or a Mexican fiesta.

Reba Mae set her plate down and scooted into the seat
next to me. "While you've been sippin' wine, I've been gettin' the straight skinny on that party crasher over yonder."

I turned my head to look. "Her name is Tulip. She's a
friend of Rusty Tulley's."

"From the way she's all over him, I gather she's a friend
with benefits." Reba Mae buttered a slice of pumpernickel.
"Her full name is Tulip Jackson."

"Should that ring a bell?"

Reba Mae rolled her eyes at my apparent ignorance.
"Tulip is the wild child of the family. Spoiled rotten since
birth. Her father is Jax Jackson."

"Jax?" Doug stopped cutting a knockwurst mid-slice.
"*The* Jax Jackson?"

Even I, who seldom ventured onto the information su-
perhighway, knew Jax Jackson was a former rock star
turned music producer. He was reputed to be one of the
most influential—and wealthiest—moguls in Hollywood.
I studied the young woman more closely. Lots of smoky
eye makeup, lots of bright red lipstick, black leather mi-
cromini, and five-inch stilettos, the woman certainly knew
how to maximize her assets.

Reba Mae sampled Doug's sauerbraten. "Tulip happens to be the youngest of Jax's three daughters. His other girls are Daisy and Marigold."

Now it was my turn to roll my eyes. "How do you know all this?"

"Hmph!" she sniffed. "I read *Entertainment Weekly. People. Us Weekly.* I like to keep up on what's goin' on in the world."

Conversation eventually veered away from Tulip and reverted to talk of food and Brandywine Creek's hopes for a football championship. No sooner had the plates been cleared than Zeke Blessing, his round face split in a wide grin, announced, "Time for y'all to kick up your heels. Do a little dancin'. Work off that fine dinner."

At the fast-paced notes of "The Clarinet Polka," Reba Mae jumped to her feet and grabbed Doug by the hand. "Don't mind if I borrow your date, do you, Piper? I want to see if the man can polka as well as he can shag."

Doug half rose, obviously up for the challenge. "Sure you don't mind, Piper?"

"Have at it," I told him, and sat back to enjoy the show. Seconds later, Doug and Reba Mae joined the dancers bouncing about as Zeke put them through their paces.

"Mind if I join you?"

I looked up to find McBride standing beside me. "No, of course not."

McBride lowered himself into the chair Reba Mae had vacated. Dressed head to foot in black, he could have passed for the leading man in a James Bond movie. I began to notice small details: the tiny scar that bisected one brow, the electric blue of his eyes, the small nick on his jaw where he'd cut himself shaving.

Clearing my throat, I tried to steer my thoughts to more pressing matters—such as finding Chip's killer before Melly landed behind bars. I leaned closer. "You won't believe what I just learned." I hurried on, not waiting for an answer. "Cheryl Balboa and Rusty Tulley were lovers."

"That so?"

I stared at him, disappointed by his lack of response. As usual, his expression was schooled, making it impossible to know what was going on inside that head of his. It would be easier figuring out why Mona Lisa smiled. "Is that all you're going to say?"

McBride kept his gaze fastened on the dance floor. "I came to the same conclusion after reviewing Mrs. Balboa's phone records. The number of calls between her and Tulley raised a red flag. There were far too many for a casual acquaintance."

Before I could conjure a suitable reply, McBride's cell phone shrilled. After listening intently, he climbed to his feet. "Sorry, duty calls."

McBride wasn't the only one to whom duty called. Time had come for me to get busy as well. With everyone in town here at the party, it was now or never to check out the Beaver Dam Motel.

"Psst," I buzzed in Reba Mae's ear the first chance I got.

"What's up, honeybun?"

"We need to take a little ride and check something out."

"Jeez Louise, can't it wait?" she whined. "I been eyein' that Black Forest torte ever since I got here."

"We'll be back in a jiffy. I'll drive."

I gave Doug a lame excuse about a raging headache and needing to rest a bit and told him not to worry. Luckily, Doug, the darling of pet owners, was surrounded by a host of adoring fans. Before he could question me further, he was commandeered by Ruby Phillips, who clutched his arm and started chattering about Mugsy, her Pekingese.

My bright green VW stood out like a beacon amid the

ocean of dark sedans and SUVs. Fortunately, Joey Tucker had left the keys inside.

"Why the cloak-and-dagger?" Reba Mae protested as we left the Oktoberfest behind.

"We need to check the Beaver Dam Motel for rear exits. If they have them, Cheryl could easily have sneaked out a back door and pushed Chip down the stairs while Danny Boyd was out front, providing her alibi. All we need to do is take a quick look, then back to the dessert table."

"If it's so freakin' simple, why do you need me ridin' shotgun?"

"Because," I sighed, "it's safer this way. Don't forget there's a killer on the prowl."

Less than ten minutes later, we pulled into the motel's parking lot. I noticed a total of four cars parked in front of various rooms. I switched off the engine, turned off the headlights, and climbed out of the car. "Let's circle the building."

Reba Mae followed close on my heels. "Don't suppose you thought to bring a flashlight."

Leave it to my friend to find the glaring flaw in my plan. "There's enough moonlight. We'll be okay without one."

In the flickering of the motel's neon sign, Reba Mae's expression looked dubious. "If you say so."

I hurried down the side of the building, rounded the corner, then came to an abrupt stop. Reba Mae plowed into me. Knee-high weeds choked the narrow strip of property that bordered the rear of the motel and tapered into a dense woods.

"Eww!" Reba Mae gasped. "Think there are snakes back here? I hate snakes."

"Remember the old saying, black on yellow kill a fellow, and you'll be fine." Using my outstretched hand to guide me along the worn brick wall, I waded through the tall grass.

Reba Mae inched behind me. "It's too dark to see colors on a snake. What if I get bit?"

"Don't worry, I'll rush you to the ER."

"Thanks," she grumbled. "I'll do the same for you."

I stopped and swept my gaze across the back of the motel. Not a single rear exit in any of the guest rooms. So much for my theory. I was about to admit defeat when a thought occurred to me. Although they didn't have a door, each room had a window—probably a bathroom window—that faced the woods. Ones that to my mind looked large enough for a person to wriggle through.

"Reba Mae"—I turned with a grin—"you and I are about to embark on a scientific experiment."

"I hate when you use that tone of voice. It usually spells nothin' but trouble."

"Follow me," I said.

I entered the motel office while Reba Mae elected to wait outside. "I'd like a room," I announced.

The desk clerk, a stoop-shouldered man with frayed gray strands of hair valiantly trying to camouflage a bald spot, barely glanced up. In a bored voice, he stated the price and slid an old-fashioned plastic key ring across the counter.

I marched down the concrete walkway to room 127, two doors away from the one Cheryl and Troy had occupied, threw open the door, and switched on the light.

Reba Mae wrinkled her nose in disgust. "What a dump!"

I couldn't disagree. The room exuded a musty odor not even disinfectant sprays could dispel. The furnishings consisted of faux walnut bed and dresser, dingy shag carpeting soiled in places, and faded gold-colored spread and drapes. "No wonder Cheryl bailed in favor of the Turner-Driscoll House."

"Can we go now?" Reba Mae asked plaintively.

"Five minutes, tops. Soon as you climb out the bathroom window."

"Me? Why can't you be the one doin' the climbin'?"

"Because I'm smaller than Cheryl, but you're about the same size. If you can fit through, so could she. You don't want Melly arrested while Cheryl gets off scot-free, do you?" I added when she looked about to refuse.

"Orange is the new black, you know," she informed me.

The bathroom possessed the essentials: commode, sink, and a chipped porcelain tub. Just as I thought, the window was located over the tub, covered by a thin curtain on a metal rod.

"If this isn't the dumbest idea ever." Reba Mae wagged her head but gamely stepped into the tub and shoved the curtain aside. "There's a screen. What do I do now?"

"Slide those two little doohickeys out of the way, and the screen should pop out."

It did, falling into the tub with a loud clatter. Reba Mae and I froze. Ears peeled, we strained to listen. I released a sigh of relief when I didn't hear any sounds to indicate someone else had heard the crash and was coming to investigate.

"Okay," I said in a stage whisper. "Let's get this over and done with."

Reba Mae muttered something unintelligible under her breath as she cranked open the window. A welcome blast of cool night air burst into the room. "Good thing I took gymnastics as a kid."

I watched as she levered one foot sideways against the rim of the tub, braced both hands on the sill, and heaved herself up. In a flash, she disappeared out the window—at least the top half of her body did. She wiggled her hips, once, twice, but nothing happened.

"Stop it, Reba Mae," I scolded. "Quit clowning around."

"I'm not cuttin' up!" she yelled back. "I'm stuck!"

"Hush! Let me help." I climbed into the tub, grasped her thighs, and shoved.

Nothing budged.

"So help me, Piper Prescott, if you don't get me out of here this instant, I'm gonna scream bloody murder."

"Shh, Reba Mae! I'm coming outside to yank on your arms."

I scrambled out of the tub, across the room, and out the door. A man's face peered through a slit in the drapes of the adjoining room as I raced past. Reba Mae dangled half in, half out a partially open window from a room midway down the back of the motel. Now that I was outside, I could see the problem. The window was the crank kind, the sort that opened from the bottom outward.

"Good news, Reba Mae," I said to my red-faced BFF, who looked angry enough to spit nails. "It's not you, it's the window that's stuck."

Reba Mae pounded on the brick with both fists. "Get me out of here. Now!"

"Stay put," I told her, as if she had a choice in the matter.

I ran back inside, placed a chair in the bathtub and, standing on tiptoe, gave the window frame a solid whack with the palm of my hand. It might have been wishful thinking on my part, but I thought it budged just a fraction. Taking that as an omen, I whacked it again. The metal frame screeched in protest, but the window shifted slightly.

"Okay, hang in there. I'll have you out in a jiff."

I sprinted outside and around the building. "Give me both of your hands. I'm going to count to three."

Reba Mae complied. "I swear to God, Piper, if I live through this, I'm gonna be a new woman. I'm goin' on a diet, quit colorin' my hair, and givin' up pizza."

"Don't go making promises you know you won't keep." I tightened my grip, planted one foot against the brick, and tugged as hard as I could. Reba Mae popped out like a shot from a cannon. Her time in gymnastics stood her in good stead as she executed a neat tuck and roll. My tumble wasn't nearly so graceful. I landed with a *plop* on my bottom, my skirt rucked up to my waist.

"Freeze!" a voice commanded.

I shielded my eyes from the blinding glare of a flashlight aimed in my face.

"What the——?"

Reba Mae was the first to recover her wits. "Hey, Wyatt, that you?"

"Might've known." McBride lowered the powerful Maglite in his hand and reholstered his weapon. "You two have some explaining to do."

I shoved my skirt down and scrambled to my feet. Hovering behind McBride, I recognized the desk clerk as well as the occupant from the next room. Summoning a weak smile, I asked, "Suppose it's too late for dessert?"

CHAPTER *31*

In a frenzy born of frustration, I cleaned and scrubbed until not even a marine drill sergeant could have found fault. The floor was spotless; the counters gleamed. My freshly laundered clothes smelled like a bouquet of spring flowers. And I'd consumed enough coffee to rival rush hour at Starbucks. I still smarted from the dressing-down McBride had given me the previous night. A dressing-down so acerbic, not even a thick slice of Black Forest torte could sweeten it. Granted, in hindsight, having Reba Mae attempt to climb out a motel window to prove a point seemed rather . . . silly. Yet, at least in my mind, it had eliminated Cheryl Balboa for once and for all as a possible suspect. McBride's lecture, on the other hand, had had the opposite effect he intended. It left me more determined than ever to discover the truth. I needed to prove to him I wasn't a complete moron.

I plunked myself on the sofa and grabbed a magazine. The apartment was much too quiet. Lindsey had deserted me in favor of hanging out with her friends. Melly had accepted CJ's spur-of-the-moment invitation to brunch at a new restaurant in Augusta. I flipped through the glossy ads without really seeing them. I sensed a trap about to spring shut on Melly's freedom. I could almost hear the hinges squeak.

Tossing the magazine aside, I snatched the television remote and idly scrolled through the channels. Time had come to move on to the next person of interest on my checklist. Rusty Tulley's name was on the top. Rusty wanted Chip out of the picture for reasons both personal and professional. I wasn't nearly so satisfied as McBride was with Rusty's alibi. The men had argued. Rusty wanted Chip to resign. And killing him would be a resignation of the permanent variety. Supposedly, Rusty had been alone in his room. But when it came to alibis, home alone was a tough one to prove.

I clicked off the remote. "C'mon, Casey. Let's go for a ride."

Once again, I found Rusty Tulley comfortably sprawled in a rocker on Felicity's front porch. A squishy tobacco-brown leather courier bag rested on the floor at his feet. At my approach, he looked up from his laptop. "If you're here for Felicity, she just left for the country club. A friend of hers is playing in a tennis tournament."

"That's all right," I said, taking a seat in the adjacent rocker. Casey sat, too, rested his head on his paws, and looked out toward the street. "You're really the one I wanted to talk to."

"About what?"

I peered over my shoulder. "Where's your friend? Tulip, right?"

"Napping. She complained she had jet lag."

A gentle push of my toe started the chair rocking. "Planning on heading out soon?"

Rusty flipped his laptop closed. "Another day or two. I'm thinking of attending a trade show in Orlando, then flying back to L.A. Why the interest?"

"I was just curious as to why you were still in Brandy-wine Creek now that Chip is . . . no longer with us."

He drummed his fingers on the arm of the chair. "I thought you knew. Chief McBride 'requested' some of us to stick around until he has a suspect in custody. Meanwhile, I discovered that without all the distractions of L.A., I can get a lot more work accomplished."

I gazed out over the manicured yard with its meticulously groomed shrubs. A bright green gecko darted across the walk and disappeared under a loropetalum bush. I rocked back and forth. "Certain people might leap to the conclusion you had a lot to gain from the death of your partner."

Rusty's affable pose vanished in the blink of an eye. "What are you hinting at?"

Casey's ears pricked up at Rusty's sharp tone. Reaching down, I stroked my pet's head to reassure him. "You and Chip had a bitter disagreement the night he died. From all accounts, Trustychipdesign was floundering. In your opinion, Chip was too preoccupied with marital woes to give the company the attention it deserved. To make matters worse, he messed up the deal with Melly by reneging on the initial offer."

As Rusty lunged to his feet, I noted the top button of his polo shirt dangled by a thread, but didn't think this was the time to mention it. In his haste to stuff the laptop into his courier bag, the contents of one of its pockets spilled. Highlighter, Montblanc pen, iPhone charger—and a small bottle of Visine.

"Eyedrops," I gasped. "You use eyedrops?"

"What of it? Lots of people do." He stuffed the items back into the bag and closed the flap.

"Did you know eyedrops contain a chemical called tetrahydrolozine?" I asked, my heart beginning to beat faster. I was suddenly aware that except for my mutt-of-

dubious-breeds, no one else was around. The street was
as quiet as a church on Monday morning. A wiser person
would've turned tail and run. Instead, I soldiered on.
"Tetrahydrolozine can cause symptoms such as blurred
vision, headaches, and dizziness. It can kill."

"I don't ingest the damn things," he snapped. "I have
allergies."

I rose to my feet and edged toward the steps. "The lab
found tetrahydrolozine in Chip's stomach contents."

"You need to go. Now!"

Casey growled deep in his throat.

"C'mon, Casey." I tapped my thigh, a signal for him to
follow. "We know when we're not wanted."

I felt proud of myself for sedately driving away when I
wanted to burn rubber. My encounter with Rusty Tulley
had revealed a nasty temper beneath the charm. Had Chip's
behavior provoked Rusty until he lashed out? The men had
known each other since college; they knew which buttons
to push. It wasn't inconceivable to think Rusty had killed
Chip.

On autopilot, I cruised out of town and turned onto
Route 78. I needed a sounding board. Doug immediately
came to mind. He was a terrific listener. He had a way
about him that made you feel every word you spoke was
important. He'd listen to me politely, but I already knew
what he'd say: Step away from the crime. Then he'd lecture me on the dangers involved. Problem was, I wasn't in
any mood for another lecture. Doug would conclude by reminding me that finding Chip's killer wasn't my job. And
he was 100 percent correct; it wasn't.

But I knew whose job it was.

Since I was more than halfway there, I decided to take
a chance and see if McBride also had the day off and might
be home. Minutes later I pulled into his drive. I immediately spotted his pickup, but there was no sign of the man

himself. My knock at the door went unanswered. I sat on the porch steps prepared to wait him out while Casey romped through grass in need of mowing. Resting my elbows behind me on the top step, I closed my eyes and tipped my head back to feel the warm kiss of the sun on my face. Birdsong filled the air, interspersed with a rustling sound as Casey scampered through a carpet of oak leaves. I felt a heavy lethargy starting to overtake me when the spell was broken by Casey's excited barks.

My eyes popped open to see McBride emerge from the woods that surrounded his property. He held a fishing rod but nary a fish. In a denim shirt that flapped open over a grungy T-shirt and faded jeans, he could have posed for an ad in *Outdoor Life*. *Sign me up, sister, for a five-year subscription.*

"Looks like you scared the fish, McBride."

"Saves me the trouble of throwing them back." He climbed the steps and propped the pole in a corner of the porch. "What's the occasion?"

"What makes you think there's an occasion? Maybe I just wanted to see how the handyman special was coming along."

"Work's at a temporary standstill." He shoved a shock of black hair from his forehead. He was wearing it a bit longer than the military-style cut he'd favored when he first came to town. "Clay tells me I need to make some hard decisions right quick if I want to have a kitchen before cold weather sets in."

"What seems to be the holdup?"

"In a nutshell?" he asked with a rueful grin. "Blame it on a pretty redhead who keeps finding dead bodies, and a grumpy old mayor demanding the poor, befuddled police chief find the culprit."

"Ohh . . ."

He seemed to find my woefully inadequate response

amusing. "I know you don't care for beer, but if I look real hard, I might find a Diet Coke hiding at the back of the fridge."

"Sure," I said. "Sounds good."

He left only to return minutes later with a diet soda in one hand, a beer in the other. Sinking down next to me on the porch step, he took a long pull from a frosty, long-necked bottle.

I pulled the tab on my Diet Coke and drank. "You don't look like the type to keep diet soda on hand. So what's the deal? Afraid of losing your figure?"

"One can't be too careful." He took another swallow of beer, then slanted me a look. "Okay, now tell me what you're doing on my doorstep."

I looked out across the yard to a stand of sweet gums that were turning bright gold. Shadows were starting to lengthen as dusk crept in. "I want to use you as my sounding board."

"Use away."

"I'm afraid you're about to charge Melly with the murder of Chip Balboa. True or false?"

"True." Casey bounded up the steps, and McBride absently scratched the sweet spot behind the pup's ears. "Someone's responsible for Chip Balboa's death. The man deserves justice. Gotta go where the trail leads."

"But what if you're following the wrong trail?"

"What other trail is there?"

"Are you aware Rusty and Chip argued the night Chip died? Do you know that their software company is in jeopardy? Rusty blamed Chip for the trouble. He even asked for Chip's resignation."

McBride zapped me with a look from his cool blues. "How do you know all this?"

I resisted the urge to squirm and took a swallow of diet soda instead. "Felicity let it slip about the argument. I had

Melly research Trustychipdesign.com. She confirmed the company is losing market share. Rusty didn't deny it when I asked him. And he doesn't have an alibi for the night Chip died. He insists he was alone in his room the entire time but can't prove it. But that's not the best part—"

"I'm afraid to ask." McBride's grip on the beer bottle tightened.

I tucked a curl behind one ear. "Rusty uses the same brand eyedrops you confiscated from Melly's house. I saw them when they fell out of the courier bag where he keeps his laptop. Rusty was furious when I asked about them. He ordered me to leave."

"That all?" he asked, his voice taut.

"Don't you see how simple it would've been for Rusty to sneak down the servants' stairs, kill Chip, and return without Felicity knowing? A perfect slam dunk."

"Here all this time, I thought you were dead set on Cheryl Balboa and Troy Farnsworth being the perps."

"I eliminated Cheryl, but Troy's still a possibility," I said in defense of my original theory. "I'm pretty sure he uses eyedrops, too."

McBride peeled the label from his beer bottle with a thumbnail. "I ran a background check on Troy Farnsworth and got a hit. Farnsworth was arrested for bilking an older woman out of her life savings, but the charges were dropped."

I nodded thoughtfully. "I can see that happening. Troy's good looking, probably a smooth talker, when the mood strikes, who could ingratiate his way into a woman's bank account."

"How many times do I have to remind you this is a murder investigation, not a frivolous party game?" McBride's tone was even harsher than last night, his eyes colder. "The stakes here are life and death. Killing comes easier the second time around. If you get too close for comfort, you could be next. Stop meddling!"

I rose to my feet, chilled by his words, and left without so much as a backward glance. I knew McBride meant well, but I couldn't stand idle while someone I cared for was about to be sent to prison.

It wasn't until I was almost home that I recalled my conversation with Danny Boyd at Friday night's football game. Danny had denied seeing a BMW in the motel's lot the night Chip died. Where had Troy been? Was it far-fetched to think a man who had possibly cheated a gullible woman out of her savings would be averse to shoving a man down a flight of basement stairs? Rusty Tulley. Troy Farnsworth. Both men stood to profit from Chip's death—and both used eyedrops.

Let the next elimination round begin.

CHAPTER *32*

When I returned from McBride's place, I found a note from Melly anchored to the kitchen table with a pepper mill. Apparently, Mavis Gray had invited her for a light supper and then to play bridge. Ever so thoughtful, she instructed me not to wait up. It wasn't exactly like she was a teenager with a curfew. Next, she'd want me to "friend" her on Facebook. A glance at the clock told me Lindsey wasn't due home for another hour.

Adrenaline still fizzed through my veins. Even though it was dark outside, it wasn't late. There was still time for a quick jog. I changed out of my jeans and into an old pair of sweatpants, a hoodie, and my sporty running shoes. After chasing squirrels all around McBride's yard, Casey didn't seem eager to join me, so I let him snooze.

After a brisk walk to warm up my muscles, I broke into a slow, steady gait. I opted in favor of a residential route and turned down Jefferson Street. Fall wreaths adorned the front doors of many homes that I jogged past. Cheery yellow and orange mums had replaced plantings of petunias and impatiens. Soon lawns would begin to sprout Halloween decorations.

My feet seemed to slow of their own volition as I neared Melly's home, which I had come to view as the "scene of the crime." I stopped and studied the house. Déjà vu all over again. Nothing had changed from several nights ago, when I'd discovered Melly unconscious in her living room. *I'm not a believer in coincidence.* McBride's mantra came back to haunt me. For once, we were in total agreement. The blown fuses, faulty heating system, and cut phone line had been intentional, not coincidental. A deliberate attempt on Melly's life.

I gnawed my lower lip in indecision. A survey of the street assured me the neighbors were hunkered down in front of their television sets for the evening. Before I could talk myself out of it, I hurried around to the back of the house. I tried the rear door but found it locked. I fervently wished I had the key ring with me that held Melly's house key. Not wanting to jingle while I jogged, I'd opted to carry only the key for the rear door of Spice It Up!

Not ready to concede defeat, I struggled to recall where Melly kept a spare key hidden. A flower pot? A ceramic frog? A plastic rock manufactured to look real? Then the answer came to me. I lifted a small panel on a decorative birdhouse next to the walkway and—presto!—felt the cool metal.

I let myself into the kitchen and flicked on the light, grateful someone—McBride, perhaps?—had thought to replace the fuse. Everything looked neat and tidy. Blue and white place mats rested on a pine table. Except for a glass canister set and a stoneware crock filled with kitchen utensils, the counters were clutter-free. The *ticktock* of a distant clock sounded overly loud in the otherwise still house.

The closed basement door called my name. Nothing I hated more than movies where a girl without a lick of common sense and too stupid to live creeps down creaking stairs while the audience screams a warning. And here I was, a grown woman too stupid to live.

Movies were movies, I reminded myself. This was Melly's home—not a soundstage. There were no evil monsters—or serial killers—about to hack me into tiny pieces with an ax. Five minutes. In and out. That's all it would take. One fast look, then I was out of there.

Feeling marginally better after my pep talk, I flipped the switch at the top of the stairs. Light, anemic and jaundiced, illuminated a steep flight of steps. Melly apparently was a stickler for conserving energy by using low-wattage bulbs. I held on to the wooden handrail as I made my cautious descent. The thought of Melly navigating these steps carrying a heavy laundry basket was frightening. Images of an elderly woman calling for help after a fall flashed through my brain. I needed to speak to CJ about buying her one of those medical alert devices for seniors advertised on television. I don't know if Melly would appreciate having one foisted on her, but it sure would make me feel better.

Even with the dim light, I could make out a discolored area on the cement floor a short distance from the base of the stairs. A bloodstain. Even if Chip hadn't broken his neck in the fall, he would likely have succumbed from the impact of his skull colliding with concrete. McBride had mentioned a splinter in Chip's hand, made during one last, futile attempt to stem the momentum. I lightly ran my fingers along the edge of the handrail and felt the roughness of exposed wood.

I shivered. Would Melly ever be able to live comfortably in this house again after all that had happened here? A man died in her basement. She had almost died.

I needed to complete my inspection and get the heck out of Dodge. This dark basement, this empty house, were creeping me out. My eyes gradually acclimated to the pale light. Gray cinder block walls, utility-grade metal shelving loaded with plastic storage bins, washer, and dryer. A half dozen small windows spaced high up probably allowed only obstructed light even in midsummer, due to a profusion of plantings around the house's foundation. An ancient furnace squatted in the center. Huge pipes stretched upward into the exposed floor joists like giant tentacles.

I had turned to leave when something caught my eye on the floor near the furnace. I ventured closer and discovered a laundry basket half-filled with articles of clothing. I picked up one of the items and examined it. A man's long-sleeved cotton dress shirt. I frowned. How strange. Melly had been a widow for more than twenty years. Why would she keep a man's shirt? As I was about to drop it into the laundry basket, I froze.

Directly overhead came the unmistakable sound of footsteps. Did whoever was upstairs know I was here? He or she must. I'd left the kitchen light on, a dead giveaway. I swallowed a nervous giggle at my choice of words.

But why didn't the person call out a greeting? Why remain silent? Unless, of course, the goal was to terrorize me. If so, it was working.

Taking deep yoga breaths to steady my nerves, I searched for something to use as a weapon. A jug of bleach, a box of detergent? All those would achieve was clean clothes. Finally I spied a broom leaning in a corner. Not much, but it would have to do. Just as I reached for it, I saw a disembodied hand at the top of the stairs switch off the light.

My scream echoed off the cinder block walls. The next sound I heard was that of a door closing. I waited for what seemed a small eternity, but I knew, could sense, I was once more alone in Melly's house. With my heart knocking against my ribs like a woodpecker on steroids, I crept back up the stairs.

My unidentified visitor must've been as energy conscious as Melly, because he—or she—also turned off the overhead light fixture in the kitchen. Swallowing my fear, I proceeded across the room and turned it on. The room appeared the same as before—with one notable exception.

A bottle of Visine sat in the precise center of a blue and white place mat.

"Are you sure it wasn't there before?"

"Positive."

Reba Mae poured me a shot of Jack Daniel's. "Here, this will take the edge off."

"Thanks." I downed the whiskey in one gulp and welcomed its burn. I'm not one for hard liquor—margaritas being the exception—but at this point, I would have drunk turpentine if it would stop the shakes.

"So what did you do then?" Reba Mae asked.

"I did what any sane person would do and got out of there as fast as I could." After my adventure at Melly's, I found Reba Mae's familiar kitchen comforting. The script for *Steel Magnolias* was spread open on the table next to a half-empty mug of coffee. I noticed her lines were highlighted in yellow.

Reba Mae's pretty brown eyes mirrored her concern. "Want me to call Wyatt?"

"And listen to another sermon?" I asked. "Nothing McBride can do anyway. Someone was just trying to give me a scare."

"Or send a message," Reba Mae said, nodding solemnly. "I saw this movie once where the bad guy didn't want to hurt anyone, just wanted to scare the person snoopin' around."

I toyed with the shot glass. "Backing off isn't an option. If I don't give McBride a reason to stop him, he's going to arrest Melly. You know how proud she is. That would be slow death."

"So what do you propose to do?"

I dragged my hand through my hair. "Wish I knew, but I'll think of something." Reba Mae took a mug from the cupboard, poured me coffee, then refilled her own mug before sitting across from me. "Anyone with eyes could see Judge Herman's sweet on Melly. I don't think he'd send her to jail."

"If he refuses to sign a warrant, McBride will find a judge who will. Thanks to you, I narrowed the suspect list down to just Troy and Rusty."

"Shucks, ma'am, 'tweren't nuthin'," she said in an exaggerated Western accent, then turned serious. "Think Cheryl's pool boy offed Chip for his insurance money?"

"It's possible." I sipped my coffee and found it hot and strong, just the way I liked it. "Money is a pretty strong motivator. Whether an accident or a homicide, Chip's death qualifies as double indemnity. The insurer will pay twice the amount of the policy's face value."

Reba Mae whistled. "Should bring 'em a bundle."

"And if he didn't kill Chip, there's Rusty Tulley to consider." I leaned back in my chair, my hands cradling the coffee mug. "Rusty blamed Chip for Trustychipdesign. com's failure to thrive in today's market. Only this afternoon, I saw eyedrops in the courier bag Rusty uses for his laptop—the same brand McBride found at Melly's. I'm pretty sure Troy uses eyedrops, too."

"There's gotta be a way." Reba Mae tugged on a flashy earring that hung nearly to her shoulder. "Remember how detectives in old black-and-white movies like Charlie Chan—or on TV shows like *Columbo*—always used to do? They'd gather all the suspects in the same room and force the guilty one to confess. I loved when that happened."

"Me, too," I murmured. "Too bad life can't imitate art."

CHAPTER 33

"Is this yours?" Melly asked when she came downstairs into Spice It Up! the next day.

I stopped inventorying stock to inspect a small shiny object Melly held in her palm. A button? Dark, flat, and round, it looked vaguely familiar. "Where did you find it?"

"In the washing machine," Melly explained. "It was caught in the lint filter."

Taking the button from her, I examined it more closely. I was about to return it when I remembered where I'd last seen it. "It looks like the one I found at your house the day I went to collect some of your clothing. I assumed it belonged to you. I slipped it into my pocket and forgot about it until now. It must've fallen out when I did laundry."

"Mercy!" Melly clucked her tongue. "Well, it's not mine. I never laid eyes on it before."

"Hmm." I rolled it between my fingertips. "I could've sworn the button was from one of your cardigans."

"Dear, do I strike you as the sort who wouldn't replace a loose button?" Melly asked indignantly. "As a young girl, I learned to sew on buttons and darn socks along with my

ABC's. I never could understand why boys weren't taught the same skills."

Inventory forgotten, I only half listened to Melly. Where had I seen a loose button recently? The answer came to me in a rush. Just yesterday I'd noticed a button dangling by a thread on Rusty Tulley's polo shirt. Most polo shirts, I knew, sported similar-type buttons. Polo shirts, I'd observed, were also a staple in Troy Farnsworth's wardrobe. Had either Rusty or Troy lost a button while at Melly's? What business would they have had there? Unless it was Chip they'd come to see, not Melly . . .

I tried to discount the notion. True, Rusty was in Melly's living room when he'd come in search of his partner, but he'd been nowhere near where I found the mystery button. He claimed he'd been in his room the entire evening Chip was murdered. But was he? And what about Troy? If he was with Cheryl as she'd implied, why wasn't their rental car anywhere in sight? Curious and curiouser.

McBride professed he wasn't a believer in coincidence. If I happened upon a shirt minus an identical button, it would throw suspicion in another direction and away from Melly. McBride would have to investigate. Attempt to poke holes in weak alibis. Problem was, Troy and Rusty would soon be leaving Brandywine Creek. I needed to act—and act quickly.

My mind working feverishly, I tapped a fingernail against the button. "Melly," I said at last, "I have an idea. . . ."

It had taken every ounce of salesmanship I possessed to convince first Melly, then Reba Mae, to agree to my plan. The three of us were about to descend en masse upon the Turner-Driscoll House. I knew from a comment Dottie

Hemmings had made that Troy had moved into the bed-and-breakfast and shared a room with Cheryl Balboa. Dottie had expressed her disapproval to anyone within earshot. Tulip Jackson, I knew, was staying there as well.

"I'm not sure I can do this." Melly nervously fingered the strap of her Vera Bradley tote bag.

"You'll do fine." I kept my eyes on the road. "All you have to do is distract Felicity and her guests long enough for Reba Mae and me to take a look around upstairs. Nothing to it."

She nodded solemnly. "I brought wine—two bottles—and cheese straws. Everyone loves my cheese straws."

"Just remember that you're there to wish them safe travels. Tell them you feel responsible for them coming to Brandywine Creek. If not for you, Chip might still be alive. Play on their sympathy so they'll sit in the front parlor and have a glass or two of that nice California wine."

"Think this is gonna take long?" Reba Mae piped up from the backseat. "I got lines to memorize."

I parked a discreet distance down the block. Reba Mae had lost her zest for sleuthing after Saturday night. McBride had scared her witless with talk of charges such as disturbing the peace and disorderly conduct. As for me—I didn't scare that easily. "Once look is all," I said. "Not long."

We climbed out of the car and walked up the street. Reba Mae and I had dressed for the occasion in what I considered stealth mode chic—black turtlenecks, black jeans, and sneakers. Melly—surprise, surprise—wore a teal blue twinset and tailored slacks. When we reached the house, Melly squared her shoulders and purposefully marched up the drive. Reba Mae and I scooted around the back and ducked into the shrubbery to await our cue.

When the doorbell chimed, I counted to ten, then signaled Reba Mae to follow. We sprinted across the terrace and through the French doors into the kitchen. I dashed up the servants' stairs, which were located just left of the pantry. Reba Mae followed so closely, I could practically feel her breath on my neck.

"What do we do now?" she whispered.

I paused to get my bearings. If memories from a previous scouting expedition were correct, there were four large rooms, two on either side of a wide center hallway. Each of them bore a brass plate engraved with the name of a general from the Civil War era. Too bad I didn't know who resided where.

"Start with the two guest rooms at the back," I whispered. "I'll check the ones up front."

"Nuh-uh," Reba Mae grunted. "I'm stickin' to you like a burr on a jackrabbit."

"Fine." It was easier—and faster—to agree than to argue. When I turned the knob of the first room, I found my assumption that the door would be unlocked was correct. I hoped my luck would hold with the rest of the rooms as well. No reason for Felicity's current guests to worry about theft of their property with everyone downstairs in plain sight of one another. I slipped inside a room bearing the name of Brigadier General Henry L. Benning. In the narrow beam of a penlight that I'd remembered to bring, the room appeared uninhabited. "Let's move on."

The room across the hall proved just the opposite. Garments, both men's and women's, were strewn over a padded brocade bench at the foot of the bed. At the bottom of the heap, I spotted the black leather mini Tulip had worn to the Oktoberfest and so knew this was the room she shared with Rusty.

Reba Mae stood in the center of the room and clicked on a small flashlight I'd insisted she bring also. I didn't want to chance Felicity or one of her guests looking upstairs and spotting a lamp shining under a bedroom door. "Where's the dang closet?" she asked.

"There isn't one. Houses way back then didn't have closets."

"Who'd be crazy enough to build a house without closets?"

"Guess people didn't have so much stuff," I said, heading for the armoire. "Check the chest of drawers. I'll look in here."

"Hey," she said seconds later, holding up a pair of scanty panties. "These oughta be X-rated."

I flipped through a neat stack of men's shirts, mostly polo, a handful of oxford cloth. "We're not here to look at ladies' undies."

"Wow! Get a load of this." A frilly lace teddy danced from her fingertips. "If I ever get me a boyfriend, I'm gonna find out where she shops."

I gritted my teeth. "Buttons, Reba Mae. Buttons."

Since our search didn't yield any results, I quietly closed the door behind us. A runner down the center of the hallway muffled the sound of our footsteps. From below, I heard Melly launch into the topic of cheese straws.

"Cheese straws are like deviled eggs," she announced. "Every Southern cook swears hers are the best."

I hoped the Californians would be duly interested in learning Melly always added garlic powder and a dash of cayenne to hers while Felicity preferred a dash of black Tellicherry pepper.

Suddenly, a heart pine floorboard groaned under our weight. My pulse hammered in my ears. I stood stock-still, waiting. I felt Reba Mae's nails dig into my forearm. Her face told me she was ready to bolt.

"What was that noise?" Cheryl demanded.

Felicity laughed softly. "Nothing to worry about, dear. This is an old house."

Melly hurriedly inquired about the difference between Napa Valley wines versus those from Sonoma. When the conversation resumed, I drew in a shaky breath. At my signal, Reba Mae followed me into the Brigadier William T. Wofford room. This room was also occupied. A silk negligee was draped across a chaise. Judging from the array of face creams and cosmetics on a dressing table, I surmised the suite belonged to Cheryl and Troy.

Reba Mae picked up a hefty-looking blue glass jar and studied the label. "Sheesh! No wonder the woman has a flawless complexion. She must spend a bundle on skin-care products. Even if I charged folks double, I couldn't afford expensive creams like this. My motto is: If Walmart or Walgreens don't carry it, I don't buy it."

"Let's get to work," I reminded her. "Start with the half-packed suitcase on the bed. I'll check the dresser."

Guilt gnawed at my conscience as I sorted through one drawer after another. I felt like a voyeur. I reminded myself I was doing this for Melly's sake. My motives were pure. Noble. Even so, I didn't feel good about what we were doing.

I sighed. One last drawer. I tugged at the two brass handles, but nothing happened. The drawer was obviously stuck. Stuck just like the darn window at the motel had been. "Reba Mae, give me a hand."

On the count of three, the drawer burst free and fell to the floor with a resounding crash. Articles of clothing became airborne.

"Shoot," Reba Mae moaned. "Shoot, shoot, shoot."

I grabbed her arm. "C'mon, run."

We sprinted the length of the hall and clattered down the servants' stairs. My chest felt as though there were a tight band around it. We paused to catch our breath on the bottom step. Above us, I heard the buzz of angry voices.

Reba Mae peered over my shoulder. "Wyatt's gonna skin us alive," she whined. "We're toast. He'll throw us in the pokey, sure as I'm standin' here."

I eyed the short distance separating us from the French doors and relative safety. "Let's make a run for it," I whispered.

Felicity rounded the corner of the pantry. "Not so fast. I'm sure there's a reasonable explanation for your antics. I'd like to hear it."

A moment later, Cheryl, Troy, Rusty, and Tulip trooped down the stairs behind us, effectively hemming us in. I glimpsed Melly standing behind Felicity and wringing her hands.

"Well?" Felicity raised a brow. "What do you have to say for yourselves?"

Before I could answer, Cheryl pushed past us and aimed a finger at my chest. If it had been a gun, she would have pulled the trigger. "Why were you stealing my things?"

I moistened my dry lips with the tip of my tongue. "We're not here to rob you. We're looking for a shirt with a missing button."

Reba Mae nodded vigorously. "We want to return it."

"Who *are* these women, Rusty?" Tulip asked plaintively.

"Lunatics, that's who," he snarled.

Reba Mae turned to the young woman and stuck out her hand. "Reba Mae Johnson, pleased to make your acquaintance. I'm a big fan of your father. I have all his CDs."

I gave her the stink-eye. Next she'd be bragging how she used to be president of the Jax Jackson Fan Club.

Troy's face registered his bewilderment. "All this commotion because of a button?"

Angling my body to better see his expression, I pulled the object in question from my pocket. "We believe this belongs to Chip's killer. It was found at the crime scene."

Troy shrugged. "Never saw it before."

"Me neither," Rusty said, although he barely looked at it.

Irate and impatient, Felicity tapped her foot on the floor. "I need a better explanation, unless you want me to press charges for breaking and entering."

At hearing this, Reba Mae's eyes grew as large as saucers. I sucked in a deep breath and forged ahead. In for a penny, in for a pound, as Granny used to say.

"Either Troy or Rusty could be Chip's killer." I held up a hand to forestall denials. "Troy, you need financial backing for your health clubs. As Chip's widow, Cheryl would be better than a platinum credit card."

Cheryl grunted. "Troy didn't need money *that* desperately. I have a trust fund."

Rusty's dark brown eyes glittered with anger. "All the times we were in bed together, you never mentioned a trust fund."

"Wait a minute!" Troy plowed his fingers through his sun-bleached locks. "What's this about you two sleeping together?"

Cheryl pressed her lips together. "Your performance in the bedroom could stand improvement," she said, her voice frigid.

"You can sort your love lives out later." I focused my attention on Cheryl. "I have reason to believe that Troy wasn't with you during the time your husband died as you claimed. A witness can testify that your rental car wasn't in the motel's parking lot. That leaves Troy without an alibi."

"Is that true?" Felicity asked, interested in spite of herself.

A dull red crept beneath Troy's golden tan. "Cheryl's high maintenance. She forgot to pack her antiaging, antiwrinkle serum. She insisted I get her another and not return without it. The nearest mall is nearly an hour's drive. I got to Dillard's just before closing. If you don't believe me, I saved the receipt with a time stamp. Afterwards, I called Kyle and we talked. He'll vouch for me."

Cheryl whirled to confront him. "Kyle? Who's Kyle?"

"He's my friend," Troy admitted, albeit reluctantly. "My *very* good friend. As a matter of fact, I'm going to call him right now and ask him to pick me up at LAX tomorrow."

Troy turned and left the rest of us staring after him. "Well, don't that beat all," Reba Mae said to no one in particular.

So much for Troy not having an alibi, but that still left Rusty. I fixed him with a hard stare. "What about you, Rusty? Do you still expect us to believe that you were in your room? It would have been child's play to slip out the back, shove your partner down Melly's stairs, and return with no one knowing."

Rusty snorted, a very unmetrosexual reaction to my accusation. "All you have to do is check the call log on my phone. I had FaceTime with Jessica Moran for hours that night."

"Jessica Moran?" Tulip batted his shoulder with her hand. "You've been fooling around with my best friend? I knew you were a player, Rusty Tulley, but this is a new low even for you. I'm out of here."

She turned and fled up the stairs with Rusty chasing after her. "Tulip, wait up. I can explain."

"Piper Prescott"—Felicity glared—"it's high time you stop this nonsense and leave the crime-solving to the police. If you ever pull a stunt like this again, I won't be so lenient. Please leave this instant before I suffer a change of heart and have you and your sidekick arrested."

I didn't need further encouragement to do as requested. Melly, Reba Mae, and I were a subdued trio as we returned to my VW and drove away.

"I don't think I've ever seen Felicity so upset," Melly said. "Or so angry."

"Look at the bright side, honeybun," Reba Mae counseled from the backseat. "Felicity Driscoll is one more person you can cross off your Christmas card list. Think of the money you'll save on postage."

CHAPTER 34

"You've had dumb ideas in the past, Piper, but tonight's takes the prize." Melly stared straight ahead out the windshield, her Vera Bradley tote bag in her lap. "Why I agreed to go along with your harebrained scheme, I'll never know. I should have my head examined."

Melly hadn't stopped haranguing me since dropping off Reba Mae. Problem was, I deserved it. Dumb idea? Check. Harebrained scheme? Check. Need a shrink? Check.

"A word of advice, dear. From now on, leave the detective work to a *real* detective."

"Yes, ma'am," I said meekly. "At least I gave everyone a chance to unburden their secrets."

"Oh, they unburdened their secrets, all right, no doubt about it. Let me see"—Melly ticked off the revelations on her fingers—"Rusty was having an affair with Tulip's best friend. Cheryl has a secret trust fund. And as for Troy, well, Troy has Kyle."

I felt like a complete fool. An idiot. "If McBride gets wind of this, he'll laugh himself silly. Even worse, if Dottie Hemmings or Jolene Tucker hears about what happened tonight, she'll spread the story while playing bunco. The next morning, I'll be a laughingstock."

"Don't worry, dear. Fortunately for you, by tomorrow your suspects will be gone."

"Great." I flipped on the turn signal and headed for the business district. Besides Melly, that left only Reba Mae and Felicity as witnesses to my folly.

"Well, at least one good thing will come from this night. We'll have a brand-new garbage disposal by the time we get home." Melly patted the paisley tote bag on her lap. "Now that Ned's headaches have disappeared, he wanted to finish the job he started."

I turned down the street behind my shop, where I usually parked—a city ordinance forbade overnight parking on Main Street—to find a white cargo van in my usual space. "What's the van from Gray's Hardware doing behind my shop?"

Melly couldn't come up with a plausible explanation as we trooped up the stairs to my apartment. The lower half of Ned Feeney's body protruded from the cabinet below the kitchen sink. Thompson Gray squatted next to him. "Give that bolt another quarter turn," Thompson instructed, "and the job's done."

"Thompson," Melly said, depositing her tote on the counter. "What are you doing here?"

"Yes, Thompson, what *are* you doing here? And," I said, looking around, "where's Casey?"

Thompson got to his feet. "Your dog thought Ned's tools were chew toys, so we put him in the bedroom to keep him out of mischief."

Ned scooted out from beneath the cabinet. "Hope you don't mind me askin' Thompson over. Garbage disposals are tricky buggers. I didn't want to make any more mistakes."

"I'm thinking of stocking this particular model so folks don't have to drive all the way to Lowe's," Thompson explained.

I bit back a retort. I didn't feel it prudent to remind Thompson that his prices were the real reason people were willing to make the drive.

Ned pulled a handkerchief from a back pocket to wipe his hands. "Mr. Gray is goin' to appoint me his chief installer once I get the hang of things—and quit droppin' the dang thing on my head."

Thompson ran a hand over his mousy hair. "You ladies have a pleasant evening?"

"I'd hardly call it pleasant." Melly slipped off the light sweater she had worn on the way home. "Piper insisted on playing amateur detective and took me along as her assistant."

Ned shoved up the bill of his ball cap. "Did you find out who shoved the guy down Miz Melly's stairs?"

"No." I must have sounded as dejected as I felt. "At first, I was certain it was Cheryl Balboa in collusion with her friend Troy. Next, I thought Chip's partner, Rusty Tulley, might be the culprit."

Melly folded her sweater neatly and set it alongside her tote bag. "Turns out they all had ironclad alibis."

Thompson began helping Ned collect the assortment of tools scattered about. "For the life of me, I don't understand why McBride is trying to turn a simple fall into a murder investigation. Personally, I'm convinced the man likes being in the limelight. Don't think I haven't noticed the way women follow his every move."

"Well, I'm not one to give up easily." I stooped to pick pliers off the floor and handed them to Ned. "I plan to keep asking questions until I find out who's responsible for killing Chip Balboa."

"Chief will figure it out." Ned shoved the pliers into his

tool belt. "In the meantime, be extra careful. Good thing you have Mr. Gray watchin' your back, Miz Melly. I was takin' a shortcut through your yard—hope you don't mind—the night that feller got hisself killed. I saw Mr. Gray comin' out your back door. I said 'hey,' but he musta not heard me. When I asked him about it later, he said he was checkin' your locks. If that ain't bein' neighborly, I don't know what is." Ned tipped his hat. "G'night, ladies."

Thompson made no move to follow.

I stole a glance at Melly, but she fiddled with her pearls and avoided looking at me. "Thompson," I said slowly, "why were you at Melly's the night Chip was killed?"

He shrugged. "Ned was mistaken. You know he's not the sharpest tool in the shed."

Hard to argue Ned's mental acuity, still . . . Tipping my head to one side, I watched Thompson closely. "Even so, Ned was quite specific about the exact night."

"Piper, really," Melly objected, but her protest sounded weak.

Why didn't Thompson leave? Did he expect us to offer coffee and cookies? Furthermore, it made no sense that he had been at Melly's the night Chip was shoved down her basement stairs. I felt my stomach knot. Unless . . .

But that didn't make sense, either. What reason could Thompson possibly have to kill Chip?

Thompson stood in front of the door leading to the stairs, effectively blocking the exit. "You just can't stop nosing around, can you, Piper? You can't leave well enough alone."

"I need to check on Casey," Melly said, making a move toward the bedroom. "The poor thing must be tired of being cooped up."

"Stay where you are!" Thompson snapped. He reached under his loose-fitting shirt and withdrew a small but lethal-looking revolver from a holster clipped to his belt.

My eyes widened at the sight of a gun in his hand. *Oh my God!* Melly saw it, too, and let out a strangled scream that set Casey barking and scratching at the closed bedroom door.

"Keep that mutt quiet before I shoot it."

"Casey!" I called out in my sternest pet-owner voice, terrified Thompson would make good his threat. "Hush!"

"Thompson, put that thing away before it goes off," Melly ordered, a quaver in her voice in spite of her bravado.

My thoughts flew to Lindsey. Thank goodness she was spending the night at CJ's. I needed to do something. But what? It was hard to think, to plan, above the buzzing in my head. All I could do was stare at the pistol, which seemed as big as the cannon in the town square.

"Um, Thompson, what were you really doing at Melly's that night?" I asked, stalling for time. "And don't lie about checking the locks. Melly never locked her back door. She had no reason to ask you to check it—until *after* Chip was killed."

"It's all your fault, Piper. Or should I call you Nancy Drew?" he sneered. "You just can't resist meddling, can you?"

I noticed Thompson's hand shaking, which only added to my fear. "Thompson, why don't you do as Melly suggested and put the gun down before someone gets hurt? It'll only make matters worse."

"And then what?" he said with a choked laugh. "You call that cop friend of yours and have me arrested?"

Melly edged closer to me, her face blanched of color. "Why are you doing this, Thompson? You've always been such a good boy, never given your mother a moment's worry."

A trickle of sweat ran down his temple. "I'm tired of being a 'good boy.' I'm tired of my life. I saw a chance to change things, but you had to come along and ruin everything."

"M-me?" Melly stammered. "What did I ever do to you?"

"I designed a software modification of my own, superior to yours in every way"—he swiped at the sweat—"but while I was tweaking it, working out the bugs, you submitted your version. Can't prove it, but I think you even stole my ideas."

Melly's hand fluttered to her chest. "Thompson, I'd never steal from you. You know me better than that."

All this chitchat was enlightening; however, it wasn't removing the gun from his hand. I looked around frantically, searching for a weapon. I had knives, of course—didn't every cook?—but Thompson stood close to the knife drawer. I had household chemicals I could throw in his face, but I'd first have to wrestle off the childproof, tamperproof screw tops.

Stall, stall. Think, think.

"Why did you kill Chip?" Not exactly brilliant repartee, but at least I'd die with my curiosity satisfied.

"I invited him to visit my workroom at the back of the hardware store. I wanted, practically pleaded with him, to reconsider my proposal. I was willing to accept a fraction of what he'd offered Melly." Thompson nervously licked his lips. "Once there, I offered him a drink of an expensive scotch I'd bought especially for the occasion. He drank my scotch, then laughed in my face. Said I must be crazy if I thought my product compared to Melly's. He humiliated me. I was furious!"

My cell phone was in my purse, which I'd carelessly tossed on the kitchen table. Did I have time to make a dive for it? How good a shot was Thompson, anyway? Everyone in town knew he had a concealed carry permit and kept a loaded .38 under the counter to thwart robbers, but how often did he visit the gun range? Was shooting a skill you had to practice to maintain? Or was it more like riding a bike—once learned, you never forgot? If I lived through this, I'd ask McBride.

"And then what did you do?" I asked Thompson, barely able to form the words. My mouth felt drier than the Sahara during a drought.

"I remembered a scene from my all-time favorite movie, *The Wedding Crashers*, where this guy put eyedrops in another guy's drink to give him diarrhea. Payback time. A joke. The long hours staring at a computer screen gives me eyestrain. I always keep Visine near my computer. When Balboa wasn't looking, I gave the bottle a good squeeze— right into his scotch. Nothing happened at first, so I assumed the trick wasn't working."

"How did Chip wind up dead in my basement?" Melly inched closer to me still and clutched my arm.

Thompson gestured with his gun hand. "Balboa told me he was meeting you, so I followed. I watched the two of you through the kitchen window. When you went upstairs, I thought, what the heck, one last pitch. He refused to listen. Complained about feeling dizzy. Said if I didn't leave, he'd call the police. He got up—guess he thought fresh air might help—but he opened the door to the basement by mistake. He'd made me so angry by this time, I shoved him hard as I could."

"And Melly would have gone to prison for a crime she didn't commit."

"My software program was my ticket out of here. I spent years of my life working on it only to discover that I'd wasted my time. With the money I'd earn from my software, I thought I'd go to an island in the Caribbean, maybe buy a boat."

Melly tried to reason with him. "It's not too late, Thompson, to see something of the world."

Thompson gave a mirthless laugh. "Hell with the hardware store. I'm sick to death of being the good son. I wish I'd never returned to Brandywine Creek. Every time I mention moving on, Mother has a spell of some sort. When it comes to guilt trips, she's the queen. Like it or not, I'm stuck here."

"So what are you going to do now that we know the truth about Chip?" I darted a look toward Melly. Her eyes were distended with fear, her skin milky pale. By her own admission, she didn't do well in a crisis. And as crises came, they didn't get much bigger than this.

Perspiration dotted Thompson's upper lip. "I tried to kill Melly once by tampering with her furnace. I planned to make it look like a suicide. It was easy to swipe a piece of Melly's notepaper. I've seen her handwriting often enough to forge an 'I'm sorry.' With her out of the picture, McBride would drop the case. No more worries. Now I have a different plan."

Calmer, Thompson almost smiled, which frightened me even more. If he let his guard down even for an instant, I was going to slam into him, try to knock the gun from his hand, then grab Melly and run like crazy.

"Too bad you nice ladies interrupted a robbery in progress and, in the bargain, got yourselves shot. To make matters worse, the shooter got clean away." He motioned with the barrel of his .38. "Turn around and head downstairs."

"I think I'm going to be sick." Melly clutched her stomach and groaned as her knees folded.

That's all it took. Instead of falling to the floor, Melly pivoted, latched on to her Vera Bradley tote, and hit Thompson upside the head. Dazed, he wobbled like a Weeble, then dropped the gun before sinking to his knees.

Before he had a chance to recover, I dived for the pistol. It felt big, heavy, awkward, but I didn't let that stand in the way. Using both hands to keep them steady, I pointed the barrel at Thompson's chest. "Call nine-one-one," I told Melly.

"First things first, dear." Melly calmly removed a bottle of wine from the tote bag and set it on the table. "Nothing like a nice bottle of California Chardonnay, I always say."

CHAPTER 35

The calm after the storm. It was peaceful sitting on a bench in the town square. A gray squirrel industriously gathered nuts. A goldfinch rested on a branch in a willow oak. The statue of a Confederate soldier, frozen forever at his post, guarded the town with sightless eyes. Puffs of white clouds floated across a bright blue sky. A picture-perfect day. If I closed my eyes, I could pretend last night had never happened—almost.

Reba Mae interrupted my musings. "Melly is sure a tough old bird."

"A real steel magnolia," I agreed.

Reba Mae took a bite of her chicken pesto wrap, a swallow of sweet tea. "Melly actually clobbered Thompson with her tote bag?"

"It wasn't the tote bag so much as its contents." I wiped a dab of sauce from the corner of my mouth with a napkin. "Felicity insisted we take the extra bottle of wine we'd brought along home with us. I suspect the Piggly Wiggly isn't Felicity's usual source of vino."

"What's going to happen to Thompson?"

"McBride hinted he plans to plead temporary insanity."

"Nutty as a fruitcake, if he thinks he can get away with claimin' he's crazy."

"As for Chip Balboa, Thompson said all he wanted to do to him was give him diarrhea. Things sort of . . . escalated."

Reba Mae finished her sandwich and bunched up the wrapper. "What's goin' to happen to the hardware store, now that Thompson's been arrested?"

I polished off the last of my Diet Coke. "According to Melly, Mavis Gray plans to put it up for sale. Use the money for Thompson's defense."

"Did you ever find the owner of the button?"

"Lindsey recognized it as hers. She said it came off at her meemaw's one day while roughhousing with Casey."

"Don't know about you, honeybun, but I'm ready to get back to normal. I've had enough excitement to last awhile." She brushed crumbs from her leopard-print slacks. "Say, did Lindsey happen to mention what's goin' on with Sean Rogers's knee?"

"After reviewing the CT scan, the orthopedic doctor diagnosed it as a bad sprain. Sean's hoping he gets the green light to play in the homecoming game."

"Great! Folks have been worryin', what with the rumor Dottie's been spreadin' about him bein' crippled."

I shouldn't have been surprised at hearing this. "Dottie's a Grand Master of the Outwardly Cheerful, Inwardly Morbid Society. But there is a bright side to all this," I said, smiling. "As a result of Sean's injury, Lindsey is determined to become a physical therapist—or a nurse."

Reba Mae grinned. "Knowin' your girl, she's liable to change careers another dozen times before makin' up her mind. Speakin' of schoolin', I've got news, too. Clay enrolled at the junior college as a full-time student, come the winter semester. He has his sights set on a degree in criminal justice. Wants to be another Wyatt McBride."

"I'm happy for Clay." I began to gather up our lunch debris. "McBride, I'm sure, will make a great mentor. By the way, when do play rehearsals begin?"

"Seven o'clock tonight." Reba Mae fluffed her blond bouffant do. "Sandy promises to be a real stickler. Some of the cast members are grumblin' already."

"I'm sure the play will be a huge success. Sandy has seen stage productions in both New York and London, so her standards are high."

"Yeah, I guess." Reba Mae stood to leave. "Time to get back to work. Mary Lou Lambert begged me to squeeze her in between a perm and two color-and-cuts. This time, she decided to try cuttin' her own hair. Now she's bawlin' her eyes out and expects me to work a miracle. Says not even her Yorkie recognizes her."

Reba Mae headed off to the Klassy Kut, me to Spice It Up! The instant Melly caught sight of me, she whipped off her apron and grabbed her purse. "What took you so long?"

I glanced at the regulator clock on the wall, but it read the same as my wristwatch. From my vantage point across the street, I hadn't noticed a horde of tourists descend, all of them eager to purchase spices. "Melly," I protested. "I was barely gone a half hour."

"Cot—er, Judge Herman—called while you were out. He invited me for a late lunch at the country club. He said there are some things he wants to discuss with me."

"Things?" I asked, instantly suspicious. "What kind of 'things'?"

She waved her hand airily. "Get your mind out of the gutter, dear. Not those kinds of things. The judge is considering stepping down from the bench, maybe travel a bit while he's still able. He said he values a woman's perspective. He's missed that since his wife passed. If I leave now, I'll have just enough time to change into something pretty.

Perhaps the blue silk blouse that brings out the color of my eyes."

Bemused, I watched her hurry off for her luncheon date. She had a certain bounce in her step I'd never noticed before . . .

. . . and a certain twinkle in her eyes.

During the remainder of the afternoon, townspeople flowed in and out of Spice It Up! Curiosity prompted most of the visits, but many neighbors left with a jar of this, a bottle of that. All of them, however, expressed shock and disbelief at Thompson Gray's actions.

It was nearly closing time. I was at the counter, totaling the day's receipts, when Doug came through the door. We'd talked at length earlier about the events of the previous night. As I'd anticipated, I received a well-meaning lecture about staying out of trouble, which translated meant "minding my own business."

"Hey, pretty lady." He kissed me soundly, then held me at arm's length to inspect for damages. "Lucky for me, my hair already turned gray. Hearing about your recent escapade made me a little bonkers."

Casey was more interested in doggy treats than in my "escapades." He danced at our feet until Doug produced a dog chewie, then went off in a corner to gnaw on it.

"I would have been here sooner, but the president of the Humane Society dropped by and asked for help writing a grant. Naturally, instead of thirty minutes, it took most of the afternoon. If they get the grant, however, it'll be used for spaying and neutering."

I thought I saw Casey wince at hearing "spaying and neutering." "Besides wanting to see for myself that you're still in one piece," Doug continued, "there's something I need to talk with you about."

Uh-oh. "It sounds serious."

Smiling sheepishly, he massaged the nape of his neck

"I've got good news . . . and bad news. Well, actually, they're one and the same."

"All right," I said warily. "Why don't you tell me the bad news first?"

"My daughter called last night. She's dropping out of Northwestern."

Well, I don't know what I'd expected to hear, but that certainly wasn't it. He'd told me his only child, a daughter, had elected to live with her mother in Chicago following their divorce. Doug usually referred to her simply as "my daughter." I tried to recall her name. If memory served, she was named after a city or a street. Finally, her name came to me—Madison.

"Madison said she's failing all her classes and needs a break."

I placed my hand on his arm. "I'm sorry, Doug. I know how proud you are of her accomplishments."

"There's more," he continued. "Madison and my ex-wife are at odds. My daughter is quite upset by what she views as her mother's irresponsible . . . behavior."

"Exactly what type of 'behavior' are you referring to?"

"Since my ex and her former high school sweetheart, now a pilot with Delta, are no longer an item, Tracy's heavily into Internet dating—and the bar scene. Madison is unhappy with her mother's choices in male companions. Both Tracy and I feel a change of scenery might be beneficial. Even though Madison's twenty, she took our breakup hard."

I nodded sympathetically. "Lindsey is still experiencing fallout from my divorce."

"Well, the news isn't all bad. Madison is coming to live with me. While she's here, she's going to act as my receptionist/assistant until she figures out what she wants to do with her life."

"That's wonderful, Doug. You've wanted to hire a

person for some time. I'm sure your daughter will be a great help."

"I can't wait for the two of you to meet," he said, drawing me into his arms. "I'm sure you'll hit it off."

Closing time now, I started across the shop to lock up for the night when McBride pushed through the door. "Don't suppose you can offer a poor underpaid public servant a cup of coffee?" he asked.

I was about to explain the meaning of "closing time" but relented when I noticed the dark smudges of fatigue under his eyes. He looked exhausted. "Sure," I said. "I was just about to brew a fresh pot."

"Liar, liar, pants on fire," he said with a tired smile. After flipping the sign in the window to CLOSED, he followed me to the rear of the shop. "I thought you might be interested in knowing what's going on with Thompson Gray."

I measured French roast into the basket of my coffeemaker and added water while he watched. "Have a seat," I said, indicating a couple of stools nearby.

Casey trotted over to sniff McBride's pant leg and was rewarded by having his ears scratched. "Your mutt probably smelled my cat."

"How's Fraidy doing these days?" I asked, setting out mugs. "Is she any less timid?"

"I'm happy to report she's making progress. It's just certain redheads she avoids like the plague."

"I tend to rub some people—and some animals—the wrong way. But"—I smiled brightly—"to know me is to love me."

"Pretty sure of yourself, aren't you?" He chuckled.

When the coffeemaker ceased gurgling and hissing, I poured us each coffee and sat next to him. "Sorry, but I'm fresh out of goodies to go along with the coffee."

McBride took a deep swallow. "Mmm," he purred. "This makes me feel almost human after only four hours' sleep last night. Darned if Thompson Gray didn't want to press charges against Melly for assault and battery."

"You're kidding!"

He shrugged broad shoulders. "Truth is stranger than fiction."

"If Thompson really feels that way, maybe the judge should accept an insanity plea. If not for a bottle of Chardonnay, Melly and I would be in the morgue right now."

"I reminded the man, he'd tried to kill Melly Prescott not once but twice—and almost killed you in the bargain." McBride's laser blues studied me over the rim of his coffee mug. "Thompson finally admitted to tampering with the chimney vent at Melly's house by stuffing it full of clothing. He planned to return later and retrieve the evidence."

"But discovered me instead. Thompson scared the beejeebers out of me." My hands tightened around the coffee mug, remembering the spooky basement, the disembodied hand at the top of the stairs. The eyedrops that had been centered on a blue and white place mat as a warning. "The entire time I was convinced Chip died at the hands of a stranger in town—Cheryl, Troy, even Rusty—while the real killer operated a business two doors down. He was the man who replaced my broken lock and helped install a garbage disposal. I never guessed Thompson capable of violence."

McBride drained his cup. "Everyone's capable of violence given the right circumstances."

"That's downright cynical, McBride."

"Occupational hazard."

I sipped my coffee, which had cooled by now. "What happens next?"

McBride set his empty cup aside. "A good defense

attorney might've gotten Gray off with voluntary man-
slaughter if he'd quit his murdering ways with Chip Balboa.
Now he's also charged with two counts of attempted
murder. The nuts and bolts in his hardware store will have
rusted long before he sees the light of day again. Time
comes"—he got to his feet—"we'll need you and Melly
to testify."

"I'll circle the date on my calendar in red," I said as I
walked with him to the door.

"Almost forgot to tell you," he said, pausing. "Beau
Tucker's no longer on probation. He's not the only one you
wheedle information from. I can't in good conscience hold
Beau to one set of standards and myself to another. I'm just
as guilty when confronted with those big green eyes of
yours."

Was McBride flirting with me? No way. Impossible. I
wasn't a Hollywood starlet; he was out of my league. And
then there was Doug. Sweet, dependable Doug.

"Even without homemade goodies, the coffee tasted
great." McBride gave me one of those rare smiles, the kind
where the cute dimple in his cheek flashed in and out. The
kind that made me weak in the knees. "See ya," he said.

"See ya," I echoed.

Hmm. Maybe I'd ask Melly if she'd share her gingersnap recipe with me. I could keep the cookies on hand for
certain unexpected visitors. Probably not a wise idea,
yet . . .

CINNAMON

Who doesn't like cinnamon? Whether it's mixed with sugar and sprinkled on toast or added to our favorite baked goods, cinnamon is a hands-down favorite with most people. The bark from an evergreen tree in the laurel family, cinnamon was traded in biblical times. Arab merchants risked life and limb to transport it to customers. Egyptian pharaohs sent expeditions on quests to find it. Crusaders brought cinnamon back from the Holy Land, thereby making it a staple in medieval kitchens. There are two main types: cassia, native to Southeast Asia, which has a strong, spicy-sweet flavor; and Ceylon or "true" cinnamon, which is less sweet with a more complex flavor. In many countries, cassia and cinnamon are used interchangeably. Harvesters cut paper-thin slices of bark, then hand-roll them into quills more than three feet long to be dried. Cinnamon should be kept in a tightly sealed glass container in a cool, dark, and dry place. Ground cinnamon will keep for about six months, while cinnamon sticks will stay fresh for about one year. The shelf life may be extended by storing them in the refrigerator. The smell test is a reliable way to check for freshness. If it doesn't smell sweet, discard.

MELLY PRESCOTT'S GINGERSNAPS

2 cups all-purpose flour
2¼ teaspoons ground ginger
2 teaspoons baking soda
¾ teaspoon ground cardamom
¾ teaspoon ground cinnamon
½ teaspoon ground coriander
⅛ teaspoon freshly ground black pepper
¾ teaspoon salt
⅓ cup finely chopped crystallized ginger (approx. 1.3 oz.)
1 cup packed brown sugar
½ cup (1 stick) butter, room temperature
¼ cup vegetable shortening, room temperature
1 large egg
¼ cup honey
1 teaspoon vanilla extract
¾ cup granulated sugar, for rolling

Whisk the flour, ground ginger, baking soda, cardamom, cinnamon, coriander, pepper, and salt in a medium bowl until blended. Mix in the crystallized ginger and set aside.

In a large bowl, beat the brown sugar, butter, and shortening with an electric mixer until fluffy, being careful not to overbeat. Add the egg, honey, and vanilla, and beat until blended. Stir in the flour mixture with a wooden spoon or spatula, mixing just until well blended. Cover and refrigerate for 1 hour.

Preheat the oven to 350°F. Lightly spray cookie sheets with nonstick cooking spray or use parchment paper. Spoon the granulated sugar onto a small plate.

Using wet hands, form the dough into balls of approximately 1¼ inch; roll them in the granulated sugar to coat. Place the dough balls on baking sheets 2–3 inches apart.

Bake the cookies until they are cracked on top but still soft to touch, about 11–13 minutes. Cool them on sheets for 1 minute. Carefully transfer the cookies to wire racks; cool completely. Yields 3½ dozen cookies.

DOUG'S SAUERBRATEN

2 cups water
1½ cups red wine vinegar
½ cup dry red wine
1 medium onion, chopped
1 large carrot, chopped
1 celery stalk with leaves, chopped
1 tablespoon plus 1 teaspoon kosher salt, additional
    for seasoning meat
8 black peppercorns
2 bay leaves
4 whole cloves
6–10 juniper berries
1 teaspoon mustard seeds
1 (3½- to 4-pound) bottom round pot roast
1 tablespoon vegetable oil
⅓ cup sugar
½ cup old-fashioned gingersnaps, crushed*

In a large saucepan over high heat, combine the water, red wine vinegar, red wine, onion, carrot, celery, salt, peppercorns, bay leaves, cloves, juniper berries, and mustard seeds. Cover and bring this to a boil; lower the heat, and simmer for 10 minutes. Set aside to cool.

Rub the meat with the vegetable oil and salt it on all sides. Heat a large sauté or fry pan over high heat; add the meat and brown it on all sides.

After the marinade has cooled, place the meat in a nonreactive vessel, and pour the marinade over it. Place the roast in the refrigerator for three days. If the meat isn't completely submerged, turn it over once a day.

After three days of marinating, preheat the oven to 325°F. Add the sugar to the meat and marinade, cover the pan, and place it on the middle rack of the oven. Cook until tender, approximately 4 hours.

Remove the meat and keep it warm. Strain the liquid to remove solids. Return the liquid to the pan and place it over medium-high heat. Whisk in the gingersnaps and cook the sauce until it thickens, stirring occasionally. Strain the sauce through a fine mesh sieve to remove any lumps. Slice the meat and serve it with the sauce.

*If the sauce needs additional thickening, either use more crushed gingersnaps or mix 1 tablespoon cornstarch with ¼ cup water and whisk the mixture into the sauce as it cooks.

PIPER'S LEBKUCHEN

1 egg
¾ cup brown sugar
½ cup honey
½ cup dark molasses
3 cups sifted all-purpose flour
½ teaspoon baking soda
1¼ teaspoons ground nutmeg
1¼ teaspoons ground cinnamon
½ teaspoon ground cloves
½ teaspoon ground allspice
½ cup slivered almonds
½ cup candied mixed fruit peel, finely chopped

Glaze
1 egg white, beaten
1 tablespoon lemon juice
½ teaspoon lemon zest
1½ cups sifted confectioners' sugar

In a large bowl, beat the egg, brown sugar, and honey until smooth. Stir in the molasses. In a separate bowl, combine the flour, baking soda, nutmeg, cinnamon, cloves, and allspice. Stir the dry ingredients into the molasses mixture. Stir in the almonds and candied fruit peel. Cover the bowl or wrap the dough, and chill overnight.

Preheat the oven to 400°F. Grease cookie sheets. On a lightly floured surface, roll the dough out to a ¼-inch thickness. Cut the dough into 2 x 3-inch rectangles (or squares). Place the cookies 1½ inches apart on the cookie sheets.

Bake the cookies for 10–12 minutes in the preheated oven, until firm. While they are still warm, brush the cookies with the lemon glaze.

To make the glaze: In a small bowl, stir together the egg white, lemon juice, and lemon zest. Mix in the confectioners' sugar until smooth. Brush the glaze over warm cookies.

Read on for an excerpt from

CURRIED
AWAY

the next Spice Shop mystery by Gail Oust, available
soon in hardcover from Minotaur Books!

CHAPTER 1

"You're fired!"

I stopped chatting with the mayor's wife, Dottie Hemmings, and my ex-mother-in-law, Melly Prescott, as Reba Mae Johnson, my BFF, stormed into my shop, Spice It Up!

"What's up, girlfriend?" I asked.

"Just like that!" Reba Mae snapped her fingers. "*She* fired me."

"Silly girl." Dottie giggled. "You can't be fired. You're self-employed."

"What's wrong, dear?" Melly *tsk*ed sympathetically. "Did you have an irate customer at the Klassy Kut?"

"Did a perm go wrong?" Dottie patted hair that would have qualified as a helmet in the NFL.

"Did highlights turn into lowlights?" I asked. As Reba Mae drew closer, I noted her blotchy face and reddened eyes.

"No, of course not." Reba Mae's tangerine-sized hoop earrings swayed as she stalked back and forth across the heart pine floor. "Y'all know I run the best little ol' beauty shop in Brandywine Creek, Georgia."

"But you still haven't said *who* fired you?" Dottie's inquiring mind demanded an answer.

"*She* said my *services* were no longer required. Imagine!" Reba Mae flung her hands in the air. "And after all my hard work! I'm so mad I could spit nails."

"Honey, why don't you sit down and tell us what's going on?" I motioned toward one of the stools behind the counter.

"Fine." Reba Mae flounced over and plopped down. "When I think of the hours I spent learning my lines, I want to scream. I even started teasing my hair. I haven't teased my hair since high school—no offense, Dottie," she added for Dottie's benefit. With this, Reba Mae put her head in her hands and burst into tears.

Dottie, Melly, and I exchanged worried glances. This was totally out of character for Reba Mae. She wasn't the type to indulge in bouts of weeping or histrionics. Not even when her husband, Butch, had drowned while bass fishing. Instead of wallowing in self-pity—and who would've blamed her—she enrolled in beauty school, paid off a heap of credit card debt, and started her own business. She was more of a pick-yourself-up-by-the-bootstraps-and-soldier-on kind of gal. I can't remember the last time I saw my friend so . . . agitated. And that scared the bejeebers out of me.

Melly cleared her throat and gave me a look that clearly translated as: *Don't just stand there like a ninny; do something*—so I did. Perching on the adjacent stool, I rubbed Reba Mae's back in small, soothing circles like I used to do when my Chad and Lindsey were babies. "There, there," I crooned. "It can't be that bad."

"Y-yes, it c-can," she blubbered.

Dottie grabbed a fistful of tissues from a box on the counter and pushed them at Reba Mae. "Here, hon."

"Let me get you a nice glass of sweet tea," Melly offered, springing into action. "Sweet tea always makes us Southern girls feel better."

"S-Sandy Granger *fired* me," Reba Mae sobbed. Tears pooled in her pretty, golden-brown eyes and rolled down her cheeks. "I still can't believe it."

The pieces of the puzzle were starting to fall into place. Reba Mae had been over the moon ever since being chosen for the role of Truvy Jones, the outspoken, wise-cracking beauty shop owner, in the Brandywine Creek Opera House's production of *Steel Magnolias*. So over the moon she'd even dyed her hair Dolly Parton yellow in honor of the singer/actress who'd portrayed Truvy in the movie version.

Before I could question her further, Melly emerged from the kitchenette at the rear of the shop. "I found these in a cupboard," she said, placing a plate of cookies along with a frosty glass of iced tea on the counter near Reba Mae's elbow. "Ginger snaps always go well with sweet tea."

"Thanks," Reba Mae sniffled. "This was my big chance for folks to see me with talent for somethin' other than with scissors and a bottle of hair dye. I wanted to make my boys proud of their momma."

"Honey, your boys adore you. Clay and Caleb think you're the best momma in the universe—bar none." I nudged the glass closer. Sweet tea and sympathy were what my friend needed, so sweet tea and sympathy were what she'd get.

"You poor thing." Dottie rested her plump elbows on the counter and leaned forward. "Tell us what happened. Getting it off your chest will make you feel better."

Make Reba Mae "feel better"? More likely provide breaking news for Dottie to broadcast to her network of cronies. Nothing the woman loved more than gossip. I could almost see little antennas sprout from her beehive and twitch in anticipation.

"Did Sandy give a reason for . . . replacing you?" I asked as gently as I could. I'd almost slipped and used the word "fired." That would've resulted in yet another "gully washer," as they say here in the South.

Calmer now, Reba Mae took a sip of sweet tea. "Sandy claims I kept forgettin' to call the characters by the right names."

Nodding, I considered the possibility. "Did you?"

Reba Mae avoided eye contact with me. "Maybe, a time or two."

"Uh-huh," I said, trying to keep my tone neutral.

"Whoever heard of a woman called Ouiser—or 'Weezer,' as Sandy insisted it was pronounced? What kind of name is that anyway?" Reba Mae fired back. "Can't help it if I kept callin' her Wowser."

"Weezer, Wowser," Melly said with a forced smile. "Not much difference, if you want my opinion."

Reba Mae shot Melly a grateful look. "That's what I tried to tell Sandy. Why, I've known all these women—except Madison Winters, who plays Shelby—my entire adult life. It seems downright . . . weird . . . to call 'em by other than their Christian names."

I gave her shoulders a squeeze. "I'm sure you would've nailed it by opening night."

"Darn right I would've." Reba Mae slapped the counter for emphasis. "If Sandy isn't careful, the entire cast is goin' to mutiny. Why, just the other night, Bunny Bowtin left rehearsal in tears 'cause of somethin' Sandy said."

Dottie helped herself to a ginger snap. "I ran into Jolene Tucker at Piggly Wiggly. She told me Bunny threatened to quit, but her husband talked her out of it. Seems Dennis forked over money for Bunny's sister, husband, and their two kids to fly down from New Jersey for opening night. He said the airfare was nonrefundable."

Melly snapped a dead bloom from a pot of mums I'd

set on the counter as a reminder that Thanksgiving, my favorite holiday, was only a week away. "Sandy isn't the easiest person to work with," she said, "but to be fair, as both director and producer she's under considerable pressure."

"Easy for you to say, Melly, since all you have to worry about is collecting props," Reba Mae said. "Behind Sandy's back, the rest of the cast and crew refer to her as the Wicked Witch of the West. And"—she winked—"y'all know what 'witch' rhymes with."

Melly clucked her tongue in disapproval, but Reba Mae remained unfazed. "I'm just sayin' is all. . . ."

"My husband the mayor says Sandy is a real asset to Brandywine Creek. An ambassador of sorts. He calls her a marketing dynamo." Since no one else seemed interested in the lone cookie that remained on the plate, Dottie helped herself. "Harvey claims the publicity she's generating will have a positive impact on the entire town. Said it's bound to attract tourists by the busload and bring in business."

"I hope Mayor Hemmings is right," I said, tucking an unruly red curl behind my ear. "I've just increased my inventory in anticipation of an influx of playgoers."

"Not only is Bunny unhappy," Reba Mae continued, "but I saw Wanda Needmore and Dorinda Kunkel—Wanda plays Clairee, the grande dame; Dorinda plays 'Wowser'—with their heads together."

"You don't want to mess with that pair." Dottie brushed cookie crumbs from her pink polyester blouse. "Those two are the most strong-minded women you'd ever want to meet." Dorinda had raised her daughter, Lorinda, single-handedly after her husband, Skeeter, ran off with a waitress from High Cotton.

"And Wanda doesn't take guff from anybody," Melly added. "She runs CJ's law firm with an iron fist."

This brought a smile to my lips. Even CJ confessed to

being intimidated by his paralegal's forceful personality. "Wanda will be the first to tell anyone who'll listen that a lawyer is only as good as his paralegal. I've heard that said so many times I've been tempted to cross-stitch a wall hanging with her words embroidered on it."

"What's stoppin' you?" Reba Mae wanted to know. "It'd make the perfect gift."

I rolled my eyes. "Reba Mae, have you ever known me to be artsy-craftsy? I tried knitting once, remember? I was better at tennis, and we both know what a disaster that was."

"Yeah, I remember. You dropped so many stitches that the afghan you were workin' on had more holes than a block of Swiss cheese."

"Well, if Wanda and Dorinda are in cahoots, whoo-ee!" Dottie clapped her hands in glee. "Sandy Granger better steer clear. She's going to need eyes in the back of her head if she wants to stay out of trouble."

"Did Sandy say who was going to replace you?" There, I'd gone and done it: addressed the elephant in the room.

Silence stretched like mozzarella on a hot pizza. Dottie studied an advertisement the butcher across the square had dropped off early that morning touting a special on pork chops. Melly nervously fingered her ever-present pearls. I wished I was in Bora-Bora.

Finally Reba Mae let out a long sigh. "Mary Lou Lambert. I hate that woman's guts." When none of us had a comment to add, she continued, "Truvy Jones is a main character; she's in *every* scene. Mary Lou can't read the directions on a box of hair color without messin' up. How can she be expected to memorize pages of dialog?"

"Maybe Sandy will realize she made a big mistake firing you, and ask you to come back," I said hopefully.

"Yeah, maybe." Reba Mae grinned for the first time since entering Spice It Up! "With opening night only three

weeks away, she might just do that. She'll come beggin'
me to save her bacon."

"Thata girl!" Dottie beamed approval. "Don't get mad;
get even."

"Good advice, Dottie. I'll keep that in mind." Reba Mae
slid off the stool. "Ladies, thanks for givin' me a chance
to vent. I feel better after havin' a good cry. Don't know
when I've been so furious, or so hurt. For an instant, all I
wanted to do was wrap my hands around Sandy's scrawny
neck until she squawked like a chicken. Gotta run," she
said, heading out the door.

"Better mad than sad, I always say," Dottie rattled off
another cliché. "Nice talking to y'all, but I have to see Pete
at Meat on Main about some pork chops. My husband the
mayor sure does love his pork chops. Toodle-oo."

"Harvey Hemmings doesn't love pork chops nearly as
much as Dottie loves gossip," Melly observed drily as we
watched Dottie bustle across the street as fast as her short
legs would carry her.

"News of Reba Mae being 'fired' will be all over town
before the first chop sizzles in a frying pan," I said.

"Poor Reba Mae." Melly wagged her head. "She had her
heart set on being onstage."

I nodded agreement. "If I know Dottie, the tale of her
losing the part to Mary Lou Lambert will be embellished
with each telling."

CHAPTER 2

Alone with only Melly for company, I reached into a drawer and removed an e-mail I'd printed out from Doug Winters, local vet and closet chef, that he'd sent the previous night. "From comments I've overheard, Sandy can be a hard taskmaster," I said.

"I thought my job as prop mistress was going to be fun, but, so far, all it's turned out to be is a headache." Melly collected the empty cookie plate and iced-tea glass from the counter. "I'll load these in the dishwasher upstairs for you before I go."

"Hmm, thanks, Melly," I replied absently, scanning Doug's list of ingredients for the third or fourth time. After months of coaxing and cajoling, Doug had finally relented and agreed to do a cooking demonstration for my customers, which was slated for tomorrow morning. I wanted everyone to know his talents extended beyond snips-and-tucks at Pets 'R People.

Before the sound of Melly's footsteps on the stairs had faded, I plucked a small wicker basket from a stack I kept near the counter for shoppers' convenience. I slowly cruised the freestanding shelves, picking up a jar of coriander here, a jar of cardamom there, and added them to my basket. As I did this, I was filled anew with a sense of pride and accomplishment. I loved my little shop, Spice It Up! Loved everything about it. From the gleaming heart pine floors to the exposed brick walls, but most of all—I took a deep breath and let it out—I loved the heady aroma of spices from around the globe. Long before Spice It Up! became a reality, it had been a dream. Little did my ex, CJ, suspect that when he dumped me in favor of chasing ambulances and a former beauty queen in a short skirt, I'd morph into a businesswoman. Maybe I should send him flowers as a thank-you.

Humming to myself, I proceeded to fill my basket with the ingredients Doug had requested. Spicy chicken curry happened to be one of his specialties. Although most customers would probably opt for curry powder that was readily available, Doug preferred to concoct his own version which he admitted was never the same twice. Besides coriander and cardamom, he needed fennel seeds, a stick of cinnamon, a nutmeg, whole cloves, and gingerroot for tomorrow's blend.

I paused, then turned, at hearing the front door open. Two well-dressed women waltzed in—Sandy Granger accompanied by her pal Vicki Lamont. The pair looked strikingly different, but they were startlingly similar. While Vicki was tall, brunette, trim, and mid-forties, her companion was average height, her hair colored golden walnut. Sandy, the older of the two, preferred card games; Vicki favored sports such as tennis and golf. Both women, however, exuded that confident, manicured, I-belong-to-a-country-club aura. The Kate Spade and Michael Kors handbags—or perhaps their designer footwear—might also have been clues.

"I don't know why I let Vicki talk me into going to lunch this afternoon when I have a million things to do,"

Sandy Granger said by way of a greeting. If she was harried, it didn't show. Not a single hair of her chin-length bob was out of place and her makeup was Hollywood perfect.

"You know what they say about all work, no play." Vicki waved her companion's complaint away with a flick of her wrist. "We just had a fabulous meal at Antonio's."

"I persuaded Tony to part with some of his wonderful minestrone," Sandy said. "With rehearsals and whatnot, I don't have time to cook. Since Craig's out of town on business, there's no reason to fuss."

I'd never tasted Tony Deltorro's wonderful minestrone. The man still considered me persona non grata because of a minor misunderstanding concerning a dead body. Tony obviously held a grudge but, then again, he was Sicilian. "Ladies"—I plastered on my friendly shopkeeper's smile—"what can I help you with this afternoon?"

Sandy adjusted the silk scarf around her neck. Hermès from a trip to Paris? I wondered. "Vicki insisted on stopping to find out the time of Doug's cooking demonstration tomorrow."

"Ten o'clock," I said. "I expect a full house, so best to come early."

Vicki extracted her iPhone from her oversize handbag and keyed in the information. "Ever since the weather turned cool, I've been in the mood for bread pudding," she said after she finished. "As long as I'm here, I want some of your vanilla. Sylvia Walker raved about its flavor. She advised me to throw out the cheaper, imitation variety and splurge."

I made a mental note to thank Sylvia for the recommendation. Vanilla, next to saffron, happened to be the highest-priced spice in the world. "Let me suggest vanilla from beans grown on Bourbon Island, now called Réunion Island, in Madagascar. It sets the standard when it comes to pure vanilla flavor."

Sandy wandered over to a coatrack I'd discovered in Yesteryear Antiques on which I'd hung a collection of chef aprons with catchy slogans. "Bread pudding is a favorite of Craig's."

"What a coincidence!" Vicki exclaimed. "It's my favorite, too. My recipe makes far too much for one person. Why don't I wait until Craig returns home? I'll whip up a pan, then bring some over. I know how busy you are, Sandy, with the play and what-have-you. Something homemade will be a nice treat."

"Have you heard from Kenny?" I asked Vicki, reaching for a four-ounce bottle of pure vanilla extract. She and her husband had split months ago. Since then, she'd been trying to woo Kenny back with gourmet meals and Victoria's Secret. I had it on good authority the breakup was the result of Vicki's fling with a local chef, now deceased. Also on good authority, Vicki missed her American Express Gold credit card even more than her estranged husband.

"Not a single word from Kenny since he hopped on his Harley and headed for Fantasy Fest in Key West." She gave a head toss, flinging glossy, dark locks over her shoulder. "He told me that his lawyer would contact my lawyer—or words to that effect."

"Sorry." I busied myself ringing up the sale. Vicki's announcement didn't sound promising for a Vicki-Kenny reconciliation.

"Did I hear someone mention Fantasy Fest?" Melly inquired as she returned downstairs. "Is that anything like a *Star Wars* convention?"

Sandy ceased riffling through aprons. "Ha!" she snorted. "Melly, dear, I can't believe you're so naïve. Fantasy Fest makes New Orleans's Mardi Gras seem like a child's tea party. Fantasy Fest is ten days of parades and parties—sans clothing but lots of body paint."

"Ohh . . ." Melly murmured.

I chuckled at seeing Melly's cheeks turn rosy as Sandy's description sank home. Fortunately, further discussion of body paint and naked bodies was forestalled by the arrival of Doug Winters with Casey, my mutt of many breeds, under his arm, and his daughter, Madison. Seeing him instantly brightened my day.

Beneath a mop of prematurely silver hair, Doug's boyishly handsome face broke into a grin at his spotting a cluster of women. Chocolate brown eyes behind rimless eyeglasses twinkled with good humor. "Ladies," he said.

I smiled back, feeling a bubble of happiness well up inside me. Many folks in town regarded us as a "couple." Truth is, I'd even begun to think of ourselves that way for lack of a better term. Our coupleship, however, had suffered a serious setback since his daughter, Madison, had arrived from Chicago to live with him. Madison demanded all his free time, and Doug—out to acquit himself as father-of-the-year—gave it willingly. Every weekend, father and daughter ventured far and wide. To the best of my knowledge, the father-daughter team had thus far shopped in Atlanta, taken carriage rides in Savannah, and toured historic homes in Charleston. He'd let it drop that Hilton Head Island was the next place of interest to be explored. While I applauded the fact that Doug wanted to bond with his daughter, I wouldn't be totally honest if I didn't admit to being a little hurt by his defection.

Upon spotting me, Casey started to bark in short, excited yaps. Doug set the squirming little dog on the floor. "There you go, boy."

Casey bounded across the shop, leaped into my outstretched arms, and lathered my face in doggy kisses.

"All right, already!" I said, laughing. "Let me see how you look after your day at a spa." Doug had recently leased space to a dog groomer from a neighboring town who came into his clinic once a week. This had been Casey's first visit to the groomer. He'd been washed, brushed, trimmed, and styled until I hardly recognized his usually scruffy self.

"I adore animals." Vicki gave Casey a tentative pat on his head, then batted her lashes at Doug in a coy gesture that predated hoop skirts. "I'm so looking forward to your cooking demo tomorrow. I plan to sit in the front row and take notes." She turned her attention to Madison. "This pretty young lady must be the daughter I've heard so much about."

Madison stepped closer to her father's side. From the pinched expression on her heart-shaped face, I could tell she wasn't happy with Vicki's flirtatiousness. Madison was a pretty girl, or least she would be if she smiled more often. She'd inherited her father's eye color, but the resemblance ended there. She was petite with delicate features and wore her long, golden-brown hair scraped back in a ponytail.

"Madison is a natural onstage." Sandy idly examined packets of recipe cards displayed on a nearby shelf. "I'd initially cast Brittany Hughes, Trish's daughter, for the role, but the girl didn't take it seriously. She was too young, too immature."

"And too interested in boys," Vicki added. "I ran into Trish at the club the other day. She's madder than a wet hen that the apple of her eye isn't going to be in *Steel Magnolias.*"

"Well, she'll just have to get over it," Sandy said briskly. "Unlike Madison, Brittany never came to rehearsals prepared and constantly missed her cues. I had no choice but to replace her."

I glimpsed the self-satisfied smirk on Madison's face before it vanished beneath her perpetual petulant expression. "Daddy," she whined, "how much longer? We need to pick up my car before the garage closes."

"Right, right," Doug said, digging into his shirt pocket and pulling out a folded piece of paper, which he handed me. "I added a few more items to the checklist I e-mailed yesterday. I want my first cooking demo to be glitch-free."

"What are you making?" Sandy asked.

"Spicy chicken curry." Doug took off his rimless eye-glasses and polished the lenses on the sleeve of his sport shirt. Satisfied they gleamed, he slipped them on again. "I like to experiment with Middle Eastern cuisine."

"I wasn't going to attend, but I changed my mind. As Vicki reminded me, all work and no play isn't good for a person. I'll encourage some of the cast and crew to come as well. A get-together outside of the theater will help create a sense of camaraderie." Frowning, she consulted her wristwatch. "Are you ready, Vicki?"

I set Casey down on the floor and handed Vicki her purchase, then watched the two friends depart.

Madison hitched the strap of her purse higher on her shoulder. "If Sandy thinks Daddy's cooking will turn the cast and crew into one big, happy family, she's sadly mistaken. If the curtain goes up before someone kills someone, it'll be a miracle."

Doug frowned at his daughter's words. Melly hugged her cardigan closer. I felt the hairs at the back of my neck prickle. Only Casey, who lounged near my feet, seemed oblivious of the tension.